Aftermath I
The Fight For Survival

By James A. Graves, Jr.

Second Edition

CRYSTAL DREAMS publishing

Oshawa, Ontario

Aftermath I: The Fight For Survival
by James A. Graves, Jr.

Managing Editor: Kevin Aguanno
Copy Editor: Susan Andres
Typesetting: Peggy LeTrent
Cover Design: Troy O'Brien

Published by: Crystal Dreams Publishing
(a division of Multi-Media Publications Inc.)
Box 58043, Rosslynn RPO, Oshawa, Ontario, Canada, L1J 8L6.

http://www.crystaldreamspublishing.com/

This is a work of fiction. Any similarity to real persons or organizations is purely coincidental.

Paperback	ISBN-10: 1591462487	ISBN-13: 9781591462484
Adobe PDF ebook	ISBN-10: 1591462495	ISBN-13: 9781591462491
Microsoft LIT ebook	ISBN-10: 1591462517	ISBN-13: 9781591462514
Mobipocket PRC ebook	ISBN-10: 1591462509	ISBN-13: 9781591462507
Palm PDB ebook	ISBN-10: 1591462525	ISBN-13: 9781591462521

This is the second edition. First edition published under ISBN 9781591460022.

Published in Canada. Printed simultaneously in the United States of America and the United Kingdom.

CIP data available from the publisher.

Dedication

To my family:

Thank you for enduring my many writers' tantrums, but mostly, thanks for trying to understand how much music and writing mean to me.

I can only imagine how confusing it must be when you can see that I am home, yet in my mind, I'm not really there at all.

In some circles, that's defined as insanity.

To my good friends:

Chuck, thank you for your advice and for volunteering to do the initial editing.

Craig, thank you for the technical support, both in II and I. I still wonder how you acquired it, but on second thought, I probably don't need to know.

Thanks to everyone, too numerous to mention, for the encouragement and moral support; you're part of my reason for never giving up.

Aftermath I: The Fight For Survival

Prelude

The year is 2006, and an asteroid impact has severely damaged the Earth's environment.

Desperate nations turned all available resources to the task of producing and obtaining food and water. The highest security priority was protecting these stockpiles of food and water. The survivors relied on the military to provide that protection.

Terrorism flourished as attentions turned from policing crime to national survival. The terrorists stole weapons of mass destruction and held nations hostage with threats of violence and devastation. Thus, they obtained food and supplies and grew mad with power.

The greatest fear was a terrorist with control of a nuclear weapon. Nations shared intelligence data and combined personnel and resources to combat the threat. The reality was that it was just a matter of time before their worst fear was realized.

Sometime after the Reaper hit, an elite group of volunteers from the Intelligence Community formed to help protect North America from an airborne terrorist attack.

This is a story of but a few of those brave people...

Aftermath I: The Fight For Survival

One of Those Days

Skip was having one of those days that no pilot even wants to think about. At the moment, he was sitting on the ramp at Base One, leaning against what remained of a baggage pod. The pod was only one piece of debris among several, including a right landing gear assembly, part of a nose gear, and a mangled piece of something that might have been a gun barrel.

Skip and this scattered, smoldering collection of recently created junk were several hundred feet from a burning heap of metal and composite fiber that Skip had just "landed," promptly exited, and sprinted away from at a very impressive speed. He was now trying to collect his composure, catch his breath, and try his best to find the courage to walk back to the burning heap of metal and composite fiber to survey the damage.

Reminding himself that any landing that you can walk away from is a good one, he spoke to himself, "After all, it didn't explode; maybe that's a good sign!"

As he toyed with an unidentifiable piece of his former jet, Skip chuckled at the thought that his aircraft *not* exploding might be the highlight of the day.

He was just getting to his feet when the cavalry arrived—lights and sirens, trucks and cars, screaming toward the scene—just like in the movies. Unfortunately, no director was going to yell, "Cut!" and thank everyone for the great job. One of the people racing to the scene was hoping the pilot was alive for a different reason than most—he intended to chew a certain hotshot pilot's ass.

"Well, if it ain't Colonel Bass. What a surprise to see you here," Skip said sarcastically as he struggled to stand with the help of the mangled baggage pod.

"Don't even start with me, Ramjet," the colonel said as he stepped out of his Jeep, "you're in enough trouble as it is."

His accent is undeniably Texan. Colonel John Theodore Bass, Commander of the North American Air Defense Agency (NAADA) Base One, tends to be an arrogant, military hard-ass. He is actually a good commander because, deep down, he is a decent guy and cares deeply for his troops. He does not always get along with Skip, but Skip does not help matters any by giving the colonel a hard time. The colonel prefers that military pilots, not civilians, fly for NAADA but knows he needs the skill and expertise of pilots such as Skip.

Colonel Bass surveyed the crash scene and commented, "It's too easy to find you, Ramjet. All I gotta to do is look for a crashed airplane, and you'll be at the scene... usually bleedin'!"

"Aw, come on, John T., gimme a break; I almost put it down in one piece."

"Yeah, I can see... one piece here, another piece there, and a mess all over my ramp. Are you hurt?"

"No, just sore... or gonna be. Only my pride's hurt," Skip answered as he pried the baggage pod open and collected his flight bag.

"Well, get in. We'll go to my office, and you can do the post-crash report there," the colonel said as he started the Jeep.

"I sure wish you wouldn't call me Ramjet all the time," Skip complained as he slumped down in the passenger seat.

"I'll stop calling you Ramjet if you'll stop crashing airplanes."

"Very funny." Skip sulked as they drove across the Base One ramp, now crowded with curious onlookers, toward the colonel's office.

Col. Bass entered the outer office with Skip a few steps behind. He spoke to his personal secretary. "Candy, we don't wanna be disturbed."

"Yes, Colonel."

"He don't want to be disturbed...," Skip said and motioned toward the colonel.

"He *is* disturbed," Candy whispered.

"I heard that!" Colonel Bass yelled from his office.

Candy blushed, and Skip laughed despite himself.

"Laugh it up, Ramjet," Col. Bass said sarcastically, "You won't have anything to laugh about when we're finished with this report. Get in here, and shut the damn door!"

Skip shut the door, went straight to the colonel's bar, and poured two glasses of Jack Daniels.

"Help yourself to my last bottle of whiskey."

"Don't mind if I do, John T." Skip handed a glass to the colonel and sat down, propping his feet on the colonel's desk with a grunt for his aching ribs.

The colonel took a sip and scowled, "I'm gettin' damn tired of picking up pieces of your airplanes. This report better be good or you're grounded."

"Colonel, sir, in the first place, it was *my* damn bird, not *yours*, and second, you ain't gonna like this report."

"Why not?"

Skip looked down at his drink. "Because you probably won't believe me."

The colonel sat back in his chair, studied Skip for a moment, and said, "You're not in the habit of lyin' to me, so why wouldn't I believe you?"

"Because," Skip lowered his voice to almost a whisper, "I was nearly shot down by a Mustang."

The colonel's eyes narrowed. "A what?"

"You heard me—a P-51 Mustang. Republic Aircraft Corporation, 1200-horse Rolls-Royce Merlin V-12..."

Colonel Bass cut him off. "I know what a Mustang is; I've got a few hours in Mustangs, and there ain't no way a Mustang could take you in air combat."

"Thank you," Skip replied.

"That was no compliment; my grandmother could take a Mustang if she was flying that hybrid, chemical-burnin' monster of yours."

"I'm glad you acknowledge the Viper-6 is mine."

"Look, let's get this straight once and for all," the colonel said, becoming visibly aggravated. "You and Pop find the damn things and put 'em together. I'm the dumb bastard that finances the project, and I own it!"

"Okay, fine, you own my damn airplane!"

The colonel backed down a bit and smiled.

"You sure don't like anyone holding any strings attached to you, do you?"

"Not really."

"Well, well, Skip is a real person after all." The colonel spoke with an honest kindness in his voice.

"What do you mean, 'real person'?"

"I mean that you are not the master of the air. You're a normal person, just like the rest of us."

The office went silent for a few moments, and then the colonel said, "So, tell me how a Mustang almost shot you down."

Then, the colonel sat back and waited for Skip to gather his thoughts.

***

Eight years earlier, in March of 1998, Tim Tenslick was not having a very good day, either. A Radio Astronomy major at Cal Tech, Tim was at the Palomar Observatory, analyzing data received from the Very

Large Array (VLA) radio telescope located in Socorro, New Mexico. The location in space, chosen at random, had not been of special interest to Tim. Actually, the location was causing the problem.

Unfortunately, at this time of the year, Jupiter just happened to dominate the radio telescope's field of view. Initially, he considered choosing another location, but he had let the computer choose at random, and before he realized it, the array had already been aimed. Changing locations would have required moving the antennae again, and he could just hear the technicians giving him a hard time for overworking the drive motors.

Besides, time on the system was limited and valuable. It was a routine procedure, and Tim was not about to make it complicated, or so he thought. However, for the past several hours, he had been crunching numbers, and the data just did not make sense.

He was working on his master's thesis, and the last thing he needed was a problem like this one. He had completed the scan, finished with the radio telescope array, and started the process of analyzing the data. Each time he ran the analysis, it showed Jupiter's magnetic envelope surrounding the planet to be 10% larger than normal. This was now his fourth attempt at running the data through the computer in the rapidly fading hope of seeing something—an error, a power surge, whatever— just anything that might help explain what he saw.

Then, one of the doctoral students complained that he was using up too much memory on the mainframe. That was the last straw. Tim was frustrated to the point of trashing the whole session and starting over. There was only one problem with starting over—time. There was not another opening on the VLA for six months. He would have to put his name on the standby list and wait. Assuming an unlikely cancellation, if he was lucky enough to be at the top of the waiting list, he would have to cut two days of classes to do the entire session over again. That was definitely not the way to get his thesis completed on time. So, once more, logic overrode frustration. Reluctantly, he compressed the data onto his zip drive and left for the university.

Back at home, he called a friend in the computer department, did some first-class horse-trading, and got unlimited time on the university's

Cray mainframe. Well, maybe it was not first-class trading… he would miss his Moody Blues CD collection.

Watching the super computer crunch numbers never failed to fascinate Tim. It was like watching a fast forward video of a mathematics genius doing math problems. Unfortunately, the magic did not work this time. When the analysis finished, the data was the same.

Disgusted, he picked up his backpack and threw it across the room. Then, while he was sitting there sulking, he had an idea. Eliminate Jupiter. Just wipe it right off the scan. A few keystrokes, and it was done.

Fifteen minutes later, the computer completed compiling the data, sans Jupiter. This time, he was livid. He stood up and yelled at the monitor, "This… is… not… possible!"

He could not believe what he was seeing. The numbers had changed very little. It was as though the computer had put Jupiter back in and just manipulated the gravimetric field readings slightly, changing the numbers.

Suddenly, he had a suspicious thought. What if that mischievous roommate of his had been up to his crap again? Once, Danny had changed the data on a visual scan and made him think he had discovered a comet. Tim had to write a formal apology to the dean of students for the erroneous article in the paper. Sometimes, Danny went too far. It did not help that Tim tended to be somewhat high strung. Or, as Danny put it, "Tim's brain stem was wound too tight."

"Danny? Are you in here? You criminal rodent!" Danny did not answer. Tim suddenly felt silly. Danny had gone to Mexico for the weekend with Elizabeth.

"Sorry, Danny!" he called out, still standing in front of the terminal, staring at the screen.

All at once, he felt very tired. He should; he had been at this now for twenty hours. Reluctantly, Tim logged off the system, retrieved his backpack from across the room, and stashed his laptop away. It was eleven o'clock, Sunday evening. Tomorrow, it would be back to classes. The next opportunity that he would have to log onto the Cray system would be during his two-hour lab on Tuesday. He could barely stay awake to drive back to his apartment. Danny was not home yet. Tim put on his pajamas and fell into bed for some much-needed sleep.

Hours later, he suddenly awoke with a start.

"I've got it," he whispered, and then louder, "I've got it!" He then repeated it, over and over, while he searched for his backpack. He ran downstairs and slid into the kitchen in his sock feet, looking for his sneakers.

Danny and Elizabeth were sitting at the bar having morning coffee. Since Tim was yelling at this point, they were both anticipating his entry. He made a pass through the kitchen and headed for the living room, found his sneakers, and hopped back into the kitchen as he put his sneakers on. Then, he ran up to Danny, put his hands on Danny's shoulders, and yelled, "I've got it! Danny, I've got it!"

"Uh, that's great. Tim, what, exactly, did you get?"

"Oh, hi, Elizabeth. Elizabeth! I've got it!"

"Hi, Tim. That's nice," she replied with her usual beautiful smile.

Tim poured himself a cup of coffee and then said, "I just don't believe it. I dreamed it. Can you believe it? I dreamed it, and now, I've got it. And I gotta go!"

He left his untouched coffee cup sitting on the bar and headed for the door.

"But, Tim! Wait!" Danny called after him. "You still have your..."

"No time for that; gotta go!" Then, Tim was out the door and gone.

And Danny finished, "...pajamas on."

Elizabeth and Danny looked at the door, then each other, with expressions of total confusion.

At the university's Astrophysics Department, Tim ran into Professor Gunderson's office and began telling him about his latest radio telescope scan, his theory, and his possible discovery.

"...You see, I thought that the program had an anomaly that was causing the mathematical error in the gravimetric calculations, but there is no error," Tim continued excitedly. "It has to be an object positioned in the field directly behind Jupiter and close enough to affect the intensity of the field. It's just beyond anything I've ever imagined!"

The professor calmly listened, slowly drinking his morning coffee. When Tim was finished, he cleared his throat and asked, "Have you been experimenting with LSD again, young man?"

"Of course not. I have been working on my thesis all weekend. Aren't you listening to me?" Tim replied indignantly.

"Yes. Are you aware that you are wearing your pajamas?"

"Oh. Well, yes, sort of... I left home in somewhat of a rush. But, Professor, I dreamed it; I dreamed the solution! I was totally hosed last night, but now, I know I'm right. Would you come with me and look at the data? I have no doubt that you will agree. There just could be no other logical conclusion."

"Perhaps, you should go to the infirmary."

"Professor! I'm serious!"

"So am I. You're not making any sense, and you're not dressed. Do you intend to go the computer lab in your pajamas?"

"Well, I suppose Spider Man doesn't really fit the academic motif, but this just can't wait."

"Very well, I'll humor you," The professor sighed. "Then, you will go home and get dressed, correct?"

"You got it," Tim replied with a smile.

In the computer lab, Tim brought up the data for which he had dreamed the solution and waited for Professor Gunderson to review his findings.

Presently, he spoke, "I'm sorry, Tim, I just can't agree with your conclusions."

"What other explanation could there be?" Tim asked in amazement.

"There are too many variables here. I suggest you run the scan again."

"I'll have to wait six months! This can't wait that long."

"Why not use data that is already in the system?" the professor suggested. "I realize it isn't an original analysis, but it will fit all of the criteria required to finish your thesis."

"That's not the point! We need to know what this object is," Tim argued, almost pleadingly.

"I fail to see how you can come to such a conclusion, based on this data alone. Your desire to conclude your analysis so quickly is highly unprofessional. You are only setting yourself up for ridicule and embarrassment."

"God, I hate professional arrogance!" Tim said in disgust.

The professor removed his glasses and turned his chair to face Tim. "Young man, I agreed to come here and view your theory. I have thirty years in this field, and I'm telling you, not out of professional arrogance as you call it, but from wisdom based on experience—your theory is foolish."

Tim gathered his things and left the lab without saying another word. He did not go to any classes that day. When Danny arrived home later that afternoon, Tim was sulking on the patio, still in his pajamas.

"Hello, Professor. Why aren't you in class?"

"Screw class!" Tim snarled.

"Okay, what's going on?"

"Nothing. Nothing is going on because Gunderson is too damn blind to see a pig in a punch bowl!"

"Oh, that makes a lot of sense."

Just then, Elizabeth arrived. She was also an astronomy student in the graduate program. Tim had met her in class, they dated briefly, and then Tim introduced her to Danny. Danny and she had immediately become an item, but Tim and Elizabeth remained friends, often sharing lunch and studying together.

"Lizzy, will you use your killer charm on Mister Fusspot and find out what in heaven's name is bothering him?"

"What's wrong with Tim?"

"Beats me. Maybe you can find out."

She went out on the patio and sat on the edge of the lounge chair beside Tim.

"Hi," Liz said sweetly.

"Hi." Tim sulked, sitting cross-legged, his head propped on his fists.

"I missed you in class. Have you been home all day?"

"Since I left the lab this morning."

"I heard about the deal with Gunderson. I'm sorry he treated you that way. Will you tell me exactly what happened?"

"It's not important," Tim replied, still sulking.

"Not important? I saw you leave here this morning in your pajamas! I like Spider Man, by the way," she said, leaning over to make eye contact.

He smiled. "My little sister gave them to me for Christmas. They're comfortable."

"Can I wear them some time?"

Tim formed an immediate mental image of Elizabeth wearing his pajama top... totally sexy.

"I'll wear the bottoms; you can wear the top," he answered, smiling devilishly.

"You would sleep with your roommate's girlfriend?" Elizabeth asked, astonished.

"Only if I had the chance," Tim replied in a whisper.

"You two should be roommates; you think alike!" she said and nudged him with her elbow.

Suddenly, Tim grew serious. "I don't know, Liz, I was so sure that I had discovered something fantastic. I just feel like crawling in a hole."

"Tell you what, let's go out, and get something to eat. We'll talk about this some more, and I'm sure we can help you plan a whole new approach to this problem. Okay?"

"Well, I don't know...," Tim resisted.

"Come on. Get up, and let's get you out of this blue funk you're in." Elizabeth pulled him up, directed him to his bedroom, pushed him in, and closed the door. "Get dressed."

Tim stuck his head out and asked, "Help me?"

"You're incorrigible!" Elizabeth declared, smacked him on the head, and pushed him back inside.

Danny did not believe Tim either, saying he was just chasing another one of his crazy ideas. However, Elizabeth did what she had promised. During dinner, Tim and she devised a plan to get on the Internet and e-mail his theory, complete with his data files attached, to every astronomer, astrophysicist, and radio telescope facility in the world. Somewhere, someone might take an interest and have a look.

"After all," Elizabeth commented, "what do we have to lose?"

Within a week, e-mail replies and phone calls streamed in to the university. Responses came from Operation Space Watch, the Near Earth Asteroid Tracking Facility at the Alaska Volcano Observatory, the Space Scout Armory, and many other facilities and independent astronomers.

Most of the replies were similar to Professor Gunderson's, but one reply was different. Dr. Fred Adkins, retired German astronomer, with a lot of political pull, had managed to get the Max Planck Institute's 100-meter radio telescope turned in the right direction. The data that was attached to his e-mail message rocked the Astrophysics Department to its core. Tim's theory had been correct.

When Tim got the message, he barged into Elizabeth's class and told her the good news. This, naturally, embarrassed her and got Tim thrown out of the class, but she was touched that he would come to her first.

That night, Tim took her out to dinner to thank her for giving him the courage to keep going. They left Danny at home.

Several days later, Danny moved in with a young actress. Tim immediately went to Elizabeth to ask her to take over Danny's room.

"I'm not sure, Tim. I would feel strange, moving into Danny's room... I'm just not sure."

"I can see your point. I don't want you to feel uncomfortable. I know I've kidded around with you, flirting and stuff... but I..."

"But you...?"

Tim took a deep breath. "I don't want you to move in just because you're beautiful and sexy. I think you are the sweetest girl I've ever known, and I enjoy the pleasure of your company. There, I said it!"

Elizabeth smiled sweetly and simply hugged Tim. That evening, Elizabeth and Tim moved her things out of her apartment and into Danny's old room. A few weeks later, Elizabeth slept in Tim's room. His imagination fell far short of what she actually looked like wearing his pajama top.

Unable to ignore the situation any longer, Professor Gunderson gained access to the Very Long Baseline Array (VLBA). The VLBA is an array of ten dishes positioned across North America, from Hawaii to the Virgin Islands. Using data from the VLBA, he and Tim made a close study of the gravimetric anomalies that were emanating from behind Jupiter.

Strangely, with each consecutive scan, the intensity increased by a measured amount. When calculated out, the data suggested that the planet's magnetic field was growing at a tremendous rate. The question was, "how?" Was the mass of Jupiter increasing by some unknown means? If so, why didn't the orbital characteristics change? Jupiter was not showing any orbital variations that would be consistent with the theory that internal changes were occurring within the planet. Was only the magnetic field increasiith enough mass to change Jupiter's gravimetric field, become trapped in orbit without being previously detected? That area of space is studied constantly. Someone would have spotted the object before it became somehow locked in a strange orbit, hidden behind Jupiter. Astrophysics just was not explaining the anomalies in the data, and Professor Gunderson was baffled.

As the end of May quickly approached, Tim received an e-mail message from Dr. Adkins. The doctor had a theory, but he could find no one who would concur with him. Dr. Adkins had concluded that the source of the changes in magnetic field density could be a small object, with an extremely high mass, approaching from outside of the solar system. The location was incidental. The trajectory just happened to place it behind Jupiter, as viewed from Earth. That would explain why visual systems had failed to locate the object.

His justification was to extrapolate the magnetic field strength, as viewed from an axis of ninety degrees from the poles of Jupiter and out to the orbit of Uranus. By calculating the flux density of the magnetic field, it appeared that the object was several million miles out in space. However, calculating the mass that would be necessary to generate such an intense magnetic field worked out to be an object six times larger than Jupiter. Being nearly the diameter of the Sun, it should be visible, but it was not. There could be only one logical conclusion—the object had to be composed of collapsed stellar matter with extremely high mass—the equivalent of a microscopic black hole. Unfortunately, Earth was about to be visited by a real falling star.

Tim rushed to the lab and added Dr. Adkins' findings to the data collected from the VLBA. Then, he let the Cray crunch the numbers again. When the results came back, Tim went pale, became nauseous, and almost threw up. But, he managed to have the computer calculate an estimated impact point. When those calculations were finished, he immediately e-mailed the results to Dr. Adkins and left a copy for Professor Gunderson. Then, he added the data to the university's Web page and left the campus. Tim went immediately and explained the situation to Elizabeth. Upon learning the news, Elizabeth went with him to their apartment, and they packed their belongings. Next, they went to the home of Tim's mother. Within the hour, they were en route to the farm of Elizabeth's parents in Arkansas.

Two weeks later, newspapers carried the following article:

June 8, 1998
A Real Falling Star

A small, rogue asteroid, approximately the size of a basketball but estimated at 7.38 x 10^{19} metric tons, or the approximate mass of the Moon, has been discovered hurtling toward our solar system. Designated A-1106, or as some in the scientific community are calling "the Grim Reaper," the asteroid was discovered by a Cal Tech graduate student using a radio telescope.

The object, traveling at approximately 60,000 miles per hour when discovered, is accelerating as it grows nearer to our Sun. Most scientific theories suggest the asteroid is a fragment of dense matter thrown from a supernova that somehow defied all known laws of physics and escaped the massive gravitational forces of an exploding star.

Experts claim that systems, such as the Near Earth Asteroid Tracking Facility in Alaska, failed to sight the asteroid visually due to the orbit of Jupiter blocking the field of view.

The Reaper should pass near our solar system around July 10 of this year, causing some disturbances due to the intense gravitational forces, but experts say it will not pass near the Earth.

***

At 1420 Zulu, July 18, 1998, the Grim Reaper, with a hundred times more mass than the news services had published, skimmed the earth with a fatal glancing blow. The impact point was northeast Siberia, creating a crater two miles deep and the approximate length of California.

Estimated instantaneous death toll was 800 million. In the next six months, another two billion died.

The impact changed the Earth's orbit by 0.5 degrees, changed the tilt by three degrees, and increased the Earth's tilt-wobble cycle. These changes caused the Southern Hemisphere to remain in winter for ten months; consequently, the Northern Hemisphere remained in summer for ten months.

Initially, the debris thrown into the atmosphere reduced available sunlight and, within months, caused global temperatures to fall by twenty degrees. Consequently, millions upon millions froze to death or starved.

Within two years, the global temperature began to rise again, especially in the Northern Hemisphere, because of the greenhouse effect. Initially, the climate improved, and some crops would grow again, but the temperature continued to rise. Worldwide starvation returned as crops died or simply would not grow.

The impact partially vaporized or melted the Arctic ice cap. As the global temperature rose, the remainder of the Arctic ice cap began melting along with the Antarctic ice cap, seriously reducing the Earth's available supply of fresh water. The increase in global temperatures also caused the oceans to heat up. The warming seawater expanded, causing islands and coastal cities to disappear beneath the surface as ocean levels rose at an alarming rate.

After the asteroid impact, the world fell into chaos. Living became a matter of survival, and survival for many was not possible. An estimated five thousand species of animals died the first year and in smaller numbers in successive years, finally leveling off as animals adapted to the changing climate. Only the animals and humans that could find food and adapt would survive; the rest simply died. Food and water became life itself.

CHAPTER TWO

Surprise

Skip walked from the entrance of his outpost that he called "Owl's Nest," propped one foot on a large stone, and sipped at a cup of imitation coffee. He watched in amusement, as his pet Rottweiler appeared to be trying to catch fish in the small mountain pond several hundred feet from where Skip stood.

Razer was standing completely still, watching the water with the intent eyes of a deadly predator. Suddenly, he would lunge forward and dive beneath the surface. Seconds later, he would come up, looking like a grizzly bear shaking his huge head, and then return to his watchful stance. He never actually caught anything, and Skip was wondering if his dog was actually playing with the fish.

The giant red sun illuminated the thin, hazy air as it silently peaked over the horizon, bathing the mountaintop with pale red and yellow hues. A slight breeze stirred, and a memory from what seemed like a century ago flashed in Skip's mind. He felt a twinge of an old familiar pain and turned his thoughts to something else... anything else. This time it was not difficult to redirect his thoughts because, on the breeze, came a strange sound to the usually peaceful mountaintop.

Razer suddenly perked up and turned in the direction of the sound. He immediately rushed out of the pond and shook off the water, continuing to stare in the direction of the sound, motionless and alert. Razer gave Skip a quick glance to see if his master was aware of the new sound.

Skip looked at Razer and asked, "Whadda ya hear, pal?"

The sound was upwind, fading, and then drifting back to Skip's ears. It was becoming somewhat familiar but yet out of place. Skip instinctively turned toward the cave where his aircraft was hangared. He had completed the preflight on the Viper-6 while his morning coffee was brewing. The plane was now ready to fly. Skip looked at the Viper as if he was trying to communicate mentally with the flight computer to initiate engine start. Something just did not feel right.

Just as Razer growled, the noise, coming from over Skip's right shoulder, revealed itself clearly. Skip spun around to see a gleaming silver fuselage, almost inverted, in a tight climbing turn toward the pond where he now stood. The sight left Skip in total awe. A beautiful, gleaming silver P-51 Mustang was rolling into a classic, low-altitude strafing run. The Mustang's supercharged Merlin V-12 was singing the sweet notes of raw power as the bird rolled, wings level, in a nose down attitude, accelerating directly toward him and the Viper-6.

Skip was quite helpless. Shock and amazement were competing in his brain. He knew that he should hit the dirt. He wished he could dive into a hole, knowing that one fifty-caliber round into a fuel cell, or a rocket into the hangar, and he and the Viper-6 were history—perhaps even the mountaintop if the highly volatile hydrogen/alcohol fuel cells went simultaneously with the JP-8 fuel and munitions stored in the cave.

All of these thoughts were screaming in his mind, and yet, he could not take his eyes away from the Mustang. It was simply beautiful. Powerful, quick, and capable in its best environment, low and fast, the P-51 was a master of close air ground attack. Skip knew beyond any doubt that this could very well be the last thing he would ever see.

Twenty feet above the ground and little more than fifty feet from where Skip stood, the attacker suddenly pitched up into a steep climb, completed a victory roll, and dove out of sight behind the mountain toward the rising sun.

The sound was gone, and except for a very agitated Razer, it was as if nothing had happened. No guns or rockets fired. No bombs dropped. It was a very anticlimactic event.

Skip stood breathless, heart pounding, coffee cup in hand, looking toward the rising sun, stunned and speechless. Razer suddenly stopped barking and growling and looked directly at Skip, causing him to break out of his mental state and look back at Razer. They stared at each other for a moment, and then Skip regained his composure.

"I gotta catch that Mustang!" he yelled and dashed for the Viper.

Razer barked after him as if to cheer him on.

Skip grabbed his helmet, hanging on the nose of the left in-board missile, and leaped into the cockpit, barely touching the climbing cleats on the fuselage. He immediately plugged into the Viper's computer audio interface, turned on the master switch, and barked an order, "Engine start!"

The computer sprang to life with a monotone response, "Ignition sequence initiated, engine start in twelve seconds, systems check in progress, stand by."

The fuselage shook as the hybrid engine's first stage ignited the JP-8, and the massive turbine blades began spooling up. The flight computer responded again, "Engine start complete. All systems go. Begin taxi."

As Skip released the brakes, he stabbed the throttle forward, and the Viper lurched out of the cave.

"Excessive power for taxi, reduce throttle," the flight computer ordered.

"Emergency override. Initiate intercept. Owl's Nest has just been flown over by an unidentified and possible hostile aircraft; we are in pursuit."

"Do you require intercept vectors from Air Defense?"

"Negative. If Base One had seen it, they would already have an alert on the net. This bird is avoiding detection," Skip replied. "Bring up the TFR on maximum range, and let's see if we can find this rascal."

"Initializing Terrain Following Radar, stand by. Define search."

"The pilot headed southeast, probably followin' the terrain down the valley."

"Do you require a terrain map?"

"Negative, just bring up the TFR, and go weapons hot."

"Terrain Following Radar is ready, weapons standing by."

***

The Nation, now considered the United States and Canada, had its resources taxed to the limit, providing and protecting the production, shipment, storage, and distribution of food and water. The military forces were combined, named the Free Forces of North America (FFNA), and dispersed throughout the globe. However, most FFNA ground troops were deployed throughout North America. Their primary duties were riot control and to protect and distribute food supplies. The naval and air forces and the remainder of ground forces were deployed worldwide. Their primary duty was to provide protection for food production, transport, and distribution. With the nation's military otherwise occupied, perimeter defense of the North American borders fell to the security agencies.

Within months after the disaster, terrorist organizations worldwide seized the opportunity to obtain power. With a myriad of fanatical agendas, these organizations gained access and armed themselves with an unlimited array of sophisticated weapons, including aircraft of all types and descriptions.

General Lewis M. Gray, working for the National Reconnaissance Office, had recognized North America's susceptibility to being undermined by these well-armed terrorists. As a commander in the intelligence community, he met with Canadian and U.S. leaders and convinced them to form the North American Air Defense Agency (NAADA). General Gray then organized an all-volunteer group of highly trained and experienced personnel from the civilian and military intelligence community.

The primary task for NAADA was to augment the military by protecting North America from terrorism from the air. The FFNA were protecting the coasts from a visible enemy. But, terrorism was often an invisible enemy. If a terrorist organization were able to establish a secret base within North America, they would be able to strike at the very heart of the government. Earth's entire civilization was already on the verge of anarchy; neither the U.S. nor Canada could recover from such an attack. NAADA became North America's last line of air defense. Bases were set up in strategic locations, forming a ring of protection along the entire border.

Base One, guarding the Western and Southwestern borders, utilized the runways and facilities of Lowry Air Force Base. Lowry, located near Denver, Colorado, had been closed years earlier by defense cutbacks. It was an excellent choice for Base One, geographically situated to provide air intercept for the Western Defense Zone, large enough to accommodate the aircraft and personnel, yet small enough to be easily defended against air and ground attacks.

CHAPTER THREE

You're Never Too Old to Learn

The Viper's speed increased as it rolled onto the short runway that ended with a cliff, which dropped just over seven thousand feet to the hot desert below. Skip scanned the instrument panel, verifying systems status and flight control settings, as the flight computer repeated the checklist, "Hot nozzles go. Afterburner and thrust assist go. Checklist complete."

Skip shoved the throttle forward and lit the afterburner. The added thrust supplied the familiar push toward rotation speed. He then rotated the hot nozzles toward vertical thrust. The nozzles immediately directed part of the pre-afterburner thrust downward, instantly pushing the Viper off the runway. Roaring into the morning sky, the aircraft climbed with a slight nose-high attitude, the vertical and horizontal velocities almost equal. Skip continued pulling back on the stick, and the Viper responded as advertised, rotating to a vertical climb. As the nose passed through the twelve o'clock high position, Skip eased forward on the stick, laying the speeding jet gracefully on its back, five hundred feet above the runway.

The hot nozzles automatically rotated back to full rearward, diverting all thrust into the afterburner stages, as the flight computer reported, "All systems go."

"FC, initiate thrust assist on my command," Skip ordered.

"Thrust assist standing by for ten-second burn," FC replied.

"Three, two, one, go!"

The results pressed Skip deeper into the seat, inflating his G-suit to keep blood in his upper torso and brain, as the Viper accelerated past three hundred knots. He looked through the top of the canopy toward the short runway he had just left, then quickly snapped the Viper into a roll to wings level. He then looked in the direction the Mustang had disappeared and snap rolled into an inverted six-G diving right turn. The thrust assist automatically shut down at the ten-second timeout just as the Viper shuddered through the first ripple, exceeding Mach 1.

Back at Owl's Nest, Razer watched intently as the Viper rolled to the right and descended into the valley out of sight. Moments later, Skip leveled out at a thousand feet above the desert floor and throttled back to maintain Mach 9.

"Sensors operational, terrain following radar is go, weapons systems on hot standby, verify FLIR video."

"Video is good; bring up weapons radar, please, FC," Skip replied.

"Weapons radar is online; verify video. Do you wish to lock autopilot to terrain following?"

"Radar video is good. Negative on the autopilot; I have it. Please advise Control of our status."

"Stand by," the flight computer responded.

Skip scanned the horizon, the FLIR video monitor, and radar screen alternately as the terrain rolled beneath him. The valley was several miles wide and meandered toward the southwest for nearly a hundred miles before opening out into rolling terrain. He knew that the Mustang must stay beneath the rim of the valley and would probably fly as close to the desert floor as possible to avoid being seen by the Viper's radar and infrared sensors.

"Base One Control does not respond. Radio unusable due to atmospheric magnetic dust layer."

"That figures."

Two long-range RADAR systems guarded the Western Air Defense Zone—one located on a mountain peak near Owl's Nest and the other on a mountaintop in Utah. Neither was very reliable, with severely limited operational capabilities. Only one surveillance satellite, a KH-11 "Keyhole," remained in orbit to provide real-time infrared reconnaissance and high-resolution video. Unfortunately, communication to, and video from, Keyhole was sporadic and unreliable due to constantly changing magnetic fields and high levels of magnetic dust particles and debris in the atmosphere. Long-range RADAR data from airborne and ground-based radar systems was only partially reliable for the same reasons.

The only other defense was a dedicated group of air surveillance pilots, stationed at a string of remote outposts located throughout North America. Their job was simple—fly armed reconnaissance missions and protect the Air Defense Zone (ADZ). Standing orders were to shoot down any unauthorized aircraft in the ADZ, unless the aircrew responded to warnings and obeyed escort to the nearest NAADA or FFNA Base. There, the pilot, crew, and any passengers would be arrested and charged with several serious federal crimes. Not the least of which, "Suspicion of intent to inflict terrorist acts or actions against North America," had only one penalty if convicted—death.

No pilot in his right mind would fly into the ADZ without permission. This was a fact that sometimes weighed heavily on Skip. He had seen his share of death and destruction, but the thought of shooting down a civilian aircraft was not a pleasant one. He hoped that he would never be faced with that option but realized it was a possibility, however remote. Terrorist activity was at an all-time high. The intent to undermine the remaining strength of the U.S. and Canada was a very real threat. Worldwide, all nations were barely surviving. In sad truth, a very small attack force, armed with the right weapons, could deal a fatal blow to the interim governmental authority of North America. Intelligence warned to expect anything, including thermonuclear and biological weapons.

Skip searched intently through the length of the valley and saw nothing unusual. The vast expanse of desert stretched ahead of him as he scanned the horizon and wondered aloud, "Where did that Mustang come from? There must be a base of some sort nearby. But where?"

He had flown over the ADZ more times than he cared to count and never saw any runway that could support an aircraft like a Mustang, at least not without some serious reconstruction. Reconnaissance photos indicated that every runway in the West showed evidence of severe earthquake damage.

Suddenly an alarm interrupted his thoughts as the flight computer warned, "Aft sensors have detected a heat bloom at seven o'clock high!"

Skip turned to look behind him.

"The Mustang!" Skip yelled. "But where the hell did he come from? And how's he stayin' with us?"

The flight computer answered, "The intruder is traveling at Mach 0.85. Sensors indicate a probable... Warning! Incoming fire!"

Skip heard the warning but had already seen the cannon pod on the right wing of the Mustang as it erupted with fire. He tried to maneuver to evade, but the cockpit of the Viper flashed, and Skip heard the familiar agonizing sounds of bullets penetrating the fuselage.

Suddenly, smoke filled the cockpit as the flight computer reported, "Electrical system malfunction. Aft sensors down. Communication down. Possible damage to flight controls. Variable thrust inoperative. FLIR system down. Weapons systems down. Evacuating smoke."

Skip listened but concentrated on flying. The instant the rounds hit, he broke left and pulled the Viper into a hard turn, attempting to get behind the Mustang. He did not dare try a vertical loop because the Mustang could decelerate much quicker and that could put the Viper at point blank range, directly in front of the Mustang. Deep in the turn now, he tried to keep the Mustang in sight but lost it, straining under the G-forces of the tight turn.

The Mustang pilot, knowing the Harrier's capabilities, immediately broke pursuit and initiated a diving left turn, followed by a hard right turn. Before Skip could complete his turn, he spotted the Mustang at twelve o'clock low, head on, the gun pod blazing.

"Damn, this guy is good!" Skip exclaimed as he instinctively selected the 25-mm cannon, but before he had time to pull the trigger, the computer was already droning the bad news, "Weapons systems inoperative."

"Damn it! I had a shot!" Skip swore as he pulled up, applying full power and afterburner simultaneously.

The Viper responded, but not with the kick that Skip expected.

"Afterburner and thrust assist nonfunctional," the flight computer droned.

"Well, ain't *that* just bloody great?" Skip swore as more rounds hit the nose and raked back toward the leading edge of the left wing. "And this day started out really good..."

It seemed like an eternity for the Viper to pull away from the Mustang. Actually, Skip was already at the maximum range of the Mustang's 20-mm Vulcan cannon pod when the last burst of rounds hit. The Mustang pilot watched as the Viper pulled away, and then turned the Mustang toward the secret desert base.

Skip leveled the Viper at ten thousand feet and started to assess his situation.

"FC, any status change since our encounter with the Mustang?"

"Negative. Flight controls status remains unknown. Engine fluids and fuel status unknown. All other systems down," the computer reported.

"It would help if the damn warning system was workin'," Skip remarked, and then added, "Well, at least the smoke's gone."

The thought of punching out was not a very pleasant thought. Daytime temperatures of 130 to 150 degrees Fahrenheit were not Skip's idea of a day on the beach.

At the moment, he was not certain that the Viper would make it back to Base One, but Owl's Nest was out of the question. He was going to need a lot of runway and maybe a fire truck or two as well. Skip began carefully testing the control inputs with gentle turns. The controls were sluggish, but at least his bird was flying.

"We just might make it after all, FC," Skip reported after the checks.

"Make it after all? Insufficient data," the computer replied.

"Get this wounded bird, with you and me in it, down intact," Skip answered.

"Systems analysis unable to determine if aircraft is go for landing," the flight computer dutifully reported.

"Well, I'm not so certain either," Skip chuckled. "We just got our ass shot up by a Mustang."

Then Skip mumbled to himself, "*I* just got my ass shot up by a Mustang. And just when you think you've lived long enough to see it all."

***

William "Skip" Scott was not exactly new at his job. Born April 1, 1952, he grew up traveling from base to base with his father, an Air Force pilot; his mother, a schoolteacher; and younger brother, Bobby. He joined the U.S. Army in 1969 at seventeen, just after graduating high school, entered flight training after basic training, and graduated Army flight school with honors. Skip volunteered for Vietnam after qualifying in the Huey Cobra Gunship.

He returned home after his first tour of duty, entered the Bootstrap Program, and went to Auburn University. He earned his BS degree in science and in 1973, joined the U.S. Air Force, transitioned to the T-38 Talon after OCS, and transferred to Williams AFB, Arizona, as an instructor. A year later, he transitioned to the F-4 Phantom and transferred to Shaw AFB, South Carolina, flying the RF-4C. Along the way, Skip earned his MS in Aeronautical Engineering from Embry-Riddle University.

In 1975, he was selected as test pilot for the Compass Sight Test Project and later transferred to Eglin AFB, Florida, as chief test pilot on the Quick Strike Reconnaissance Test Project. In 1980, he resigned from the USAF and formed Tree Top Flying Service whose primary services were crop dusting, air taxi, cargo hauling, flight instruction, full-service FBO, and aviation repair facility. Skip holds certificates as air transport pilot, certified flight instructor, and instrument in fixed wing and rotary wing, single and multi-engine, reciprocating engine, and jet engine.

During the years between 1980 and 1998, Skip and his partner, Dr. Pop Hackland, worked on various projects with U.S. intelligence agencies, primarily with Aeronautical Intelligence and Reconnaissance Systems Development. The Viper Series jets were designed, built, and tested at Tree Top Flying Service during this period.

His wife, Holly Ann; twin girls, Jessica and Veronica; and son, William, Jr. were all killed because of the asteroid impact.

He is presently an air surveillance pilot for the FFNA, NAADA, assigned to the Western Frontier Air Defense Zone, NAADA Base One, Denver, Colorado. His post is a remote mountain top base site called Owl's Nest, located in the southern section of the Western ADZ.

CHAPTER FOUR

Time to Get to Work

Skip was ninety miles west of Denver, Colorado, inbound for Base One and a full-stop landing. He was certain it would be a full stop if only because he doubted the Viper would make it into the air again. Engine power had been steadily dropping for the last two hours. He did not know why because the engine instruments were dark, and the flight computer was unable to access the engine status bus interface. Just as a precaution, Skip had been looking for possible emergency landing sites along the way. He was determined to fly the Viper to the ground, unless an in-flight fire decided otherwise.

In the last four years, Skip had lost three aircraft. Two aircraft had simply quit flying due to engine problems. The third had a catastrophic engine failure while at full power. In the first two accidents, he tried to put the aircraft down safely, and both times, he had been forced to punch out, left hanging there beneath the parachute canopy, watching his aircraft plummet to the ground and explode in a ball of fire. Skip punched out of the third aircraft less than two seconds before it exploded.

Pilots feel a certain connection to their aircraft, as if it was a living thing. An aviator takes it personally when his bird develops a problem. If the problem results in a crash, he tends to blame himself, even if it was not his fault. Somewhere in the back of his mind, despite all of his efforts to save the aircraft, he cannot help but feel he could have done something more to save it. That attitude was especially strong with Skip.

Skip knew home was not far. "Come on, sweetheart, you can do it," he pleaded. The throttle was now firewalled, but the Viper was wallowing just above stall speed, and Skip was fighting the control stick just to stay in the air. Normally, his left hand would be on the throttle, but considering the situation, Skip decided to keep his left hand on the ejection handle.

Base One appeared on the horizon, and Skip spoke to the flight computer, "FC, start emergency landing procedures."

"Systems status unchanged; check seat harness, and don't forget to check leg straps. Transponder is set to emergency squawk, but may not be transmitting. Communications systems down. Communication with the tower will be visual. Advise if you need verification of light gun signals," the computer concluded.

Skip replied, "Harness check complete. I intend to fly by the tower for a gear check, unless they send up an escort. Gear down."

"Unable to comply."

"I knew that. Why did I ask?" Skip mumbled to himself.

Skip manually activated the landing gear switch. Knowing he could not use variable thrust, he had to depend on the landing gear. If any part of the landing gear were to fail on touchdown, the situation could get real in a hurry. Skip heard the landing gear motors cycle and stop. Four green lights appeared on the landing gear status panel.

"Hey, FC, somethin' actually works!" he exclaimed.

"Systems check unable to confirm gear status."

"Now ain't that just ducky," Skip said to himself.

"Define 'ducky'."

"Well, ducky normally means somethin' good, but in this case, it's sarcasm."

"Define need for sarcasm."

"Sarcasm ain't always necessary; it just helps me deal with certain situations. In this case, I didn't like your answer," Skip replied, and then added, "We've got to improve your vocabulary... if we're still in one piece after this."

"Computers are not 'one piece'," FC replied. "The flight computer exists as 298 files totaling 12.3 gigabytes of data. Skip Scott, are you 'one piece'?"

"Technically, yes. I could still function with a few parts missin', but given the choice, I'd rather not. I'm definitely not immortal like you."

"Immortality applies to living beings. The flight computer Core Program is backed up and protected by Dr. Hackland. Computers have redundancy."

"Well, FC, you got me there. My wounds heal. Well, most of 'em anyway, but that's not exactly redundancy. Jesus! Does this mean I'm inferior to a machine?"

"Insufficient data to formulate a response."

"Good answer."

Minutes crept by as Base One's control tower came into full view. Skip had dropped to two hundred feet AGL, and he flew by the tower, slowly wagging his wings to indicate no radio. He could see the controllers inside, looking over the Viper with binoculars.

Skip then negotiated a long sweeping turn, passing by the tower again. This time, a white light flashed four times from inside the tower cab, indicating the main gear, nose gear, and the wingtip gear all appeared to be down and locked.

"Well, we've got landing gear anyway."

Then, an alternating green and red light signal flashed from inside the tower.

Skip decoded the message orally, "Clear to land with caution." As he slowly wagged his wings in reply, he spotted the fire trucks and other emergency vehicles responding to his crisis and remarked, "I wonder just how bad this bird looks from the outside?"

On the ground, controllers were relaying information, via radio, to the emergency crews "Emergency aircraft now turning long final for Runway Two One. Aircraft is trailing smoke and appears to have severe battle damage. The pilot is unable to communicate. We have transmitted his situation in the blind, but there is no indication that he copied the message."

The emergency response team commander replied, "Firefighter One copies; aircraft in sight; we are in position and standing by."

Seconds slowly ticked by as Skip nursed the wounded Viper toward the runway. He wanted to descend gradually and touch down as gently as possible, just in case the landing gear had been damaged. Unfortunately, the flaps and speed brakes were inoperable, so airspeed would have to be high to avoid stalling on final approach.

The Viper did not have a tail-hook, so the runway's arresting cable was useless. Landing hot would require a very long rollout, even if the brakes worked. If not, the overrun at the end of the runway was just long enough to say a short prayer and eject. Thus, it was imperative for Skip to set the Viper down as near to the runway threshold as possible. The problem was, with no extra power available, his glide path had to be steep and nearly perfect.

About a half mile from touchdown, as he crossed the ILS middle marker, Skip nosed the Viper over to increase airspeed. But just as the wounded fighter crossed the runway threshold, it suddenly pitched down sharply and yawed to the left.

"Flameout!" Skip yelled as the engine quit.

He struggled with the stick, trying to get the nose up and back on the runway centerline. In the distance, he could see emergency vehicles as he managed to swing the nose back toward the runway. Just then, the Viper stalled, yawed to the right, and slammed down on the runway. It bounced back into the air, and then slammed down again, this time onto the taxiway. Not knowing where the crippled Viper might go, emergency vehicles scattered. Skip was trying to keep the nose up, but the elevator was not responding. The nose gear hit hard, immediately folded, and separated from the fuselage, taking other pieces from the nose area with it. This caused the aircraft to spin to the left, and the right wing gear separated from the wing. As the right wingtip hit the ground, the main gear tore away from the undercarriage. Fire erupted from the ruptured hydraulic lines, ignited by the sparks created as the aircraft spun on the concrete. Skip blew the canopy and resisted the temptation to eject. He intended to ride it out, praying the aircraft did not flip onto its back.

As if in slow motion, the burning Viper finally slid to a halt. Skip released his harness, scrambled out of the cockpit, and sprinted away from the aircraft, following the trail of debris the Viper had just created. Emergency vehicles were already tending to pieces of flaming debris and spraying water onto the fuselage as Skip stopped where his baggage pod had come to rest.

At that point, Skip ended his recollection of the story by saying, "Well, you know the rest, boss."

"What was the point of riding that thing to the ground? Are you crazy?"

"You mean, like, clinically crazy?"

The colonel did not reply; he only looked at Skip with guarded suspicion.

Avoiding the first question, Skip replied, "You know full well that none of my shrinks has ever come to any definite conclusions about my sanity... or insanity for that matter."

"Humph" was the colonel's only response. He studied Skip for a moment and finished his drink, and then he spoke, "We have a serious problem. We have to get more information on that Mustang. Where it came from, who was flying it, where it's based..." The colonel broke away from what he was saying and called to his secretary, "Candy, will you get Ron Taylor for me, please?"

"Right away, sir."

Colonel Bass turned his attention back to Skip. "Why don't you go get examined by the flight surgeon. Maybe your head would be a good place to start. And get cleaned up. I'm gonna set up a debriefing with Ron's folks. I'll let ya' know when they can see ya'... and don't worry 'bout the viper. If Pop can't fix it, I'll getcha another one!"

Skip stood up, speechless, but continued to look at the colonel, as if waiting for him to say something else.

"Well?" Colonel Bass asked quizzically. "You need something else, Ramjet?"

"No, sir!" Skip replied and saluted.

The colonel started to salute, and then smiled. "Get your civilian butt outta here. I've got business to tend to!"

Just as Skip was closing the office door, Candy announced over the phone to the colonel, "I have Captain Taylor on line two for you, sir."

"Got it."

She laughed as she hung up the phone and said, "I've worked for the colonel for two years now, and I've yet to see him use the intercom."

"He's an old fashioned guy, I reckon," Skip commented. "I really thought I was gonna get my butt chewed in there today."

"You should have heard him when he left the office on the way to your crash," she whispered. "I've never heard such language!"

"I'll bet," Skip replied. "I haven't had anything go right yet today, so I figured leavin' a piece of me in there would end the day just about right."

He reflected a moment, and then said, "I hope I don't have to thank that Mustang pilot who almost shot me down for keepin' Colonel Bass from havin' me for lunch!"

"I really doubt that," Candy replied. "Oh, by the way, you have two messages. Pop Hackland called and said, 'If he's still got an ass after the colonel is done with him, send him on down to the O-Club, and tell him to plant what's left of it on a barstool and order a bottle. I'll be along just as soon as I get a good look at what's left of the Viper.' Then, the flight surgeon called and said you are to report to the base hospital for a post-crash physical and x-rays ASAP."

She studied him for a moment and then said, "If I had to guess, I'll bet you're going to the O-Club and won't even show up for that physical."

Skip smiled back at her, winked, and said, "You'd win the bet. See ya' later, Candy."

Skip collected his helmet, survival pack, and G-suit and headed for the Officers Club. Except for his left side, most of the aches and pains had faded, and he was almost beginning to enjoy the day.

He thought about Pop and wondered what he would think when he saw what was left of the Viper. Skip suddenly had a painful thought and wondered what he would do if he ever lost his old friend.

Dr. Gregory "Pop" Hackland, a graduate of the University of Arizona and Cal Tech was the son of an American father and a Taiwanese mother. He held an engineering degree and a Ph.D. in physics. His mother, a research scientist, always wanted her son to follow in her footsteps, but Pop was more interested in airplanes and flying.

Pop co-designed the Viper Series Aircraft and engineered the modifications that created the ABTX-6 hybrid-fuel engines that powered them and the flight computer that controlled them.

He and Skip met in Vietnam, and Pop later joined Skip's flying service, Tree Top Flyers, as partner and chief scientist. He smokes cigars (when he can find one), loves food (although the present fare does not always fit that term), and drinks anything with alcohol. Presently, he is Base One's chief engineer.

It was late afternoon, and a dust storm was blowing in from the west, painting the gray sky dark red. As the wind began to kick up, Skip wondered how Razer was doing. He had only planned on a brief stopover at Base One, and he could not help but think about his dog. Razer had been his constant companion for the last five years, most of that time spent at Owl's Nest.

"Looks like a big one," Skip said to himself as a distant rumble pulled his attention to the north. A thunderstorm was brewing, and it looked as though it would be another monster. Fond memories ran through his mind. Skip missed the days before the Reaper hit. He missed the smell of the rain and the feel of the cool breeze ahead of a thunderstorm. Now, there was rarely ever rain. The breeze was hot, and the storms were like an artillery assault, often raging for hours. When it was finally over, you were glad just to be alive. The howling winds and relentless lightning and thunder were intense and terrifying. If it did rain, it poured, usually causing severe flooding. No one looked forward to rain anymore. Skip reflected on the contrast of what was looming on the horizons to the west and to the north, and somehow, the events of the day seemed far away and insignificant.

Presently, his path brought the Officers Club into view and with it came the delightful aroma of meat grilling on an open fire. Skip was suddenly aware that he had a ravenous appetite. He crossed the short distance to the club, went directly to his locker, and put his flight gear away. As he followed his nose toward that delightful aroma from the grill, he encountered a fellow pilot, Jake Spade. Jake was well into a typical evening at the club. This was typical for Jake.

"Well, looky what I found," Jake laughed, loud and obnoxious as usual, "If it ain't our one-man airplane wrecking crew, in the flesh! Can I have your autograph?"

"Go away, Jake," Skip snarled. "Goin' for your daily liquor quota?"

"I ain't drunk yet," Jake retorted. "Besides, you're the one who needs to drown his sorrows, huh, Ramjet?"

"Bite me." Skip's reply was cold as ice.

Jake held up his glass. "The bar has a brand new batch of moonshine. Can I buy the great pilot a drink?"

"Spade, get out of my face. This ain't the time."

"Can't take it from a better pilot, eh?"

"Spade, know what your problem is?"

"I don't have a problem."

"Oh, yea, you do… It's your continuin' delusions of adequacy."

Chuckles came from the direction of the bar.

"Now, that's funny. You're a real funny man."

Then, from across the bar, someone shouted, "Better leave him alone, Spade. He'll be all over you like gravy on a biscuit!"

"Screw you!" Spade yelled back.

"You've gotta strange way of talkin' to your boss."

Spade realized his error and looked in that general direction. "Sorry, Major. Ah, hell, I'm on his shit list most of the time anyway."

Skip was weighing the consequences of decking Spade and the damage it would do to the rest of the evening when he heard Pop's booming voice behind him.

"Whadda we got here?" Pop said laughing. "A couple of hotshot pilots, puffin' up like two bull snakes! I don't know about you, but I'm as hungry as a grizzly. Let's get some of that mystery meat grillin' out back."

Pop put his arm around Skip's shoulder and dragged him toward the grill and away from the explosive encounter with Spade.

As they walked away, Spade yelled after them, "I don't eat with losers!" and headed back toward the bar.

"Are you okay, pal?" Pop asked sincerely.

"Yea, I'm fine," Skip replied, rubbing his painful ribs. "Give me another minute with that arrogant jackass, and I'll be great."

"Come on now. I'm serious," Pop insisted. "I've just finished inspecting what was left of Viper-6. What, in the livin' hell, did you get into?"

Skip gave him a bewildered look and said, "Buy me dinner, and I'll tell you the whole, sordid story."

"Deal," Pop replied. "But you've got to buy the beer."

"I hope it's better than the last batch…," Skip mumbled.

An hour or so later, Pop leaned back in his chair and said, "Not a bad meal, even for mystery meat."

Skip was taking a sip of beer, and he almost spit it out trying to contain an involuntary laugh.

"Why do you call it mystery meat, Pop?" Skip asked after he regained his composure.

"Oh, I don't know, I guess I just don't believe it's actually beef," Pop explained. "I mean, it's been years since I've even *seen* a cow. Well, at least we know it's not rat; the pieces are too big."

Skip grimaced, "Gross. Tell you what—if you do find out, don't tell me, okay? I don't wanna know."

"Hmmm…," Pop uttered mischievously, ignoring Skip's plea. "There's always soylent green."

"Don't even go there. Cannibalism is still a serious problem."

"Well…, it could be dog."

"I'm not listening!" Skip immediately plugged his ears and began to hum loudly.

Pop let out a generous belly laugh and raised his hands in surrender, "Okay, I won't say anymore! But, man, that was some story you just told me," Pop observed, changing the subject. He thought for a moment, his eyes sparkling with the fascination of a little boy as he continued, "I would give my left one to get my hands on that Mustang."

"I'd give more than that to get my hands on the pilot."

"I'll just bet you would," Pop said, laughing again.

"Speaking of getting my hands on a pilot, look who's coming this way," Skip warned, indicating Spade, staggering his way toward them.

Pop spoke seriously, "Look, pal, I know you'd like nothing more than to kick this joker's ass, but if the colonel is serious about replacing the Viper, we've got a load of work ahead of us… starting early tomorrow."

Skip got the point and turned to address Spade, "Well, Ace, you got a tank full yet?"

"Not even close, Ramjet. I burn fuel so fast, my tank is always empty," Spade shot back.

"You keep callin' me 'Ramjet,' and you're gonna have to fuel up through a soda straw!"

"Ooooo, I'm really scared now. Old man, you couldn't lay a hand on me if you were twins."

"Don't press your luck," Skip warned, and then he turned to Pop and said, "Let's get outta here and leave this drunk to his booze."

At that point, both men stood up to leave.

Before Skip could walk away from the table, Spade grabbed his arm and said, "Hey! Don't walk away when I'm talkin' to you! Don't you know how to show respect to a better pilot?"

Skip could barely restrain himself, "Better pilot! You arrogant dipshit! I've got more time taxiin' aircraft than you've got in the air!"

"Well, at least I can keep my aircraft in the air!"

"Better let him go, Hotshot," Pop warned.

"Why? You gonna do something about it, Grandpa?"

"No, I am!" Skip replied, then effortlessly removed Spade's hand from his arm, grabbed him by the throat, and pushed him backwards, slamming him into a sitting position in one of the chairs.

"I'll kick your sorry ass!" Spade yelled and started to stand up, but Skip planted a solid right to Spade's jaw. He sank back in the chair, out cold.

Skip looked down at Spade sprawled out on the chair. "Too bad it's illegal to kill assholes."

Pop chuckled, "If it was legal, there would be a bounty on 'em!"

Then, Skip turned to Pop and said, "It's time to get to work; let's go."

CHAPTER FIVE

Time to Go Shopping

The storm, looming on the western horizon earlier in the afternoon, blew in with a vengeance and raged most of the night. The next day dawned hot and dusty but calm and promising.

After an early breakfast, Pop and Skip were on a flight toward the Boneyard. The Boneyard was one of the few places left on earth where flyable military aircraft were stored. Located in the far western section of the Defense Zone, the former Davis-Monthan Air Force Base was all that remained of a once thriving Arizona town.

"Pop, you spent a lot of time in Tucson before the Reaper hit, didn't you?" Skip asked.

"You could say that," Pop answered. "Just after I graduated from the U of A, I hired on as a junior engineer with the CIA at Ft. Huachuca in Sierra Vista. We had a couple of intelligence-gathering birds and flew missions out of the fort. We'd put in at Tucson every chance we got for repairs, crew rest, or any other excuse we could come up with and hit a few watering holes while we were there, of course. Man, that town sure had some good-looking gals!"

Skip added, "I had a few TDYs over the years and a bunch of fuel stops at DM when I was flying the Commando Solo birds. The food was sure good, too."

"You got that right," Pop agreed. "It's hard to beat a town that has good food, good booze, and fine women."

They laughed, Pop thought for a moment, and then continued, "After three years at the U of A, I got to know that town pretty good."

"Too bad about Tucson; it was a nice place."

"Too damn hot!" Pop replied.

"You never did like the desert, did ya?" Skip asked but already knew the answer.

Pop answered anyway, "If I want to bake, I'll crawl in an oven."

The Tucson Valley gradually appeared on the horizon and with it, the jumbled, scattered remains of the city. The shock wave of the asteroid impact and the months of earthquakes that followed literally destroyed every city in North America.

"You remember that old country song, 'Ocean Front Property'?" Skip asked.

"Oh, yea, that's a George Strait song, ain't it?"

"Yep. I was just thinkin' that it's actually true now."

"Whaddya mean, Sport?" Pop asked.

"Well, the song goes, 'I've got some ocean front property in Arizona, from my front porch you can see the sea.'" Skip sang the lyrics and continued, "In the song, he's saying something that no one would really believe, but now it's true."

"Yea, you're right," Pop agreed, "I'll bet Yuma's under fifty feet of water at high tide."

"At least," Skip went on. "You know, if the weather ever gets back to somethin' close to normal, the islands of the Baja north of where Encinada was might be a nice place to do some fishin'."

"I've given up waitin' on the weather," Pop grumbled.

"I know what you mean," Skip agreed, and then changed the subject. "I guess we better let 'em know we're inbound before we get shot down."

Skip pressed the mike button on the control yoke and spoke, "Boneyard Control, this is Eagle Two-One, inbound for full stop."

"Eagle Two-One, Boneyard Control, we have you. Please ident."

Skip dialed in the proper security code and pressed the button on the aircraft's IFF system to flash the code on the radar screen.

The Boneyard responded, "Ident code received and verified. Wind is calm; altimeter is thirty-one point two five; surface temp is one two eight degrees. You are cleared for the option."

"Copy cleared to land. I'll take Runway Three-Zero, Eagle Two-One," Skip echoed back and began setting up the aircraft to land.

"I get a little jumpy every time I fly into this Godforsaken place."

"Really, why is that?" Pop inquired.

"Well, it's like this," Skip answered. "Since the Mount Lemmon long-range radar is almost useless, they decided to use a short-range system. I flew the parts and pieces out here for 'em. The primary concern was security, so they installed a SAM air defense system to protect the base. They use the SAM's radar for controllin' airplanes too."

"I see why you're jumpy," Pop replied soberly.

Skip went on, "I'm not all that comfortable around this crew out here anyway. And the thought of bein' tracked by a radar system with twenty hypersonic surface-to-air missiles tied to it, just one touch of a button away from bein' blown out of the sky… I mean, man, that could ruin your whole day!"

Pop laughed and said, "I wouldn't worry too much; I don't believe these jokers are crazy enough to let loose one of those birds on a friendly."

"I sure hope you're right, Pop," Skip replied.

As Skip taxied up to the Boneyard Security Headquarters, a security guard, armed with an MP-5, met the plane and marshaled them to a parking spot.

Skip shut down the engines; Pop opened the door and lowered the steps. Before either one could get out the door, the security guard positioned himself on the steps, pointed his MP-5 in their direction, and ordered, "Your identification and authorization papers!"

"Keep your shorts on, trooper; we ain't terrorists," Pop replied sarcastically.

In response, the guard pointed his weapon directly at Pop and demanded, "Now!"

"I guess he don't like you talkin' about his shorts," Skip said dryly.

Just then, a booming voice ordered from outside the aircraft, "Ease off, Mack."

The voice was Big Sam Thomas. The guard lowered his weapon and slowly backed out of the plane, his eyes never leaving the two men.

"I'd know that smart mouth anywhere!" the big man said as he greeted them at the door. "How have you been, Skip?"

Skip grasped the big man's extended hand. "Well, howdy, boss! I didn't expect to find you here. Damn, it's good to see you!"

"Actually, I've just returned," Big Sam explained as he bear-hugged Skip. "It's good to see you too!

"Hello, you big rascal!" Pop said as he stepped out of the plane.

"Hey, Pop!" Sam shook Pop's hand and continued, "Actually, I'm just filling in for the manager, and I thought I might take care of a couple of personal projects at the same time."

"Great! We need as much help as we can get," Pop confessed.

"Let's get out of this heat, go to the watering hole, and celebrate," Sam offered.

"I'll drink to that," Skip replied.

"Amen! Now you're talkin'," Pop added enthusiastically.

The three friends spent the evening catching up and talking about old times. Early the next morning, they met Big Sam at his office.

"Good morning, fellas," Sam greeted them.

"Top o' the morning to you," Pop replied.

"Mornin', boss, we need to borrow a jeep and a map," Skip announced.

"Why don't you let me give you the nickel tour?" Sam offered.

"That would be great," Skip replied.

As they followed Sam to his jeep, Pop looked out across the rows of aircraft and said, "This place has always overwhelmed me."

"I know what you mean," Skip said.

"It may not be quite like you remember," Sam cautioned as he started the jeep.

Skip gave Sam a quizzical glance as he climbed into the rear passenger seat. Sam steered the jeep toward the tarmac. Hundreds of military aircraft stood before them, lined up in row after row, each stored with a process called "pickling," which protects the internal workings of aircraft. The exterior aluminum, stainless steel, titanium, and composite skin are unaffected by the dry desert air and scorching sun.

"Sam, why wouldn't it be like we remember?" Skip finally asked.

"Well," Sam explained, "some of the planes may be missing, or if they're here, they're probably not in the same condition they were the last time you were here."

"What do you mean, exactly?" Pop asked. "I know the Reaper must have caused a lot of damage."

Momentarily, Sam stopped the jeep at the edge of a huge field. A massive pile of twisted metal lay before them.

"That's not the problem...," Sam remarked.

"Holy socks!" Pop exclaimed.

"Okay, explain," Skip replied.

"I should have told you last night, but two weeks ago, that junk pile was 296 flyable aircraft. Now, there are very few salvageable parts left. Just mostly scrap metal."

"What, or who, did that?" Skip asked.

"Terrorists hit the yard. They had planned the strike for some time, and it was executed with the precision of a Seal team."

"Damn!" Skip said, and then asked, "Why haven't we heard about it?"

"And how can you be sure it was planned for some time?" Pop added.

"Well," Sam explained, "Intelligence is playing this one close. I just don't know why. The planning part is simple. It takes a good crew about a week to pull a bird from storage and get it flyable. There are a lot of variables, but the average is about six days. When the first alarm sounded, the attackers had already been on the base approximately six hours. We know that, because all of the surviving guards were jumped at about the same time. After they gained access to the base, they planted explosives in a selected number of planes. That pile of scrap is all that's left of those birds and others nearby. The sound of jet engines running triggered the alarm. Then, explosions started going off everywhere. They used the explosions to pin down our security force. Four guards tried to get to the runway to block the takeoff, but they were all killed by explosions. Debris was flying everywhere. During the confusion, eight F-5E Tiger IIs were stolen," Sam concluded.

"Now, I see why Intelligence is keepin' it quiet," Skip said knowingly.

"They knew everything about those aircraft before they hit the base," Sam continued. "The crews here worked for months getting those F-5's flyable, and we were hit the very day we had planned to fly them out to duty stations. These people are so good, it's scary."

"Think they had help from the inside?" Pop asked.

"Well, if they did, we can't find a clue. Everyone, alive or dead, has been looked over with a microscope. We didn't find a thing. Not a thing." Sam's tone was that of near desperation.

"Maybe the help is much deeper," Pop offered.

Sam looked at Pop but said nothing.

"You believe it'll happen again, don't you?" Skip asked.

"Yes, I do, old friend, yes I do..." Sam's voice trailed off, as if lost in thought.

The trio sat in silence, staring at the results of the terrorist attack.

Suddenly, Sam slapped the steering wheel, breaking the silence. "Well! You didn't come here to look for junk. Let's go find something you can turn into Viper-7."

They drove toward the location where most of the flyable Harriers were stored. One row of twenty, and several partial rows, was still standing and intact.

"Well, at least they didn't do these in," Pop remarked.

"What we need to do," Skip explained, "is identify ten or twelve likely candidates, then get the records and look them over closely. We can narrow the field down to four or five, then pull a few inspection panels and make our final decision."

Skip and Pop surveyed the Harriers one by one, checking for evidence of battle damage, crash damage, over-stress, and signs of substandard maintenance. Within a few hours, they had compiled a list of ten aircraft. The next step would be to review the records and pick the aircraft meeting the requirements established for Viper candidate aircraft.

"Man, it is hot out here!" Pop complained. "What time is it anyway?"

"It's just after eight," Sam answered. "Heck, it's not hot yet, probably no more than 105 degrees. It will be 130 by afternoon. Now, that's hot!"

"No, Sam," Pop corrected. "A hundred and thirty degrees is a damn oven!"

Skip laughed, and then suggested, "Why don't we get out of this oven and get this list back to the records section."

"Excellent idea, young man," Pop said.

Back at security headquarters, the trio went directly to the aircraft records section and began to collect the maintenance and flight logs for each of the Harriers on the list. After several hours, the large stack of files had been collected in several boxes.

"Gentlemen, you have a big job ahead of you," Sam suggested.

"You are right," Pop agreed as he sat down on one of the boxes.

"Let's get to it," Skip sighed. "I need to get back to Owl's Nest and check on Razer. Pop, do you think we can have the list narrowed down to four or five by morning?"

"Sure, I mean, who needs sleep?" Pop answered.

"Listen, guys," Sam offered, "why don't you scan the data into our mainframe? I have been doing a software inventory, and there's a nice database program in there that will save you a whole lot of time. Then, when you're done, leave the list with me. I'll crunch the numbers, then have the crew pull the candidates into the main hangar and have them waiting for you when you return."

"Now that's an offer we can't refuse."

"You got that right, Pop," Skip agreed. "We owe you for this one, boss."

"Ah, forget it," Sam answered. "This new Viper is gonna help hunt down a certain bunch of terrorists, right? Just let me be in on the kill!"

"That's a deal," Skip replied, slapping Sam on the shoulder.

Early the next morning, Sam watched as the graceful King Air climbed into the desert sky, and then turned toward the giant red sun and home.

CHAPTER SIX

Intelligence, I Wonder

fter an uneventful flight, Skip was taxiing to parking when he spotted the colonel on the ramp ahead. "Well, we've had a fairly routine trip until now..."

Pop saw the reason for Skip's sarcasm and asked, "I wonder what Colonel Butthead wants."

"Now, Pop," Skip cautioned as he shut down the engines, "remember that he gave us a blank check for the Viper-7 project. Be civil."

"I won't say a word." From his tone, Skip doubted that Pop meant it very much.

Pop opened the door and lowered the steps. At that point, he sat down in one of the passenger seats, propped his feet up, and said, "He's all yours, Mister Diplomacy."

"Thanks a lot," Skip replied and stepped out to find Colonel Bass walking toward the aircraft with Lieutenant Colonel Ron Taylor in tow.

Neither of the two was smiling. The colonel looked to be in his usual 'I've got to deal with Ramjet again' mood.

Taylor, himself, was dressed as if he was ready to join a Marine recon team on a mission behind enemy lines, looking paranoid and acting suspicious of everyone and everything.

Taylor spoke first, "Mr. Scott, you are under arrest!"

Skip ignored him and greeted the colonel, "Colonel Bass, good to see you, sir."

"Welcome back, Skip, how did the shopping trip go?"

"We've got five good birds picked out. They're bein' prepared for inspection right now and will be ready for us by the time we get back to the Boneyard."

"Excellent!" the colonel exclaimed, obviously pleased.

"Mr. Scott, did you hear me? You are under arrest!" Taylor repeated with more volume.

Skip turned his attention to Taylor. "What's the matter with you? Somebody steal your magic decoder ring?"

The colonel smiled. Pop laughed so hard, he fell out of his seat.

Taylor, failing to see the humor, continued with his initial attack, "You were ordered to report to Base One Intelligence for debriefing. You failed to report. Therefore, I am placing you under arrest for disobeying a direct order."

"I received no such order, Colonel Taylor," Skip lied.

"You didn't?" Taylor asked, taken off-guard.

Skip continued, "No, and I'm returnin' now, specifically to see you."

"You are? Well, If...I...ah...good," Taylor sheepishly replied. He then quickly regained his composure, "Let's go."

"Lead the way." Skip turned toward Pop and winked. "See you later."

"Have fun," Pop said with a devious smile.

As they walked away, Colonel Bass was greeting Pop. Skip turned to look in their direction, and just as Pop emerged from the aircraft, Skip saluted Pop. It was a sarcastic reminder to play nice with the colonel. Carefully, out of the colonel's view, Pop returned Skip's salute with an upturned middle finger. Skip laughed, completed his salute, and continued following Taylor.

Oblivious of the event, Taylor asked, "Do you find something particularly amusing about this situation, Mr. Scott?"

Skip answered his question with a question, "Ron, why don't you relax just a bit? And while you're at it, I'm Skip, remember?"

"I don't forget anything," Taylor said arrogantly.

"Well, then, I'm sure you haven't forgotten how to relax."

"I will relax when what is left of the free world is free from terrorism."

"Then, you'll die stressed," Skip bluntly predicted.

"I am confident that you are wrong."

Skip's tone became serious, "I hope you're right, sir."

Taylor looked at him quizzically, but said nothing. They continued walking in silence.

At Base One Intelligence Headquarters, the debriefing team was ready, and the debriefing began immediately. Several hours into the debriefing, Skip had renamed it "interrogation" and had adjusted his opinion of Taylor to a considerably lower level.

"Mr. Scott, why do you think the terrorists overflew your remote outpost?" Taylor asked.

"My opinion hasn't changed since the first and second times you asked me that question," Skip replied.

"Just answer the question," Taylor insisted.

"Okay, if I wanted to see something, I would look at it!" Skip answered sarcastically.

"Do you mean that you have some inside knowledge of how the terrorist organization operates?" Taylor asked suspiciously.

Several of the interrogation team members made gestures of embarrassment as Skip, contemplating the consequences of physical violence, replied, "Taylor, your paranoia is only exceeded by your stupidity."

The interrogation team members were making large efforts to conceal laughter as Skip continued with more intent, "They made a classic recon run over Owl's Nest. Maybe, they didn't expect me to be there. Or maybe they knew I was there and wanted to determine the capabilities of the Viper. Or maybe they just wanted to take me out in a dogfight. Quite honestly, sir, I don't friggin' know!"

"Hmm, those are interesting theories..., and I will ignore the insult. This debriefing has taken quite a long time, but I assure you it was time well spent. Thank you, Mr. Scott, you may go," Taylor concluded and abruptly left the room.

As he walked out, Skip called after him, "Next time you have an interrogation, *don't* invite *me*!"_

Then he addressed the debriefing team, "How in the hell do you work for that conspiracy-obsessed security Nazi?" Most of the six smiled, but no one answered his question.

Then, Major Bud Cooper, Deputy Chief of Intelligence, spoke, "Skip, I apologize for the excessive length of the debrief. Ron isn't so bad after you get to know him. He's very thorough and just a little overzealous."

"A *little* overzealous?" Skip exclaimed. "And Attila the Hun was a *little* warlike!"

Maj. Cooper laughed and then grew serious. "You have to admit— we do have a serious problem here, and it could get a lot worse."

"Yes!" Skip replied with urgency in his voice. "It could get completely out of hand, Bud. Just like it did with the food riots. And the last thing we need is to be chargin' every direction at once, actin' like a bunch of Nazis, interrogatin' everyone as if we're all suspected of bein' terrorists. It wouldn't be long before we'd all become as paranoid as he is and start killin' each other!"

"I understand where you're coming from, and I agree with what you're saying," Bud replied. "Just don't let Ron get to you. We need your help."

It was late afternoon. Most of the team had left the debriefing room, heading home.

"Why don't we get out of here and let me buy you a drink?" Bud offered. "Thanks, after this ordeal, I could use one," Skip replied.

Arriving at the Officers Club, they found Pop and the colonel. The pair had been there for most of the afternoon. Upon seeing Skip and Bud, Colonel Bass heartily welcomed them and immediately ordered a round of drinks. The colonel and Pop, both half-sloshed, acted as if they were old comrades.

Skip observed the pair with amused amazement for the next hour or so, and then Colonel Bass declared that it was time to go home and departed.

After he left, Skip could not resist asking, "What happened to the disharmony between you two?"

"Aw, hell, he's not such a bad guy. Especially, after he's had a few," Pop remarked and laughed heartily, and then declared, "Gentlemen, it's time for this old man to turn in. I bid you goodnight."

"Goodnight. Don't forget our trip to Owl's Nest tomorrow," Skip reminded.

"Right. I'll be ready."

Bud asked, "You and Pop have been friends for a long time, haven't you?"

"Yep, we sure have," Skip said with a faraway look in his eyes.

"Where did you meet?" Bud inquired.

"Vietnam," Skip replied.

"Vietnam!" Bub replied in surprise. "You were in the Vietnam War? I didn't know you were that old."

"I'm not *that* old!" Skip replied defensively. "Besides, I thought you worked for Intelligence. You people are supposed to know me down to my underwear size."

"Honestly, I haven't read your file. I'm a little embarrassed to tell you that, but I have a hard time taking all of Ron's investigations seriously."

"You don't suspect me of bein' a terrorist sympathizer?" Skip asked, teasingly.

"Of course not. I know you, or at least, I know your reputation. I think you're right when you suggested they may be trying to take you out," Bud replied.

Skip looked at Bud for a moment, and then said, "I wish I could find their base. The problem is the range of some of the Mustangs was greater than two thousand miles. That covers a lot of territory."

"Maybe not," Bud suggested, "I've been doing some thinking about that... their main problem would have to be concealment. We have some pretty good terrain maps, and I've isolated four areas where I think a small base could be hidden."

"Then, we need to get a closer look at those areas," Skip said enthusiastically.

"And I have an idea how we could do that too," Bud offered.

"How?" Skip asked and lamented, "We're spread too thin to call in a recon bird from another outpost, and all we have are offensive aircraft. Man, I wish Viper-6 was still flyin'."

"How about a bona fide reckey bird?" Bud asked.

"What do you mean?"

"I mean an aircraft designed for reconnaissance with a reputation for getting the job done. I mean an RF-4C." Bud sat back and smiled, acting pleased with himself.

"You have access to a Phantom?" Skip asked in total awe.

"Very possible. I'm also a qualified RSO. If you can fly it, I can run the sensors," Bud announced triumphantly.

"If I can fly it!" Skip exclaimed. "The Phantom is my all-time favorite aircraft. My dad flew Phantoms in Vietnam. I instructed for the 33rd Recon Wing at Shaw and flew as test pilot for the Quick Strike

Test Project at Eglin. I have a slew of hours in the Lead Sled. Where can we find an airworthy Phantom?"

"I delivered one to the Wright-Patterson Museum," Bud answered, "just before the Reaper hit. I was on a detail to take one of the last RF-4C birds to the museum and prepare it for display. We got it there, then all hell broke loose, and the museum was closed permanently. That bird is probably still sitting right where we left it and ready to fly."

"That is fan-damn-tastic! If you can get us a ride out there, I'll be ready as soon as I get back from Owl's Nest the day after tomorrow," Skip announced.

"That is a deal," Bud replied as they shook hands.

Making his way to his apartment, Skip could see an electrical storm now raging on the western horizon. He hoped it would be gone by morning. The thought of time wasted trying to fly around a massive thunderstorm did not appeal to him. Flying through a storm was not an option he would even consider, and he had to get back to his mountaintop home and check on Razer tomorrow. He was anxious to get at the controls of that Phantom.

Thunderstorms fascinated Skip, and since he was too wound up to sleep for thinking about the Phantom, he poured himself a drink and watched the storm for a long while before finally going to bed. Sleep came quickly, but rest was elusive. His dreams were filled with visions of a P-51 Mustang eluding his aim as he tried to lock weapons on the evasive machine through the heads-up display. The Mustang would suddenly disappear, and then reappear dead on his tail with the cannon pod blazing. Flames would suddenly engulf his cockpit as he saw the ground racing up to greet him. Alone and helpless, hanging beneath his parachute, he would see his aircraft explode, scattering across the desert floor.

Later that night, an electrical storm blew in with ferocious intent. During the storm, Skip suddenly awoke in fright, his heart pounding, his body soaked with sweat. Realizing that he was having a nightmare, he got out of bed and splashed a bit of precious water on his face. He dared not go back to sleep and see another rerun of the Mustang's victorious kill, so he poured another drink, opened the curtains, and watched the storm rage.

In his life, he had been bombed, mortared, shot at, shot down, shot, and had generally taken just about everything the enemy could throw at him, with intent to kill, and survived it all. However, nothing he could recall was more terrifying than the storms that began appearing after the Reaper hit, and the sky grew dark. The lightning was relentless, hitting anything and everything, knocking holes in the ground and setting fire to anything that would burn. The crack from a lightning bolt and the thunderclap that followed would leave ears ringing and rattle one's insides. Seconds later, another strike, then another—on and on for hours. People were killed inside buildings— buildings that were considered lightning safe. It was fortunate that most survivors had chosen to live underground to escape the ravages of the climate. However, to venture outside during one of these monsters meant almost certain death.

Firefighters, always considered by Skip to be the bravest souls alive, were now held in even higher regard, as they faced the storms to fight lightning-sparked fires. Many firefighters died in the line of duty, but thanks to their selfless sacrifice, many potential victims were rescued from a fiery death.

Skip's thoughts dwelled on the firefighters as he heard sirens in the distance, the signal of yet another fire. Then, his thoughts flashed to his new foe, the Mustangs. Those mysterious Mustangs... If I ever get another chance, that gray camouflage bird will be mine... "Hey, wait a minute!" he spoke aloud. "Gray camouflage. Gray camouflage?"

His mind was racing now. "But, the Mustang that I first saw was polished aluminum... reflectin' the sun... there's two! There are two! Damn! I was set up! They knew that I would follow. It was just a matter of waitin' in ambush and then pouncing. Next time, it won't be so easy. You bastards should have done me in on the first try. You won't get another shot!"

The storm diminished and slowly marched toward the east, but Skip was too wound up to sleep, so he dressed and gathered his flight gear for the trip to Owl's Nest. It was 04:15 by the time he was in his flight suit and ready. He decided to get an early breakfast at the Officers Mess.

When he arrived, the place was mostly deserted. Skip noticed his friend and fellow pilot, Major Phil Blake, sitting alone, studying a terrain map. He poured himself a cup of coffee and walked over to the table where the pilot was sitting.

"Hey, pal, mind if I join you?"

"Skip! Pull up a chair. What have you been up to?"

"I've been better," Skip replied, sat down, and stared at his cup.

His friend smiled and slapped him on the shoulder. "Don't let it bother you, partner. Intelligence is taking this very seriously. We've set up a series of sorties to gather more data and maybe draw the terrorists out in the open. This is just too interesting to pass up. I have the first run. Going out on patrol this morning." Phil beamed proudly.

Skip was caught somewhat off guard by this turn of events. He had not expected much to come of his strange encounter. It all seemed surreal somehow—a nightmare that had not yet ended. But this was good news. For Skip, it was personal, and he needed an answer.

"I'm glad they picked the best man for the job."

"Thanks." Phil saw the look on Skip's face and asked, "Something bothering you about this deal, pal?"

"No, not really, just a lot of unanswered questions. One thing, though, I know there are two Mustangs. The one that made the recon run was polished aluminum, but the one that almost got me was gray camouflage. So, keep your head up, and check six; they like to jump you from behind."

"I'll give 'em a twenty-millimeter message for you." Phil smiled and gathered up his charts. "Briefing in fifteen minutes; see ya' later."

"Good huntin'," Skip offered and watched his friend head for the first official terrorist-hunting mission.

Skip had a feeling that this was not going to be over for a long time. He also had reservations about what Base Intelligence was doing. Phil Blake was one of only twenty intercept pilots for Base One. The interceptors were on alert around the clock. There were only twenty operational F-16's assigned to Base One, and all of the aircraft were primarily assigned for air intercept and air combat. Pilots and aircraft would be out of their element, flying low and slow for reconnaissance. The pilots were all well trained and experienced, but so was Skip, and a Mustang almost cleaned his clock.

CHAPTER SEVEN

Some You Win; Some You Lose

Later that morning, just before sunrise, Skip had the MD-500 helicopter loaded with supplies for Owl's Nest and was doing the preflight. He liked the Loach. It had been a while since he had logged any time in the nimble little bird, and he looked forward to the trip. Just as he was finishing the preflight, Pop arrived with a large bag in one hand and an ice chest in the other.

"Good morning, kid," Pop said as he put his things in the baggage compartment.

"Mornin', Pop, what's in the bag?"

"I thought Razer might like a surprise."

"That's nice of you. I'm sure he will."

"I also thought we might like a surprise," Pop continued. "That's in the ice chest."

Skip lifted one eyebrow, "Hmmm, and what might that be?"

"You'll see, just get this whirly-jig in the air."

"Aye, Captain." Skip saluted with a proper British Navy salute and climbed in the left seat.

Skip spooled up the Loach and called Ground Control to get taxi instructions for departure.

"Base One Tower, Chopper Three-Five for departure."

"Chopper Three-Five, Tower, you are number two for take-off following Eagle Flight. Taxi to Last Chance and hold."

"Copy number two for departure, Last Chance and hold, Chopper 35."

Skip lifted the MD-500 from its parking spot and hovered two feet above the pavement. Then, following the taxiway, he set down near the Last Chance checkpoint. He and Pop watched as the ground crew performed the final safety checks and armed the air-to-air and air-to-ground missiles on the two F-16's called Eagle Flight.

"That's Phil Blake takin' the first hunt for our suspected terrorists," Skip said to Pop on the intercom. "I wonder who his wingman is."

"It's that jerk, Spade," Pop replied. "Look what's painted on the side of his bird—'Bad Ass'. Now, ain't that cute?"

Finally, the Last Chance crew chief signaled, "armed and ready" to the pilots, saluted smartly, and gave the hand signal to taxi to the runway.

The lead pilot returned the salute and came up on the radio, "Tower, Eagle One, we're ready to roll."

"Roger, Eagle Flight, wind is calm, altimeter two niner two five. You are cleared for immediate departure, Runway 21... good hunting, sir."

"Eagle One, copy; clear to go. We'll bring back one or two tied across the hood."

"That'll do, sir, that'll do."

As Phil applied power and swung his F-16 around toward the runway, he saw the Loach and called on the radio, "Hey, Skip! I thought that was you on the radio. Headin' home today?"

"Yep, makin' a supply run; gotta feed Razer and the fish."

"Have a good flight, and say hello to Razer for me, would ya'?"

"I'll do it. Good huntin', partner," Skip replied, and alluding to their conversation at breakfast, he added, "and remember, check six."

"I'll let you watch the video. See ya later. Eagle One out."

Suddenly, the radio erupted again, "Don't worry, Old Man. Let the real pilots get the job done." Jake Spade was looking at Skip as he spoke on the radio.

Skip recognized Spade's voice and looked toward Eagle Two. Spade flipped him off as Eagle Flight taxied to the runway. Then, the afterburners lit on both aircraft, sending them roaring down the runway on a mission with an unknown outcome.

"You know," Skip reflected thoughtfully, "if ignorance is bliss, Jake must be the happiest bastard on the planet."

"I sure don't have much confidence in the outcome of that mission," Pop commented.

"The choice of wingman ain't exactly brilliant, either," Skip added.

"Roger that," Pop agreed.

Just then, the Control Tower announced, "Chopper 35, you are cleared for take-off, Runway 21. Have a good flight."

"Cleared for 21, Chopper 35. See ya'" Skip brought up the power, lifted off, and headed for Owl's Nest.

Later that morning, the master of Owl's Nest perked up and turned his ears toward a new sound. Razer had not heard this sound in a long time. He was not sure if this was a good sound or a bad sound. As the sound grew nearer, Razer waited and watched. Soon, the strange machine with blades whirling over its head came into view. He had seen machines like this before. His master had brought him to his mountaintop home in one. Perhaps this machine was bringing his master. The noisy jet with fire in its tail had taken Skip away and brought him back time and again. Maybe this time, the noisy jet would not be the one to bring him home.

Razer watched as the Loach circled overhead and then began descending toward the concrete pad that, on any other morning, would be occupied by a jet known as Viper-6. Razer sensed something familiar about the whirling machine and the manner of its approach; he relaxed a little but watched closely, just in case.

The little helicopter quickly settled to the landing pad and shut down, the rotor blades slowly spinning to a stop. Razer carefully approached the aircraft, sniffing and watching the two occupants, waiting to see what they would do. Suddenly, he recognized the man in the left seat and bolted up to the aircraft, just as Skip opened the door and stepped out. Razer leaped up on his hind legs and placed his front paws on Skip's shoulders.

Skip was expecting the greeting but still couldn't throw off the 190-pound mass of dog, happy to see his master. Skip continued backward, landing flat on his back with Razer standing on his shoulders, licking his face.

Just then, Pop came around the front of the Loach. "What have you been feeding this dog—steroids?"

Skip was laughing too hard to answer but did manage to command Razer, "Back." Pop offered his hand, but Razer knew what to do; Skip held onto Razer's collar, while Razer simply backed up, pulling Skip directly to his feet.

Pop watched in awe and exclaimed, "Jesus!"

After the supplies were unloaded and stored, they rested on the patio adjacent to the hangar cave. Pop was stretched out on a patio chair, hands behind his head, his feet propped up on the ice chest that he had brought on the trip, obviously enjoying the benefit of the high elevation and cooler temperature.

"You know, I could get accustomed to this... all I need is a hangar large enough to build Viper-7, and I'd be good to go."

"I'd enjoy the company," Skip replied. "When I first came to Owl's Nest, I needed the solitude. Razer and I have explored every inch of this mountain from top to bottom. It did me a lot of good to get out here, but now that I have, at last, made peace with the past, I need a more conversational companion than Razer."

Pop laughed and said, "Hey, that reminds me. I have a little surprise for him."

At that, Razer perked up and looked at Pop.

Pop looked at Razer and said, "Yes, I'm talking about you. How would you like a little something to sink those deadly teeth into?"

Razer jumped to his feet and walked over to Pop, sniffing the bag that Pop was just opening. Pop brought out a huge rawhide bone that weighed almost ten pounds.

Skip laughed with surprise and asked, "Where on Earth did you get that?"

Pop replied, "You know me; I have a few outstanding favors here and there, and besides, I never reveal my sources."

Razer watched as Pop removed the massive rawhide bone from the bag and handed it to Skip for closer inspection. He grunted noisily, licked his chops, and wagged his stubby tail.

"I think he approves of the gift," Skip said, watching Razer trying to contain his obvious desire for the bone.

Skip handed it back to Pop who was now sharing part of his chair with Razer as the big dog stretched to reach the delicious gift.

"Okay, big fella, what do you say?" Pop asked the dog.

Dropping back to the ground, he let out a small, excited bark, then accepted the bone and held it for just a moment, looking first at Pop and then at Skip. Realizing that he would not have to share, he trotted off to one of his favorite spots to enjoy his treat.

"He should be busy for a while," Pop remarked as they watched Razer disappear behind a mound of rocks near the pond.

"That was really nice of you, Pop."

"If you liked that, you're gonna love this!"

At that, he reached for the ice chest, slid it over to Skip, and opened the lid. Inside, along with a chunk of dry ice, were fresh vegetables, beer, and meat.

"Oh, man! You sure know how to make my day. I'm not even gonna ask where you got this stuff."

"That is wise," Pop replied. "That is very wise, indeed."

Several hours later, all three companions were beside the lake, sitting around a fire, full and contented. Pop refilled Skip's cup from a coffeepot that was sitting near the fire, and then refilled his own cup.

"You know, pal, life don't get much better than this," Pop observed as he lit a cigar.

"Looking back, I would not have guessed we would ever be enjoying life this much again," Skip observed.

"I know what you mean," Pop replied. "Until the Reaper hit, I thought that I had really missed out by not having married and raised a family. Then, I saw firsthand how devastating it would be to lose everything. After taking part in the cremation of a hundred thousand dead bodies, each of whom was once part of someone's family, I came to the conclusion that I might have made the best choice after all."

Skip was silent for a few moments.

Pop made an effort to repair a possible mistake, "I hope I didn't get too personal... sometimes I have a big mouth."

"No, not really," Skip replied. "I was just thinkin'..."

"You have a very serious expression. I thought I might have offended you."

"No, not at all. I was just thinkin', I've never told you exactly what happened during the months after the Reaper hit."

"Well, no..." Pop was caught off guard with Skip's comment. "I thought that you were laid up for a while with that cut on your leg."

"Yea, I almost died from blood loss and was down for a few weeks in the basement of a hospital in North Platte. Meanwhile, we went under marshal law, and I was ordered to report to the nearest military base. But, you know me; I ain't much for followin' orders, so I got out of there as quick as I could. I just had to find my wife and kids, so I headed West. I made it almost to Oregon before the situation went so far to hell that I finally gave up and started to make my way back home.

"My ID, flight suit, and the story of my crash got me through most of the checkpoints, plus food in most places. But before long, I was ordered to help a squad of National Guard soldiers. They were trying to prevent looting and distribute food and water. It was just the beginning of the food wars. They handed me an M-16 and a flak vest, so I pitched in. For the past few weeks, I had watched otherwise civilized people turning into animals. Now I had to try to help 'em or maybe shoot somebody trying to feed his family. I lasted for a few days. Finally, I just got sick of seein' all of those helpless faces that I could do nothin' for, and I just walked away.

"My leg was givin' me a fit. I knew that I wouldn't be able to make it on foot, so I went back and stole a Hummer. A couple of days later, I found myself taking refuge beneath an overpass during one of the debris showers. It had been months since the Reaper hit, and debris was still fallin' out of the sky. I've yet to figure that out... Anyway, as I lay there, a young mother with three small children took refuge too. Shortly, three skinheads showed up. They were rough lookin'—swastikas tattooed on their scalps and everything. Right away, they started screwin' with the young mother. I stood up and yelled at 'em to get the hell away from her, and the one nearest me, probably twenty feet away, pulled a .44 magnum and shot me.

"The round hit me in the chest, knocked me backwards about ten feet, and son-of-a-bitch, it hurt! I thought I was dead, but thanks to the flak vest that I was still wearin', I just ended up sore as hell and bruised. I was wearing a hooded poncho, so they didn't see the vest. I guess they figured I was dead too. I woke up several hours later. My Hummer was gone. The skinheads were gone. They had raped the young mother and killed her and the kids.

"I also found two other people dead and tire tracks heading towards a nearby town. I was so enraged that I followed the tracks, determined to find them bastards. Sure enough, I found 'em. They had stopped at a drug store, ransacked it, and were takin' pills and drinkin' whiskey. I just watched from a distance and waited. In a few hours, they were all three passed out.

"I tied 'em up while they slept and then woke 'em up. I told them that I was the ghost of the guy they had shot just before they raped and killed the young mother and kids. They actually believed me! Then, I slit the carotid artery on each of the bastards, took their supplies and whiskey, and left them to die.

"I had finally descended to the level of all of the other animals out there. If I live to be a hundred years old, I'll never forget that sorry, friggin' day."

"You can't blame yourself for that. Hell, I would have probably done the same thing." Pop meant what he had said, and then asked, "What happened then?"

"I managed to make my way to Colorado Springs. I found out that General Grey had taken command of Cheyenne Mountain, so I contacted him. I worked for him for a while, and after that, I was assigned to Base One."

Skip suddenly changed the subject, "When we get back to Base One, I'm gonna fly out to Wright-Pat with Bud Cooper. We're gonna try to bring back a RF-4 that was there before the Reaper hit. Do you think that you could go on to the Boneyard and get started on Viper-7? I should be able to join you in a few days."

"I don't see why not," Pop answered. "We've got a generous budget on this project. I'd like to get started as soon as possible. If the recce is airworthy, and you can get it back to Base One, do you think we can get any useful data from a limited number of reconnaissance missions?"

Skip reflected for a bit, "Well, we've only seen infrared data gathered by Viper-6, and that was taken on three consecutive patrol missions at ten thousand feet, almost eight months ago. The reason I flew those missions is that Keyhole managed to punch through a few holes in the blanket and detected something out of the ordinary. Intelligence said they needed a wide sweep, so that's what I gave 'em. No follow-up was ever ordered, so I figured they didn't find anything and forgot about it. But, if terrorists had established a base in the mountains, a lot of work could have been done in eight months."

"You have a valid point," Pop agreed. "I suppose any data is better than what we have now."

"Speakin' of missions," Skip said, "I wonder how Phil and Dickhead did on their mission today."

"I hope Mr. Bad Ass didn't shoot down his flight leader by mistake," Pop said sarcastically.

***

Major Phil Blake, flying Eagle One, flight leader of the search and destroy mission, discontinued afterburner and throttled back slightly to conserve fuel. He was about to give his wingman an order to join up on his wing, when Spade's F-16, still in afterburner, shot directly over his cockpit, missing him by a scant few feet.

Major Blake was not an excitable person and disliked the rigid military-style discipline that was customary in dedicated, career officers. He was, however, a very contentious pilot and did not consider this particular moment the best time to play grab ass.

"I don't need to remind you that you're the wingman, and I'm flight lead. Assume your position and conserve fuel."

"Da, Comrade Flight Commander."

Spade pulled his aircraft into a vertical loop, sliding tightly into position on the right wing of his flight leader's aircraft. One hour and fifteen minutes later, the two fighters were approaching one of the areas suspected to be the location of the terrorist base.

Major Blake gave Spade further orders, "Stay on my wing. We'll make a few passes over the area at three thousand feet. If we draw anything out, watch my back."

Spade replied, "I'm with you."

Major Blake confirmed, "Roger, break on one...—three, two, break!"

Both F-16's rolled, as one, into a fast descent from their cruising altitude of twenty thousand feet, descending to three thousand feet above ground level. Making wide sweeps, they made several passes over the area from different directions.

On the fifth pass, all hell broke loose. A missile streaked past Eagle One; another followed almost immediately, and this one exploded a few feet above his starboard wing.

Major Blake gave a command to his wingman, "Break right to one eight zero, and get low!"

Blake broke left and went into afterburner. As the two fighters split in opposite directions, another missile went by but missed by a much larger distance. Major Blake looked left through the top of his canopy, as he rolled almost inverted into a steep dive, looking for his wingman. Eagle Two was in the position Major Blake expected to find him, also diving for the ground.

He gave another order to Spade, "Level at 500, and join up. Let's get that joker!"

Major Blake intended to turn and bring his air-to-ground missiles to bear on the point from where he thought the missiles had been launched. Since there was no indication of a weapons radar track or lock from his defensive sensors, Major Blake assumed the missiles were shoulder-launched infrared tracking, similar to Stingers. *The one that exploded must have malfunctioned*, Blake thought, *or have been rigged with a proximity fuse.*

This confused him, and he thought *who would go to the trouble to set a proximity fuse on a missile with such a small warhead? It couldn't do enough damage to disable an aircraft.* In the back of his mind, the thought occurred that perhaps the ground fire could be used as a distraction. That might explain the proximity-fused missiles. He only hoped they could draw more fire or see the enemy with enough time to mark and fire on the launch point.

As Eagle Two slid into the right wing position, Major Blake initiated a hard, climbing right turn to put them in a good firing position and line up on the spot that he hoped was the target.

Suddenly, his aircraft shuddered. He heard a noise from behind, and before he could identify it, the noise identified itself as machine gun rounds. Fired from above and behind, the rounds ripped through his left wing as tracers zipped by, inches from the top of his cockpit canopy. Major Blake immediately went to full throttle, lit the afterburner, and looked back, trying to locate the source of the incoming fire.

He shouted on the radio, "Where is he? Where is he?"

Eagle Two said nothing.

Major Blake looked for Eagle Two and found him, trailing behind, still on his right wing. Directly behind him, four black F-5's bore down on the two F-16's.

He shouted into the mike, "Break left! Break left! Four bandits on your six! Full AB! Full AB!"

Eagle Two broke left and went into full afterburner, but only one F-5 followed. The remaining three stayed on Eagle One. Suddenly, Major Blake heard the unmistakable sound of a hostile radar warning in his headsets.

"They're trying to get a lock on me," he said aloud. "Well, just watch, assholes!"

He quickly jettisoned his air-to-ground missiles. That lightened his load and reduced aerodynamic drag considerably.

Still in afterburner and pulling away, he selected an AIM-9X Sidewinder, fire and forget, air-to-air missile, but the infrared tracking system could not lock on a target. Unable to get a lock and not knowing how long he would have before his attackers fired, he decided to turn the tables. He then made an abrupt 9.5 G, 180-degree turn and met the three F-5's head-on. Knowing he had, at most, two seconds, he targeted one of the F-5's and fired a Sidewinder. As he initiated another hard right turn, a flash lit up his cockpit. He looked over his left shoulder and saw the remaining pieces of the F-5 falling to the ground. The Sidewinder had entered the F-5's left engine intake, and the fighter exploded in a ball of fire.

"Gotcha!" he said and turned his attention to the remaining two F-5's continuing the pursuit.

Major Blake called on the radio, "Two, One, how are you doing? I could use some help; I've got two on my tail."

After a few seconds, Eagle Two answered, "Boss, I'm havin' trouble shakin' this guy. I'll be there as soon as I get rid of him."

Spade said nothing else.

Aftermath I: The Fight For Survival

The hostile radar tone was continuous in Major Blake's ears as he struggled to evade the two F-5's.

Suddenly, a voice came over the radio, "Surrender your aircraft, and we will not fire."

"How in the hell did they get our frequency!" Major Blake exclaimed aloud, and then keyed his radio, "I'll give it to you all right; I'll shove this Falcon up your ass!"

Unsure what missiles they carried, he could only trust his electronic-warfare defensive system to provide the necessary data he needed to avoid being hit. He kept watching his six o'clock, slowly pulling away from the F-5's. The tone in his ears changed, indicating a weapons radar lock. He looked back to see several missiles leaving both aircraft simultaneously. The rocket motor exhausts suggested more than one type, and the EWS tones in his ears confirmed it. He immediately ejected several magnesium flares and pulled a short 10-G left turn. Then, he rolled the Falcon inverted, went into a dive to gain airspeed, then ejected several more flares, plus chaff. Several flashes lit up his cockpit, indicating that heat seekers had hit the flares.

He then pulled another 9.0-G right turn, rolled out straight and level at Mach 1.8, and looked back to see two of the missiles still on him and gaining ground. Suddenly, his weapons system indicated lock.

"Kiss your ass good-bye!" the major said as he fired a Sidewinder. The AIM-9X left the rail, made an abrupt 180-degree turn, and headed for the F-5's. Immediately, he put the nose down and made for a mountain pass, hoping he could get through it and rid himself of the remaining missiles if his F-16 did not disintegrate first. The aircraft was vibrating so badly that he was having trouble reading the instruments. Major Blake was sure that he had exceeded the maximum speed for this altitude, by at least 0.8 Mach, and he did not know how badly his Fighting Falcon was damaged.

The F-5 flight lead and his remaining wingman saw the Sidewinder launch and split apart, hoping the Sidewinder would choose a target early enough that the missile could be avoided. The Sidewinder's internal processor compared the received infrared data and chose the most likely target. The Sidewinder turned slightly, heading to the left.

As the F-5 wingman began evasion tactics, the flight leader turned his F-5 back to the job at hand. Major Blake looked back just in time to see the second F-5 explode in a ball of fire.

"Two down!" he shouted.

The mountain pass was coming up fast. The tone in his ears and a quick look back verified that the missiles were almost on him. Suddenly, the peaks flashed by, and directly behind him, he saw the blinding flashes as the missiles exploded from the compression of the F-16's shock wave in the mountain pass.

"Man, that was close!" he exclaimed as he pulled up and continued accelerating. Suddenly, an EWS tone indicated a missile had been launched from eight o'clock low. It was a heat seeker, and it was close.

"Damn!" he exclaimed.

Another aircraft had been waiting in ambush on the other side of the mountain range. Major Blake immediately broke left and descended, looking for the aircraft that launched the missile. Looking back, he saw the missile turning in trail, accelerating at a tremendous rate. He selected a flare and hit the pickle switch. Just as the flare ejected, his weapons radar indicated a target. He turned his F-16 towards the blip and saw the F-5 ahead, descending away, trying to escape. As the radar locked on target, he fired an AIM-7 Sparrow, and it streaked away toward the target.

Then, he looked back to see the flare still burning. The missile had slipped past. A second later, Phil Blake felt a thud from behind and reached for the ejection handle as Eagle One exploded.

F-5 number four looked back to see the ball of fire and, in the same frame of vision, saw the Sparrow as it sprinted toward him. He knew he might not brag of his victory today. Turning hard to avoid the missile, the nimble F-5's wings gave way to the excess G's and separated from the fuselage. The pilot pulled the ejection handle, but before the seat fired, the missile completed its job, and the F-5 exploded into hundreds of flaming pieces.

The F-5 flight lead watched as the pieces of debris from the F-16 and his wingman's F-5 fell to the ground. He would not forget this battle and the three comrades that had been lost, nor would he forget the valiant bravery and airmanship displayed by the F-16 pilot. The superior fighter pilot had not won this victory and, if not for a twist of fate, the results would have been different. Of that, he was certain.

Seeing no parachutes, he made an abrupt turn and headed for home. He would not remember this fight as a victory; he was just happy to be alive.

***

The next day dawned with final preparations to depart Owl's Nest. Razer knew that his master would be leaving that morning. He was by the bed when Skip woke up, and he would be within a few feet of his master until the flying machine took him away again.

While Skip added a hundred pounds of dog food to Razer's automatic feeder and verified that it was working properly, Pop checked the operation of the solar-powered pond filter system and cleaned the filters. The final duty to perform was to set the security system, and then it was time to go.

Skip knelt down by the big dog and looked him in the eyes, "Well, pal, it's time for you to go on duty again. You watch the place until I get back, okay?"

He rubbed Razer's head, scratched behind both ears, and patted him on his massive neck. "Oh, by the way, your old pal Phil Blake asked me to say 'hello' for him. Do you remember Phil?"

Razer recognized the name and paused for a moment, then barked.

"Pop, did you see that?"

"Yes, I did," Pop replied. "You think he remembers Phil just from hearing his name?"

"Apparently, he does," Skip said and studied Razer for a few moments, then continued, "He probably spent as much time with Phil as he did with me when I was stationed at Base One. They seemed to have a connection of some sort. Razer would just go with him. Phil never had to call him; Razer just followed Phil by choice. When I was on a mission or gettin' crew rest, I never had to worry; he would always be with Phil."

Skip spoke to Razer, "I wish I could take you with me, boy. I know you and Phil would get a kick out of seein' each other again. Well, I'll see ya', pal."

Then one last, firm command, "Razer, protect."

Skip spooled up the Loach, lifted off, and headed for Base One. Hours later, he set the little chopper down in front of Base Ops.

Pop noticed that the American flag was flying at half-mast as they walked toward the Ops building. "I wonder what that's about?"

"I don't know," Skip answered, "but I'll bet it ain't good."

Except for the staff sergeant on duty at the desk, the Ops room was deserted.

"Howdy, Sarge," Skip said, "here are the keys to the Loach."

Skip actually handed him the aircraft logbook.

"The little bird flew like she knew what she was doin'. No write-ups. Would you know if Bud Cooper has scheduled a flight to Wright-Pat for tomorrow?"

"Yes, sir." The duty sergeant quickly checked the schedule book and continued, "He has T-38, 72388 scheduled for departure at zero six hundred tomorrow morning."

"Great. Thank you, young man," Skip said and added, "I think it's time to get some liquid refreshment."

The sergeant replied without expression, "You might as well, that's where everyone else is today."

"It wouldn't have anything to do with that flag out there, would it?" Pop asked.

"I'm afraid so," he answered.

Skip suddenly had a very bad feeling and asked, "Who?"

"Eagle Flight ran into some trouble yesterday. Major Blake didn't make it back."

Skip showed no outward reaction, but just said, "Damn."

"I gather his wingman is okay?" Pop asked.

"Yes, sir," the sergeant replied. "He reported that they were jumped by five or six F-5's. You should see his F-16. I'll bet it has fifty machine gun hits. The memorial service for Major Blake is today at 1600 hours."

Skip left without saying another word. Pop thanked the duty sergeant for the information and caught up to Skip just as he made it to the front door.

He grabbed Skip by the arm and stopped him. "I think I know what you're up to, and I would like to do the same thing, but you need to let this one go."

Skip paused and looked at the floor. "You're right, as usual," Skip agreed. "I just know, as sure as the sun rose today, that Phil went down because that jerk didn't do his job."

"Let's just not convict and sentence the jerk today. You and I won't make much of a lynch mob... although we could probably recruit enough folks!"

Skip smiled and said, "We've got Colonel Bass on our team, at the moment, and if I beat the crap out of Spade, it won't exactly make any points."

"I don't think I could have said it better myself," Pop agreed.

Then he put his hand on Skip's shoulder and said, "Now how about let's get some of that refreshment you mentioned earlier?"

As they walked past the flag fluttering at half-mast, Pop looked up and said, "As that old saying goes, 'Some you win, some you lose, and some are rained out,' but we could have done without losin' one like this..."

CHAPTER EIGHT

Friends in the Right Places

Early the next morning, Major Bud Cooper was at the Base One Operations Office, signing out the T-38 Talon for the trip to Wright-Patterson Air Force Base. Skip joined him, flight bag in hand, ready for a trip that he truly looked forward to making.

"Good mornin'," Skip said to Bud as he approached the counter.

"Good morning. I'm just getting the keys to 388. How's the old man this morning? Ready for a fun trip?" Bud asked Skip and smiled mischievously.

He was referring to the previous evening at the Officers Club. The entire Base One population had attended the memorial service for Phil Blake. In a time-honored pilot tradition, an Irish wake and celebration of the life of Major Phillip Blake was held after the memorial service. By midnight, there was not a sober soul in the place. Bud Cooper was sporting a hangover that would kill a lesser person. He naturally assumed that Skip was in the same shape. Skip, on the other hand, never felt better.

"I'm ready. Never felt better. Just anxious to get back in a Phantom again."

Bud knew that when it came to flying airplanes, Skip was like a kid in a candy store. But, he was certain Skip was lying about how he felt.

"Well, I've requested a full fuel load and flight prep," Bud informed his co-pilot. "All we need to do is a preflight, and we're ready to roll."

"Fantastic! Let's get to it," Skip replied.

Thirty minutes later, they were climbing through ten thousand feet, en route to Wright-Patterson Air Force Base, Ohio.

Bud leveled the Talon just beneath the overcast level at eighteen thousand feet, set the Inertial Navigation system for a direct flight, and engaged the autopilot. He intended to relax and nurse his hangover.

Skip spoke to Bud from the rear seat, "Since I'm flying the rear seat, do you mind if I navigate just a bit?"

"Sure, go right ahead. What did you have in mind?"

"Well, I thought it might be interesting to have a look at the Mississippi River. Since salt water invaded the Great Lakes, the Mississippi and Missouri are mostly salt water. I was wonderin' how that has affected the river delta. We could turn east, intersect the river, and then run north along the river. It shouldn't add more than an hour to our flight time."

"Sounds okay to me. In fact, you have the airplane. Wake me up when we make the river," Bud said, taking advantage of the opportunity to nurse his hangover.

"You're on," Skip said and disengaged the autopilot. "Let's get a bit lower and go VFR."

He pulled the throttles back and descended to fifty-five hundred feet, set the throttles back to cruise power, and said, "I'll try to keep it straight and level, just for the sake of your hangover."

"Hangover? Who has a hangover? I don't have a hangover."

"Right. I got news for ya'; it's all but written on your forehead. If your hangover were any worse, your head would explode. That homemade rot gut will eat your lunch."

"Skip, do me a favor. Next time you see me drinking like that, shoot me!"

Skip just laughed and said, "Go to sleep."

Almost two hours passed as Kansas and Arkansas slipped by below. Just north of Memphis, Skip made a descending turn and headed north along the Mississippi River. Leveling out at fifteen hundred feet, they had a bird's eye view of the big river.

Increased flow had extended beyond the banks, and the river was now four miles wide in some spots. The river delta was devoid of plant life, caused by lack of sunlight and salt water flowing to the Gulf of Mexico. Only an occasional water bird could be seen along the river.

The two men flew along the river in silence. No words came to mind. Comments were unnecessary. The scene spoke for itself.

At the confluence of the Mississippi and Missouri, Skip said, "I've seen enough." He pushed the throttles forward and pointed the nose of the T-38 skyward. Climbing to 7500 feet AGL, he throttled back and leveled off. For the next fifteen minutes or so, they said nothing, the river scene still occupying their thoughts.

Finally, Bud broke the silence, "I was wondering about something..."

"What's that, Bud?"

"Well, you know, we've gotten away from call signs somewhat. I guess the Navy and Marines have stayed with the tradition pretty much. But the defense force hasn't. Why do you think that is?"

"Well, the force is mostly small detachments. Bein' smaller, I suppose we're more team oriented and less competitive. I think call signs are kinda like a badge. The unique name gives a pilot a way to stand out in the crowd—like the family banners carried by the knights of the Middle Ages. We probably don't feel the need as much because we have a stronger sense of pride within our organization from what we've all lived through."

"That makes sense. But, certainly, you once had a call sign. Why don't you use it now?"

"I do."

"Pardon me?"

"I do use a call sign."

"What?"

"Skip."

"I thought Skip was your nickname."

"Nope, my nickname is 'Bill'."

"I don't mean to be nosy, but I am deputy chief of Base One Intelligence. I should already know this, but... how did you get 'Skip' as a call sign?"

"Well, it's a long story and goes back to the days just after Vietnam. In '72, I enrolled at Auburn University on the GI Bill. I would fly every chance I got, tryin' to get my multi-engine instrument rating and commercial ticket. Holly and I got married during the summer break and soon realized that we were not gonna live very well on my GI Bill income.

"Holly was also goin' to Auburn and workin' part time too. We barely made enough to buy food after the bills were paid. I was gonna have to quit flyin' and get a better payin' job. I just couldn't go for that, so I sold just about everything I had and used the money to pay for the remainder of the flight time that I needed to get my commercial ticket. Then, I went to every airport, flyin' service, FBO, and pilot I could find, lookin' for work. I mean I would do anything, short of hauling dope, to make a few bucks.

"I got jobs flying sight seein' tours and jobs haulin' everything from canceled checks to explosives. I even had to haul a load of pigs once! I got ferryin' jobs to various places, bringin' planes into maintenance facilities, delivering planes fresh out of maintenance and brand new ones too. Some of the ferrying trips were really long hauls.

"And one of those long hauls was a reconditioned DC-3 that had to be delivered from Atlanta to Sondistrom, Greenland. It was in the summer, and I was lookin' forward to the trip. I'd never been to Greenland.

"On the morning that I was scheduled to depart, Charlie, the boss of the FBO that had reconditioned the old bird, wanted to go along. I figured that was better for me; we could take turns at the yoke, and the trip wouldn't seem so long. So, we left Atlanta, flew along the coast, and topped off the tanks at a small airport in upstate New York. We jumped off there and headed out across the North Atlantic.

"We were about five hours out when, suddenly, the left engine quit. No warning, it just sputtered once and quit. Like the fuel had been shut off. We turned back and started goin' through the water ditching procedures, when the other engine quit. Again, no warnin'; it just stopped.

"I set up best glide angle, and we tried everything in the book to get one or both of the engines started. We did everything but climb out on the wing and spin the props by hand. Nothin' worked. We prepared to ditch, and I was tryin' to set her down as gently as possible. But, on the first contact with the water, we felt the jolt and salt spray hit the windscreen, but we must have skipped off the top of a wave, and then both engines started!

"It seems that during our frantic efforts to get the engines started, we had ignored the final steps of the emergency checklist... you know, chop the throttle, turn off the fuel, kill the ignition... that stuff. So, there we were, both engines sputterin' to life, barely a wave height above the ice-cold North Atlantic, skippin' off the crests of the waves, tryin' to get enough airspeed to climb.

"We were no more than fifty feet from the surface when I looked over at Charlie, and he was just lookin' down at the ocean sayin', "I don't believe it; I just don't believe it!"

"Then he turned to me and said, 'How are we going to explain this to the FAA? Hell, how are we going to explain this to anyone? You just started both engines by skipping this crate off the ocean! From now on, I'm calling you Skip!'

"He did, too. I worked for him, off and on, until I joined the Air Force. It seemed that everywhere I went, my new nickname preceded me. So, when the subject of call signs came up, and I wasn't able to use my old call sign from Nam, I already had one, 'Skip'."

"What was your original call sign?"

"Viper."

"So, that's the origin for the name of your aircraft?"

"Yep. Pop thought it was a good name and insisted that we use it for the whole series."

"That's a fascinating story. You've had an interesting flying career."

"It's been fun. It has been fun."

"Well, Bud, we're approaching Wright-Pat airspace—time for you to take over."

Within an hour, they were in a van, heading for the hangar where the Phantoms were stored. At the wheel was Frank Levins, the person in charge of aircraft storage.

In the process of procuring the Phantom, Bud had been handed off to Frank. It seemed that, while security of food and weapons was a high priority, the duty of caretaker for surplus weapons, such as older airplanes, was a very low priority. Frank was the authority and had the final word about the disposition of most of the aircraft now stored at Wright-Patterson Air Force Base.

"Are you gentlemen familiar with the base?" he asked.

"Not really," Bud answered, "I ferried the Phantom here and a few other birds, but I never stayed over for very long."

"It's been years since I've been here," Skip said.

"Well, we have taken on quite a few aircraft over the last few years. When the coastal bases began flooding, many of the aircraft were sent here on a temporary basis. Then it was decided, due to the change in our defense posture, that the aircraft would be stored here permanently. We stuffed the existing hangars full, and then more birds were brought in. It was ordered that all of the aircraft were to be hangared, but we were out of space, so we covered 'em as best we could with camouflage netting and the like. I guess it's smarter to keep them 'out-of-site, out-of-mind,' so to say.

"Except for the security detachment protecting the base, we're a small unit. I'm pretty much on my own deciding what to do with these birds. Now, I don't want you to get the idea that you've got an open expense account, but I really appreciate the job that you're doing out there in the Badlands. So, if you need more aircraft, just remember me; I'll do my best to get you what you need."

"We really appreciate that, Frank, and don't worry, we won't forget you," Bud replied.

Presently, they arrived at the hangar. Frank spoke as he disabled the security system, unlocked the access door, and activated the switch to open the hangar doors, "I had to do quite a bit of rearranging to get your bird to the outside. I also had it prepped, inspected, and serviced. The only thing remaining is fuel... we can't hangar a fueled bird."

"Frank, you're priceless," Bud said. "You sure have made this a piece of cake."

"Thanks, Major, I really appreciate that."

Just then, the doors opened enough to reveal the inside of the hangar. There were Phantoms of every model and description, with wings folded, parked as close as possible to each other. At the front, near the center of the hangar, was the Phantom they sought.

Skip suddenly laughed and said, "I don't believe it. It's7463!"

Bud and Frank both gave Skip a look of confusion.

"This is my airplane," Skip explained. He walked up to the Phantom and ran his hand along the pitot tube and radome as he had done many times before, during each preflight. "This is the Sensor bird used on the Quick Strike Test Project. I have several hundred hours in this machine, testin' FLIR and the Pave Tack pod. Man, if we had one of those to hang on this bird, we could do some serious reconnaissance."

"Does the pod look like a centerline fuel tank with a big ball on a gimble at one end?" Frank asked.

"Yep. And the ball has a flat side with three oval windows," Skip added.

"I have two of those things in crates in the hangar next door," Frank announced.

"I must be dreamin'!" Skip exclaimed.

"The crates came with the rest of the spares," Frank explained. "I've also got four complete engines, a full set of avionics spares, tires, cameras, including two AAD-5 infrared cameras... heck, a whole list of stuff. I opened the crates to inventory the contents. I had no idea those were Pave Tack pods. The forms just listed them as camera pods, part of 7463's spares."

"We should have brought a C-130," Bud said.

"You can borrow one; heck, we've got thirty," Frank offered.

Skip looked at Frank and said, "If you were younger, I'd adopt you! Would you like to be written into my will?"

Frank laughed and said, "Just keep them damn terrorists from taking over, and we'll call it even."

Simultaneously, Skip and Bud said, "You got a deal!"

The next morning, a C-130 with Bud at the controls departed Wright-Pat with a load of RF-4C spares. A few minutes later, Skip lit the afterburners on 463, roared into the sky, and joined Bud for the trip home.

They had come to get a RF-4C Phantom of unknown origin and condition. All they knew was that it was airworthy. They were now headed home with an old friend, a proven test platform, with a history of outstanding performance, including a full complement of spare parts and the best prize of all—two operational Pave Tack pods.

All thanks to one guy, working in the right job, at the right time. Skip and Bud were not sure how they would repay Frank, but somehow, they would.

It sure was nice to have friends in the right places.

CHAPTER NINE

A Needle in a Haystack

Back at Base One, Skip and Bud set to work immediately on the Phantom project. Skip propped his foot on the loading ramp of the C-130 and looked into the cargo bay, "Well, pal, we've got enough spares to keep the Phantom flyin' for a bunch of missions."

"I hope so," Bud replied. "Man, this is like Christmas! All of these boxes to open and explore… Our next step is to go over the aircraft with a microscope and find out which systems are operational and which systems need maintenance."

Many months previous, Major Brandon "Bud" Cooper had initiated Operation Deep Search and accepted the duty as the Operation Commander. Deep Search began after intelligence reports indicated a high probability that a terrorist group planned to establish a base of operations somewhere in Western North America. The primary obstacle to gathering additional intelligence data was accurate tactical reconnaissance. The primary goal was to find the base. With the right crew and equipment, the RF-4C could find it.

"I'd like to stay and help," Skip said wishfully, "but I know this baby is in good hands."

"Skip, you're needed with the Viper project. I'll keep you updated and see you when you get back."

Bud would stay with the Base One aircraft maintenance team until the job was done. Skip knew that, so turning his attentions to helping Pop Hackland get Viper-7 flying was not a problem.

As soon as the Phantom's spares could be unloaded and the salvaged Viper-6 spares loaded, the C-130 was refueled, and Skip was in the air, bound for the Boneyard. Pop was already there, in the process of evaluating the AV-8 Harrier candidates. One primary bird, with parts from several others, would become Viper-7, serial number 01.

Pop had recently paid a visit to a secret engine design and test facility at Sandia Labs near White Sands Missile Range in New Mexico. The Jet Propulsion Laboratory, teamed with NASA engineers, had been testing the Viper-7 Engine, designated the ATBX-6A prototype for several months. Pop had been on site for the design, fabrication, and most of the early tests. The reason for his recent visit was to review the final dimensions and performance estimates of the new hybrid engines. He then returned to the Boneyard and turned his attention to modification of the Viper-7 airframe.

Since Viper-6 had been severely damaged in the crash, the project had to be accelerated. The importance of the project was increased considerably by Skip's Mustang encounters. Since the loss of Major Blake and his F-16, the project was on the front burner.

Skip was overseeing the unloading of the Herk when Pop joined him. "Welcome back, kid. Your Phantom hunt go well?"

"Better than that. Not only did she turn out to be my old bird, 463, but we found a shit-load of spares, too, including two FLIR pods."

"Well, Junior, you're gonna like my news; I had a great visit to Sandia. The new engines are performing perfectly, and four will be operational and ready for install by the time the airframe is ready. That means two spares readily available. We've never had more than one spare."

"Two? Now that's cool."

"I'm not finished… the work on the new flight control computer is also going well. We'll probably have to flight test with the existing computer, but the new one will be ready for operational testing within a year."

Skip beamed at him, "Man, you're just full of good news!"

"Umm," Pop grunted, as though he was disinterested. In truth, he was beside himself with excitement. Pop was in his best element and loving every minute of it. Skip knew it but went along with Pop's attitude, just as if he believed him.

***

It was an old practice, using an existing aircraft to combine new technology with proven technology. The trick was to pick the right machine to modify. With so many variables involved, aerodynamics and airframe strength determined success or failure. The power of the new engines made supersonic speed a reality, but acceleration from hover and maneuverability at low speeds were far more important for an aircraft fulfilling the dual roles of reconnaissance and attack. An aircraft designed for supersonic speed was ideal for air intercept and strategic reconnaissance but virtually useless for close-in air combat and close air-ground support.

In addition, utilization of the flight computer was extremely important. The flight computer was capable of acting as a second crewmember, but how the computer was utilized could mean the difference between victory and defeat in air combat. Obviously, programming was very critical.

All these variables had to be weighed and studied. It was almost easier to design an aircraft to fit the new technology. However, the days of putting billions of dollars and millions of man-hours into a new technology project were gone. Many of the scientists and design engineers were dead. Much of the government infrastructure was gone. Existing weapons resources were being pushed to the limits of availability and capability.

The Viper project had moved from a pre-disaster technological experiment to a major player in the post-disaster air defense of North America. Everything associated with this project had to be done right the first time. There was no room for failure.

Skip, Pop, and Big Sam Thomas stood around a table in the second-floor office of the main hangar on the Boneyard. They were reviewing the blueprints of the Viper candidates and discussing the status of the project.

The Boneyard director had returned to duty, and Big Sam was now serving as Viper project director. A team of twenty aircraft engineers and technicians were busily working on various sections of each of the six AV-8 Harriers parked in the large hangar.

Pop pointed to the main wing area on one of the prints and said, "The most difficult part of the project will be to reinforce the main wing. We don't have the luxury to assume that all six are suitable, so we must x-ray each to determine the best one."

"We have an NDI (non-destructible inspection) Lab with both portable and fixed x-ray units," Sam informed. "Which aircraft do you need to inspect first?"

"Actually, I think we need to separate the main wing from the fuselage. I don't want to miss something by trying to x-ray the entire aircraft," Skip replied.

"I'll get with the teams and set up a schedule ASAP," Sam said and headed toward the hangar floor.

"I'm glad the boss is back. We needed a man like Sam on this project," Skip told Pop.

"He indicated, during our first meeting, that he would like to be on the project if it were possible," Pop replied. "He's a busy man. Did you know that he's been working on a project of his own out here?"

"No. What is it?" Skip asked.

"General Grey has granted him authority to pull and rehab an OV-10," Pop replied. "He's been working on it, off and on, for several years."

"He was a Bronco driver in Nam. One of the best too. We could use him on Project Deep Search," Skip said.

"Well, he's got it almost ready to fly, but it will need some avionics work. I hope to give him some help when we finish the Viper project."

"Maybe we can utilize the flight computer from Viper-6," Skip suggested.

Pop smiled, "You read my mind."

***

A week later, Skip returned the C-130 to Wright-Patterson and brought the T-38 back to Base One. A functional test flight for 463 was scheduled, and he was really looking forward to putting it through its paces. After the test, a series of flights to test and calibrate the sensors were scheduled. For the test crew, a busy week lay ahead.

Skip brought the T-38 to touchdown on Base One and taxied to parking at Base Ops. As he shut down the engines and opened the cockpit canopy, Bud walked up to the aircraft and activated the latch to lower the climbing steps. Skip removed his helmet and threw it to Bud.

"Welcome back!"

"Thanks. It's good to be back. How's it goin'?"

"Climb out of there; let me buy you a cup of coffee and get you caught up."

"Deal." Skip then signed the aircraft logbook, handed it to the crew chief, and they headed for the coffee shop.

Over coffee, Bud updated Skip on the status of 463, "The inspection went well. No major problems found. The Wright-Pat crew did a good job. We're also checking out all of the spares. The Sensor shop found a problem with one of the three AAD-5 cameras, but the other two checked out good. The third camera should be repaired this week. That will give us two spares. We loaded each Pave Tack pod and hangar tested the systems, including the helmet mounted site, joystick, monitor, and video recorder. They all work as advertised."

"Did you test the laser designator?" Skip asked.

"We were only able to determine that the laser will calibrate and fire. After it's bore sighted, we'll run a few more tests, but range and accuracy testing will have to be done in flight," Bud answered.

"We don't want any surprises," Skip said. "I would like to give each pod a complete shakedown, including one or two missile shots. How's the Laser Maverick inventory?"

"We should have about twenty primed and about a hundred ready to assemble."

"I know we don't need to waste resources, but I would rather throw away a dozen at test targets than screw up one mission because the Pave Tack System couldn't track a live target and keep it illuminated with the laser."

"I sure as hell can't argue with that," Bud agreed and then changed the subject by asking, "How is the Viper project going?"

"It's goin' great. We've got an excellent team assembled. To be honest, the Phantom is the only reason I'm here. I should be at the Boneyard right now, but she just kept callin' me... 'Come on, let's go ballistic!'"

"Well, since you're so hot to fly this 'lead sled,' let's go schedule a functional check flight."

"I was wonderin' when you were gonna get around to that!" Skip said and grabbed his flight gear.

After scheduling a FCF at Base Ops, they stopped by the hangar to have a quick look at 463, and then continued on to a brief meeting with Lt. Col. Ron Taylor. The meeting was informal, but very little seemed informal with Base One's chief of intelligence. Taylor was working at his desk when they arrived.

"Good afternoon, Ron," Bud said, greeting his boss. "We just stopped by to let you know that we've scheduled 463 for an FCF at zero seven hundred hours tomorrow. If all goes well, we should also be able to get two test sorties in, as well."

"Good," Taylor replied, "I have scheduled a briefing for the day after tomorrow at zero eight hundred hours. The meeting is mandatory for all Deep Search teams—that includes you, Mr. Scott."

"I wouldn't miss it for the world."

"Very well, see you there." Taylor smiled and returned to the work on his desk.

Both men departed the office and remained silent until they were out of the building.

Then, Skip commented, "If I didn't know better, I'd swear he's in a good mood."

"You read him correctly. He's been in a much better mood since Deep Search started. I think he feels like he's needed again. A guy like that can go nuts if he doesn't have a purpose in life or a goal to work toward."

"I can relate to that," Skip said. "The Viper projects sure kept me out of a padded room."

"I think Ron's character is a little different. It wasn't a personal tragedy or anything like that; he's just not friendly and never has been very sociable. He's not much for family, either. Oh, he has a mom and dad, but they're about as close as a family of sharks. I've known Ron for a long time. We went to college together. He has always been the same as he is right now. He keeps to himself. I've never even known him to go anywhere or do anything with his own family."

"Jesus, he sounds like the perfect candidate for a mass murderer!" Skip said, half joking.

Bud laughed and said, "Believe it or not, he's very non-violent. Hates confrontations. He was a bookworm in school. During his senior year, he was offered a scholarship to West Point."

"Wow!"

"Yea. But, believe it or not, he turned it down and went to Yale. Paid his own way too. At eighteen, he convinced the bank to loan him the entire tuition for four years, plus expenses. He began getting job offers during his junior year, but the very day he graduated, he applied for a commission in the Air Force. He completed OCS at the top of the class and had his choice of assignments. He chose the Security Service and asked to be assigned to Space Command. During the security investigation, they put that guy through more tests than a lab rat, and he came through looking like an All-American."

"Damn, why don't he wear his cape with the "S" on it!"

"I think I know someone who just might consider him Superman," Bud hinted.

"Who?" Skip asked and turned to look at Bud, uncertain what he was going to reveal.

"Candy Simms."

Skip looked at Bud in amazement. "You're kiddin'!"

"Serious as a heart attack."

"Candy Simms?"

"Yes," Bud chuckled.

"Sweet, gorgeous, strawberry-blonde, intelligent Candy Simms?"

"Read my lips—y-e-s."

"No kiddin'… I need a drink," Skip admitted, shaking his head.

"What a coincidence, there's the O-Club."

For the rest of the afternoon, they sat and talked about the Phantom and Viper-8, planning mission sorties and schedules.

One of the focal points was resource management. This was a very high priority in the aftermath of the Reaper. It was also the hardest thing to manage. Defending the interior air space was NAADA's primary job. Getting that job done was a very big challenge. Doing the job with limited resources was, at times, impossible. However, telling anyone on the NAADA team that a particular thing could not be done was a waste of breath. The standard response to being told "no," was, "define no." "No" was not an option. It just was not in their dictionary.

The next morning dawned hot and dusty, leftover from a dust storm that blew through during the night. By 0500 hrs, the Phantom had been pulled out of the hangar and parked on the ramp, fueled and ready to go.

Skip and Bud had been up since 0430 hours, or "Oh-dark-thirty," as Skip called it. They were making final checks and preparations for the functional check flight (FCF) and operational test missions later in the day.

The center of attention on the flight line was7463. Line vehicles from various maintenance shops were parked on both sides of the Phantom. A team of Sensor specialists were busily working near a mobile FLIR/Pave Tack test set, parked just forward of the right wing. Another truck, marked RADAR, was parked directly in front of the nose. That team worked at a mobile TFR (Terrain Following Radar) test station that encompassed most of the nose radome.

It was now 0630 hrs. The noise of a Dash 60 turbine power cart dominated the scene. Conversations were via the Phantom's intercom system.

Bud was in the rear seat, running various tests in response to requests from specialists. Skip was on the ground, plugged into the Ground Intercom Buss, listening to the conversation as he performed the ground portion of the preflight. The crew chief, Staff Sergeant Sandra Mitchell, stood nearby.

The crew chief is the focal point of any flight line operation. The pilots fly the bird, and the specialists fix what breaks, but the crew chief owns the aircraft. The crew chief is the one who signs for it and takes on the tremendous responsibility of determining if the aircraft is airworthy. If you need to know something about a particular bird, you ask the crew chief. Nothing happens with an aircraft without the crew chief's approval, period.

"Sandy, don't let that old fart pull the wrong plug and drain the oil," Bud said, jokingly referring to Skip.

"Don't worry, sir, he's only allowed to look. I don't let him touch anything outside of the cockpit."

"Say, Sandy, how does this 'cockpit canopy jettison handle' thing work?" Skip asked as he looked up at Bud. "If I pull it, will that smart ass in the rear seat get a thrill?"

"Oh, excuse me, sir; I'm sure that handle is just fine," Bud said, trying to sound as sweet and humble as he could, "We'll be needing this canopy in a few minutes."

"What's the matter, don't care for open-cockpit airplanes?" Skip asked, laughing.

"No, sir, not at Mach 2! Just a tiny bit too breezy for me."

Skip winked at Sandy. "That's what I like, a conscientious, but humble, RSO."

"That's me, boss, the most conscientious and humble reconnaissance systems officer in the agency." Then, extending his arms in the air with both thumbs up, Bud said, "All right! Are we good, or what? Checks are complete, and all systems are go. Looks like we have a bird to fly!"

"Let's saddle up," Skip said as he unplugged from the ground cord and handed it to Sandy, climbed up the ladder, and entered the cockpit.

The crew chief was right behind him, first checking Bud's seat harness and ejection seat, then Skip's. She then removed all of the safety pins and devices in the cockpit area, made one more safety scan of the front and rear seats, then went back down the ladder, removed it, and carried it clear of the aircraft.

Meanwhile, on the ground, the assistant crew chief cleared and attached the Dash 60's auxiliary air hose to the number one engine, as the various maintenance specialists moved their vehicles and equipment out of the way.

At 0715 hours, Sandra announced, "Ready for engine start on your command, sir."

"Okay, Sandy, gimme some air," Skip replied, and the crew chief flipped the air compressor switch on the Dash 60. The hose immediately jumped as the air compressor inflated it like a fire hose, blowing highly compressed air into the Phantom's engines.

Skip spoke a running account of events, "I have rpm... ignition on... fuel pressure in the green... compressor start... fire in the hole... spoolin' up... and in the green. Kill the air. Sandy, we'll start two with bleed air from one."

"Aye, sir, air is off." The assistant crew chief went beneath the Phantom. There, he disconnected the compressor hose and power cable, closed and secured the access doors, and continued the preflight checks.

As the assistant went from point to point, responding to the checklist being followed by the aircrew, he would repeat the name of the system and announce the completion of each check with, "Go."

When he was done, Sandy continued talking to the aircrew, "Air lines and power cables are clear, sir; BLC system is good. You have plenty of aux air over the wings. Checks are complete. You are ready to go."

As she spoke, she walked toward the left main wheel well to disconnect the ground cord from the intercom system. "I'll be going to hand signals now. You two have a fun flight but take care of my airplane; she and I are just getting to know each other."

"Will do. Thanks, Sandy, and don't worry; she's in good hands," Skip replied.

"I'll reach up and smack 'em on the back of the head if he gets too rowdy!"

Sandy laughed, "Just don't knock him out. You're a SR-71 pilot. Can you still fly something this slow?"

"Hell, we taxi faster than this thing flies," Bud bragged.

"You two gonna reminisce all day, or are we gonna go play sky tag?"

"See ya! Ground out." Sandy pulled the plug and then signaled to the assistant to marshal the Phantom out of the slot. He pulled the right wheel chocks, moved to the front of the aircraft, and raised his arms, signaling to Skip to apply brakes. This allowed Sandy to remove the chocks from the left wheel. He then checked for a clear path for taxi and signaled Skip, "Clear to taxi."

"Base One Tower, this is Flight Test One, ready to taxi," Skip announced over the radio.

"Flight Test One, Tower, you are cleared for taxi to Runway 03. Wind is zero niner zero degrees at twenty two knots; altimeter is thirty-one point zero eight; current temperature is ninety-two degrees Fahrenheit. Check density altitude."

Skip read back the information to Tower and signaled "ready to taxi" to the assistant crew chief. As he eased the throttles forward, the twenty-five-ton Phantom slowly rolled out of the parking slot. The assistant then signaled the turn, and Skip steered toward the main taxiway. As 463 swept through the turn, Sandy and her assistant came to attention and saluted the aircrew. Both men returned the salute, and Skip gave a thumbs up to the ground crew.

The ground crew then broke in a run to the nearest vehicle. They would join a large group of line trucks, fire trucks, and security vehicles parked near the end of the runway where, in a few moments, the Phantom would roar past on its way to the sky.

As 463 taxied to Runway 03, Tower came on the radio again, "Flight Test One, you are cleared for takeoff at your convenience. If you're go for takeoff, I'll be on our handheld transceiver outside on the catwalk."

"Tower, Flight Test One, we're ready. Enjoy the show."

Bud looked toward the ramp, "Would you look at that, the whole base must be out here to watch this old bird show her stuff."

"Well, heck, do you blame 'em? If we weren't puttin' on the show, we'd be out there watchin' too."

"Everybody loves the Phantom."

"Well, let's give 'em a good show," Skip said as he turned 463 onto the runway and applied the brakes.

He began applying power and watching the instrument panel, again giving a running narrative, "Gauges are in the green... spool up is smooth, and power is even... brake release... burners coming up... feels good... and max power... here we go!"

As Skip was talking, Bud activated the Forward Looking Infrared Reconnaissance Camera on the Pave Tack pod, turned on the video recorder, and slewed the FLIR ball toward the tail. He could see the bright flash as the afterburners lit and adjusted the optical contrast to compensate.

"Man, you're gonna love this video," Bud said, but Skip was still talking through the takeoff and watching the airspeed.

"Rotate... and gear up." As the gear doors closed, Skip lowered the nose. Holding the Phantom to no more than six feet from the runway surface, he rode the ground-effect compression wave and watched the airspeed indicator quickly climb...

"One fifty knots... two hundred... two fifty... three hundred... three twenty-five... here comes the overrun..."

As the Phantom approached the end of the runway, all eyes were trained on the powerful aircraft as she roared by, a scant fifty feet from the personnel along the sides of the runway. Just as the end of the runway flashed past, Skip pulled back on the stick and pointed the nose toward the sky. Both men grunted as they strained under the G-load.

Skip then continued his narrative, "Oh, sweet thang! Gauges in the green... three seventy... four hundred... four fifty... five hundred... climb, baby, climb... five fifty... she's losin' steam now... passing through fourteen thousand AGL... let's go over a bit."

As Skip pulled further back on the stick, the Phantom lay gracefully on her back and began accelerating again. A slight left aileron input on the stick, and the jet snapped rolled to wings level. An easy forward push on the stick, and the Phantom nosed over, sending the airspeed past Mach 1 knots.

"First ripple," Skip said, as the slight shudder rippled through the airframe, signaling transition to supersonic speed.

"Let's make some noise!" Bud exclaimed. Still accelerating, Skip initiated a sweeping 180-degree turn to a heading of zero three zero degrees, retracing the path they had just made, returning back over the base.

The ballistic Phantom was now pushing a sonic shock wave, emanating from the leading edge of the wings and rolling across the countryside. On the ground, a solid, quick "boom-boom" was heard and felt, as the sonic boom shook the entire base and most of Denver. Everyone watching applauded.

Skip began a gradual climb and called out the altitude and airspeed again, "Passin' angels eleven at Mach one point eight. If we don't lose the Pave Tack pod, this should give her a good shakedown."

"You can say that again," Bud said, obviously enjoying himself. "The FLIR is working great. The video has been flawless, and it's going to be killer!"

"You got this whole FCF on tape?" Skip asked, just realizing what Bud had been doing in the rear seat.

"Sure. You didn't think I was just along for the ride, did you?"

"Cool! Good job! Let's hold her here at Mach two point two for a minute or so, then we'll be bingo for fuel. Everything's in the green. She's lookin' great. This old gal still has what it takes to get it done."

Skip leveled out just below the solid canopy at twelve thousand feet and initiated a long 270-degree left turn, rolling out on a compass heading of 120 degrees. That would put them back over the base again, this time, greater than twice the speed of sound. The crowd on the ground continued to watch the jet as it passed over the base, drawing a contrail line across the sky and dragging a double sonic boom along to rattle the windows.

Finally, Skip pulled back the throttles and let the mighty Phantom glide to the runway they had just left only a short time ago.

The remainder of the day went as well as the Functional Check Flight. The Phantom completed two missions intended to test the FLIR/Pave Tack System. It was necessary to determine the capability to find a target and hold the laser designator on target long enough for a laser-guided weapon to acquire the beam, fire, and hit the target. Both missions were flawless. With the airborne systems working as advertised, the remainder of the scheduled test missions would be used to hone the skills of the aircrews and prepare for attacking real targets.

That evening, the test team gathered at the O-Club to celebrate a successful flying day and to discuss the upcoming missions.

The next morning, at exactly 0800, Colonel Ron Taylor, looking something like General Patton sans baton, brought the meeting of the Deep Search project to order....

"Ladies and gentlemen, you have all been briefed on the intent of Deep Search; now it is time to describe the enemy. We have just received intelligence data, gathered over the last three months, that has enabled us to get a great deal of insight about what we're up against. You should also know that many lives were lost obtaining this information. Your Deep Search commander, Major Cooper, will continue with the briefing."

"Good morning, folks," Bud began with a more casual tone. "First, I would like to thank all of the team leaders for your reports. All reports have been on time and complete. That makes my job a lot easier. Now, to the reason we're all here… about a year ago, we began getting alarming information about quantities and types of weapons being stolen all over the globe.

"As you can see by the figures projected on the screen, the weapons and equipment that have been disappearing are all high tech and specific. Unlike the earlier, random weapons pillaging, these thefts have been well planned and executed.

"If aircraft are stolen, so is all of the associated support equipment, including spares. They will raid a warehouse and take only specific equipment, leaving valuable weapons behind. Obviously, these are not thefts for profit. The raids are often staged simultaneously around the globe, always with specific targets in mind.

"To date, enough transport-type aircraft has been stolen to make this group one of the most mobile terrorist groups in history. We have recently learned that this group is called Bushmaster. Their political agenda is somewhat unclear, but we know that two organizations have recently joined forces with Bushmaster. The first, called Red Death, claims that the enemies of the Free Forces of North America are also their enemies. They insist that the West has been moving toward Socialism for many years, especially during the 1990s. We are, they say, 'An impotent giant.' They take action, while we do nothing. Unfortunately, they are not entirely wrong. In the past, we have sanctioned them to carry out certain operations, events with which we did not want to be connected.

"One operation, in particular, in 1996, went sour. We had promised command and control support. The support was terminated during the operation, and they lost over half of their forces. Understandably, that left them with hard feelings toward us, which may have led them to join forces with Bushmaster.

"The second group was called Red Scorpion. Their slogan was, 'The Earth now belongs to the Sons of Mohammed.' The Sons of Mohammed, another terrorist faction, was unfortunate enough to be on the Asian continent when the Reaper hit. They are considered by the Islamic Nation to have been slaughtered by the West and are now worshipped as martyrs. According to Red Scorpion, we somehow orchestrated the disaster and directed the Reaper at the Asian continent with the intent to wipe out the Sons of Mohammed. Apparently, we decided it was worth destroying the Earth, just to kill a handful of saber-rattling terrorists. Talk about collateral damage. Obviously, these idiots have a slightly inflated view of their importance.

"Mohammed Za-Ved Raazmahd, a self-appointed general, is the son of the notorious Sheik Dasheed Raazmahd and the reported mastermind of Bushmaster. The Army of the Bushmaster, under his command, is estimated to number between 2500 and 3000. As I said, we don't know their political agenda, but it's obvious that Raazmahd's agenda is death and destruction, and his ultimate goal is to destroy the West.

"We understand that the selection of the name, Bushmaster, best defines their attitude, 'Quick to kill.' They have consistently proven that by not leaving any witnesses. Death toll, thus far, from their raids and attacks is estimated to be in the thousands.

"In more than one instance, they have used chemical weapons, and we are now investigating the possibility that a biological weapon was used last month in Russia. It is rumored that Bushmaster has access to bioweapon technology from labs in the Middle East. A former deputy director of the Soviet Biopreparat reported that Castro obtained bioweapon technology directly from top-ranking Biopreparat generals and scientists who made repeated trips to Cuba to provide advice and training during the late 1980s and early 1990s.

"During the same period, there were Cuban transfers of dual-use biotechnology to Islamic countries closely connected to Middle Eastern terrorist networks. The transferred technology involved biological agents, pathogens, and germ-strengthening processes that are applicable to weaponizing bacteria.

"The deal with Iran was transacted through banks in the United Arab Emirates (UAE). Castro also visited the states of Libya and Syria. The UAE was an odd destination for Castro. But the UAE was one of the main international money-laundering centers of the Arab world, with bank accounts and financial companies directly linked to al-Qaeda and the Iranian-backed Hezbollah terror network.

"Soviet biotechnology simultaneously was transferred to Cuba, Iran, Iraq, and other Russian allies that shared similar bioweapons programs. The Soviet Union organized courses in genetic engineering and molecular biology for scientists from Eastern Europe, Cuba, Libya, Iran, and Iraq. Some forty foreign scientists were trained annually. Many of them headed biotechnology programs in their own countries before the disaster. Bushmaster could very well have access to some of these scientists.

"If the deaths in Russia were the result of a bioweapon, then the number of Bushmaster's victims will rise to over two thousand. The entire population of a base was wiped out by, what was thought to be, an accident involving the destruction of biological weapons. It seems that Bushmaster, to divert attention away from the theft of over fifty pounds of weapons grade plutonium and ten nuclear triggers, may have staged the accident.

"We are certain that the F-5's that shot down Major Blake were stolen from the Boneyard. If you're wondering why Bushmaster left most of the Boneyard crew and Defense Force alive, it was not intentional. A low-yield nuclear weapon was found near the Yard. How they got it there, we don't know. The only reason we found it, instead of a big hole in the ground, is that it failed to detonate because the trigger misfired. Apparently, they're better magicians than they are bomb builders.

"Unfortunately, they may have solved that problem, if Bushmaster did, in fact, steal the ten nuclear triggers from Russia. The Russians have informed us that this particular model trigger is very reliable.

"The tactical reconnaissance portion of Deep Search will begin in two days. We have a photographic interpretation team assembled and ready to receive data. If all goes well, we should have an abundance of data available. Finding that hidden base is going to be like looking for a very small needle in a very large haystack. To be honest, we are at a considerable disadvantage. Let's do our best to turn that around. That will be all for now—dismissed."

CHAPTER TEN

Insurmountable Odds

As Bud plowed through the stack of reports on his desk, he realized just how glad he was that he had made the decision to assign another aircrew to fly recon missions with 7463. Although he and Skip wanted to fly every mission, three missions a day, seven days a week was far too much for one crew to cover safely.

Taking on more than one can handle can be as unproductive as doing almost nothing. Both men already had a heavy workload. Bud was ultimately responsible for the entire Deep Search operation, and Skip was spending as much time as possible on the Viper-7 Project.

Operation Deep Search was taking its toll on many of the team members in hours and stress. Most of the team worked fifteen-hour shifts, seven days a week. It was now six weeks into the operation, and none of the reconnaissance data had produced anything that might suggest a remote base or signs of increased activity such as vehicles or even vehicle tracks.

Either Bushmaster had found out about the additional aircraft that had been added to the operation and were lying low, or they were waiting for something to happen before they made their next move. Worldwide, intelligence gathering had discovered the same thing—Bushmaster had simply vanished.

Skip had returned to Base One early this day to prepare for another week of flying. He was in his Base One quarters, going over the maps and plans for the upcoming missions. Pop would be returning to Base One later in the day, and they had plans to meet with Bud later in the evening. Unexpectedly, the phone rang...

"Oh, hey, Bud, I was just goin' over the mission..."

Bud interrupted, "Skip, there's no way to make this easy... Pop has gone down en route to Base One."

"Was he able to call in on the Range Net? Any idea where he went down?"

"Not exactly, he was several hours out of the Yard. He filed IFR for nine thousand feet. The controllers had intermittent radar hits for most of his flight when the King Air just disappeared off the scope. Weather was not good, visibility less than a half-mile and getting worse. The controller thinks she heard a short transmission, but it was very noisy and almost unreadable. Also, our listening posts in the area did not pick up a thing, so it's not likely that there was an explosion. And, Skip, one more thing... it's near the same area where we lost Phil."

"I'll be in your office in five minutes."

"Skip, meet me at the Command Post in ten."

"You got it." Skip gathered up his flight gear and headed for the Command Post.

When Skip arrived, Bud was already in the control room, discussing the situation with Col. Bass and Lt. Col. Taylor.

"Skip, we have the audio log of the last radio transmissions from Pop's aircraft," Bud said, drawing his attention to a computer station. "We're bringing it up now..."

"This is the first contact at twenty zero five Zulu."

"Western Defense Zone Control, this is Eagle Two-One with you at niner thousand."

"Eagle Two-One, this is Zone Control, turn to heading zero two five and climb to flight level one seven zero."

"025 at seventeen, Eagle Two-One."

"The next one was at 2035Z..."

"Zone Control, Eagle Two-One, I'm gettin' into some chop and heavy scud up here, do you have a better altitude?"

"Negative, Two-One, we've got a heavy layer from flight level 560 down to almost eight thousand."

"Control, Two-One, can you flight follow at or below eight thousand?"

"Roger, Two-One, we have intermittent radar coverage down to six thousand, but this area is a possible hot zone. Are you requesting a descent to eight thousand or below?"

"Roger that. Just get me out of this rough scud."

"Roger, Two-One, descend to eight thousand, turn to heading 030 and ident, report on reaching eight thousand, and watch your six."

"Eight thousand at 030 and ident; I'll see you in a bit. And I always watch my back. Two-One."

"Now at 2055Z..."

"Control, Two-One, with you at eight thousand. It's much better down here; I have at least three miles and smooth air."

"Two-One, Control, we have you. Glad we could help. Be advised radar coverage is intermittent, and you can expect radio coverage problems too."

"Thanks, Control. And what's new?"

"I heard that. Just stay heads up, and call if you need us."

"Rog, will do."

"Here it comes, just twenty minutes later, at 2115Z"

"Control, what in the hell... (unreadable) ... get your...," static is heard, then a buzzing sound, and then dead air.

The Zone Controller responds, trying to contact Eagle 21, "Two-One, Control, say again... Eagle Two-One, this is Zone Defense Control, say again... Do you read? Eagle Two-One, Control... Eagle Two-One, Control..."

"We haven't received anything since—no emergency beacon, nothing," Bud commented.

Just then, the room was called to attention.

"At ease." The voice was General Lewis M. Grey, Commander of NAADA. He was en route to Base Two when he received the information about the missing aircraft. When he learned that Pop was the pilot, he ordered his pilot to fly directly to Base One.

General Grey, always aware of protocol, extended his hand and greeted the base commander first.

"John T., it's good to see you. I'm sorry I dropped in on you like this but..."

"No need, sir, I know how much your old friend means to you. We were just reviewin' the radio log. There has been no radio contact with Pop since 2115 Zulu. We dispatched two F-16's and the Loach to the area at 2145. We have also received offers for assist with recon flights out of Base Two, and Big Sam Thomas is en route from the Boneyard in his restored OV-10. Western Defense Control is coordinatin' the air search."

"Excellent, John T., you're on top of things, as usual."

"How have you been, Skip?" General Grey asked as he shook Skip's hand. "It's been a coon's age since we've seen one another."

"Good to see you, sir. I've got a few irons in the fire, as usual."

"How is the Viper-7 project coming along?"

"We're makin' excellent progress. Pop was on his way back here to work on the software for the new flight computer. He was scheduled to meet with the engine design team next week. Until this situation came up, we had a tentative flight test date set for next month."

"Well, let's see if we can't keep that schedule." General Grey turned to Col. Bass, "John T., pull as many search aircraft as possible from Base Two. My G-4 is available and so am I, for that matter. Bud, I understand that another RF-4 is here at Base One?"

"Yes, sir; in fact, 7455 rolled out of maintenance today. Skip and I were going to fly a recon mission with it tomorrow morning, but I am having it prepped for flight right now."

"How about 7463?" The general asked.

"It's being turned around now. The crew had to return for fuel; otherwise, they would still be on the search," Bud answered.

"Let's get both C-130's and my G-4 in the air with as many people with good eyes as we can muster. Ron, I would like to have a couple of your Insertion Team specialists on each of the 130's in case we need to get someone on the ground in a hurry. And we need to make sure every aircraft and everyone is well armed; we just don't know what we're up against out there."

"Aye, sir, my entire team is ready right now," Lt. Col. Taylor replied.

For the next four days, day and night, the search teams scoured the area where Pop disappeared from the radar track, covering thousands of square miles. They found nothing—no sign of Pop, the King Air, or any signs of an aircraft crash. What were found were the wreckage of Eagle One and the crash sites of three aircraft that were assumed to be F-5E's.

General Grey reluctantly called off the search at the end of the fifth day. More questions were raised by the search than were answered.

Skip and Bud returned from the last search mission and set the F-4 down on the runway. As they were taxiing to parking, Skip said to Bud, "I would like to make one more run over the area just to the west of where the first F-5 wreckage was located. Somethin' tells me that Phil would not have waited very long to splash one of those jokers. If I'm right, maybe the hidden base is closer to the crash site than we first thought."

"Well, pal, the search for Pop has been called off, but we've got to continue the Deep Search project... maybe we can just deviate a bit from our mission plan and make a sweep over that area tomorrow morning," Bud said.

"Sounds like a plan to me," Skip replied.

Aftermath I: The Fight For Survival

When Skip and Bud reported in to the Command Post, the general called a meeting of all the participants in the search and rescue operation. He addressed the entire group:

"I would like to personally thank each and every one of you for your unselfish efforts and dedication during the search operation. I don't want any of you walking away from this thinking that you failed to do a good job, or that if you could have done something more, we might have been successful. We did everything but turn over every rock within the search area. It is my opinion that other forces are involved here, and the outcome of this has yet to be determined. Again, thank you all. Well done."

At that, General Grey went with Colonel Bass to the colonel's office. Over a drink, they reflected on the events of the last five days. Finally, the general told the colonel something that was bothering him...

"John T., I've had something on my mind for a couple of days, and I just can't seem to shake it off."

"What's botherin' ya', Lew? You know you can bounce anything off me."

"Well, you saw all of the crash sites out there. There are three F-5's and one F-16. All destroyed before they hit the ground. I also read Captain Spade's report of the incident. Something just don't fit. I mean, Spade said he and Phil were outnumbered, they were separated in the first engagement, and that he barely escaped. Damage to his aircraft attests to that, but if he didn't take out any of the F-5's, that suggests that Phil got all three. Now, if they were jumped and broke and ran during the first engagement, how in the hell did Phil get three F-5's and no one pursued Spade? And if Phil did manage to get all three, how were the crash sites separated by almost a hundred miles? I mean, it doesn't take a genius to do the math if all that happened during the first engagement... son-of-a-bitch. Can you imagine a scenario like that?"

"I follow you, Lew. To tell the truth, I have been thinkin' about that myself. I can't explain it, and I can't imagine it either. I've flown a bunch of F-15 intercept missions, and I have gone up against F-14's many times on the ACMI Range. I've also gone up against SU-27's in the Middle East. I've been in a number of low altitude runnin' dogfights, but for one engagement involvin' quick turnin' aircraft like F-5's and F-16's to get spread over a hundred miles... I just don't know."

"I don't want to step on anyone's toes here, but I would like to talk to Capt. Spade if you don't mind," General Grey responded.

"Not at all, Lew. If you can get straight answers from that cocky rascal, it would ease my mind too. I'll have my secretary call him in."

"Let's set it up for tomorrow morning. Right now, I think we need to unwind a bit."

"How about a few rounds of golf? We've got some new, hellatious sand traps during the last sandstorm," Colonel Bass offered, and then added, "We might just work up a bit of thirst too."

"Your folks still brewing your own beer and whiskey?"

"Yes, sir. The best brew west of the Mississippi!"

"It's been a long while, but you've got permission to get the boss plastered tonight."

"I might just be able to arrange that, boss." Colonel Bass answered, "I'll make sure you get safely to your quarters too."

"You're a good friend, John T." The general replied with a chuckle.

The next morning, a very hung-over General Grey walked softly into the mess hall. Just as he passed through the door, a young sergeant noticed the general and came to attention.

The general looked at the young man and tried to smile, "Son, never mind that, why don't you pour us both some coffee." Then, he leaned closer and whispered, "If I don't sit down with a hot cup of something pretty quick, this hangover is going to kill me."

Then, he walked directly to the nearest table and slowly sat down.

Momentarily, the young sergeant brought the coffee, "Here you go, sir, I figured you needed... er, ah, wanted it black."

"Bless you, son, bless you." The general took a sip and closed his eyes. When he opened his eyes, the young man was about to walk away.

"Sit..." The general winced, and then more quietly repeated, "Sit down and join me, son. I don't want to die alone."

The young man chuckled in spite of himself, returned to the table, and sat down, "Excuse me, sir, but I've never seen..."

The general finished, "... A flag grade officer looking like a college kid the morning after a frat party! Is that about right?"

The sergeant could not contain it any longer and totally broke up laughing.

"I deserve this... I truly deserve this...," the general continued talking, his elbows on the table, his head propped on both hands. "I know better than to get that shit-faced. I know better than to drink that horrible brew that you Base One people foolishly call whiskey. I swear to God, I have no idea how I got to my quarters last night."

The young man was just about to regain his composure when the general said, "Thank God I didn't wake up with a strange woman!"

The young man lost it again. This time the general just looked at him mournfully and covered his face with his hands. At that moment, Colonel Bass, Skip, and Bud joined the general and his amused young guest. The young man tried to regain his composure and come to attention, but was not very successful. All three of the men sat down, looked at the general, and smiled.

Without looking up, the general asked the sergeant, "Do we have an audience now?"

"Yes, sir."

"Who?"

"I think it's probably the guys responsible for your present condition, sir."

"Then they are probably getting a real kick out of this, aren't they?"

"Judging by their expressions, I would say so, sir."

"John T., when I said you had permission to get the boss plastered, I thought you understood that I wanted to *survive* the occasion."

"Lew, your coffee's getting cold."

"I know, John T. I can't taste it. Your so-called whiskey has killed my tastebuds."

At that point, everyone at the table cracked up.

The general finally looked up and then addressed the young sergeant, "Son, have you ever been in my, ah, this condition?"

"Yes, sir, in fact, I have, once or twice."

"Well, so have these guys, and I have seen it! Just so you know that... you're a witness!" he said, glaring at the three men.

They cracked up again.

"I know this is an undignified situation for a general, but just because I have four stars on my lapel doesn't mean that I've been promoted out of the human race."

"Actually, that's good to know, sir," the young man said. "Thank you for inviting me to have coffee with you."

"Well, it's actually my pleasure. And the coffee... with the entertainment (glaring at the trio again) is on me." The general smiled and shook the young man's hand. "I didn't get your name."

"Saxon, Sergeant Bill Saxon."

"Bill, do you know these three criminals?" indicating the trio with his thumb. They cracked up again.

"Yes, sir, I work for Major Cooper."

The general looked suspiciously at Bud and asked, "Bud, you and Sgt. Saxon didn't set this up, did you?"

"No, sir. I think you are suffering enough as it is; we wouldn't have the heart to take advantage of this situation. Would we, Sergeant Saxon?"

"Absolutely not."

"Just checking," the general explained. "You Intelligence guys are all alike."

"Sir, aren't you the head Intelligence guy?" Bill Saxon asked.

"That's what I mean. I know you people."

"Bill, remind me someday to tell you some of the pranks that 'General Hangover' here has pulled during his career. Some are real classics," Bud said, looking at the general.

"I've done my share of trying to get demoted," the general reflected. "In fact, I did get demoted a couple of times." Then he smiled, "But it was worth it. I wouldn't change a thing, even if I had the chance."

"Say, ya'll want some breakfast? I'm hungry," Skip suggested.

"You actually want food?" the general asked.

"Unlike some people, I remember how I got home last night."

"If you are you suggesting that my evening of drink and merriment affected my memory... you are correct. It has also spoiled my appetite. I think I need an hour or so in the gym. Bill, would you care to join me for a game of racquetball?" the general asked as he stood up.

"Yes, sir, I'd be delighted."

"You're on. Any of the rest of you miscreants want to get trounced at racquetball?" the general challenged.

Three immediate negative responses followed.

"I thought as much. If you can't run with the big dogs, stay on the porch."

As the general and Sergeant Saxon left for the gym, Skip commented, "I think we just got insulted."

Colonel Bass, still looking in the general's direction said, "Yep, we did."

Shortly after breakfast, Skip and Bud headed west in 7463, making one last run over the area where the King Air had disappeared. Somehow, Skip knew Pop was alive.

***

Later that morning, Captain Jake Spade reported to the base commander's office for a meeting with General Grey. The general and Colonel Bass were waiting in the office.

"Captain Spade reporting as ordered, sir."

"Have a seat, Captain. I just had a few questions about the F-5 encounter. The report was vague on a couple of items, and I was hoping you might be able to clear them up," General Grey explained.

"Well, sir, I can't imagine what I might be able to tell you that I didn't include in my debrief."

"Humor an old man, if you would, and maybe we can make some headway."

"I'll do my best, sir."

"Good. Now, I see in the report here, at the moment you were jumped by the F-5's, you and Major Blake were forced to split up. Did Major Blake call a split?"

"Yes, sir, we were on an attack run after being fired on from the ground. When the first missile went by, nearly hitting my aircraft, I called bogie at six o'clock. Major Blake was unable to see the enemy aircraft and stayed on the target run. At that point, my aircraft was hit by machine gun fire. I called 'in coming' and indicated I was hit. Major Blake called ten seconds from weapons release and commanded me to stay on target. I advised Major Blake that we might not have ten seconds. At that point, Major Blake broke off the attack and called break. By that time, they had us point blank. I still don't know how I made it out of there."

"Did you or Major Blake try to regroup after the split?"

"Despite numerous attempts, I was unable to establish contact. I figured Major Blake didn't make it out."

"Yes, that was in your report."

"So, you believe that Major Blake was shot down during that first engagement?"

"Yes, sir."

"Why didn't you try to verify your assumption?"

"The area was too hot. I couldn't risk losing my aircraft as well. I was outnumbered four to one."

"Are you aware that the crash site of Major Blake's F-16 is almost a hundred miles from the point where you first encountered the F-5's?"

"Yes, sir."

"Are you also aware that the wreckage of three F-5's are scattered along a direct line from the estimated ambush point to that crash site?"

"Yes, sir."

"Do you have any idea how these aircraft went down?"

"We must have done more damage to the F-5's than I first thought."

"So, during the first engagement, while you were trying to evade, you were also able to turn and fight?"

"I was able to get off a few shots. I don't know whether Major Blake did or not."

"Captain, I'm just unable to piece together a viable theory of how this occurred, based on your analysis of this situation."

"Sir, I would like to figure this out too. I wish I had more information."

"I'm going to be straight with you, Captain. This is off the record. I am looking for answers that only you can provide. I need a logical series of events that puts these aircraft on the ground. What I have so far suggests that a wingman left his flight leader. The flight leader, an exceptional fighter pilot, proceeded to engage three or more F-5's, despite the attackers' advantage. Using his extensive knowledge of air combat tactics and the superior performance of his aircraft, he turned the attackers' advantage around and took out two, maybe three, of the enemy before they got him.

"Now, that is just my theory, and I don't have a thing to back it up. But if I'm known for anything, I'm known for my intolerance of deceit. I am not suggesting that you intentionally falsified your report. But, I am saying this, if I learn that you broke and ran, leaving Major Blake to fight against insurmountable odds, I guarantee you will regret the day you were born! Dismissed."

Captain Spade left the colonel's office without saying another word.

***

Skip and Bud were now over the search area, using the FLIR to scan the area in detail. Unfortunately, the Data Link Relay aircraft, 7455, was down for maintenance and no live video was being sent to Base One. Running a standard grid search pattern, they swept the area at one thousand feet above the terrain, cruising at two hundred knots. While cruising parallel to a steep, jagged ridgeline, Bud spotted something unusual.

"Well now, what might that be?" Bud asked as he watched the FLIR screen intently.

"What do you have?" Skip asked.

"I'm not sure. I zoomed in on a heat source. It looks like a vehicle. Do a one eighty and drop down to five hundred feet."

On the next pass, Bud locked the FLIR on the target, zoomed in again, and continued describing what he saw on the FLIR screen, "It's a truck with a camouflage paint scheme. Even the windows are painted over. Looks like a '90s model Suburban. And Skip, the engine is hot! It's not running, but it's been running within the last hour. I can see a faint trail leading from the base of the cliff, but it just seems to end into a rock wall."

"Yeah, I can see the trail. Slew the FLIR along the rock wall, about a mile to the east of the trail. You see that wide crevasse? What is that line about halfway up the side of the cliff on the edge of the crevasse?"

"Man, you got good eyes! Hit your HMS." (Bud was asking Skip to look at the target, select the Helmet Mounted Sight Mode, and press the trigger on his control stick. This commands the FLIR pod to swing around and focus on the spot where the pilot is looking.)

"Good, now I'll zoom in a bit... it looks like a steel cable attached to the rock face, but I can't tell where the cable goes, it just seems to disappear into the shadows of the crevasse."

"We need a team on the ground. Let's get some altitude and contact Base One." Skip said and pushed the throttles forward.

At that moment, a burst of tracer rounds streaked across the nose of the Phantom. Before Skip could react, a camouflaged Mustang, complete with a cannon pod and Sidewinder missiles, dove past them from left to right, pulled up into a hard left turn, and came wings level just off their right wing, parallel to their flight path.

Then, the Mustang pilot came on the radio. "Set your speed to 150 knots and follow me. Deviate and you will be destroyed!"

"How in hell do they know what frequency we're on?" Skip asked, amazed.

Bud noticed something on their six o'clock in the rear-view mirrors, and swung the FLIR pod around to get a better look. "Better do what he says, Skip. We've got an F-5 and another Mustang on our six o'clock low."

"Well, I wonder where they're takin' us," Skip said sarcastically.

"I'll bet we're about to find out where Bushmaster's hidden base is," Bud replied.

"I'd say you win your bet. Check this out..." Skip directed Bud's attention forward.

As they followed the camouflaged Mustang, the pilot led the formation toward the small crevasse they had flown by earlier, except this time, a large opening near the base of the mountain came into view. Then, the approach end of a runway appeared, extending into the dark opening.

The pilot came on the radio again... "Directly ahead, you see a runway. As I land, you will make a simulated approach to landing. When I call 'no joy', break left, and set up for a full stop landing. You will follow the silver Mustang that is now on your six. The Mustang will land first. Then, you will follow. The Tiger will land last. You must clear the runway immediately upon landing. Set up for a standard barrier engagement. Use the Precision Approach Path Indicator Lights to set up your descent rate. The goal here is not a perfect "three wire" carrier landing. We have six cables and a barrier net. Keep your descent on the established glide path, and you will engage the barrier. Do not, I repeat, do not attempt to go around! You cannot go around. Do you understand?"

"Roger, I copy," Skip answered and stayed on the Mustang's left wing, observing the pilot's procedures.

"No joy in three, two, one. Break."

The camouflaged Mustang continued his approach to land. Just as Skip broke left, the silver Mustang pulled ahead, lowering the landing gear and increasing the flap angle, slowing slightly.

"I guess this guy don't believe in usin' the radio," Skip commented as he struggled to configure the Phantom for slow flight and maintain the Mustang's approach speed.

"Apparently, they're aware of your flying skills."

"I hope they're aware of the stall speed of a Phantom. We get any slower, and we're gonna be walkin'!"

Skip struggled to stay behind the Mustang, the big jet wallowing just above full stall. As the Mustang turned toward the runway on a long final approach, he commented, "That's the one that flew over Owl's Nest."

Skip continued his line of flight, extending the distance from the silver Mustang. The F-5 pulled up alongside the Phantom, and the pilot looked toward Skip and Bud. When they looked back, the pilot applied power and accelerated away.

"Just a small reminder not to try to escape, I suppose," Bud commented.

"That might be the one who got Phil," Skip said coldly and turned the Phantom toward the hidden runway.

"This ought to be interesting," Bud said as he used the FLIR to pry into the darkness where the runway led. "You should see this. There's quite a facility in there. Aircraft, fuel trucks, the works."

As they came closer to touchdown, the details of the runway became clearer. It had the look of a stage with the curtains pulled back. The touchdown point, marked with a white strobe on either side of the runway, had no more than a hundred feet clearance from edge to edge. Beyond the runway, on either side, were jagged rock walls. The runway extended into the mysterious darkness and appeared to be longer than an aircraft carrier deck. Each of the six arresting cables was marked at the side of the runway by a large, lighted yellow circle.

Skip planted the Phantom down hard, catching the third cable. The arresting gear stopped the heavy aircraft within the span of two hundred feet. Skip immediately retracted the arresting hook and applied power to taxi off the runway. Ahead, the silver Mustang was pulling into a parking spot. Near the Mustang, an armed ground crew member stood with arms raised, ready to marshal the Phantom to parking.

Beside the ground crew member, stood Major Andre Vosh, the Hidden Base flight leader and second in command, wearing his flight gear and holding his helmet. He had been piloting the camouflaged Mustang. A former member of Red Death and son of French Freedom Fighters, he is a ferocious warrior and deadly fighter pilot. He is also an avid rugby player and keeps himself in top physical condition.

As Skip parked the aircraft, Bud watched the helmeted Mustang pilot climbing out of the cockpit and remarked, "That silver Mustang pilot sure has a nice..."

"A nice what?" Skip asked, as he shut down the engines.

"Oh, nothing. Never mind."

Actually, Bud thought the pilot had a sexy bottom but did not say it because he was heterosexual. He could not think of a way to say, "That guy sure has a nice ass" and make it sound right.

Just then, the F-5 landed, and behind it, the curtain of camouflage netting closed, covering the opening completely. Overhead, hundreds of feet up, what appeared to be the same netting was stretched across the top of the steep canyon, creating the atmosphere of a huge cave.

The ground crew member displayed her weapon and motioned for both men to exit the aircraft. The silver Mustang pilot was standing beside the aircraft, watching as the men climbed down. Just as they turned to face the ground crew member with the gun, in the distance, the silver Mustang's pilot removed her helmet and out tumbled shoulder length, chestnut-brown hair.

Skip's mouth dropped open.

The ground crew member looked directly at Skip and said, "Lieutenant Cohen has a picture of you, just like that."

Skip gave her a confused glance and returned his gaze to the Mustang pilot.

Bud exclaimed, "Well, I'll be damned, the pilot's a girl! That's a relief."

By then, the F-5 had parked alongside the silver Mustang. The pilot shut down the engine, opened the cockpit, and removed her helmet, revealing long black hair.

This time, both men looked on in total amazement.

Bud said, "Son of a bitch!"

Skip was speechless.

Colonel Albert Fronz, wearing a dark gray flight suit, emerged from a large tent at the canyon wall near the aircraft. He approached, unnoticed by the two men, who were still preoccupied watching the two women pilots.

The colonel, a West German and former commander of Red Death, is the commander of Bushmaster's Hidden Base. A graduate of MIT, he is intelligent, fair minded, and impartial. A good commander but an unlikely terrorist.

"Not what you expected, are they?" he asked, as he joined Skip and Bud.

Both men looked in his direction, but said nothing.

The colonel has short, blonde hair and green eyes, over six feet tall, with broad shoulders. His flight suit has no rank insignia and only one small patch of a dark green snake with black eyes on a white background.

"Put away your weapon; these men are our guests. You may return to your duties. Gentlemen, welcome to our little base away from home. I am Colonel Fronz, commander of this outpost."

Bud spoke first, "None of this is what I expected."

"Bushmaster is not noted for doing what our enemies expect."

"Except for leavin' dead bodies behind wherever you go," Skip said hotly.

"Ah, you must be William Scott, the Viper pilot," Colonel Fronz said, smiling. "And you are Major Cooper, Deputy Chief of Intelligence."

Bud and Skip looked at each other in surprise.

When the colonel offered his hand in greeting, each man accepted it as a gentleman.

"Come, you must meet some of our pilots and officers."

He led them to the tent from where he had emerged. Inside was a mission briefing room with a large map board and several worktables. The two women pilots were sitting at one of the tables, writing in pilot logbooks. They stood as the men approached, presenting themselves with military bearing consistent with greeting senior officers.

The colonel introduced the ranking officer first, "Gentlemen, may I present Captain Vanya Petrovich, intercept and attack pilot."

Captain Petrovich, also a former member of Red Death, is the only daughter of Russian General Vladimir Petrovich, commander of the Russian Air Force. Her light, creamy complexion was in marked contrast to her dark eyes and jet-black hair. While attending college, she participated in sports, and she had been selected as a gymnast candidate for the Olympics. However, when it was evident that sports would conflict with her goal to pursue a flying career, she resigned as an Olympic candidate. Her choice to join with Red Death caused a serious conflict between her and her father, and he consequently severed all ties to her.

She extended her hand and responded with a firm handshake, direct eye contact, and a formal demeanor. She appeared to Skip as if she could be an athlete. She looked directly into Skip's blue eyes and maintained that gaze as if she was preparing to speak, but said nothing.

"Lieutenant Ahana Cohen, tactical reconnaissance, attack, and air combat."

Lieutenant Cohen, an Israeli, is stunningly beautiful, with long, chestnut-brown hair that covers her shoulders, golden brown skin, and piercing gray-blue eyes. Strong, healthy, and full of energy, she stands five-eight, almost as tall as Skip. She offers her hand. Her grip is painfully firm. She is warm and friendly with a beautiful smile.

The lieutenant had been a fighter pilot and a member of Red Death most of her adult life. Mistaking the lieutenant as only a beautiful woman was a mistake made only once, especially by those who competed against her piloting skills in air combat. Her kill ratio is the highest in the unit. When an enemy comes into her sights, they go down. She has never boasted of that fact. To her, it is just part of doing the best job she knows how to do.

"Lieutenant Cohen might be persuaded to show you some of her recent reconnaissance photos; right, Ahana?"

The colonel, Vanya, and Ahana all looked at Skip. Then, Bud looked quizzically at Skip. Skip had an expression of total confusion on his face.

At that point, Ahana spoke, "Yes, I think I might have some interesting photos to show our guests."

Her accent was Middle Eastern and sounded to Bud like Israeli.

"Gentlemen, if you please." The colonel motioned toward a door at the back of the room.

They entered the room, set up as a pilot's lounge and furnished with comfortable chairs and cots, several computer workstations, a library of books, and detailed wall maps of North America. There, three more officers were involved in various tasks. They looked up, and two of them immediately stood. The other went back to his work.

Before the colonel could speak, the ranking officer introduced himself, "I am Major Vosh, flight leader. I was flying the camouflaged Mustang. I know who you are, and I am aware of your positions and abilities. It is an honor to meet you. What do you think of our small base?"

"I can't say that I'm honored to meet you," Skip frankly replied. "I must admit, however, we are both impressed with your accomplishments."

"We've flown over this area many times and haven't seen, or suspected, a thing," Bud added.

"Actually, NAADA aircraft have overflown our base numerous times in the last three years," the other officer said, smiled and extended his hand. "I am Lieutenant Sharee (Sha-ray) Reshond, intelligence officer."

Lieutenant Reshond was previously a member of Red Death. A young, handsome, Western-educated, and idealistic Arab, he is very proud of his position as intelligence officer.

"Your count may go up slightly in the next few days," Bud predicted.

The lieutenant and the major both laughed. The pilot who had remained seated, stood up, scowled, and left the room.

"You must excuse Captain Draxon. He considers your presence here an insult. The recent death of his younger brother has only fueled his fire. It would be wise to keep a safe distance from him," The colonel warned.

Captain Draxon, a German soldier of fortune and fighter pilot, hates everyone, keeps his anger with him, and shows it often. The recent death of his younger brother, Tiger, killed by Major Phil Blake, has left him very bitter. Draxon is a dangerous man.

"His anger is affecting his judgment," The major commented.

"If he becomes a liability, I will deal with it," the colonel said bluntly, then turned to his guests, "We must not trouble our visitors with internal squabbles. We have much more interesting things for them to see. Lieutenant Reshond, will you please continue with the tour?"

"Yes, sir. Gentlemen, please follow me."

The young lieutenant trotted ahead, so Bud took advantage of the brief moment to speak privately, "Well, what do you think so far?"

"I think Lieutenant Cohen is the most beautiful woman I've ever seen."

"Now there's a tactical reply if I ever heard one."

"Huh?"

"Don't 'huh' me. Our first duty is to escape and you're scoping out the pilots!"

"Not 'pilots', pilot," Skip corrected. "The drop-dead gorgeous one."

"Captain Petrovich isn't bad either."

"And what was that about our first duty?"

"Well, we may be here for a while… it never hurts to survey all of the ass…"

"Hey now! We're supposed to be gentlemen!"

"Assets! I was going to say assets!"

"That's an interesting term for it."

"You're a gutter-brain."

"I think I'm in love."

"I don't believe I just heard Skip Scott say that. Are you sure you're not an imposter?"

"Who in the hell but me would want to look like this!"

"Good point."

Lieutenant Reshond had stopped at the center of the compound, saying nothing, waiting for the men to catch up. He was looking around the compound, as if seeing it for the first time, so Skip and Bud followed his example and surveyed the area in silence.

The canyon was positioned near the center of a steep, jagged mountain range. The walls were almost vertical and allowed maximum use of the canyon floor. What fascinated both Bud and Skip was the brilliant use of the camouflage netting.

Bud leaned over to Skip and whispered, "Do you see the cable bundles running up toward the netting?"

"Yea. I'll bet it's Stealth Net."

"That's what I was thinking too."

Aftermath I: The Fight For Survival

The entrance of the canyon was a huge rectangular opening about a hundred feet wide and two hundred feet high. At the top of the rectangle, the opening narrowed and closed, forming a huge rock buttress, almost fifty feet thick, giving the appearance of a cave entrance. The buttress extended several hundred feet straight up, then opened again, spreading into the crest of the mountain. There was a heavy curtain of camouflage netting over the opening.

Overhead, the camouflage netting was stretched across the entire top of the canyon, supported in place with a network of steel cables attached to the canyon walls. From above, the netting looked like a shallow depression across the crest of the mountain. Below the net, the canyon floor widened from one hundred feet at the entrance to over four hundred feet and extended for about two thousand feet, where it then narrowed quickly from top to bottom, becoming a winding passage that disappeared into the mountain. An impressive collection of aircraft was parked along both sides of the runway. The utilization of space made the operations area look like an aircraft carrier flight deck.

Near the two Mustangs, five F-5's were parked nose to tail. Four Mig-31's were next, along with two YAK-36 Russian VTOL attack jets. Along the wall on the other side of the runway were three Mig-29's, one SU-27, one Tornado F-3 Multi-role Fighter and one Tornado GR-1A, Tactical Reconnaissance Variant. There was also a Helio Stallion, STOL, single-engine propjet.

Skip was surprised to see a Helio here. Base One had a Helio Super Courier that he loved to fly. These rugged aircraft, used primarily by the CIA, had amazing short field performance.

Along the wall, an impressive collection of armament was stored, including bombs, missiles, gun pods, and ammunition.

Lieutenant Reshond finally spoke, "I was reflecting on the efforts to construct this base. One year ago, I stood here with Colonel Fronz, surveying this canyon. Our Recon Team had found three possibilities for a hidden base and this was, by far, the best choice. The work ahead was monumental in scope. We had to get heavy equipment in here, to remove tons of rock that had to be blasted away. The entire canyon floor had to be leveled and landscaped to accommodate facilities for base personnel, a runway, and aircraft parking ramp, plus handle water run-off during torrential rains.

"The runway had to be capable of launching and recovering aircraft with the same efficiency as an aircraft carrier. With no possibility of going around after a missed approach for landing, the challenge was to design arresting barriers that were fail-safe. Obviously, one failure to stop a landing aircraft could mean destruction of the whole base.

"We hauled over fifty thousand gallons of jet fuel and avgas here. It is stored in synthetic bladders beneath the runway.

"All of this had to be accomplished while remaining unseen and unheard by your defense forces. There were the occasional and unpredictable reconnaissance satellites, the two long-range radar facilities, listening posts in secret locations, and your continual, incessant, unscheduled sentry flights. Yet, we accomplished all of this in less than four months." He took a deep breath, obviously pleased with the results, and continued to take in the scene.

"You have a lot to be proud of," Skip commented, "too bad your purpose is for all the wrong reasons."

"That, my cynical adversary, is a matter of opinion. You may be in for a surprise."

"A philosophy of elitism does not justify aggressive terrorism, theft, destruction, and murder," Bud responded with conviction. "And that is not an opinion; it's a simple, logical fact."

"You are in the middle of your greatest enemy's secret base, a guest of the base commander, and you have the audacity to call us thieves and murderers!"

Skip and Bud looked at each other, unsure how to respond, when the lieutenant continued, "I am impressed! I knew I would like you. Our intelligence network is truly the best."

Then he added, "In all sincerity, much work and sacrifice has gone into this base. We lost ten workers during the project. Many believe in our quest and would gladly sacrifice their lives, if necessary, to see it come to fruition."

Realizing the conviction in the lieutenant's voice, they decided to keep silent, avoiding an inevitable argument.

Their tour continued. Lieutenant Reshond answered all of their questions without hesitation, holding back nothing. At one point, the lieutenant had to tend to some business, leaving Skip and Bud alone.

"Would you reveal this much information to a captured enemy?" Skip asked.

"I would if I were certain my captured enemy wouldn't live to report it."

"That's what I was thinkin', too."

"Well, there's an old saying that goes, 'When faced with insurmountable odds, do the unexpected.'" Bud said, philosophically.

Skip looked at Bud in amazement. "I'll say one thing, you're the biggest…"

Bud cut him off, "Now be nice!"

"I was gonna say, optimist. The biggest optimist I've ever known. What're you plannin' anyway?"

Suddenly, Bud spotted something familiar in the half-light at the far end of the canyon. He drew Skip's attention and asked, "What does that white object look like to you?"

"It looks like a wing tip… like the wing tip of a King Air. Do you think…?"

At that moment, Lieutenant Reshond returned and said, "I thought you might find that interesting. Yes, it is the missing King Air. And the old man is here and quite well, if he hasn't provoked someone into killing him this morning."

"That's Pop," Skip said smiling.

"Do you mean he is like that all of the time?" the Lieutenant asked in amazement.

"He's just very opinionated," Skip explained.

"*We* are opinionated. He is impossible. If anyone even tries to speak with him, he starts an argument. I have refused to speak to him since he thumped me."

"Thumped you?" Bud chuckled.

"Yes, thumped me."

"As in, hold-your-bird-finger-back-with-your-thumb-and-let-it-go, thump?" Skip asked with an amused tone as he demonstrated the deed.

"Yes!" the Lieutenant snapped.

"He was just lettin' you know that you were bein' a jerk," Skip explained, "That thump is his substitute for knockin' you on your ass, which is what he probably wanted to do. I've seen him thump his nephews a few times. The victim always seemed to get the point."

"Oh, I got the point all right. And I must admit that I was being a jerk. But I truly don't know how he has survived thus far. Each one of us has contemplated killing him just to shut him up. Everyone, that is, except Colonel Fronz. I think the colonel finds all of this amusing somehow."

"Really?" Bud commented with a question.

"Well, we intercepted the King Air, assuming a VIP or, at least, a commander of some sort would be traveling in such an aircraft. Instead, all we got was that old fossil."

"I wouldn't let him hear you say that...." Skip cautioned.

"Too late. I grew impatient with him on the second day and called him an old fossil. Things went rapidly down hill from there."

"I can believe that. May we see him?" Bud asked.

"Certainly. In fact, his quarters are over there, next to the colonel's tent. Please follow me."

CHAPTER ELEVEN

For All the Wrong Reasons

Lieutenant Reshond led the men to a tent, the largest of a group of tents used as living quarters for the entire base. A guard was posted outside. Lt. Reshond approached the guard and whispered, "Is he sleeping?"

Before the guard could answer, a familiar voice from inside the tent roared, "I'm not asleep, you Commie Twerp!"

The lieutenant turned to the men and explained, "He insists that we are all Communists, and since I am the base intelligence officer, I am the worst 'Commie' of our group."

"What do you want with me now, you Red Bastard?"

"Visitors, Mr. Hackland. You have visitors."

"Well, I'm almost positive that you can find your way inside..." Pop's reply was thick with sarcasm.

The guard opened the door and Skip and Bud entered, followed by the lieutenant. Pop was working at a computer station, in a well-furnished room, complete with a bar. He continued with his work, not bothering to look up and see who had entered.

"I might've known you would have the most comfortable quarters in the place," Skip commented.

At that point, Pop quickly stood up and spun around with a look of total surprise, "What, in the name of Christ, are you two doin' here?"

"Oh, we just thought we'd drop by and say 'hello'," Bud said sarcastically.

"Okay, you got me, smart ass. How long have you been here?"

"About three hours. The lieutenant was just givin' us the nickel tour," Skip answered.

Pop scowled at the lieutenant and asked, "Don't you have some terrorist act to commit somewhere?"

The lieutenant ignored Pop but took the hint and addressed Skip and Bud, "If you should need anything, or when you have had enough of this... person, tell the guard, and he will summon me." Then, Lt. Reshond departed.

Pop looked at the door after it closed and said, "Red bastard."

"Jesus, Pop, how are you keeping these people from killing you?" Bud asked.

"Hell, they ain't gonna damage me. I'm valuable to them; they need me. Their computer system crashed, and they couldn't fix it. When they discovered who they had, naturally, they knew that I'm somewhat of a computer genius, so they've had me digging into their system for several days now."

"Pop, you're ever so humble," Skip joked.

"Humph!" Pop replied and continued, "They have a very sophisticated data base on every one in NAADA and all of the other federal agencies as well. Some of the files date back over ten years. They must have had a team of expert hackers at one time. Most of this data was extracted from protected systems—some guarded with the highest possible security levels. But, it's sort of strange. From what I can determine from the archived files, the most recent data is over six months old. The computer crash isolated them from their own intelligence network."

"How do they get into the Net way out here?" Skip asked.

"Apparently, they have tapped into one of our long-line fiber-optics cables that were installed through this area several years ago. Until their system crashed, they were getting news, movies, and all that other crap."

"You mean they have access to all of the encrypted data that we send and receive?" Bud asked, somewhat alarmed.

"Yes. At least until their system crashed."

"Now, that's disturbing," Bud commented, and then continued, "but, on the other hand, how could an outfit like this function without any communications from their commanders? And why waste the time and effort to capture us? They set up this elaborate, expensive, hidden base and operate out of here for over a year, and the only reason we discover they're here is that they decided to show their hand. Don't you find all of this rather strange?"

"Yes, I do," Skip replied. "We need to get some answers. Maybe Lt. Reshond was trying to tell us something when he said, 'We might be surprised...' You know, I think I've got the answer to that question I asked you a while ago."

"What question was that?" Pop asked.

Skip explained, "Bud said, 'When faced with insurmountable odds, do the unexpected,' and I asked what he had in mind. We were distracted by the King Air and he didn't answer, but now, I think I know the answer."

Then, he looked at Bud and asked, "What would be the most unexpected thing for us to do?"

Pop suddenly realized what they were up to, "Oh, no! Oh, no! You're not thinkin' that. You can't be thinking that."

Bud looked at Skip and said, "Offer them an opportunity to join the FFNA."

Pop exclaimed, "I knew it! I just knew it! You two have come up with some of the damnedest, hair-brained schemes before, but this one takes the cake. Both of you ought to be committed, I swear to God!"

"Well, hell, Pop. What's the worst they could say?" Skip asked.

"They could say, 'Up against the wall, Red Neck Mother!' is what they could say!"

Skip and Bud looked at each other with expressions that acknowledged that Pop could be right, but now, they did not want to discuss those consequences.

***

Back at Base One, the report of the over-due reconnaissance flight was making its way through the channels. An overdue aircraft alert was sent out on the NAADA communications net. When three more hours had passed with no word on the fate of the RF-4 and her crew, the alert was upgraded to "Aircraft missing and presumed down in possible hostile area."

From that point on, the search and rescue operation was handled differently from the search for Pop and the missing King Air. Every unarmed search aircraft was provided a fighter escort. Enough chances had been taken, and it was just too coincidental for two aircraft to disappear in the same general area within the span of a week, leaving no trace or evidence of a crash.

***

At the Bushmaster base, the "guests" were assigned living quarters. Then, Lt. Reshond returned, introduced them to the other pilots, and resumed their tour of the base. The technical details of the design and construction continued to fascinate them, and the lieutenant was willing to answer any, and all, questions.

One question was from Skip, "How do you avoid the temperature differential across the camouflage net?"

"That is an excellent question," the lieutenant commented. "We would not have even considered this location, had it not been for the special camouflage net. It's called Stealth Net. It was invented by a scientist who was trying to solve the problem of heat protection of ground forces operating in hostile environments. It has been designed using nano-technology. Special components and materials in the fabric allow it to change color and temperature, matching the colors and surrounding surface temperature of the existing terrain. That makes it virtually invisible to optical and infrared sensors. It is a simple matter to match it to the shape of the terrain during installation. If the placement is done properly, it is extremely hard to pick out of the surrounding terrain, even in close proximity. We are considered among the best in the world at camouflage."

"What about radar?" Bud asked.

"The net contains fibers made from titanium oxide and aluminum wire. If the net is scanned by synthetic aperture radar, it would only appear to be a layer of…"

Bud realized the significance and finished his sentence, "…metal oxide. Son of a bitch! I remember the comment in the report about the unusual return seen in this area. But we concluded it was a vein of metal oxide."

"Fascinating, but quite correct. The net does its job very well."

"How do you heat and cool the net?" Skip asked, "It must require a sophisticated and power hungry system to accomplish that."

"Yes, certainly. Coolant gas is circulated throughout the net. Heating is done much the same as an electric blanket is heated. We power the net, and the rest of this facility for that matter, with power cells."

"Hydrogen or nuclear power cells?" Bud asked.

"Both. We have seventeen hydrogen cells and ten nuclear cells positioned at various locations throughout the facility. They are silent and efficient. The best choice for our operation."

"Where did you acquire those?" Skip asked.

"The Russian space program donated most of them; NASA provided the rest… involuntarily, of course.

"Naturally," Bud added.

"I guess there is one advantage to bein' a ruthless terrorist organization," Skip commented.

"What's that?" Bud and the lieutenant asked, simultaneously.

"No worries about nuclear waste, contamination, that sort of thing... A total lack of morals equates to, no conscience, no guilt, no worries."

Again, simultaneously, Bud and Lieutenant Reshond said, "Good point."

As evening approached, Colonel Fronz stopped by to invite Pop, Bud, and Skip to dine with him and the crew. Skip and Bud accepted. Pop said he would be there if he did not have any other pressing engagements.

After the colonel left, Pop commented on the food, "They serve the same crap that we have to eat... MRE's, rat meat, dog, and freeze dried, artificially flavored, and heaven-knows-what. If the illustrious Bushmaster is so damn good at stealing whatever they please and so well financed and resourceful, why don't they have real food?"

"There are any number of logical reasons why a remote, hidden base don't have 'real' food." Skip replied, "However, in a roundabout way, you do have a good point. And it's just one more reason to take a hard look at these people and try to determine their intentions."

That night, all three "guests" joined the Bushmaster crew for dinner. Colonel Fronz was particular to thank Pop for joining them and pointed out, to his companions, that it was the first time he had accepted the invitation.

Except for the posted guards, everyone dined at the same time and in the same place. No rank or special privileges were observed during meals. It was a time set aside for the crew to associate as a team, treat each other as equals, and share friendly conversation. For each of the three "guests," it was an unexpected and pleasant surprise. It also afforded an opportunity to observe most of the Bushmaster crew in close quarters. The only absentee was Captain Draxon.

The meal was tolerable, even for Pop, and the participants talkative and friendly. The conversation alternated between comments and questions from both sides. It was apparent that the Bushmaster personnel were very knowledgeable about NAADA and its personnel. Some of the questions were somewhat personal, especially about Owl's Nest. Often, when commenting on Skip's mountaintop base, Lt.

Cohen would be referred to as the foremost authority. She would laugh, occasionally, but more often, blush and smile shyly. She was obviously modest about her abilities as a pilot.

Major Vosh was not so hesitant to boast of the pilots' abilities. As flight leader, he was visibly proud of his role and of the pilots with which he flew. He trusted his life to his comrades and made it known. It was obvious why he was flight leader.

After dinner, Lt. Cohen approached Skip, "Sir, I apologize for any embarrassment I might have caused for you."

"I was fascinated, but not embarrassed... and please, as a civilian, I might outrank you, but I'm Skip, not 'sir'," Skip said and smiled.

Lt. Cohen blushed again and said, "I'm sorry, I thought you were called William."

His mind flashed back to a very special moment in his distant past, and the lieutenant noticed the change in his expression.

The lieutenant was suddenly concerned that she had offended him. But before she could speak, Skip's expression softened, then he smiled, looked directly into her eyes, and said, "It's been a long time since someone as pretty as you called me William."

"Thank you." Lt. Cohen believed his compliment to be sincere and offered, "I think I can explain most of this... gossip... if you would allow me to show you some reconnaissance photos that I have in my quarters."

"I would appreciate that very much."

She led him to her quarters. Inside, he found a very modestly furnished tent, reminiscent of the accommodations of a Marine training base barracks room. Among the exceptions, included a very impressive collection of aerial reconnaissance photographs.

"Wow! All of these are from your recon missions?"

"Most of them. I have collected a few from other pilots," she answered. "It's a hobby. Helps keep me busy."

The one that drew Skip's immediate attention was the explanation to which the lieutenant had been referring. The photograph was of

Skip, taken at the instant he first saw the silver Mustang, standing near the pond at Owl's Nest, in his flight suit, coffee cup in hand, mouth agape, looking completely dumbfounded.

"Now I know why the ground crewman said that…," Skip commented, mostly talking to himself, and then explained, "I had just watched you remove your flight helmet. She saw the look on my face. I was taken completely by surprise, just like that mornin' at Owl's Nest."

"I understand your reaction to my Mustang, but I do not think I will ever completely understand the reactions that I sometimes cause."

Skip looked directly into her eyes and said, "I'd get used to it if I were you, 'cause I can guarantee it ain't gonna stop."

She blushed, and he noticed that her gray-blue eyes showed a hint of green that was not normally visible. Realizing that he had noticed, she blushed even more and looked down at the floor.

"Blushin' complements your beauty," Skip said, matter-of-factly.

She looked at Skip with curiosity. Lt. Cohen was not accustomed to getting sincere compliments about her beauty. She was not certain he was sincere, until she saw his face. Skip was simply stating a fact. He did not expect anything in return, and it showed. No one had ever impressed her as much as Skip did at that moment.

The lieutenant's look of curiosity faded, she smiled, and softly replied, "Thank you."

"Young lady, you are most welcome."

They remained facing each other for several minutes, each unsure what to say. Skip looked at the floor, fidgeting, then looked at her and asked, "Lieutenant, why did you join Bushmaster?"

"Please, call me Ahana."

"Okay, Ahana, tell me, why do you waste your talent and ability with these people?"

Ahana hesitated, as if considering whether or not she wanted to answer, then she said, "Please, have a seat. It is a long story."

Skip waited for Ahana to be seated first, then he sat down, and she began, "I am a Jew. My father was a foreign diplomat and a very traditional man. So, when he was assigned to various posts, my family traveled with him. We were treated well by people in most of the countries, but it is inescapable that Jews are hated people.

"We children had to live on the embassy grounds in most places. We went to school, played, and lived, isolated from the native children. We only knew children of other diplomats and dignitaries. Sometimes, when we ventured out among the populace, we would be taunted, threatened, and, occasionally, attacked. Our mother insisted that we were not to burden our father with those type problems. He was working very hard to make our world better, she would say, and so our lives went on.

"When I was twelve, my father was reassigned to a post in South America. We had been in-country for about six months when my father learned of a plot to overrun the embassy. He made immediate plans to return us to Israel, but the embassy was attacked before we were able to leave. My father and brother were killed, my mother raped and killed, all while we were forced to watch.

"Then, my younger sister and I were taken, along with four other girls, to the rebel stronghold. There, we were abused and raped repeatedly over the next several days. My sister and two of the girls died from the abuse, but somehow two other girls and I survived.

"One who died was the daughter of a member of the terrorist group Red Death. Her father was a spy stationed at the embassy. He and his wife were killed, but before he died, he managed to get a message to his people.

"Less than a week later, a small force of Red Death soldiers attacked the rebel stronghold, and we were rescued. The Red Death soldiers killed all of the rebels. Then, swearing vengeance for the lives of the Red Death spy, his wife, and daughter, they killed the relatives of the rebels and everyone associated with the rebel group and all of their families.

"I was taken to a hospital in Germany, where I recovered. I was so bitter and full of hate. My life had been turned inside out, and I was totally alone. They gave me security and comfort and provided care and understanding. Eventually, I regained my pride and confidence. It was then that I asked to join Red Death.

"I have always been treated with respect, allowed to be myself, and to do what I love, which is flying airplanes. I have been provided the best education possible. The colonel has been like a father to me. This is the only life I have known since I was thirteen."

"Ahana, if I could show you a way to a better life, would you consider leavin' Bushmaster?"

She looked at him with surprise, and then grew very serious, "I am willing to listen."

"Good. I know you'll make the right decision," Skip said and smiled confidently.

So, Skip began to tell Ahana what it was like to live in North America and work for NAADA and the FFNA.

Pop had excused himself early and returned to his quarters for the evening. Bud lingered after the meal and was having an interesting conversation with Major Vosh and Captain Petrovich. She appeared to be fascinated by this American pilot.

"Tell me, Major Brandon Cooper, deputy chief of Base One Intelligence, what do you find most fascinating about our organization?" She asked.

"Well, Captain Vanya Petrovich, fighter pilot, I find it most fascinating that so many bright and capable people would follow a madman like General Za-Ved Raazmahd."

Captain Petrovich smiled deviously, as if she was preparing to tell him the real reason she belonged to the Bushmaster organization, when Major Vosh spoke, "Why do you call our leader a madman? Perhaps your judgment is clouded by your allegiance to a government that has deceived you for too many years?"

"I call Raazmahd a madman because it is the only plausible explanation for his actions. My judgment, if affected at all, is made clearer because of my government. I have been afforded the opportunity and privilege to view unfiltered, raw intelligence data. Information that is not available to most people. You have access to the very same information, and I find it humorous that you actually believe the bullshit that Raazmahd feeds you. You're certainly not stupid. Why do you fight like lions, yet follow like sheep? It appears to me that you do this for all the wrong reasons."

"You sound just like my father," Capt. Petrovich observed.

"It is your government that has deceived the rest of the world," Major Vosh said.

"Deceived the rest of the world about what?" Bud asked.

"It is widely known that the West controlled the asteroid," Captain Petrovich answered. "Your so-called Grim Reaper was used to kill innocent people, throw the Third World nations into chaos, and place control of the world's economy into your hands alone."

Bud laughed, "Raazmahd has been preaching that to anyone who would listen, and I'm telling you that it's complete nonsense. We did not control the Reaper. No one controlled it. Hell, no one with the authority to do anything would even believe that the asteroid was on a collision course with the Earth, until it was too late to do anything. We were just as helpless as you."

"Helpless?" Major Vosh replied. "The asteroid did not hit North America; it hit Asia. We have documents that prove you are lying. We should have you in chains instead of treating you like visiting dignitaries."

Their discussion had drawn the attention of the entire room. Colonel Fronz had heard most of it, as did Skip and Lt. Cohen, who had returned to the mess tent.

Suddenly, Lt. Cohen addressed Maj. Vosh, "Andre, why don't you insist that Major Cooper prove what he claims?"

"How can he do that?" Capt. Petrovich asked.

"I will only believe what he says when I see it for myself," Maj. Vosh replied.

Then, Colonel Fronz intervened, "I think it is time to let our guests retire and consider their position."

Skip looked at Ahana and winked. She returned a curious smile, wondering what he was thinking.

As he and Bud walked back to their quarters, Bud asked Skip, "I saw that confident wink you gave Lt. Cohen. What do you have in mind? These people are convinced that we're a bunch of monsters."

"Not all of them think that way. Most of these folks are followin' this path by choice and with a belief that they made that choice based on facts. We may not be able to sway everyone, but if we can prove they've been lied to, then they'll realize that they've been followin' that madman for all the wrong reasons. Then, we'll have a good chance of gettin' outta here alive and, just maybe, takin' some damn good pilots with us."

Early on the second day, as the air search intensified, the guard was doubled on the "guests" of the Bushmaster's hidden base. Bud and Skip were in Pop's quarters, discussing their situation, when Colonel Fronz paid them a visit.

"Gentlemen, I apologize for the inconvenience, but it would be unfortunate if one of the search aircraft were alerted to our position. Things should return to normal in a few days. That will give Major Cooper more time to prepare his response to Major Vosh. If you need anything, please do not hesitate to ask."

After the colonel left, they returned to their discussion...

"Pop, since we seem to have plenty of time on our hands, why don't we dig a little further into their computer system?" Skip suggested.

"Good idea." Bud agreed.

"Just tell me what you'd like to see...," Pop said and sat down at the terminal.

***

Back at Base One, the atmosphere was tense. The base was on full alert that morning. There were a number of reasons for the alert, the least of which was the search for the missing RF-4 and her two crew members.

The Stage 3 nuclear alert was in full effect, and to make things worse, Intelligence had learned that a small force of elite Bushmaster recon troopers were en route to North America to detonate a nuclear weapon. Aircraft were departing for the search area at forty-five minute intervals. The entire Base One security force was on duty, conducting patrols of the base perimeter and other areas. At Base One Headquarters, at 0600 hrs, Candy Simms was busy coordinating the final phase of the Perimeter Defense Weapon System (PDWS) upgrade.

Based on the LifeGuard/DeadEye System developed by Lawrence Livermore National Laboratories and later deployed by the USAF under the name Backlash, the PDWS is an array of passive infrared detection devices tied to a sophisticated computer system. The system continually analyzes the external heat signature of the base perimeter, alerting security of any activity that might indicate unauthorized entry. If a weapon of any type is fired toward the base, the computer will instantly analyze and identify the projectile's signature and point of origin. The computer then commands the PDWS to fire on the projectile and its source. The current upgrade that Candy was coordinating would be supplementing the existing 7.62-mm cannons with the Navy's 20-mm Phalanx Ship Defense System.

The Phalanx Systems, using the 20-mm Vulcan Cannon, are being placed at specific targeting locations around Base One, so that each gun position will cover a maximum area of thirty degrees horizontally and forty-five degrees vertically. That will allow the PDWS to locate and fire on an identified target, within a range of five thousand yards, in less than two seconds. Since the Phalanx System was designed to protect naval vessels from attack by Exocet and Harpoon missiles, any threat to Base One's perimeter had a high probability of a short life span.

"Good morning! How is my Intel boss today?" Candy said, talking into her telephone ear set.

"Much better now that I've heard your voice. How is my best girl?" Ron Taylor replied.

"I'm in the process of coordinating the PDWS operational test and evaluation. The install crew has completed tests on the passive system, and we're ready for tests on the weapons system. I have notified security and set up a meeting for all interested personnel at 0900 hrs this morning. If all goes well, the testing should start later today. I'm planning base-wide announcements, starting at 1000 hrs and repeating every thirty minutes. I'm told that, when just one Phalanx fires, not only will the gun be heard all over the base, it will also be felt as well. If that is true, I can't imagine what firing a salvo will be like."

"You really have a handle on this project," Ron commented.

"Thank you, sweetie. Now, what can we expect when they fire all of those guns at once?"

"It's going to be like a high frequency earthquake. I suggest that anyone outside wear hearing protection, and you probably should protect any fragile items that could fall and break. You might want to include that in your announcements."

"Good idea, big guy. Gotta go! I'll see you later. I love you, bye!"

"Call me, maybe I can make it for lunch. Love you, too. Bye."

Later that day, Candy had a break in her busy schedule and arranged to meet Ron at the base cafeteria. It was just after midday, and the mess hall was crowded. When she arrived, Ron was waiting at the door.

"Hi, beautiful," he said, kissing hello.

Candy smiled and replied, "Hi! How is my favorite fella?"

Ron opened the door for her, and just as she entered the doorway... suddenly, he felt a blast and realized he was flying through the air, and then, everything went dark.

CHAPTER TWELVE

Sometimes the Truth Doesn't Hurt

At the Bushmaster hidden base, three days had passed uneventfully. Several of the search aircraft had flown directly over the base, but none had lingered.

Pop had been digging into the computer system with a great deal of tenacity. To cover his efforts, he had set aside enough free memory to allow the system to operate on a limited basis. That was enough to convince Lieutenant Reshond that Pop was actually trying to repair their computer system's damaged programs. Actually, Pop had discovered, almost immediately, that a computer virus had damaged the system. He analyzed the software virus closely, looking for the trademark message or signature that hackers typically bury within the program. An arrogant game is played within the confines of the software world—a challenge to an unknown foe... "Catch me, if you can."

Pop finally found the signature. It said simply, "Gotcha! Bitwraith." Pop chuckled to himself, thinking of the irony of this particular virus. A hacker, probably doing nothing more than entertaining himself with his mischievous deeds, had invaded a system used by Bushmaster to invade other computer systems to steal secret files and documents. The hacker, Bitwraith, had planted a software bomb in the heart of Bushmaster's system, and they were completely unaware that it ever happened. It only proved the old adage, "No matter how good you may think you are, there is always someone that's better."

Pop removed the virus and proceeded to pry into their system, digging through layer upon layer of encrypted files. Most of the files contained information about NAADA and other Free World intelligence organizations. Continuing to dig, Pop found more and more data about the Bushmaster organization and personnel. With each file he found, it became more and more revealing.

As promised, the guard had been cut back as the search aircraft came less frequently. It was early morning, and very few personnel were active. Skip had ventured out onto the ramp, enjoying the opportunity to view the aircraft. Never had he seen such a mix of aircraft types and categories in one place. He had flown most of the aircraft during his career, but he had never flown the Sukhoi SU-27 Flanker. The Flanker was ranked as the best multi-role fighter in the world, and it had held that spot for many years. As Skip stood viewing the Flanker, he mumbled to himself, "Man, I sure hope Bushmaster don't have a bunch of these things…"

Another aircraft that interested him was the second P-51 Mustang. It was obviously a modified version and had the aerodynamic design and look of an air racer. The Merlin engine had been replaced with a 2500 SHP (shaft-horse power) Rolls-Royce prop jet engine. That explained the power and performance that it displayed during their brief encounter. It had no on-board weapons, only hard-points in numerous places. The hard-point rails appeared to be designed to accept virtually any type of ordinance.

From behind Skip, Major Vosh spoke, "It is a beautiful aircraft, isn't it?"

"Yes, it is, Major. I've been admirin' all of your aircraft. You have an excellent collection of fighters here, each well suited for their intended roll and well maintained."

"Thank you. That is a quite a compliment, considering your background."

"I wouldn't say it, if I didn't mean it. I wouldn't hesitate to fly any of these aircraft." Then, Skip put on his best poker face and said, "How about a quick brief on the Flanker? I'd like to take it for a spin around the pattern... I'll bring it right back!"

Major Vosh was taken off guard for only a moment, and then he smiled and erupted into genuine laughter. "I like your wit, Skip. I truly do like your sense of humor. Unfortunately, for all of us, the Sukhoi is broken. During a launch several months ago, the number one engine ingested a stone dislodged from the rock face above the entrance. The engine was instantly trashed. We cannot repair it, and we have no spares. If not for the remarkable piloting skills of Captain Petrovich, we would have lost the aircraft and possibly revealed our position as well. She is a very talented pilot."

"Can you tell me who was flyin' the Mustang that almost shot me down?"

The major hesitated and looked at Skip with a very serious expression, studying his face intently.

"I was just wonderin'. From the viewpoint of a pilot who has had his ego cut down a notch or two. If revealing the pilot violates your security procedures, or protocol, I understand."

The major studied him even more intently, saying nothing.

"Maybe I should drop the subject."

"No, no, that is not necessary. I was just contemplating how I could tell you. Trying to put myself in your shoes, if you will, imagining how I would take the news. To be honest, I would not take it well. However, I don't believe you will react as I would... regrettably, I do not have your sense of humor."

Skip smiled a somewhat curious smile and looked puzzled.

"Captain Petrovich was the pilot."

"Vanya?"

"Yes. As I said, she is a remarkable pilot. Truthfully, she is somewhat apologetic now. She spoke with me on the first day you arrived and revealed her feelings about the matter. Vanya is unsure how to approach you or even if she should. I advised her to act with the feelings within her. She said I sounded like her father, and the discussion went to hell from there. Truthfully, it is difficult to come face to face with a pilot that you have opposed in air combat. You will be the first, since most of the pilots that she has opposed are dead."

"Well, I'll be damned!"

"Perhaps, I have misjudged you?"

"No, Major, not really. Actually, I blew the landing and destroyed the aircraft. Captain Petrovich was just the primary contributor; I finished the job."

"Somehow, I doubt that. And, please, call me Andre."

"Well, Andre, I guess I should tell her that she didn't fail after all, except that I'm still alive," Skip remarked.

"I shouldn't tell you this, but in all confidentiality, she is glad that you survived."

"Really? Me too! And I'll keep it just between us."

Skip extended his right hand, which Andre readily accepted. At the moment they shook hands, Skip realized that he had just made another friend and perhaps gained an ally as well.

Suddenly, Andre grew very serious, looked directly into Skip's eyes, and said, "Skip, I must tell you of the F-16 pilot that we recently shot down."

"Will you tell your story to Bud and Pop as well?" Skip asked.

"Certainly."

Skip and Andre went to Pop's tent, where Andre gathered the men together and began his story:

"Often, I find it's not easy to tell of the death of a comrade, even when he died a hero. I am not one to tell of the glorious battles and hard-fought victories. I like to win, but I do not like to lose my men, nor think of the losses of my enemy in those terms.

"On that day, we lost three good pilots. We were stalking the two F-16's, and we surprised them, but our first shots failed to get the intended results. Our intentions were to overwhelm and force surrender.

"They immediately split up, but only the flight lead reacted as a disciplined pilot. The wingman hesitated, and I can only say that his luck was holding that day. I am certain that I hit the mark with sufficient shots to bring him down, yet he broke and ran. Considering the damage and expecting easy prey, my number four pursued, and we remained on the leader.

"I have gone up against countless battle-hardened and experienced pilots, but I have seen none that could match this Falcon pilot. His missile system did not lock on us—an apparent malfunction. The logical choice would have been to evade and outrun us. He had salvoed his air-to-ground missiles, becoming light enough to run, yet he turned and fought us head-on.

"At first, I thought he was insane, but then I realized that he had turned to lock his weapons system. He had made an extreme high-G one eighty, locked, fired, and made another evasive turn more quickly that I could think. The missile took out my number two. Number three and I continued the pursuit, but for all intent and purpose, we were flying defensively, not offensively. We had no idea of our opponent's capabilities.

"We fired four missiles—two heatseekers and two radar-guided. He decoyed and out maneuvered the heatseekers. Then, apparently, his rearward radar became operational, because he fired a Launch and Leave Sparrow. I evaded it; my number three did not. Then, he performed another astounding maneuver, flying his F-16 through a mountain pass that I could not fly my Tiger through. The shock wave, generated within the pass, detonated both remaining missiles.

"Unknown to me, my number four had returned from his pursuit of the other F-16. Anticipating our flight path, he positioned his aircraft to attack as our opponent entered the valley on the other side of the mountain range. With a clear shot and every advantage, my number four was unable to hit the F-16.

"When I cleared the mountain range, I saw that the F-16 was within firing range of my number four, so I acquired and launched. The pilot fired his last missile, but did not live to see it complete its task. My missile had locked on, and before he could eject, it found its mark. My opponent's last shot also found its mark, and I returned home alone.

"I will always believe that I am alive today only because we had superior numbers. We did not have superior skills. He was truly a magnificent pilot, and it saddens me that I was victorious that day. I am glad to be alive, but I am not proud of my victory." Andre finished and looked down at the floor.

"His name was Phil Blake," Skip said.

Andre looked at Skip and said, "I wish I could have met him and talked, as we are talking today."

"I think Phil would have liked that, too," Bud replied.

"What about the other F-16?" Skip asked ominously.

"He was a coward and left his flight leader to die," Andre said with much conviction, and then added, "If I knew him, I would personally slit his throat!"

"You may just get that chance," Skip said, "unless I beat you to it...."

The four men sat in silence, Bud and Andre looking at Skip, both somewhat surprised, wondering if Skip really meant what he said. Pop just smiled slightly. He knew, but he was not telling.

"Since everyone here seems to be so open and honest, I guess there is no better time than the present to show you what I found on this computer system," Pop said. "What do you think, gentlemen? Do you think Andre is ready to hear the truth for a change?"

"I think so," Skip replied.

"Why not," Bud said. "Sometimes, the truth doesn't hurt."

"I don't understand. Aren't you repairing damage to our system, so we may have access to it again?"

"Yes, in the process of the repair, I found a virus," Pop answered, and then told a little white lie, "Then, I had to search throughout the system to make sure the virus was not hiding in some unlikely place. I found it in thirty-four different places. However, as I searched, I also found some other interesting things—information that you and other members of Bushmaster are, most likely, not aware of and need to know."

"For instance?" Andre asked, showing heightened interest.

Pop accessed a file called Bushmaster WDZ Order-1.

"For instance, I'm sure you have seen this file... it's the search criteria and establishment orders for the operations base in the Western Defense Zone. This base."

"Yes, I have seen it. Please continue."

"Now, let's access the rest of the document." Pop initiated a subroutine that opened the encrypted files associated with WDZ Order-1.

"There is more? This, I have not seen," Andre said, surprised, as he gazed at the screen.

"Order-1 was written under the authority of General Raazmahd. The general wrote this additional file, personally. He has established a timeline for your operation. Specific things are supposed to be accomplished along the way, as we see here," Pop said, indicating a calendar with certain weeks highlighted and operations start and completion dates."

"I have seen this information. These plans and operations are contained in individual orders administered by the colonel."

"But look on down the calendar," Pop suggested. "Six months from now, reconnaissance of Base One and Base Two is to be completed and then, three months later, attacked and destroyed. But look, you are also to abandon and destroy this base. Now, why would you want to do a stupid thing like that? Why destroy a secure point of retreat, in the middle of a major offensive? And here, two weeks after that, he indicates a three- to four-day operation called, 'Seed Project.' Then, a one-day event called, 'Cleansing Day.' Then, nothing—the calendar just ends.

"Why all of the precise planning in Order-1? Yet, a separate timeline plan that specifies the destruction of Bases One and Two, plus destroying your own base, but no plan to pull back or relocate your unit? Where are you supposed to go after Cleansing Day? And tell me this, if his ultimate goal is to destroy the West, doesn't Cleansing

Day sound a little like 'mission accomplished'? So where is your unit supposed to be?" Pop asked, then turned and looked at Andre.

Andre had no answers.

"Want to see more?" Pop asked

"Yes."

"There are a whole series of magazine, newspaper, and various news service articles on the approach of the Grim Reaper and efforts to prevent an impact. Literally, everything you would want to know about it is in here. All of the files have accurate dates. These dates correspond with the publishing date of the articles," Pop explained.

"Yes, I have read each of these articles."

Pop continued, "Now, just days before the impact, there was a flurry of communications among several government agencies. I know that because I was at Sandia Labs. Impact was imminent, and the concern was to determine the safest location for data to be stored. Apparently, all of these classified communications were intercepted by Bushmaster and deciphered. At least, I have found most of them in here.

"Also, there is a series of e-mail messages here, to and from Dr. Alexander Pripkin, the director of Sky Watch. Most of his messages were sent to the White House chief of Intelligence. The rest were sent to Lawrence Livermore Labs, Sandia Labs, and NASA.

"The first series of messages, sent about a month before the impact, assure the recipients that the asteroid will miss the Earth. Then, about two weeks later, the doctor's analysis changes. He is concerned that the asteroid will come very close to, if not actually hit, the Earth.

"Since prevention of asteroid impacts was the sole purpose of Sky Watch, this news is not received very well. He is criticized for not acting quickly enough and not properly using the resources available to him, etc., etc. Typical bureaucratic and political finger pointing, trying to fix blame and shift the burden of responsibility as far away from Washington as possible.

"Then, a series of messages were sent to Dr. Pripkin, asking for the anticipated impact point or part of the Earth that would be subjected to the most damage. Plus, they also wanted survivability numbers. He responds with realistic numbers. Then, an order is sent to him immediately, directing him to mark his data classified and not release any information, period. He fires back that it is his duty to inform the various emergency response and relief agencies of the scope of the pending disaster. He adds that he will disobey a direct order if necessary to save lives.

"Obviously, the boys in Washington have something else in mind. They're concerned about the security of the White House. The doctor is immediately fired. He simply replies that he may not be employed, but he could still communicate. Suggesting that it would take more than a bureaucrat to shut him up."

"I like this guy," Skip commented.

Pop continues, "At this point, he is contacted by the NSA. They threatened his life. He reconsiders his options for a time; all the while, the Reaper is getting closer to Earth.

"Then, just a few hours later, a number of agencies simultaneously send out an alert. It's an emergency message, transmitted in the blind: Asteroid's speed miscalculated, impact imminent, activate Emergency Broadcast Network, transmit worldwide. Suddenly, the president, the chief of Intelligence, and the NSA are all overridden by a single, terrible message.

"Then, another message is sent to Doctor Pripkin. Orders rescinded, he's reinstated; please advise best estimate of impact point and possible survival procedures. The message is answered by an unknown source. 'Dr. Pripkin has committed suicide, sincerely hope you meet a similar fate!'

"I was aware of some of these messages, and I am certain that this is a factual record of the events. All of these messages were encrypted by the Bushmaster programmers, and the files were hidden," Pop continued. "I've also found similar files, all accessible to members of the Bushmaster organization, but there are several glaring discrepancies. Check this out."

Pop then brought up the file lists, side by side. "Here are both lists. You can see that the file names are similar; only the extensions are different. But compare the file dates. Nearly every one of the accessible files has been modified. If you compare the files, line-by-line, as I have over the last few days, you find that the content of the accessible list has been deliberately changed. The modified files falsely show that every Western agency associated with the asteroid was in control of the thing and planning to destroy the Middle East and other third world countries. It is a total fabrication, carefully and masterfully done, using facts to back up lies. All of this could be disputed, of course. The file dates are very close. Some were modified just hours after the original file was saved. There is, however, one extremely glaring error. And this one cannot be denied."

Pop brought up another file, "The message informing the White House that Dr. Pripkin had committed suicide was dated and time stamped less than an hour after the doctor died. Immediately after we received the news, a close friend of his working at Sandia Labs confirmed the time of Dr. Pripkin's death. However, the file containing the news of the doctor's death was not deleted from the accessible files; it was simply modified like the rest. And so, according to the file available to you, the doctor continued to communicate with Washington after his death. Not only did the good doctor provide information for hours after his death, he continued to communicate for days. Your general really blew this one. He used a dead man to perpetrate a lie, and I can prove it. The doctor's death is a matter of record."

Andre was speechless. He stared at the screen for what seemed like endless minutes, and then he finally spoke, "He is due to visit here in two days."

"The general, himself?" Bud asked in surprise.

"Yes, we received a very brief message just hours ago. It's the first direct contact that we have had from the general in quite some time. And you are our prize. We are planning to present you to that lying bastard like spoils of war. The colonel and Sharee must see this immediately."

Within an hour, the entire camp was buzzing with news of the hidden computer files, but not all of the ranks of the Bushmaster group believed what they heard and saw. One, especially, was not swayed in the least. In fact, he was sure it was just another hustle, like many he had witnessed as a child, victimized again by the Americans.

Thus, Captain Draxon was very vocal with his opinions, "These bastards are the liars here, not our leader. We cannot allow these Western capitalists to destroy what we have built. They are doing what Americans always do, using their money and technology to fool you into believing they are right. When they have you convinced, and you let your guard down, they will use you to get what they want, then roll over you and squash you like bugs. These people don't care about us. They want to gain our confidence, get inside our operation like a disease, and destroy Bushmaster."

The entire population of the base was listening to him, and it was obvious that there was doubt in their minds about the intentions of the Americans. Until now, their lives had a clear and defined purpose, supported by the belief that Bushmaster, with General Raazmahd at the helm, would become the most powerful army and political force on Earth. They believed that Bushmaster could take them beyond simple survival, rewarding their hard work and determination with unlimited food, comfort, and security—give them a better world.

As Skip watched and listened, he realized that it would take more than the evidence of doctored computer files to convince these people that a madman was fooling them. So, he climbed onto the wing of his Phantom, jumped up on the engine intake cowl, and stepped up onto the backbone of the aircraft.

There, where everyone could see him, he called to the group, "Bushmaster! Listen to me! Listen! We are not tryin' to trick you. We are only tryin' to show you the truth."

"Bushmaster does not need your version of the truth," Captain Draxon replied. "We know what we see. And what we see is the strength and power of Bushmaster. You would do or say anything to stop us."

"Yes, it is true that we want Bushmaster stopped. But, since I have been here, I have not seen what I expected to see. You're not vengeful murderers and butchers. But your leader is, and he is usin' you to fulfill his agenda. When you have done his bidding, he will not just cast you aside, he will kill you. I am sure of it."

Skip looked at Bud and Pop standing nearby. Bud gave him a thumbs-up sign. Skip nodded and continued.

"To show that I believe what I say, I propose this... The general is due to arrive in two days. I believe that he intends to deliver the plan personally and maybe the weapons necessary to complete his plan. All I ask is that you determine what these weapons are before you reveal that we are your prisoners.

"Why do I make this request? Because a large number of nuclear triggers have recently been stolen from Russia. I am sure that you expect to be rewarded with free reign of North America if you are victorious. In fact, I expect that the general, if he hasn't promised this already, will promise it when he arrives. I also expect him to bring you more weapons. Since he obviously must fly in, he will not be able to bring much, but I believe he will bring a token number of, what will appear to be, special iron bombs. I believe he has found a way to use the triggers stolen from Russia to manufacture thermonuclear weapons. Probably using Plutonium.

"Do you know what that will do to the target? You won't be livin' here for a few thousand years; I can promise you that!

"Somehow, he's gonna get you to drop these bombs, and he's not gonna tell you what they are. And, if you drop a nuke durin' a standard ground attack run, you know full well, your aircraft and those of your group will not survive the electro-magnetic pulse and shock wave. This is a suicide mission, except you are not kamikaze! You expect to be rewarded for your victory, and he intends to use and murder you. Read what his encrypted files say. He don't want North America. He wants it destroyed!

"All I ask is that you determine if I'm right or wrong before you make your final decision. If I'm wrong, tell the whole story to the general, and you can all have a fun time at our execution."

Colonel Fronz was standing at the front of the group, listening to what Skip had to say and watching the reactions of his personnel.

He addressed Skip, "This is a very bold challenge you are making. I know you realize that we will be forced to execute you if you are wrong. And we would be foolish if we did not accept, we have nothing to lose."

"Very well..." The colonel turned and addressed the gathering, "As commander of this base, I am willing to accept this challenge. We will keep our guests in hiding until we determine the construction of these bombs that Mr. Scott has so clairvoyantly foreseen. Our leader must not know of this until I have determined that it is prudent to inform him. These are my orders; carry them out."

It was obvious from the reactions of the personnel that respect for their commander outweighed any doubts they had; even the outspoken Captain Draxon remained silent.

Skip remained standing on the backbone of the Phantom, watching the personnel return to their duties. He wondered if he had just sentenced his companions and himself to death.

Near the Phantom, just out of his field of view, Lieutenant Ahana Cohen was watching Skip. After the people dispersed, she spoke, "William, you have placed yourself in an extremely dangerous position."

He turned and looked at her, not answering.

"I was not told of my commander's plans for you, but I cannot imagine anything that would have jeopardized your safety more than what you have just done. You have directly challenged the integrity of our leader!" Ahana said in amazement.

"If you're tryin' to give me a pep talk, it ain't workin'."

"I apologize. I didn't mean to insult you; I am just overwhelmed by your actions."

"I'm not noted for doin' things in a small way. I usually fuel the fire instead of puttin' it out."

"I would say you napalmed this one!"

Skip laughed at her candid comment and climbed down from his aircraft. They met at the nose of the Phantom. Skip grabbed the pitot tube and leaned against the radome.

Ahana reached up and put her hand on his, "I am very moved by your courage."

"Thanks," he replied, smiled slightly, turned to look at his aircraft, and patted it, as if it were a very large animal.

Ahana looked at him with a curious smile and said, "You treat your Phantom as though it were your horse."

"I know it must look silly to you," Skip said, blushing slightly, "but I've always felt a connection to the aircraft I fly. I know it's just a complicated, mindless machine, but to me, she's a great, big, powerful bird that takes me to places that I would otherwise never see."

He paused for a moment, rubbing the Phantom's radome affectionately. "God, I do love to fly." His eyes took on a faraway look.

Ahana reached out and touched his face, then kissed him on the cheek.

Suddenly, Skip was swept with a flash of hurtful memory. He was with Holly, just before he had to go away again. She was touching his face in her special way, telling him not to worry about her and the kids.

"William—just go do your fantastic pilot stuff."

She, too, would smile and kiss his cheek. The memory suddenly took his feet from under him before he knew what was happening. Ahana tried to catch him but only succeeded in cushioning his fall.

Seconds later, after he regained consciousness, he found himself lying on the ramp underneath the Phantom with Ahana cradling his head in her lap. On her face, there was a look of puzzlement, combined with fear.

"Damn! What was *that* all about?" Skip asked, his head still swimming.

Ahana said nothing but let his head continue resting on her lap, while she gazed at him with concern.

Skip could not help noting the plainly visible emotion on her face. He chuckled, "Does this happen to every guy you kiss?"

When she realized he was well enough to joke with her, she let out a long sigh and smiled.

Just then, one of the security guards approached them, "Ma'am, do you need assistance?"

Skip answered for her, "No thanks, she's just helping me inspect the floor."

The guard was not amused. He waited for the lieutenant to answer. As Skip began to rise, the guard took the couple by their hands and lifted them to their feet as though they were weightless.

"Jesus! Remind me not to piss *you* off," Skip said, impressed with the man's strength.

"I work out," the guard mumbled.

"With what, a *truck*?"

Quickly changing the subject, the guard asked, "Are you all right?"

This time, Ahana answered, "He's fine, Dave. Thank you for your assistance."

"My pleasure, ma'am." He saluted Ahana and returned to his post.

As soon as the guard was out of hearing distance, Ahana turned to Skip. "What *was* that all about? And who is Holly?"

"I said *Holly*?"

"Yes."

"Holly is... *was*... my wife."

"Oh. I didn't know."

"Bushmaster's profile didn't mention that I was married?"

"No."

"I thought they were very thorough."

Ahana looked into the distance. "Where is she?"

"She died along with our three children when the tsunamis hit the Oregon coast."

She faced Skip again. "I am so sorry. I didn't mean to cause..."

He gently placed his index finger on her lips. "It wasn't *you*. It was *me*. I've been keepin' their deaths inside me. I've fought with the reality of it since...." His voice trailed off, and Ahana picked up the slack.

"William, I get the feeling that you have not given yourself time to grieve."

"I'm not sure *how* to grieve. I was tryin' so hard to deny it, thinkin' the pain would just go away. Even thinkin' that they were alive, somehow... some way. And also ashamed that I was so self-involved with my personal tragedy when billions were dyin'. When I realized that I had actually survived, I stole a case of bourbon and tried to drown myself. For about two weeks, or so I'm told... at least, until the case was empty, I pretty much kept a bottle in my hand."

"You drank a *case* of whiskey by *yourself*, and in just *two* weeks?"

"Yeah. And I had enough brain cells left to know that it didn't work. After I sobered up, I still remembered. And I almost went nuts. Finally, Pop got me involved in the Viper project again. I guess I would have gone over the edge, if not for Pop. He's one smart guy.

"You are the first... since Holly... well, hell! I guess I forgot how good it feels to have someone like you touch me. I just lost it for a moment... that's all." He blushed. "Damn, I'm really embarrassed."

"Why don't we go to my quarters? Before you fall down again."

"I think I'm doin' a fair job at wallowin' in self-pity standin' up."

Ahana laughed at his candid comment, took him by the hand, and led him to her quarters. When they were inside, she turned and faced him.

They were eye to eye in height. Still holding his hand, she pulled him closer.

Slowly and carefully, Skip traced her cheek with his fingers. Then, he delicately stroked the length of her shiny, chestnut-brown hair, from above her ear all the way down past her shoulders. His hand came to rest on the small of her back. Looking into her beautiful gray-blue eyes, he thought he was capable of melting right where he was standing.

She closed her eyes and kissed him softly.

He studied her face for a brief moment, and then closed his eyes, half-expecting to wake up from another vivid dream and find himself disappointed once more.

Ahana pulled away and opened her eyes, but Skip's remained closed.

"Are you losing it again?" she whispered.

He whispered, "No. Just don't pinch me... I don't want to wake up."

"But, you're *not* dreaming!" she said as she pinched him.

He opened his eyes. "I want to show you how good it feels to know you are real."

"I feel the same way about you. And I want this feeling to *last*."

He kissed her with a passionate urgency, moving her in the direction of the bed they would share for the night. The *would-be dream* became complete reality.

Early the next morning, Skip was already up, standing outside, when Ahana awoke.

She called to him through the screened window near the front door, "Good morning, fly boy."

Skip walked to the window, and they touched, fingertip to fingertip, through the screen. "Good mornin', gorgeous. Did you sleep well?"

"Oh, yes. And you?"

"I can't remember when I've slept better. I just wish I could have stayed awake. I can think of a hundred things I would like to do in bed with you, and not one of 'em involves sleepin'. Definitely a waste of precious time."

"Would you please come to the door for a moment, love?" she asked sweetly.

When he opened the door, she reached out, grabbed him, and dragged him back inside.

Later that morning, they emerged together. All around them, the base personnel were busy preparing for the arrival of their leader, so Skip asked, "Say, gorgeous, since we've got some time, would you give me 'the cook's tour' of your aircraft, starting with the Mustangs?"

"Of course, William, I am honored that you asked."

She took great pride in her aircraft, personally overseeing all maintenance and modifications, thus she knew the aircraft inside and out. Skip was very impressed with her knowledge of the aircraft and was just as eager to learn, as she was eager to teach.

"Your Mustang is very close to its original configuration. Why not modify it for better performance?" Skip asked.

"Actually, the engine has been highly modified and produces almost four thousand horse power."

"Wow!"

"And many of the fuselage components have been replaced with lighter composite materials or titanium. But with this clean configuration, it is sufficiently aerodynamic, yet it keeps the characteristics that make it the beautiful aircraft that it is... why change it?"

"Good point. What's her top speed?"

"Five hundred and forty knots on a level run in a closed course."

"Damn!"

"Then, Captain Petrovich's Mustang must be as fast."

"Actually, faster. It has gone ballistic a few times in a dive," Ahana said matter-of-factly.

"That thing exceeds Mach 1?"

"Mach 1.05, according to my Tornado's Mach meter, but the stress on the airframe is far too great. We have designated them Mustangs One and Two. Mustang One is actually based on the best aerodynamic design characteristics from several of the Reno Air Racers. Both of our aircraft have had extensive structural modifications, replacing aluminum structures with composites and titanium. Number One has had additional structural modifications, plus the engine is a highly modified Rolls-Royce propjet power plant. Number One has been clocked at 625 knots on a level run in a closed course."

"No wonder the captain almost kicked my butt," Skip said with no emotion in his voice.

"I, for one, am glad she didn't," Ahana said and kissed his cheek, then added, "If you will give Vanya an opportunity, I think she needs to speak with you about that encounter."

"To be honest, I would like to speak with her too. If I'm around long enough."

"Maybe this situation will turn out..." Ahana's voice choked, and Skip could see by the look on her face that she was very upset and concerned for his safety.

He quickly changed the subject, "You know, yesterday, I sensed that you feel the way that I do about your aircraft. Am I correct?"

She smiled slightly and said, "Until I met you, my only love was aviation. I was going to tell you, just before you fainted. That is why I kissed your cheek."

"Fainted? Who fainted? I didn't faint! Guys don't faint."

"Oh, really?" she said in a doubting tone.

"I was just overcome by your passionate affection," Skip offered, intending to tease.

"Right... What? Passionate affection! I thought that what you said was very moving and sweet. Passionate affection!" Ahana exclaimed, poking him accusingly with her finger. "*You* are a first class bull-shitter!"

Skip hesitated for a moment, and then decided that he might not have another chance to say what he felt, so he decided to go for it. Holding nothing back, he kissed her, and then blurted it out, "Ahana, I have fallen head-over-heels in love with you. I need you. I think you and I were made for each other."

Ahana opened her mouth, as if she had intended to say something, but no words came out. Her expression was a most profound look of surprise.

"Speechless?" Skip asked and smiled deviously.

She considered the question for a moment, closed her mouth, but only nodded.

"I know what's goin' through your mind. We've just met, and it's too early for me to say somethin' like that. Do I say that to every girl I meet? Am I just another American playboy pilot? And so on. Right?"

She nodded again, her eyes wide with anticipation.

"Well, I'm not a teenager infatuated with a pretty girl. I'm a grown man. Old enough to be... well, your big brother anyway, and you're an intelligent, drop-dead gorgeous lady, the likes of which I have only imagined in my dreams. I've had four loves in my life, but they're gone now. Since then, all I've had was flyin'. Now, I've finally found you. I sure as hell ain't gettin' any younger, and last night... well, actually, yesterday afternoon and evenin', last night, and again this mornin', you reminded me that I'm alive. You've given me a reason to live again. If you want me half as much as I want you, I'll fight off this whole damn crew and follow you to the ends of the Earth!"

Ahana stared at him with wide, watery eyes for just a moment longer; smiled the biggest, sweetest smile; and leaped into his arms. Crying and laughing at the same time, she kissed him deeply, and then said, "I have been waiting for you my whole life! Yes, I want you! Even if this is the only time we will ever have together, I will cherish it until I die."

"Let's not talk about dyin' right now." Then Skip lowered his voice to a whisper, "And, I hope you didn't intend to keep our relationship a secret."

"Why?" She asked innocently, momentarily forgetting that they had been standing on the tarmac in view of anyone who cared to look.

Nearby, someone intentionally cleared his throat. The lovers looked, and both immediately blushed. Colonel Fronz, Lieutenant Reshond, Andre, Bud, Pop, and several guards, including Sgt. Spiker, who had assisted them the previous day, were all standing nearby, looking at them and smiling, somewhat embarrassed themselves.

"I, ahh, hate to interrupt," Colonel Fronz said apologetically, "but we need to brief you and get you concealed before the general arrives."

Then, he studied Ahana for a moment and continued, "Lieutenant, this is unexpected. You must make a choice. Do you need time to consider your options?"

Ahana answered firmly and without hesitation, "No, sir, I am aware of the consequences. I will stay with William."

"Very well, I know you to be an honorable officer. I respect your decision, and I wish you well."

"Thank you, sir. Thank you very much," Ahana said and saluted the colonel.

"Guard, escort our guests to the holding area," Colonel Fronz ordered. "We will be along presently."

"Ma'am, gentlemen, will you please proceed toward the wrecked King Air?" The large guard named Dave asked.

They began walking with Skip and Ahana, hand in hand, bringing up the rear, followed by the guard. Skip looked at him sheepishly and said, "Hello again. I didn't thank you for helpin' us yesterday."

"Lieutenant Cohen did."

"I know, but I wanted to thank you too. I'm Skip. And you are?"

"Sergeant Spiker. And you're welcome."

"Glad to meet you." Skip extended his free hand, the sergeant shook his hand, and it hurt. His grip was like a vise. Skip took back his hand, turned to Ahana, and whispered, "Ow!"

She laughed.

"Ah... Sergeant Spiker," Skip began again, looking at his painful hand, "I was wonderin'; did you hear what I was sayin' to Lieutenant Cohen back there?"

"Most of it."

"The part about fightin' off the whole crew; I mean that part, mostly?"

"Yes."

"I hope you know that I didn't mean anything personal. I mean, I know you're a part... a very large part of the crew. I was just tryin' to make the point that I really do love Ahana. Not that I want to, well, get my ass kicked. You follow me?"

At that point, both Pop and Skip broke up laughing.

"This is a man who knows well, that discretion is the better part of valor!" Bud said, laughing louder.

Ahana looked back at the sergeant, and he was smiling too. She did not recall ever seeing Dave smile before, and it made her feel good that Skip was able to get him to smile.

"Don't worry, sir," the sergeant said, "I didn't take it personally."

"Good," Skip sighed in relief, and then turned his attentions to his companions, "Laugh it up, guys. But you ain't seen this guy in action. I think he works out with a truck!"

The sergeant smiled again and said, "No, sir, only six forty."

"Pounds?" Pop asked, rhetorically.

"Shit!" Bud whispered under his breath.

"See, I told you," Skip said smugly. "Dave is one bad dude."

"Say, Sarge, why don't you call me Skip? I mean, just 'cause we're on opposite sides, we don't have to be unfriendly, do we? Besides, maybe we can talk more about this 'bein' enemies' thing..." Skip continued trying to win over the sergeant's allegiance as they walked on toward the King Air.

As they walked past the wrecked aircraft, Pop's companions got their first opportunity to view the damage. It was obviously no longer airworthy, with a missing nose gear, structural damage to the nose, and bent props.

"You sorta pranged it, Pop," Skip commented.

"Yea. First bad landing I've ever made. These damned Commies told me to do a short field landing, but didn't tell me the runway was that damn short. I locked the brakes and blew a tire. Things kinda went to hell from that point."

They continued walking, past earthmoving equipment and several, military-type, ten-wheel drive tractors hitched to long flatbed trailers. Beyond that, several militarized four-wheel drive Broncos were parked alongside a large bus. They entered the bus and waited for Colonel Fronz. He arrived within the hour and told them of his plan.

"In order to determine the validity of your proposition, I am placed in the very dangerous position of lying to my commander. We have placed your Phantom at the very end of the flight line and positioned several aircraft near it, hopefully blocking it from view. If I am lucky, the general will cut his visit short and not have time for a tour. I can only hope that my people trust and respect me enough to remain silent. If the general is told of this, I will be joining you at your execution. I have sent two men to your mountaintop outpost. If you are wrong, I will be forced to claim that you were captured there. If you are right... well, I suppose that remains to be seen, doesn't it?"

Several hours later, the alarm sounded, the runway gate opened, and a Northrop/Grumman E-2A transport landed. Moments later, a SU-27 Flanker landed, followed by another, and the runway gate closed. The supreme leader of Bushmaster, General Za-Ved Raazmahd and his Elite Guard had arrived.

For the next several hours, the general met in private with Colonel Fronz. After the meeting, a dinner was held for the general and entire crew. The general greeted each of his people personally, remembering their names and asking personal questions that sounded as though he was a close friend, interested in the most trivial aspects of their daily lives.

Colonel Fronz watched the general and continued to be amazed at his memory. The colonel had long been aware of this talent and knew how well the general used it to impress and manipulate. This occasion was no different. Colonel Fronz saw, in their faces, the irresistible attraction and power the general held over his people.

After the dinner, the general spoke to the gathering, "My people, we are on the brink of a great battle. This battle, once and for all, will show the world that Bushmaster is the One True Master. We will defeat the Free Forces of North America and destroy their military grip on our world. I must not stay here long; their intelligence agents are always on my trail and never far behind.

"I want to be with each of you, to fight alongside you, to help you win, and celebrate our victory. Since I cannot fight alongside you, I have brought weapons that you can take to the enemy in my place. My Elite Guard is now unloading ten special bombs from my aircraft. I have personally prepared ten bombs that will take my message to the enemy. I will personally honor any pilot that will volunteer to deliver my bombs to the target.

"My Elite Guard will remain behind to ensure that my bombs have been loaded on your aircraft. They will personally report your accomplishment to me, and you will be at my side when we celebrate our victory and show our superiority to the world."

The people stood and applauded. The general then said that he must retire to rest and plan his departure. Colonel Fronz escorted the general to his quarters and bid him good evening. The colonel then met with his senior staff, discussing the events of the last two days. Most of his staff was shocked to hear their leader confirm Skip's prediction. They had trusted General Raazmahd. Now they stood, in utter disbelief, that he, so easily and coldly, would waste their lives to achieve his twisted goals. Some of the officers, however, wanted to reserve their final decision until the exact configuration of the bombs was determined.

The colonel went from the staff meeting directly to the bus where Skip, Ahana, Bud, and Pop awaited their fate. Colonel Fronz spoke for his officers, "We have had our moment of truth. Most now believe that your predictions are correct. But, some of my people are not sure and have requested that the bomb's configuration be verified. I am obligated to honor their request. I elected to come to you and advise you of these developments. Our situation is still in jeopardy, but if the general departs in the early morning hours, we will then inspect the bombs and, I believe, put an end to this madness.

Although we must wait until morning for the final answer, I have suspected this for some time. I must confide that I, and several of my most trusted officers, have planned for this day for some time.

Your presence here is part of that plan, and I can only say that it is an answered prayer that events have transpired as they have thus far."

"Dang," Skip uttered.

"Is something wrong?" the colonel asked.

"No. It's just that I thought this was all *my* idea."

"Well, you must admit, great minds think alike. You perceived our plan brilliantly."

"Yeah. Sometimes, I'm so brilliant, I scare myself!"

"And so modest too," Bud interjected.

Skip flashed a cheesy grin, "Naturally."
The colonel continued, "Gentlemen, I cannot, in good conscience, consider you prisoners

of Bushmaster any longer. You are free to go, if you wish."

Skip, Ahana, Bud, and Pop all looked at each other for a moment, and then without hesitation, Skip said, "We'll stay and see this through to the end."

CHAPTER THIRTEEN

Small Moments Of Truth

Morning came, and they were still alive—a fact that did not go unnoticed among Colonel Fronz, his officers, and former prisoners. Before dawn, they watched as General Raazmahd and his aides departed for an unknown destination.

"I'll bet it is not anywhere in North America," the colonel commented sarcastically.

Unfortunately, the general had kept his word and left five of his Elite Guard behind. They were menacing in appearance, wearing green camouflage combat fatigues, black robes, and black berets with the green snake emblem. They each carried a large curved-blade knife, similar to a scimitar, and a .45 caliber M.A.C.-10. Highly disciplined and very unfriendly, they guarded ten large, shiny black bombs—each blazoned with the emblem of the green snake.

Inspecting any of the bombs would prove to be a difficult task. The guards apparently had some type of electronic device attached to one of the bombs. If anyone approached, the guards would cover the device with a black cloth.

And there was more bad news. Before the general left, Lt. Reshond had positioned himself, unseen, near enough to the guards to hear normal conversation. He reported what he had heard, to the colonel and the others, "The general told the guards that the battle must begin at dawn, the day after tomorrow. He ordered them to use the interface device to detonate a bomb if they suspected their situation was compromised."

"That's just great!" Bud exclaimed, "Tell a bunch of paranoid, saber-rattling fanatics to blow themselves up, which they would gladly do at any moment anyway, I might add, and they are to base that decision on whether or not they feel compromised!"

"I was afraid the general might do something like this. He is a shrewd man," the colonel admitted.

"We must proceed quickly," Major Vosh informed them. "Draxon told the general that one of his escort pilots had taken ill, and he volunteered to take the pilot's place. I am concerned that he may return and launch a missile into our base."

"If he believes the general," Captain Petrovich offered, "it would not be logical to destroy our base. If the bombs are conventional, we will deliver the weapons to the enemy, so it would be to the advantage of Bushmaster to keep us alive. Had Draxon remained, and we determined that the bombs are nuclear, as we suspect, he would be trapped here, outnumbered and helpless. He is simply covering his bets. Either way, he wins."

"Good point, Vanya," Colonel Fronz said.

"It makes sense to me," Skip commented.

Vanya smiled at Skip, and then looked away, as if she was embarrassed.

Just then, one of the base guards approached and said, "Excuse me, sir, but we have a problem. We have found the general's escort pilot that Capt. Draxon reported to be ill. He's dead. His neck has been broken."

"Hide his body immediately. By all means, do not let the Elite Guard learn of this."

"Yes, sir." The guard left immediately to carry out the colonel's orders.

At that point, the colonel turned to the group and said, "We must devise a plan to inspect one of the bombs. I need suggestions and ideas."

For the next few hours, the group brainstormed, discussed, and planned. At one point, they took a break.

"William," Ahana said, "this is a good opportunity for you to talk to Vanya."

"Will you come with me?" Skip asked.

"I think Vanya's pride will be harmed less if you alone hear her words."

"You're a smart lady," Skip said, kissed her on the cheek, and went to talk to Vanya.

Vanya was sitting on the tailgate of one of the trucks, staring down at the ground.

"Hi. Am I intruding?" Skip asked.

"No, I was just thinking about our situation," Vanya answered.

Skip sat down by her, saying nothing. She glanced at him, and he smiled. Ahana watched discretely from the bus window.

"Ahana gave me a nice tour of your aircraft. I especially like Mustang One," Skip said, trying to make conversation. "That is one awesome fighter. I hope I don't have to go up against it again."

She glanced at him, looked back at the ground, and said, "I think I would not do as well in a rematch."

"I don't know about that. I understand your combat-kill ratio is very impressive."

She looked somewhat surprised that Skip would be impressed with her combat record and asked, "You are impressed with my kill ratio, when you could have been included in those numbers?"

"No, I'm impressed with a damn good fighter pilot."

Vanya sighed and said, "I have never had to deal with anything like this. In combat, it is a simple thing—kill or be killed. I am ashamed that I thought of you as my enemy. I would feel better if you were more like an enemy. I try to dislike you, but I cannot. It is most frustrating."

Then, she looked him in the eyes and did not look away.

"You know, in your heart, that we were never enemies. You were just followin' orders, caught up in a situation totally beyond your control. It's not always so easy to tell the good guys from the bad guys. Especially, when the people that you trust the most are lyin' to ya."

"You are a very wise man." Vanya paused, and then said, "I am sorry about your aircraft. I have never seen anything quite like it."

"Well, I blew the landing, not you. You and your Mustang definitely made the Viper a challenge to fly. But I've pulled off better landings in worse situations. Besides, any landing you can walk away from is a good one, right? I *ran* from that one, but it still meets the criteria."

Vanya laughed in spite of herself and admitted, "I am sincerely glad you are alive."

"Thanks… me too!

Vanya laughed again. Skip put his arm around her, and she laid her head on his shoulder. Through the window of the bus, Ahana looked on and smiled. She knew that Skip had just made a lifelong friend.

When the meeting ended, a plan had been devised. It would take a great deal of speed, timing, and a little luck to see it through. Within the hour, the plan went into action.

Colonel Fronz approached the Elite Guard, displaying the intentions of checking on their welfare and tending to the business of commanding the base. They came to attention but kept their positions, surrounding the bombs on all four sides.

"All is well, I presume?"

"Yes, Commander," the guard that tended to the electronic device answered.

"Do you need anything? I can assign someone to see to your needs."

"No, Commander. We have no needs."

"My people are very excited and curious about these weapons. They have many questions. May I inspect one of the bombs?"

"General Raazmahd has given strict orders that his bombs are not be touched until we load them on your aircraft."

"I am commander of this base. I have a right to know what type weapons have been brought here."

"You also have a duty to obey the orders of our leader."

"Guard, you do not tell me what my duties are."

"My apologies, Commander, but I have been given a direct order, and I must obey."

"Very well. Will you allow my people to view the bombs?"

"Yes, Commander."

"I also have several prisoners. Captured NAADA members. I would like to show them the devices that our leader has brought to drop on their bases. Is that all right with you?"

The guard considered the request for a moment. His curiosity aroused, he replied, "Yes, Commander." The guard wanted to see the prisoners for himself.

Colonel Fronz placed several of his best sharpshooters in strategic points around the base, with a reminder that a stray bullet could destroy the entire base. The general's bombs had been placed very near the armament storage area. If any of the bombs or ammunition were accidentally set off, it would trigger the rest to explode. While it is not possible to trigger a nuclear weapon without initiating the precise detonation sequence, it is possible to detonate a cell of the conventional explosives used to trigger the weapon. If detonated out of sequence, the explosion would simply destroy the bomb, but could also create a catastrophic chain reaction detonation of other explosives in its proximity.

The first part of the plan required a large group of base personnel to converge on the elite guard, all trying to see the bombs at once. They were told to be pushy and obnoxious, but not challenge the Elite Guard who might feel threatened and detonate the weapon.

Concealed within the crowd, Lt. Reshond would attempt get close enough to unlatch the data interface access cover on one of the bombs and attach a data interface cable. In order to add more confusion, the colonel would bring his "prisoners" to the scene. The personnel were told to yell and curse the prisoners, creating even more confusion. All of the women were to make a big deal about the presence of Lt. Cohen, calling her a traitor and protesting the fact that she was allowed to see the bombs.

They hoped this distraction would serve to attract the guards' attention enough that Lt. Reshond could attach the cable. This part of the operation required a bit of finesse. The data port had to be inspected to determine what type of connector it required. Fortunately, the lieutenant discovered that the interface required a standard RS-232 nine-pin din cable. The cable had to be connected to the bomb and then to a laptop computer that Pop would use to access the bomb's CPU. All of this had to be accomplished in no more that a few minutes, and one of the guards was standing only a few feet from the most accessible bomb.

As the plan went into action, the disturbance was sufficient to distract the guard.

The lieutenant and Major Voss looked over Pop's shoulder as he accessed the bomb's CPU. First, he initiated a communication program to determined the CPU's language and establish data exchange. When communication was established, a security program activated and temporarily blocked access. Pop defeated the security program by uploading a small virus, which corrupted the security subroutine. Then, a menu popped up. Choices were few and in Russian. They needed Vanya. She was on the other side of the stack of bombs with most of the others.

Lt. Reshond tried to get her attention, and when he did, the guard who had been standing no more than an arm's length away, noticed him, saw the cable, and realized what was happening. As he reached for his weapon, his attention was diverted overhead as one of the guards from the other side of the bombs came flying over the top of the stack and slammed against the rock wall.

It seems that the unfortunate guard had taken an extreme dislike to Ahana when he discovered that she was a Jew and a traitor. The fact that she was holding on to a NAADA pilot infuriated him even more.

Unable to contain his anger, the guard screamed something in Arabic and lunged at her. Skip moved to stop him, but the guard kicked Skip, knocking him down. As the guard swung at Ahana, he somehow failed to see Sergeant Spiker standing near her. Spiker simply reached out and caught the guard's fist as if it was a baseball. Everyone stopped in silence and looked at the sergeant in total awe.

There is usually a moment in every inflated ego's life when he realizes that his superiority, at least in part, was imagined. For the poor guard, this was his moment. He was one of the elite—a dedicated member of the most feared of the Bushmaster Elite Guard. What must have been going through his mind as Spiker reached out with his other hand, grabbed him by the throat, and with one smooth motion, threw him over the stack of bombs. Everyone watched in silence as the screaming guard flew through the air and landed headfirst against the wall, instantly breaking his neck.

Lt. Reshond drew his side arm, and before the distracted guard could react, fired two rounds into his face, point blank. The other three Elite Guards responded, but simultaneous shots rang out as the snipers all fired at once, and the three guards fell to the floor, dead. The entire sequence of events had occurred in a matter of seconds. It was over before most of the group realized it was happening. Vanya stood up, surveyed the scene, and then walked over to where Pop was working with the computer.

"Captain, I think this is where you come in," Pop said.

She looked at the screen, cursed in Russian, and said, "If I were you, I would *not* select number five on the menu... unless you want to detonate this thirty-kiloton nuclear weapon."

Then, she ripped the green snake emblem from her uniform, threw it on the floor, spat on it, and walked away.

Colonel Fronz was standing near by, "Well, I think that just about says it all."

Then, he addressed the entire group, "We now have our answer. We must mobilize and abandon this base immediately. Our destination is NAADA Base One. If anyone chooses to remain here, speak now."

The crowd remained silent.

"Very well. I am pleased. You have your orders. Senior officers, you know what needs to be done. Ahana, that goes for you too. And thank you everyone, well done."

At that point, everyone cheered the commander. Four hours later, the entire base was ready to leave.

CHAPTER FOURTEEN

Time to Pack Up and Go

In the first hour following the colonel's orders, a plan was devised to coordinate an airlift of personnel and supplies from the Hidden Base to Base One. Using the earthmoving equipment, they began to prepare a dirt strip in the valley below. The runway inside the Hidden Base had not been constructed to handle aircraft as large as a C-130, and they were going to need at least two of the big Herks.

Time was of the essence. If Draxon decided to tell the general what had transpired at the Hidden Base prior to his arrival, his reaction to the news was unpredictable. The general might send additional troops, if any were available; if not, he might order the destruction of the base. Regardless of his decision, it would not go well for those who remained at the base.

While Skip and Bud readied the Phantom for flight, every other flyable aircraft was prepared as well. They intended to take all of the aircraft to Base One immediately, leaving two of the fastest fighters to defend the base and remaining ground personnel.

One by one, the aircraft took off, forming up on the Phantom as Skip circled the Hidden Base. Skip would have to set their cruise speed according to the slowest aircraft, which happened to be Mustang Two. Ahana tucked her Mustang into the formation on Skip's left wing position.

Just as the last aircraft checked in, Skip called Ahana on the radio...

"Well, gorgeous, we're ready. I know your baby will cruise at 450 knots, or do you want to set speed for max range?"

"William, she can run at 450 all day, but I get better fuel economy at 410 knots."

"Well, folks, you heard the lady. Set speed at 410 knots, climb to twelve thousand, and maintain your position in the formation. My call sign is Recon One. Squawk 2121 on your transponder, and check six; we don't need any surprises."

"Why does she call you William?" Bud asked from the backseat.

"The Bushmaster file had me listed that way. When she called me William the first time, it really got to me. It's amazin' how a simple thing like hearin' her say my name can make me feel so good."

"Should I tell Connie to expect an extra guest the next time you come over for dinner?"

"You can bank on that, partner."

"Fantastic! Connie will be glad too. She's been worrying about you up there on that mountain all by yourself. She told me I should find you a partner. I told her I'd have better luck fishing in the kitchen sink."

"Have I really been that bad?"

"I was amazed that you noticed Candy Simms. You've been alone way too long, pal. You've got a lot of catching up to do."

"I'd like to spend a lifetime with Ahana, workin' on curin' that problem."

"Judging by the way she looks at you, I'd guess she's thinking the same thing."

"I hope you're right, partner. I sure hope you're right."

"I thought Bushmaster Intelligence was really good... and they didn't even know your call sign? Do you think Ahana would have gotten to you as much if she had called you Skip?"

"Hell, I would've fallen in love with her if she'd called me dip-shit!"

Upon reaching cruise altitude, Skip began calling in the blind on the Zone Control emergency frequency. He wanted to establish contact with Base One, or any friendly, as soon as possible. The last thing he needed was a confrontation with a trigger-happy surveillance pilot, thinking he had encountered an invasion force. By squawking a classified transponder code, Skip figured he could avoid a problem before it started.

"Base One Control, this is Recon One calling in the blind... does anyone copy? Base One, Base One, Recon One, do you copy?"

All they heard from the receiver was static. Since radio transmissions were often unreliable due to atmospheric disturbances, communication required persistence and patience. Therefore, for the next forty-five minutes, Skip repeated the call at five-minute intervals. Finally, someone answered...

"This is Tiger Six. Say again?"

"Tiger Six, this is Recon One en route to Base One."

"Recon One? Where the hell have you been? We gave up searching for you a week ago!"

"It's a long story, Tiger Six... you'll hear about it... trust me. Say your position."

"I'm two hours southeast of Base Two. Where are you?"

"We're in the Zone, one hour west of Base One. Can you contact Control and let them know we're on the way in with guests?"

"I think they're trying to call me now; stand by."

"Base One, this is Tiger Six on Guard, how do you read?"

Skip could not hear the reply—only more static, with a few unreadable words scattered in the noise.

"Roger, Base One, this is Tiger Six, and I am in contact with Recon One."

It was apparent that they would not be able to receive Base One's transmissions.

"Negative, Recon One is not, I repeat, not on the ground; they are airborne, one hour west of Base One, inbound. And Base One, be advised; they're bringing in another aircraft."

"Recon One, Control needs to know if you need any assistance."

"Yes, we do, Tiger Six. We need two Hercs fueled and ready to go. We'll need to turn around immediately after touchdown. We'll also need fighter escort."

"Recon One, Tiger Six. I'll relay your message... and welcome back, guys. Six Out."

"Thanks, Tiger Six. We'll see ya'; Recon One out."

Thirty minutes later, Base One control began seeing something on radar. The controller was trying to pick the return out of the clutter, when seventeen individual blips appeared on the screen, all squawking the classified transponder code 2121.

"What in the hell is going on?" he shouted and immediately got on the hot line to the command post.

"Yes, we see it, too," the duty officer said. "We've got it from here, thank you."

"Recon One, this is Base One, do you read?"

"Base One, this is Recon One, you are loud and clear. Did you get my message?"

"Roger, the 130's are standing by... Ah, how many aircraft are you escorting?"

"Base One, I have sixteen birds in tow."

"Recon One, we understood Tiger Six to say you had one guest."

"Ah, Base One, we were havin' comm problems, sorry about that. I'll need Colonel Bass to meet us on arrival. Call Ron Taylor, and tell him to have a security detachment standin' by. We also need a secured area to park seventeen fighter aircraft."

"Recon One, Colonel Bass is on the way. Colonel Taylor is not available. A security detachment will be standing by, and we are arranging for the parking now. Contact us when you are ten minutes out. Welcome back."

"Thanks. We'll see you shortly, Recon One."

When the flight was ten minutes out, Base One control sequenced them in, with the Phantom landing first. Skip and Bud briefed Colonel Bass immediately.

"Damn, Ramjet! When you do something, you really do it big," the colonel remarked.

"Well, sir, I can't take the credit. It was a team effort. Besides, these folks are the real heroes. They have taken a bad situation and turned it into a good one. I believe you will find them to be willin' to help us fight Bushmaster anyway they can."

"He is correct, sir. I will personally oversee their debriefing," Bud said.

"Very well. I will want to meet these people as soon as it can be arranged. But right now, I want the 130's in the air and the remainder of those people and supplies back here as soon as possible," the colonel ordered.

After learning that Lt. Col. Taylor was not on duty, Bud assumed command of Base One Intelligence and requested that security establish a perimeter and guard the aircraft. He also assigned personnel to provide around-the-clock security for the new arrivals and see to their accommodations. He then arranged for a debriefing to begin the following day after the remainder of their personnel arrived.

As Ahana climbed out of her Mustang, Skip met her with open arms, "Hello, gorgeous! Welcome to Base One and freedom."

"William, I can't begin to explain how good it feels to be here."

"About as good as I feel to have you here, I suspect."

"What now?"

"Bud is takin' care of your accommodations and security. I will be returnin' to bring the rest of your people and equipment."

"Well, I'm going with you."

181

"Great! You can fly second seat. You'll make one helluva copilot!"

"Okay, fly boy, let's go."

Within the hour, two C-130's lifted off, heading for the valley below the Hidden Base. Two F-16's followed in trail, providing fighter cover.

Seven hours later, the four aircraft, plus the two fighters that had remained to protect the Hidden Base, touched down at Base One. For the former members of Bushmaster, one adventure had ended, and another adventure was just beginning.

"Cleansing Day" would come and go with no attack and no nuclear detonations in North America. At Bushmaster Headquarters, General Raazmahd was furious. He screamed obscenities, breaking or throwing anything within reach. He called on his new personal pilot and ordered a new mission. Within hours, Captain Tom Draxon was airborne, making his way from secret base to secret base, refueling his aircraft, a Super Mirage 4000, many times. His destination: the Bushmaster Hidden Base in the Western Defense Zone. His mission: destroy the base.

Knowing the terrain well and augmented by the Mirage Inertial Navigation System, Draxon approached low and fast. The familiar entrance flashed by as he made a sweeping turn and activated the weapons system. As he rolled wings level, the Hidden Base lay directly ahead. Selecting the four air-to-ground missiles the Mirage carried, he fired a salvo. Instantly, the four missiles sprinted away to their target. Seconds later, the abandoned base disappeared in a massive series of explosions. Captain Draxon smiled and headed back to Bushmaster Headquarters.

CHAPTER FIFTEEN

Welcome Home

Base One was a busy place on this day. Thirty-seven former members of Bushmaster were being processed, debriefed, inspected, injected... well, you get the general idea. Colonel Bass had done exactly what he said he would do and personally greeted each and every one of the new arrivals. Although some of the personnel were Americans by birth, it was still amusing to see their reaction to Colonel John T. Bass. He was a genuine Texan, and although he did not wear a cowboy hat, somehow you expected him to have his horse tied up nearby. In fact, when the subject of his nationality came up, he always said that he was a Texan.

After Colonel Fronz scheduled all of his people for in processing, he came to Skip and the others, with concern for two members of his guard, "Do you remember when I told you that I had dispatched two men to Owl's Nest?"

"Yes, I recall that," Skip answered.

"They did not return, and I am concerned that they may be in jeopardy."

"Did you brief them about what to expect?" Pop asked.

"We don't have much information about your outpost. Primarily, I wanted them to go there and gather information about Skip. I had hoped the information could be used to my advantage if the general had caused a problem. On reflection, it was a bad idea. However, I must find out about my men and retrieve them."

"Razer will be the worst problem by far," Skip commented.

"Is Razer your horse?" Ahana asked.

"I don't have a horse."

"But, my love, some of the reconnaissance photos show a horse standing in the lake."

"Holy socks!" Pop exclaimed, "They think Razer's a horse!"

Skip turned to Ahana and said, "Sweetheart, that's not a horse; that's a dog."

Simultaneously, the colonel and Ahana said, "That thing is a *dog*!"

"Yep, a 190-pound Rottweiler, and the last command I gave him was 'protect.' He will attack anyone who invades his territory, until he sees me again," Skip said with much concern, and then turned to Ahana. "The guards know you. Will you fly with me to Owl's Nest?"

"Of course. I would like the opportunity to see your outpost up close too."

"Okay, we'll leave first thing in the mornin'. I'll request the Helio. We'll have a heavy load on the return trip. I just hope it ain't dead bodies," Skip commented ominously.

Early the next morning, they prepared the plane for flight.

"Gorgeous, have you ever flown any of the Helio series aircraft?"

"No, I haven't. We had only recently received the Courier. Only the colonel and one of the two guards have been checked out in it. I have yet to have an opportunity."

"Well, you do now."

"How sweet. Thank you, love."

"You're gonna fall in love with this little bird. She literally jumps off the ground at thirty knots and will climb all day at eighteen hundred feet per minute."

"Wow! And you don't have to get a Rotary Wing rating to fly it?" she asked, jokingly.

Skip laughed and replied, "Almost. It's just rated for *I*-STOL... Incredibly Short Take-off and Landing."

Later that day they arrived at Owl's Nest. Ahana landed the Stallion with the skill of a veteran bush pilot and taxied up to the hangar entrance. The two men and Razer could be seen near the back of the hangar. Razer watched to see who had arrived but maintained his position, ears perked, listening carefully.

"My God! He's a monster!" Ahana commented upon seeing Razer. "Thankfully, our men are alive, but they don't look very happy."

"At least, they're alive," Skip said in relief.

Razer heard him speak and recognized Skip's voice.

"Look, he knows I'm here. Watch him, now he'll treat those two guys like they were his best friends. They're not gonna know what to do."

Razer stood up, wagging his butt (no tail), and in his excitement, he ran over to the two men huddled against the far wall. He was happy now and glad to see everyone. When he got in this particular mood, he liked to lick. He tried to lick both of his prisoners, but they hit the floor face first and curled up into a ball, as if they were defending against a grizzly attack.

Skip stepped out of the aircraft and called Razer. Immediately, Razer came galloping and tackled him, as usual. Amused but cautious, Ahana watched from the safety of the plane.

Skip grabbed Razer's collar and commanded, "Stand."

Razer obeyed, walked backward, and effortlessly pulled Skip to his feet.

Ahana looked on in amazement, "I have never seen a dog that strong in my life."

"Well, let's introduce you two. Come on out, and say hello," Skip requested and then spoke to the dog, "Razer, say hello to Ahana."

Razer walked over to the door of the aircraft, sat down, and held his right front paw up, patiently waiting for her to "say hello." Unable to resist, Ahana stepped out, knelt down, and took his large paw in her hand. "Oh my, his paw is larger than my hand!"

As she patted his head and scratched behind his ears, Razer slowly lay down and rolled over, displaying his belly.

"Well, he's yours now, like it or not," Skip said.

"What do you mean?" she asked curiously.

"He's showin' submission. That's his way of tellin' you that he trusts you and that you're the boss."

"Does he demonstrate this to everyone?"

"Nope, just my closest friends."

"How could he know that you and I have become so close?"

"I have no idea. But he has demonstrated that behavior to only three other people—Pop, Phil Blake, and Bud."

While they were talking, Razer stood up. Ahana was still kneeling, and since her face was conveniently close, he gave her a nice, big, wet lick, right on the lips.

"Yeeuuuck!" she squealed and fell on her butt.

"Apparently, I'm not the only one who thinks you're kissable!" Skip said, laughing as Ahana frantically spat and wiped her mouth. "Now, take hold of his collar, and say, "Stand.""

She did as Skip directed, and Razer pulled her to her feet as easily as if she were a small child.

"I think you will find that he will be protective and affectionate with you. Although he doesn't always realize his size and strength, he's very intelligent."

"Hello! May we get up now?" The voice came from the guards, still sitting in the hangar.

"Oh... We should see about them," Ahana whispered, somewhat embarrassed.

"We're fine, considering," the guard said, and then related their ordeal to Ahana and Skip. "As we soon as we landed, we split up and scouted the area. That monster dog from hell must have been stalking us, waiting for the best opportunity to attack. He got my partner first, crushed his left forearm, and disarmed him. Then, the dog forced him into the cave. After that, he came after me. I shot him, or thought I did, but I guess he's bulletproof too! When he lunged at me, I just gave him my weapon and joined my partner. After that, he just stayed nearby and guarded us. Periodically, he would go get a huge rawhide bone and chew on it for a while. He also chewed on one of the Stallion's tires, and it went flat, so we were stranded here.

"He let us eat, drink, and go to the bathroom. But when we ran out of food, he started bringing us his food... in his mouth. He would bring a whole mouthful, then stand there, and growl until we ate some of it. Thank God, he only brought it once a day. We would really like to have some people food now."

Ahana and Skip hated to laugh at the poor guys but just could not help themselves.

"Sure, guys, we can take care of that; I have a fair stash of chow up here." Then, he went to a box on the wall of the cave, opened it with a key, and entered a code on a keypad. The doors opened, revealing the Owl's Nest hangar and the entrance to his living quarters.

An hour later, they all shared a meal. The first meal of "people food" the two guards had eaten in five days. After the meal, Skip gave Ahana a first-class tour of Owl's Nest. They wanted to stay for a few days, but the guard with the crushed forearm was in need of medical attention. On the return trip, the two guards did not much care for sharing the close space inside the Stallion with Razer, but they let him lie wherever he chose to lie.

***

Back at Base One, there was a lot of tension and some strong resentment among some of the Base One personnel toward the new arrivals. One reason was the recent bombing. The other was the loss of Major Phil Blake. It was widely known that one of the Bushmaster pilots had shot him down. No one knew which pilot, and some did not care; they just blamed the entire group.

Colonel Bass decided to make a base-wide announcement to let everyone know that an investigation was in progress. At the completion of the investigation, a judicial committee would hold an open tribunal to determine the disposition of each of the former Bushmaster members. Everyone would be given the opportunity to voice concerns and ask any questions he or she chose to ask. The announcement appeared to satisfy their concerns and help keep their fears from controlling their actions.

***

Ron Taylor awoke in total panic. The nurse had just taken his vitals, and she was recording the information in his chart when he sat up in bed and screamed. The chart and pen went straight up into the air, and she screamed too.

This commotion got the attention of several of the hospital staff, including Dr. Jack Rightson, Ron's physician. Within seconds, two more nurses, an orderly, and the doctor were holding Ron down, or at least trying. The orderly laid across his legs, two of the nurses held his right arm, the third nurse was trying to hold his left arm, and the doctor was sitting on his chest. Ron was lifting all three nurses off the floor, and the doctor looked as though he was riding a bull.

"Get something into this guy!" Dr. Rightson yelled.

"What?" one of the nurses asked frantically.

"What's ever handy!" the doctor shouted.

"Just shoot in here among us; one of us has got to have some relief!" the orderly yelled.

"But, I'll have to let go of his arm," the nurse warned.

"Do it!" they all yelled at once.

The nurse quickly returned with a syringe and three ccs of morphine. A few seconds after the needle entered his arm, Ron was a happy camper. Immediately, all five of the attendees, totally exhausted, rested in various locations around the room.

"Christ! I knew he would come out of it soon, but I didn't expect him to wake up in Superman mode," Dr. Rightson exclaimed. "At least, he's going to be all right."

"Hell, he's ready to be discharged now!" one of the nurses exclaimed.

After the morphine wore off, the doctor stopped in to check on Ron, "Well, how's Superman?"

"I'm just a little bit embarrassed, Doc." Ron said, apologetically.

"Don't sweat it. Heck, we needed a workout anyway. I assume the nurse has told you why you're in the hospital?"

"Yes, she explained that I was knocked unconscious by the explosion. Why did I wake up like that, Doc?"

"Well, you received a concussion, due to that bump on your head. I think your mind just paused at the moment of the explosion, so when you woke up, as far as your brain was concerned, it was six days ago. One thing's for sure, your adrenaline system works great."

"Everything is so foggy... all I remember is standing at the door of the cafeteria and... Candy! Oh, Christ! Candy was with me!"

"Take it easy, Colonel. She's alive."

"But, how is she?"

"She's in ICU right now and doing well. She's battered up quite a bit, but her vitals are strong, and all she really needs is a lot of rest and recuperation."

"How bad?"

"She has a fractured skull, a broken left tibia, broken left ankle, broken collarbone, six fractured ribs, and a few abrasions. Also, her lungs were damaged slightly from smoke inhalation. I know all of that sounds bad, but she is making an excellent recovery. So don't worry, she'll be as good as new very soon.

The amazing thing is, with all of her injuries, after having been literally blown through the wall, Candy went back into that burning building, not once, but five times and dragged five people to safety.

Looks like you picked the right girl, Superman; she has got to be Super Woman!"

"Do we know who did it?"

"Your people were on it immediately and have determined that it was a small bomb planted inside the cafeteria. We don't know for sure who planted the bomb, although we know that we continue to be the target of terrorism. We suspect that the targets were Colonel Bass and General Grey, who were supposed to be dining at that hour. They were delayed and arrived only moments after the explosion. As soon as I notify your office that you can have visitors, I'm certain they can fill you in with more detail."

Ron contemplated for a moment, sighed, and asked, "Doc, how will we ever stop it?"

"Terrorism, you mean?"

"Yea, I mean, they're like roaches when you turn on the lights. You can stomp on a few, but most of the nasty bastards crawl back into hiding until the lights go out again. We can't burn down the house. What can we do?"

"We vow to never give up. We get them one by one if necessary, but each of us must dedicate ourselves to fight because we are fighting for our survival."

"Thanks, Doc. Thanks for everything."

"My pleasure. Say, why don't you go visit Candy? There's no reason for you to remain in this bed as long as you take it easy. You don't need me for anything; besides, I've got more doctor stuff to do."

Downstairs, several of the former Bushmaster personnel were filling out forms and preparing for their physical exams. One of them was Lt. Cohen. Knowing this, Skip stopped by to see if everything was going all right and to ask if she needed anything.

"Hello, gorgeous. How's it going? Is everyone treatin' you okay?"

"I'm doing fine, sweetie. Everyone is so nice. They even salute me."

"Well, you are a lieutenant, right?"

"Yes. But I just didn't expect... Oh, William, I have been so wrong about Americans, especially the FFNA."

"I think a lot of our folks are findin' out that you're not what they expected, either."

"Do you think Colonel Bass will consider my request to join the FFNA?"

"I don't think so."

"Why?"

"Because I signed up as your official sponsor and personally submitted a request that you be considered for an aircrew position with NAADA, here at Base One."

Ahana hugged Skip, gave him a kiss, and said, "William, you are so wonderful!"

"I just want to keep you as close to me as possible."

"That is where I want to be too."

"I was just on my way upstairs to see Ron Taylor and Candy Simms; they were injured in the bombing. I'll see you for dinner, okay?"

"See ya, fly boy."

Just as Skip was walking to the elevator, he spotted Dr. Rightson and remembered that he never did come in for the check-up after the Viper-6 crash. Knowing how tenacious the doctor was about taking care of Base One's pilots, Skip did an abrupt about-face and headed for the nearest exit. Unfortunately for Skip, the former Bushmaster personnel had a contingent of security guards with them constantly.

The doctor saw Skip and could not resist the opportunity.

"Stop that man!" Doctor Rightson yelled, motioning to the guards in Skip's direction.

The guard looked at Skip and then at the doctor and said, "You want him? That's Mr. Scott. A Base One pilot."

"I know exactly who he is, and he has disobeyed a direct order. Arrest him!"

The guard caught Skip just before he got to the door, "Sorry, sir, I don't have a choice, the doctor is a bird colonel."

The guard brought Skip back to where the doctor stood.

"What's up, Doc?" Skip asked facetiously.

"Very funny. Do you have any idea how much I dislike having someone disobey my orders?"

"Well, if I didn't before, I'm beginnin' to get the idea now," Skip remarked, glancing at the guard.

Along with everyone in the waiting room, Ahana had witnessed the event and had come to see about Skip.

"William, are you all right?" she asked, very seriously.

"William?" the doctor repeated and looked at Skip.

Skip smiled proudly and said, "Ahana, this is Doctor Jack Rightson. Jack, I would like you to meet a very close friend of mine, Lieutenant Ahana Cohen."

"Pleased to meet you, Lieutenant. Why is someone as attractive as you hanging around with this old, rogue pilot?"

"Hey! Who's old?"

Catching the tease in the doctor's tone of voice, she played along, "I'm not really sure now, I wasn't aware of his criminal tendencies."

"Oh, very funny. You two can knock it off anytime, you know," Skip said, not very amused.

"Let me tell you, Lieutenant, just what this friend of yours did. After surviving a horrible crash right here on this base, I ordered him to come in for a post-crash physical. Not only did Skip fail to show up, he didn't even have the courtesy to call me and let me know that he had decided that he didn't need the exam. I suppose Skip thinks he's indestructible."

"Is that true, William?"

"Well, I was busy."

"Too busy to take care of yourself? I think, from now on, I'll need to watch over you a little more closely," she commented, and then turned to the doctor, "Doctor Rightson, William will take my appointment. I can wait. And, I want to know if he was injured during the crash."

"Finally, someone to keep an eye on Skip. Lieutenant, you have an impossible job ahead of you," the doctor said, then turned to the security officer, "Guard, please take Mr. Scott to Exam Room One and keep him there until I arrive."

Skip stuck out his tongue at Ahana and said, "Traitor!"

"I'll see you and the doctor after the examination," she said sternly, standing with her hands on her hips, watching as the guard escorted Skip down the hall.

An hour later, the doctor came out and called Ahana, "Lieutenant, you can come in now; I have an x-ray that you should see."

In the exam room, Skip sat on the examination table, looking like a lost little boy. Ahana kissed him on the cheek and sat down beside him.

"Since you have such a personal interest in this rascal, I thought I might get you to help me keep him in line."

"Yes, sir, I'll be happy to do that."

"Well, this is what you're up against, look at this..." He pointed to the x-ray, "Right here, you can see several small striations on the fourth rib. That is a fracture across the entire width of the bone. It has healed considerably, and fortunately, it healed correctly. This occurred about three months ago; coincidentally, so did the crash. That broken rib could have easily punctured his left lung and caused internal hemorrhaging. If he had been flying when that happened, he would, most likely, not be here right now."

Ahana looked at Skip and commented, "I thought men couldn't tolerate pain."

"I'm just tough."

"You may be tough, but you are not indestructible," Dr. Rightson began. "You're not a kid any longer, Skip. The days when you could recover from an injury overnight are gone. If you're not more careful, you're going to inflict an injury that your body and I can't fix."

Ahana walked over to Skip, gently placed her hands on his cheeks, kissed him, and said, "Fly boy, I have waited my whole life to find you. Maybe you felt that you didn't have anything to live for then, but now you have me. I want you to be here today, tomorrow, and for as long as God will let us stay together. Will you promise to take care of yourself... for me?"

Skip reached up, touched her face, and said, "Doc, I think she's serious."

"If you don't answer 'yes,' I'll have your head examined... again!"

"I promise," Skip whispered and kissed her very passionately.

The doctor cleared his throat, "Well, I'll leave you two lovers alone now. I've got doctor stuff to do."

He left the room, closing the door behind him, then he stuck his head back in and said, "Don't be too long, your exam is coming up, Lieutenant."

Two hours later, Ahana walked out of the doctor's office and found Skip waiting for her, "Hello, love. Thank you for waiting."

"What did the doc have to say about you?"

"I'm fine," she sighed. "We also talked about the possibility of me having babies. I was just hoping that maybe, modern medicine might have a new solution. Doctor Rightson understood, but he said it would just be too much of a risk to me and the baby."

Ahana was visibly distressed and about to cry. As Skip pulled her to him, she put her arms around his waist and laid her head on his shoulder. Skip held her close and stroked her hair, letting her know that he wanted to give her whatever comfort she needed.

"You really want to have babies, don't you?"

"Yes, I really do."

"There are other possibilities."

"If we stay together and perhaps, marry someday, I want so much to have your children," she explained, sounding very disappointed.

"I would like to have babies with you, Ahana, but I don't think any less of you because you're unable to have children. I want you to stay healthy. If the doc says childbirth would endanger you and the baby, then we will adopt if we want children. It'll be okay; you'll see. When that day comes, we'll face it together."

"Hold me for a little while," she whispered.

"For as long as you want, gorgeous."

They sat on a large sofa outside the doctor's office. Ahana curled up, laid her head on Skip's chest, and fell asleep. Later, Doctor Rightson came out of his office and noticed them sitting there.

He sat down very quietly and whispered, "How is she doing?"

"I think she just needs to relax a bit after hearin' the bad news yet again. I'll bet she's asked every doctor that she ever knew."

"All of her people have been under severe stress for many months. The situation that she is in now is obviously very stressful, plus the subject of motherhood is terribly painful for her." The doctor commented, "I could almost see her blood pressure soar when we were discussing her inability to have children. Her face reddened, and her body temp rose. I tried to be as consoling as possible. She may have nerves of steel at the controls of a fighter, but she can't handle that subject. Why don't you let her rest for a while in one of the empty beds down the hall? It will help her a lot if you just hold her while she sleeps. She needs your emotional support right now, very much."

"Thanks, Doc," Skip whispered, then carefully picked Ahana up, carried her to one of the rooms, and gently placed her on the bed. Then he curled up with her and held her securely while she slept. About an hour later, she woke up and was pleasantly surprised to find Skip, still holding her, fast asleep.

"Hi, fly boy," she whispered, and he awoke almost immediately. "I'm sorry I crashed out on you," she said, apologetically. "I guess it was my turn, huh?"

Then she smiled, reminded of knocking Skip out with a kiss.

"But, you didn't faint; you were just exhausted from the stress," he corrected her.

"I think I would have fainted, had you not been there to hold me."

"Well, I'm glad to be of service, gorgeous. Anytime you need some tender loving care, I'll be right here."

She kissed him, propped up on her elbow, and asked, "Do you realize we're lying here, in a hospital bed, when we could be out doing something fun?"

"Personally, I think bein' in bed with you is about the most fun I could have!"

"In our flight suits?" she asked, lifting one eyebrow.

"Well, I've never tried it, but I'll bet it's possible," he replied with confidence. Studying her flight suit as he spoke, he began to unzip it.

"I think we should just stick with the old-fashioned way. And now, in a busy hospital, is not the place." Then, she pushed him off the bed, and he hit the floor with a thud.

As they were leaving, she remembered that Skip had intended to visit friends in the hospital. "Oh, did you visit your friends? How are they?"

"Ron is as feisty as ever. And more than a little pissed at your former leader. I explained the situation to him, half expecting him to come undone, but to my surprise, he welcomed you folks. He's glad to get the help."

"That is a big relief. I wouldn't want your chief of intelligence as an enemy."

"No. He is one bear you don't want to cross. His fiancée, Candy, is in pretty bad shape, but he's well enough to be right there beside her. I'm sure they'll both be fine."

"William, I am so troubled by all of this. I feel partly responsible for what happened here. I am so ashamed that I allowed myself to be associated with Bushmaster."

Skip paused and pulled her to him, "Now stop beating yourself up. You've made the right decision, and soon, all of you will get an opportunity to make amends."

"How do you always manage to say the very words that I need to hear?"

"Hey, that's why I'm here, gorgeous."

"For that, I am truly thankful." Then, Ahana kissed him. "By the way, where are the guards?"

"I told them you would be my responsibility from now on."

"Oh, really? Think you're up to it?"

"I think I can handle you."

"Then, let's go to the gym. I noticed it on my way over here, and I really need a workout."

"You don't need a gym for that," Skip commented, suggestively.

"Oh, you!" she exclaimed as she nudged him with her elbow, "Let's just see if you can keep up with me, that is, unless that rib is bothering you."

"Rib? Oh, that rib. No. Not at all," he fibbed, then asked, "Are you sure you're up to this?"

"Well, fly boy, you be the judge."

Two hours later, Ahana was finished with her workout, and her workout was finished with Skip.

"I thought you said you wanted me around for a while," he complained as he lay on the floor of the gym, totally exhausted, "Keep this up, and you're gonna kill me for sure."

"I think you'll survive. Besides, I want you in top shape. You're a fighter pilot; you need to be solid and sharp."

"What I need now is a good rubdown."

"I might be able to do something about that," she said and winked at him.

"Forget dinner, let's go to my place!"

"You have a home here on the base?"

"Yep. I don't care much for the BOQ; it feels too much like a college dorm." Then, as he increased the distance between them, he continued, "Besides, you can't have girls and throw wild parties in the dorm."

"Girls? Wild parties?"

"Just kiddin'. Checkin' to see if you were listening!"

Ahana made a face and threw a rolled up towel at him.

When they arrived at Skip's home, she commented, "You live underground! Somehow I never expected that."

"Yep. As you can see, it's actually built into the side of the hill. About 90 percent of the house is below ground, which makes it easier to heat and cool, plus it's much safer down here. It's not as closed-in as you might expect; the den and kitchen open onto the patio, and there's a great west view." He opened the door for Ahana and said, "Please excuse the mess; I'm not much of a housekeeper."

Ahana looked around and smiled, "How cozy. I like it."

"Thanks. Please make yourself at home. My place is your place."

It was unnecessary for Skip to say that, for Ahana already felt like she was home. While he put a few things away and fixed them something to drink, she wandered around the rooms, taking in as much about her newfound mate as she possibly could.

Actually, Skip was not such a messy person. He was just typically male. His home was a lot as she had pictured it to be. He had many books, on many subjects, including several classics, poetry, science fiction, and aeronautics. He also had a collection of CDs, including rock, country, blues, classical, and jazz. Pictures of airplanes and models of airplanes were everywhere. A picture of a large log home near a mountain stream hung on one wall.

On a small table, there was a picture of a very lovely blonde woman with twin girls and a little boy with blonde hair. Ahana was certain this was a picture of his wife and children. She picked it up for a closer look, realized he was bringing her drink, and returned the picture to the table, quickly turning her attention to the mountain scene. "This is so lovely. Where is it?"

"That's my granddad's home in the Blue Ridge Mountains near Asheville, North Carolina. We spent summers there when I was a kid. I'd like to go back someday, maybe even settle there if it's livable now. It sure was pretty up there."

"America was such a beautiful country before the disaster. I visited here many times. You are fortunate to have been born here. I would like to become an American citizen," Ahana said wistfully.

"I wouldn't worry about that. I'm not lettin' you go. They'll either grant you citizenship or have to deport me." Ahana was not certain if he was serious or not. Then, he kissed her passionately and carried her to his bed. Later, as they lay in each other's arms, Ahana remembered that Skip had mentioned wanting a rubdown. She went to the bathroom, found a container of body lotion, returned to the bed, and said, "Roll over on your stomach."

"You're not gonna get kinky, are you?"

She smacked him on the head and ordered, "Roll over!"

"Yes, ma'am! You female officers are rough!"

"We have to be." Then, she straddled his legs and started massaging his back.

"Oh, that feels sooo good!"

"See, I'm not so rough. Besides, I told you that I might be able to do something about your rubdown, didn't I?"

"Oh, yea. That's why we came here, isn't it? But we would have ended up here, anyway."

"Really? Why, is that?"

"Because I canceled your room at the women's dorm. Your stuff will be delivered here shortly."

"You rascal!" She pinched him, then gave him a kiss on the back of his neck, and asked, "Why didn't you tell me earlier?"

Skip rolled over and replied, "I wanted to surprise you. I knew you wouldn't ask to stay with me. You're very capable of lookin' out for yourself. But you don't have much control over what's happenin' right now. I want to make sure you have everything that you need and that you are comfortable and safe."

"Thank you, love, you are so sweet!"

Skip pulled her to him, and she spent the next few hours in the comfort and safety of her lover's arms.

Later, as they lay together on the floor of the living room, watching a lightning storm raging in the distance, Ahana asked, "William, would you tell me about your wife and children?"

"What would you like to know?"

"I was just wondering. I know that you have much pain still inside you, and I want to take that pain away... maybe if I understood why you hurt so, I would better know how to help you heal."

"Ahana, I have never known anyone like you," Skip declared as he caressed her cheek. "Thank God, I found you."

"Thank God, we found each other," Ahana added, and then asked, "Will you tell me about them?"

Skip recited the story...

"Not long after we were married, Holly and I agreed that, if things ever got bad, she and the kids should go stay with her parents in Oregon. Rumors of the asteroid were everywhere, and people were really goin' nuts. Everyone expected the government to have some system in place to prevent that sort of thing. Maybe we could have changed the orbit of a comet or a small asteroid, but that thing's mass was far greater than the mass of the Moon. Just imagine tryin' to move the Moon. We will never have that kind of technology.

"People became violent towards anyone connected with the government. I was afraid that Holly or the kids might get hurt, so they went to Oregon. I promised that I would get there as quickly as I could. I had access to all of the information about the Reaper, so I told Holly not to worry, I would watch it closely and be there with her and the kids, no matter what.

"During the nineties, I was flyin' a Herk on a project called PsyOps."

"What was the PsyOps project? I've never heard of that."

"Well, the idea originated with a modified C-130 code named Commando Solo."

"I'm familiar with that; we used Commando Solo to manipulate radio and TV broadcasts during some of our missions. And I know that PsyOps is psychological operations, but what is the PsyOps project?"

"Believe it or not, airborne mind control."

"You're not serious," Ahana replied in disbelief.

"Serious as a heart attack."

"How is that possible?"

"Well, it all started with a neurobiologist working at Lawrence-Livermore Labs. He discovered that by stimulating the cerebral cortex with a very specific series of impulses, it is possible to invoke very strong emotions and thoughts in a person's conscious mind. The experience is similar to a vivid dream, except the subject doesn't have to be asleep."

"That's incredible. And PsyOps was a project to attempt that from an *airplane*?" she asked, amazed.

"Yep. The impulses don't have to be very strong. An amazingly low level, at the proper frequency, and modulated correctly can cause fear, anger, hunger... almost any basic emotion. So, someone in the intelligence community got the bright idea to use this technique for mass mind control. The idea was to set up a Herk in an orbit over a battlefield. If timed right, it was possible, by beamin' these signals at the troops, to instill fear into the enemy or anger into our guys and literally control the soldiers like puppets."

"William, this sounds like science fiction. George Orwell or something!"

"I know, but it really worked. In fact, it worked so well, the boys in Washington ordered us to use it on civilians. We were to try to keep folks calm by targeting an area where people were gettin' out of control and planting a sense of well-being into their psyche.

"The problem is, on a battlefield and similar situations, the front-line commanders and tactical intelligence have a much better handle on the disposition of the troops. It's their job to know that, plus what's expected in the next few hours, all that battlefield stuff.

"Well, when you're dealin' with a large mass of unruly civilians, with little or no control over what they might do next, it's virtually impossible to know how to control 'em. Certain emotions override other emotions. If you're not sure what's on someone's mind, it's not easy to know his or her emotional state. Tryin' to instill a sense of well-being into a group of people who, at that particular moment, might be feelin' anything from self-pity to fear to anger... heck, who knows what would happen?

"Anyway, we didn't seem to have much luck. Despite that, the orders were very specific. We were supposed to help keep the masses from overrunnin' Washington.

"While we were involved in that, the Reaper was accelerating a lot more than predicted as it grew nearer to the Sun, due to its tremendous mass. The trajectory of the asteroid caused Jupiter to be positioned directly between it and Earth, so gettin' good data on it was very difficult. They even tried turnin' the Mars Probe antennas toward it, anything to bounce a signal off it, but nothin' worked. Mostly 'cause they refused to believe that it was travelin' so fast. When they finally figured it out, it was just hours from Earth.

"We got the word before most people did, but it was too late. I grabbed an F-15, against orders, and left Langley, headed for Oregon. I was in the air when the Reaper hit the upper atmosphere. The first shock wave knocked that Eagle out of the air like a paper airplane. I fought it, but I went into a lake in southwest Nebraska. The Eagle sank like a rock, and I couldn't get the canopy open. It wouldn't release, and it wouldn't blow. I was under thirty feet of water when the Reaper hit. The sky lit up like nothin' I've ever seen or ever want to see again."

"I know I will never forget that horrible day. What happened next?"

"Well, I was in the process of choppin' through the canopy when all hell broke loose. A dam or somethin' must have collapsed, because

I was almost free when a surge of water just ripped the canopy out and dragged me along with it.

"After I made it to the surface, I discovered I had a huge gash in my leg, and my left shoulder was dislocated, but I managed to drag myself up on the bank. And while I was lyin' there on the bank of that damn lake, a series of tsunamis, each estimated to be three thousand feet high, swept the West Coast and took away my reason to live.... in one horrible moment, they were just gone."

At that point, Skip could no longer speak, so Ahana just held him close, "William, it's okay. I understand your pain. I'm here, my love, I'm right here."

And for the first time since he learned his family was gone, Skip cried.

After a little while, Ahana spoke, "William, you tried so hard to be with your family. No one could have known that you would never see them again. That knowledge is for God alone. If you had been there, you would have been killed, too. You could have made no difference. I know, just as sure as I'm holding you now, that Holly and the children knew that you loved them more than anything, even more than your own life. You risked your life, just to be with them. I can think of no greater love. Maybe, God has a reason for you to live. I know that nothing can bring back your beautiful family, but look what you have accomplished thus far:

"First, you are the driving force behind the design and production of a prototype attack jet that exceeds the performance capabilities of any previous design. I believe the Viper series will provide a level of air superiority that has previously been unknown.

"Second, if you had not been brought to our Hidden Base, we might never have had an opportunity to escape the horrible grip of General Raazmahd. Most likely, we would have been killed.

"Third, and most important to me, you and I would never have met. Just in the short time I have known you, you have brought me more happiness than I have known my whole life!"

Then, she gently lifted his face to hers, wiped away his tears, kissed him tenderly, and said, "I don't want to replace Holly, and I can't give you children. But if you will let me, I will love you with all of my heart for the rest of my life."

"As I said before, I have never known anyone like you. Ahana, I love you. I want you to stay with me for as long as you will have me."

"Then, I will stay with you forever."

"Ahana, my love, welcome home."

They held each other and watched the storm rage, secure in the knowledge that they would never be lonely, or alone, again. They would wake in the morning, still in each other's arms.

CHAPTER SIXTEEN

You Never Know Where You Will Find a Friend

After almost a week of intensive debriefing, Base One security had established a file on each of the newcomers. The files included a worldwide data search of the history of each person, from birth to present day. Unfortunately, the data was sketchy and incomplete.

Colonel Fronz was familiar with this information and a great deal more because he had previously compiled this data, creating meticulous archived files on each member of his unit. He had offered this data to Base One security, but the offer was promptly refused. Colonel Bass was not so hard-lined about it, so he and Colonel Fronz had spent most of the previous week reviewing those files.

When security advised Colonel Bass that the new files were ready for his review, he remarked to Colonel Fronz, "By the time we're done, I'll know more about these people than I know about my own family!"

Therefore, one by one, they reviewed each new file, comparing the recently compiled data with the data gathered by Colonel Fronz. With very few exceptions, the information was virtually identical. Then, a follow-up interview was done, questioning each person about various events recorded in the files.

One of the primary advantages for Colonel Bass was the personal insight provided by Colonel Fronz. Colonel Bass was impressed to learn that his counterpart had personally selected each one of the people assigned to his unit. Thus, Colonel Fronz had personal knowledge of each one of his people, gained by close observation. This type of information is not always available in a person's historical file and would prove to be an invaluable tool to Colonel Bass in the days that were to follow. After the final interviews, a formal review had to be conducted and decisions made, based on the personal request of each individual.

Colonel Bass and select members of his staff, base Intelligence, base security, and other base personnel, acting as a formal review board, would perform an official, final evaluation of each of the new arrivals. This evaluation would include a recommendation to accept or reject the individual's requests. The evaluations and recommendations would then be referred to NAADA Headquarters and a federal judicial board for final determination.

As chairman of the formal review board, Colonel Bass was adamant that the board would be fair and impartial. Colonel Bass and Colonel Fronz had just completed the follow-up interviews...

"Al, I want you to rest assured that I will conduct a fair and impartial review. If, at any point, I suspect that my people are basing their decisions on prejudice, rumor, or unsubstantiated information, I will either have that individual removed from the board, or I will dismiss the entire review, and we'll start over with a whole new crew."

"John, that means more to me than I can convey. Truthfully, I didn't expect this response. I am reassured by your honesty. I can guarantee that my people and I will abide by your recommendations."

"Based on what I have seen, I'm not concerned about the conduct of your folks. Every one of your people has displayed discipline, courtesy, professionalism, and a keen sense of duty. Hell, most of 'em are more aware of world events than my people are.

"I can't guarantee the outcome of the review board, but I see no reason to deny any of the requests that your people have made. To be honest, we need your help. You and your people have more knowledge of Bushmaster that we could ever hope to obtain, even if we had the luxury of time and the opportunity to plant infiltrators into the organization. I believe this advantage will give us the edge we need to stop 'em cold."

"John, I am concerned about the welfare of my people. They are the best. I picked them because of their devotion to duty. I know they will disregard personal risk, if necessary, to follow orders. They deserve a secure future, but we are labeled as terrorists. I am concerned that we will not get a fair and impartial judgment."

"When my people hear the whole story, their attitude will change. You'll see."

"I can only hope that the other members of the review board are as logical and fair-minded as you. To deny even one of us the opportunity of freedom would be a great injustice to the efforts we have made to get here. I will do everything in my power to fight for my people, because I know that any one of us would be proud to fight and die to protect the freedom that your government provides to its citizens."

"Al, I'm gonna give you every opportunity to mount a defense. I want you to tell the board what you just told me. That genuine commitment to fight for the common cause will go a long way toward convincing everyone that you and your people are sincere. As far as your innocence in all of this, of that I have no doubt."

Thus, the final decision was about to be made; it was only a matter of scheduling the final review.

***

It was the end of another day. Ahana had arrived home earlier than Skip on a singular mission... find food. When Skip arrived, he found her sitting cross-legged in front of the open pantry with the contents scattered all around her, inspecting each item for appeal and edibility. Skip walked in and peaked around the door, "Hello, gorgeous. Lookin' for somethin' in particular?"

"Not necessarily, just something edible. I am starving." She turned her face up toward him, reached and grabbed hold of his flight suit, and pulled him down to her for a very delicious kiss.

"I'll bet I know why you're so hungry," Skip offered. "Your appetite for food has finally caught up with your appetite for sex!"

"Hmmm, there is some logic in your supposition. Now find me something to eat!"

"Yes, ma'am! Your wish is my command, Oh Great Fighter Ace. But I'm afraid we ain't gonna find it here. We've got to restock this pantry. I'm not much for cookin' meals for one. Why don't we go to the commissary?" Skip suggested.

"William, don't you know that you are never supposed to go grocery shopping when you're hungry? You end up buying too much food. We must eat before we go shopping."

"Well, Pop invited us to meet him at the Officers Club this evening. Wanna go there for dinner?"

"Yes! Let's go now." And they were out the door and on their way to the O-Club.

Walking with Ahana was a delight for Skip. She was full of life and had a natural curiosity about the world around her. Ahana loved life. On the darkest, gloomiest day, she would find something good about it, and that always seemed to make it brighter. She was strong, mature, and intelligent, yet she radiated youth with an implied innocence.

As they walked hand in hand, she quietly hummed a song and took in the view around her. Skip loved just to look at Ahana. When she noticed, she smiled and kissed him on the cheek. It was as if an aura surrounded her, affecting Skip in a most profound way. This aspect of Ahana's character fascinated Skip and made her even more attractive. With her, he was content and needed nothing else. His world and his life were complete.

She looked at him thoughtfully for a moment and asked, "William, if I am allowed to join the Free Forces and I am offered the opportunity to fly, would you want me to continue flying?"

"Certainly. How could I ask you to stop flyin'? I don't even like to think about the day that I will no longer be able to fly. I would be selfish and hypocritical to expect you to turn in your wings, just because I'm concerned for your safety. I would never treat you that way."

"Thank you, my love. I hoped you would feel that way," she said, beaming her beautiful smile.

"Will the fact that I fly, despite your concern for my safety, affect your feelings for me?"

"Absolutely not! I'm proud of your determination to follow your dream. Gorgeous, nothin' can change how I feel about you. And since we don't know what happens after we die, I've decided that I'll continue to love you forever."

"How interesting. I thought that very same thing, just today," she said with a note of fascination in her voice.

"Do you remember when, today?" Skip asked, curiously.

"Yes, around ten this morning. I remember, because I was helping my mechanic work on Mustang Two."

"This is really strange. I was also thinkin' about that around ten. Did we have a telephone conversation today that I'm not aware of?"

Ahana laughed. "No, silly. We must be connected in some special way. How else can it be explained?"

"Cool!" Skip exclaimed. "We're telepathic."

Ahana laughed again, "I don't think so. But we might have a psychological link that keeps us close, no matter how far apart we are. I've heard of that phenomenon."

"Really? That is too cool."

"Well, here we are," Ahana said, as they reached the walkway to the Officers Club. She immediately headed for the door, dragging Skip along with her.

"You are starvin', aren't ya?"

"Yes!"

They found a table and ordered dinner and drinks. While dinner was being prepared, they got their drinks, and Skip gave Ahana a tour of the Officers Club. One of the highlights of the club was a collection of aviation memorabilia. The collection, dating back to the dawn of aviation, included pictures, books, personal items, uniforms, medals, and biographies of pilots throughout history. The collection also included avionics equipment from famous aircraft and hundreds of model aircraft hanging from the ceiling everywhere in the building.

"Viewing this," Ahana commented, "I feel as though I am part of an extended family. It makes me even more proud to be an aviator."

"You already have a great reason to be proud; you're a Triple Ace. Do you realize what that means? I'm honored, just to know you."

"Thank you for the compliment, but I've never really thought about my accomplishments that way. I just love to fly, and when I fly, I do the best job I possibly can," she said, matter-of-factly.

"You're the most humble ace I've ever known, that's for sure. Do you also realize that I may be the first pilot in history to marry a female fighter ace?"

Before she could answer, Skip spotted Pop and started walking in his direction.

"Well, I.... What? Did you say *marry*? William? William!"

"Ahana," Skip called from across the room, "Pop is here. Did you call me?"

She walked to where they were standing, looked at Skip curiously, but did not answer his question. Pop greeted her warmly, "Hello, beautiful lady, it's good to see you again. How has this rogue been treating you?"

"He's been somewhat mischievous, of late," Ahana replied, giving Skip a sideways glance.

Skip looked at her mischievously, trying not to smile.

Pop said, "Well, if he doesn't treat you right, just let me know; you can move into my place. I'm hardly ever there anyway."

"Dinner's ready," Skip said, as he noticed the waiter delivering the food to their table.

"We took the liberty of ordering for you, Pop," Ahana said.

"Good. I'm starving!"

"That makes two of you," Skip commented.

Skip enjoyed watching Ahana and Pop eat much more than he enjoyed the meal. It was a pleasure to see anyone enjoy the food currently served. After the meal, they stayed and talked. Skip could not remember enjoying an evening at the club as much as he was enjoying this one.

Later, Bud and his wife, Connie, joined them. This was Connie's first opportunity to meet Ahana. Nevertheless, after a short time, the two women acted as though they had been friends for years. Bud embarrassed Connie by telling Ahana how she had been trying to find a mate for Skip. Ahana thought it was sweet and thanked Connie for trying to watch over him. Connie was relieved that, finally, she did not have to worry about Skip any longer.

Then, Colonel Bass and Colonel Fronz came in and joined them for a while. At one point, Skip left the gathering, and as he was returning, he stopped to take in the unique scene. There was Ahana and Colonel Fronz, sitting at the same table with four of Skip's closest friends. Extraordinary people, who had been strangers and enemies just weeks ago, were now socializing and enjoying each other's company. Ahana noticed Skip standing there and came over to him, slipped her arms around his waist, and propped her chin on his shoulder.

"Hi, handsome. Whatcha' doin?" she asked.

"I was just takin' in this scene. Ain't this amazing? You know, you can just never tell where you're gonna find a friend."

When they returned to the table, the colonels announced that they had to leave. As they were saying good-bye, Colonel Bass leaned over and gave Ahana a fatherly kiss on the forehead, patted Skip on the cheek, winked, and said, "You're a lucky man, Ramjet."

After they had gone, she turned to Skip and asked, "Why did the colonel call you Ramjet?"

Skip laughed. "It's a long story."

Then he recited the history of his tenuous friendship with Colonel John T. Bass. Pop and Bud added their parts to the story, and Ahana began to learn the fascinating history of the people who had, so willingly, welcomed her into their extended family.

Suddenly, a disturbance at the bar caught everyone's attention. Captain Jake Spade had arrived, half-lit and looking for trouble. Pop and Bud turned to look at Skip.

Bud said "Just let it go, pal; he's not worth it."

Then, Pop said, "Oh, crap, he's comin' over here."

"Well, well, well, look who we have here, the hero pilots and their little ladies. They even brought the old man to chaperone. Are you watchin' over the Jewish princess, old man?" Spade said, laughing at his own sarcasm.

"Careful, gutless. Don't insult the lady, unless you intend to back it up," Skip threatened.

"You got a problem with me, hot shot?"

"Left any more flight leaders to die lately, asshole?" Skip shot back.

Spade pointed his finger accusingly. "You don't know what the hell you're talkin' about, Skippy! You weren't there."

"Let it go, son," Pop warned Skip.

Ahana tried, unsuccessfully, to hold Skip in his chair. Skip stood, then turned to Ahana and winked. She looked at him curiously and then looked at the others. However, no one had any idea what Skip was about to do.

"Should I try to do something?" Ahana whispered to Pop.

"I wouldn't. Let's see what he's up to," Pop suggested, and then added, "Normally, by now, the manager would be throwing us out!"

The place was dead silent. Spade recoiled slightly as Skip reached over, put his hand on Spade's shoulder, and said, "I met someone the other day that you need to meet."

"And who might that be?" Spade asked indignantly.

"He's an F-5 pilot. He's very familiar with you and your F-16. Seems he had a recent encounter with you, and he wasn't very impressed with your air combat tactics."

"You're losin' it, Skippy. There ain't no F-5 pilot that knows me."

"Oh, sure, he knows you real well, 'cause I told him all about you. Interestingly enough, he feels the same way that I do about a wingman that deserts his flight leader. He's of the opinion that someone like you needs his throat cut... I'll be glad to introduce you."

Then, Skip stepped back, looked Spade straight in the eyes, and said, "He was there, you useless son of a bitch! He saw you run, and he saw Phil die. You'll pay for that, you bastard. It's not my place to collect, but you will pay!"

Spade suddenly went pale. He stood there for a moment, as if he was not sure what to do, then he abruptly turned and left the club. After Spade walked out, everyone in the entire club stood up and applauded Skip.

CHAPTER SEVENTEEN

The Answer to the Question Is "Yes"!

The walk back home that evening gave Skip time to cool down. Ahana did not say much, although she was proud of the way he had handled the situation. She did not mention the confrontation. If he wanted to talk, she was ready to listen. Finally, Skip spoke, "I'm sorry about that scene back there. I really didn't want to insult you by exposin' you to that drunk. I just couldn't let it go."

"I wasn't insulted, sweetheart. I have dealt with my share of drunks. It's foolish to be insulted by someone like that. I consider them beneath contempt. I am proud of the way you handled him. I saw how mad you were, and I know how you feel. I was afraid the confrontation was going to become violent."

"I sure would like to clean that guy's clock. We've had encounters in the past, but this is different... Phil was a good guy and a good friend. He was an excellent pilot and considered one of the best F-16 pilots in the world.

"Phil invented new ways to utilize the F-16 in air combat. I've never known anyone who could appear to be in two places in the sky at once, but he could, and it baffled the hell out of an adversary. And he would never leave his wingman, even if it meant that he had to take the hit. Phil had a bird shot out from under him while he covered for me.

When I think of how that gutless bastard left Phil to fight alone, it just makes me sick.

"It's all so damned ironic. I mean, Major Vosh was just followin' orders. The colonel wanted a way out for ya'll and had very few options. No one in that air battle wanted Phil dead, but there was no way in the world to convince him of what their intentions were. He was just too damn good to let somethin' like that happen. If his wingman had been doin' his job, Phil would be alive today, of that, I'm certain.

"It goes against my grain to let that gutless bastard live. Major Vosh is right; Spade needs his throat cut. But, in some ways, I think he'll suffer more alive than dead. He knows what he did, and now, he has to live with it."

Ahana waited for a bit, then asked, "I know that you needed to talk about it. Do you feel a little better now?"

"Well, I'm still frustrated, but I do feel a little better. I'm glad I didn't show you my mean side, poundin' on that jerk the way I wanted to."

Ahana stopped, pulled him in front of her, put her arms around his waist, and said, "Fly boy, if you have a mean streak in you, you'll have to prove it. In the short time that I have known you, I've have seen your courage, your intelligence and humor, your dedication to duty and intolerance of evil and deceit, your decency and compassion, your kindness and generosity, your friendship, love, and passion... and I really like the love and passion part. But in all of that, I have not seen the least bit of unkindness. Standing up and speaking out, fighting for the things in which you believe and the people you care about are not acts of meanness but acts of courage and respect. It makes me feel so wonderful when someone like Colonel Bass says to you, 'You are a lucky man.' Not because they refer to me, but because they acknowledge that we are companions. For me to be chosen by you is such a great honor. Now, I can proudly say, 'He is my man, and I am his woman.'

"What we share are not just friendship, sexual attraction, and love; we have emotionally bonded. I feel like I am part of you, and you are part of me, as though I have known you all my life. William, I am so proud to be with you."

Skip smiled, and his eyes watered just a bit, but all he could say was, "Wow." Then, he kissed her with the passion she had mentioned.

Realizing the perfect opportunity, he asked, "So, you thought I was bein' mischievous earlier this evenin', did ya'?"

"Earlier at the club, you mean? Well, you did say something that caught me, somewhat, off guard. Then, when I realized what you had said, you were talking to Pop, and I didn't want to bring it up in front of him."

"Bring what up?"

"You know," she replied shyly.

"You mean, the 'm' word?"

"Yes." She nudged him in the ribs. "You said it, not me."

"I said it?"

"Yes!"

"Are you sure?"

"I'm going to punch you, fly boy!"

"Careful. You might break this..."

"Break what?"

Skip reached into one of the pockets of his flight suit and handed her a very small, dark blue, velvet box.

"Open it, and see."

Ahana smiled curiously, as she carefully opened the box. Even in the glow of the streetlights, a diamond refracts light very well.

"Oh my, William! I... I don't know what to say."

"Wait! I haven't asked you yet!" Skip took her hand, dropped to one knee, and continued, "Ahana, I want you to be mine in every way, not just my companion. I want you to be my wife." Ahana was beaming as he carefully placed the ring on her finger. "Will you marry me?"

"Yes! Yes! Oh, *Yes!*" She grabbed him around the neck, kissed him, and said, "I have prayed to Jesus, asking that one day we could marry, but I wasn't sure that you were ready. Never in my wildest dreams, did I think you would ask me now. Oh, William, I love you so..."

The couple walked around the base for a while that night, talking, dreaming, and planning. At one point, Skip asked, "Ahana, when you said you had prayed that we could marry someday, you said that you prayed to Jesus... I'm a little confused; I thought you were Jewish."

"We haven't talked about religion much, have we? I should have explained earlier, I am a Messianic Jew. We believe that Jesus is the Messiah and Savior. Since you're not aware of my beliefs, I can certainly understand your confusion."

"It sure puts a whole new spin on bein' a Christian. Do y'all consider yourselves Christians?"

"Not exactly. Let's just say, 'As for our house, we will follow the Lord.'"

"You are a true miracle for me, gorgeous. If there ever was a time in my life when I lost my faith, you have erased it forever."

***

Two days later, the Base One Formal Review Board met in its first public session.

"Attention! The room will come to order. Chairman Colonel John T. Bass will now begin the proceedings."

Colonel Bass then entered the large room and took his place in the center chair.

"Please be seated. I am Colonel John Theodore Bass, Chairman of this preliminary judicial board. During the past few weeks, we have accomplished a complete background check on every individual that is a former member of the terrorist group, Bushmaster. Not one of these people has been identified with crimes committed by Bushmaster, or any other terrorist organization for that matter. None has even received a negative security check. Frankly, we only know that they were associated with Bushmaster by the events that occurred after we lost contact with Pop Hackland over the Western Defense Zone. Before these events, if any of these people had applied individually for service with FFNA, we would have had no reason beyond their non-citizen status, not to accept their application. They have no criminal background. A lie detector test was included among the battery of interrogations that each of these people was required to pass. Each accepted the tests without hesitation. All passed.

"Thus, it has simply come down to a determination of their intentions. Why were they in the Bushmaster organization in the first place? Although that question was asked and answered during each interrogation, a public answer, provided for all to hear, is in order. However, it has been suggested that we base our decision, at least in part, on an evaluation of their political philosophies. I don't have to remind you that it is against the laws of the Constitutions of the United States and Canada to discriminate against an individual solely on the basis of their political affiliations.

"This is a most unusual situation. We are fighting for our survival. We have been saddled with the difficult task of considering the possible risk of terrorist infiltration with the offer of assistance from highly trained and capable warriors. A task, I might add, that we take deadly serious. We cannot tolerate spies within our ranks, but neither can we afford to turn away even one capable soldier.

"So, we have asked each person if they would swear allegiance to the United States, Canada, and the FFNA, and sign an oath to carry out the laws of the land and lawful orders dictated by their superiors. Each person answered affirmatively.

"Thus, I have given each individual the option of choice. These requests are now a matter of public record. All have applied for asylum, non-citizens have applied for citizenship, and all seek to join the FFNA. We have convened this preliminary judicial tribunal to consider these requests and to hear all arguments, public and private, for and against accepting these requests.

"We are obligated to treat each of these requests individually. However, since all of the applications are identical, the board has determined that we will make our recommendations consistent with a blanket request. Thus, the final decision will apply to all applications equally.

"Are there any objections to this decision?

"Very well, the decision stands. Preceding this tribunal, we requested questions and comments from the entire base population. The data was then gathered, compiled, and condensed into a number of specific questions. After these questions have been properly answered, if anyone has any comments or additional questions, you will be given the floor.

"Now, I must caution you to consider your comments and questions carefully today. We have received comments that are blatantly racist and discriminatory. The sources of these comments may well believe that their concerns are valid. But the truth is simply this: If we allowed opinions based on race, creed, national origin, and political affiliations to dictate the choosing of the individuals that protect our citizens from harm, we would not survive as a cohesive society for very long. Our forefathers, with the wisdom of experience, knew that if we were to survive as a republic, we must put aside our prejudice and hatred and base our laws upon the solid foundation of tolerance and equality. Upon this, our survival now most certainly depends.

"We will now begin the proceedings. Colonel Fronz, have your people determined who will act as the representative for the group?"

"Yes, sir, I have the honor of speaking for my people."

"Very well. Sergeant at Arms, please swear in Colonel Fronz."

"Sir, do you swear to tell the whole truth and nothing but the truth, so help you God?"

"I do."

"Please be seated, Colonel Fronz. State your full name and rank for the record."

"Albert Wilheim Fronz, Colonel, Air Force of the Republic of Germany, retired."

"Members of the committee will now ask the questions. After the question has been asked, you will have the floor. You may take as long to answer, as you need. Other questions and comments will not be allowed until you relinquish the floor. The first question, please."

"How did you come to belong to Red Death/Bushmaster, and why do you now choose to leave?"

"We are all volunteers. We joined because we each share the following basic beliefs and expectations: We have utopian expectations about how we think the world should be and could be. We believe in the individuality and freedom within the human spirit. We believe in true equality of the human condition and do not believe that one race or creed is superior to any other. The tools required to succeed in a particular thing are based on ability, desire, and drive, not ancestry.

"We believe that, given the opportunity, we could somehow make a difference and, at the very least, set the wheels in motion to make our world a better place in which to live.

"We believe that actions speak louder than words. Each of us, at some point in our lives, has fallen victim to rhetoric. Words were substituted for action when we asked for help, and we paid the price. That price was usually paid by losing loved ones or being physically or mentally abused, yet knowing for certain, that we could have been protected if actions had replaced words. While we do not condone violence, for the sake of violence, we know that action gets results. Sometimes, and unfortunately, the only action that will work is military force.

"I formed Red Death under the same precepts as those beliefs, offering a means to meet our expectations. When Raazmahd offered us an opportunity to join Bushmaster, he used deceit to achieve his goals. Unfortunately, we were not completely aware of Bushmaster's agenda until it was too late.

"It is hard to admit when you have made a catastrophic error in judgment, especially when you realize that you have willingly boarded a runaway train. We were terribly wrong, and it appeared as though we were trapped. Anyone who openly disagreed with Raazmahd, or suggested that they were considering leaving, would inevitably have an unfortunate, fatal accident. Or simply be murdered.

"I made a personal commitment to organize my people and anyone else who wanted to escape Raazmahd and find a way for each of us to accomplish that escape without sacrificing lives, if possible. Thank God, we were successful."

"Any comments or questions? Very well, next question."

"Do you, or any member of your organization believe in the holy war that the members of Bushmaster are fighting?"

Colonel Fronz laughed, then quickly regained his composure, "Please forgive me, I was not making light of your question. It is just that it strikes me as funny that you are so misinformed about General Raazmahd and Bushmaster. I will explain it this way:

"For the first six months after we joined Bushmaster, we remained at a compound in North Africa for what he referred to as indoctrination. Actually, we were being closely scrutinized. Each week, we would have a senior staff meeting, which always ended up being yet another opportunity for the general to boast of his plans for destroying the West. In one of these sessions, one of his senior commanders referred to the Jihad, the holy war. The general immediately stopped, glared at him, and asked, 'Did you just say Jihad? When have I ever mentioned Jihad?'

"Of course, the poor man was taken off guard and did not answer. The general rose from his place at the head of the conference table, went to the commander, spun him around in his chair, and screamed in the man's face, 'Never! Never! Never! This is no holy war. I spit on your Jihad! Naturally, Allah is on my side because Allah favors the mighty. Bushmaster is strong because I am strong. The leaders of the Islamic Jihad are fools! All they do is murder innocent people and gain nothing for it. I watched for years while al-Jihad and al-Qaeda postured and squawked, pissing away many fortunes on your stupid Jihad. All the while, Bushmaster was quietly stealing as much of their blood money as we could get. Now, either most of those fools have starved to death, or they have been killed. The rest of your pathetic jackals sit in their squalor, rattling their sabers, reading passages from the Quran and making references to the laws of Islam as if Allah actually cares who they are or what they do.

"'Zealous idiots like you follow these jackals, actually believing their bullshit, and together, the lot of you accomplishes nothing more than murdering innocent people for no profit! Fool, we are in this for the money! You have power because I have power. I have power because I am richer than Allah. And I intend to continue acquiring even more wealth by taking control of the West. I want it all... and I will have it!'

"The commander, growing visibly agitated, replied, 'But, your Highness, Allah dictates that we shun wealth. The West is the great Satan. The infidels must be cleansed!'

"The general replied, 'So, that is what you think? That is why you are here? That is what you believe all of this is about? You believe that I have dedicated my life to helping you and your kind wage a Jihad on our enemies?'

"'Yes, your Highness.'

"Then, with blinding speed, the general drew his sword and slit the poor man's throat, then grabbed him by his beard, looked him straight in the eyes, and said, 'I am not Muslim.'

"As we sat there in shock and disbelief, he shoved the dying man to the floor, looked around the room, waved his sword menacingly, and calmly asked, 'Anyone else wish to join the Jihad?'

"No, my friends, the general wages no holy war. I liken the general to Hitler or Stalin. He is a madman. His war is all about gaining territory, wealth, and power."

You could have heard a pin drop in the room. There was a long pause as the members of the board tried to comprehend the gravity of what they had just heard.

Then, Col. Bass cleared his throat and said, "Next question, please."

"Exactly what ties do you have to the United States, and why did you not make these requests before now?"

"Red Death was a covert organization formed as a joint venture by the CIA. As a young lieutenant in the Intelligence Division of the West German Air Force, U.S. intelligence agents approached me. They were tasked with the job of forming a clandestine unit based in Europe. I was asked to evaluate a proposal to form a group of specialists whose duties would be to carry out certain covert missions critical to the interests of the U.S.

"I was provided with a list of possible candidates and the criteria required for recruiting additional members. Financing was unlimited, but Red Death, as I chose to call my unit, could not use any weapons manufactured by the U.S.

"I was provided total protection toward my career in the German Air Force. I had an office, wore the uniform, and showed normal career progression. I operated the Red Death organization from that office. After I 'retired,' I moved our operation to a classified location. My duties were to carry out the orders given to me with the primary directive that Red Death, in no way and under no circumstances, could be tied to the U.S. It was under those conditions that I operated Red Death.

"However, in 1996, during an otherwise standard covert mission, the command and control that was being provided to us was suddenly terminated without warning. I had well over half of my people involved in various stages of an intense air-ground offensive. When our C&C was terminated, the tide of the battle turned against us. Before I could order a pullback, we lost seventy-six men and women and most of our resources.

"I received no explanation for the termination of support, and subsequently, communication with my contacts was suddenly cut off. We were summarily ignored. Unable to sustain my unit without any logistical or financial support, the remainder of my operatives was in imminent danger of being discovered and killed.

"It was at that point that General Raazmahd approached me, saying that he was well aware, but not vindictive, of our involvement with the U.S. He made a proposal that we join his newly formed organization that he called Bushmaster. Unable to make contact with any intelligence database outside of our own, we were unable to run a thorough check on Raazmahd. Despite being the son of the notorious Dasheed Raazmahd, the information that we were able to gather suggested that his goals were primarily financial gain. Although I had reservations about dealing with a criminal, on the other hand, much of the operations that my organization carried out had been criminal. Thus, I felt that he was not a severe threat. Unfortunately, we had been tricked, given false information, planted by Raazmahd's own organization.

"We were simply caught in a desperate situation, and despite our reputation as a ruthless terrorist group, we would not have survived without the finances provided by Raazmahd. If anyone had given us the opportunity to request asylum, we would have done so. But under the circumstances, thirty-six covert operatives, located in five different countries, cannot exactly go knocking on embassy doors and expect to be welcomed with open arms. Especially when, by official definition, we were terrorists."

"Any comments or questions? Very well, next question."

"Why did your group plant the nuclear weapon at the Boneyard?"

"We were completely unaware of that reprehensible act. I did not learn of it until recently. We are adamantly against the use of weapons of mass destruction and inhumane weapons, such as chemical and biological weapons."

"Any comments or questions? Very well, next question."

"Why did your pilots fire on our aircraft with apparent intentions to shoot them down?"

"We needed an influential member of your forces to come into our organization and get an unfiltered, firsthand look at our people and our situation. We could have attempted to kidnap someone, but there was a very high possibility of placing innocent people at risk. That option was unacceptable.

"We could not risk sending any form of communication for fear of discovery by the Bushmaster intelligence network. The option of approaching you with a white flag would be foolish, because we knew that you must consider the possibility that Raazmahd would not hesitate to use that tactic to expose you to attack. He has used that method before, and quite successfully. To shoot first and ask questions later is the only sure method of dealing with Bushmaster.

"I chose to make an attempt to bring a pilot into our base. I made that decision based on two things: first, a military pilot knows the risks involved with every mission. They are well trained and prepared to deal with those risks. Second, they would most likely come to us, so we could attempt a capture, or hijacking, with minimal risk to human life.

"Unfortunately, we were not able to surprise Major Blake and disable his F-16. Instead, in the first few seconds of the encounter, he initiated what I call a 'withdrawing attack.' While Major Blake was making what appeared to be a run to escape, he skillfully executed a series of deadly attacks, shooting down three of my pilots. When Major Blake's aircraft was hit, he failed to eject before it exploded. I sincerely regret the loss of Major Blake, and I would change that if I could.

"I believe that sufficiently answers the question, but I would like to make an additional comment."

"By all means, Colonel Fronz, you have the floor."

"From the outset of our adventure, starting with the decision to form Red Death, we knew and accepted the risks. Also, we did not hesitate to take the risks of leaving Bushmaster. Sometimes, it is difficult to know who your friends are. First, the people we had served and trusted abandoned us. Then, we were fooled again, finding ourselves serving the sinister purposes of a madman. We are not asking for sympathy or pity. We are only asking for the opportunity to correct our mistake.

"You have our complete life histories, and you know that not one of us comes to you as a criminal or with a sinister agenda. We want to fight for the principles in which we believe. Those principles are the same principles upon which both the American and Canadian governments were founded.

"All we ask is that you give us the opportunity to join you in your quest. Our goals are the same. We will proudly stand and willingly fight at your side."

"Any comments or questions? Very well, next question."

"Are you willing to follow through with the requests that you have made, to achieve citizenship and join the FFNA?"

"I have personally discussed these decisions with every member of my unit, and we are completely dedicated to those choices."

"Any comments or questions? Very well, the last question, please."

"Will you repeat and sign the solemn oath of duty that each member of the FFNA must sign?"

"The only answer to that question is 'yes.' On behalf of each one of us, I can say, unequivocally, yes."

"For the record, would you restate that, please?"

"Yes, each of us will proudly repeat and sign the FFNA oath of duty. We are honored to serve the FFNA."

"Any more questions or comments? Very well, Colonel Fronz, thank you for your candid and insightful answers and comments. You are now excused."

"Thank you, Colonel Bass and members of the board."

"Are there any final questions or comments? Very well, I hope that, by providing this opportunity, we have laid to rest any doubts about the intentions of these people.

"Ladies and gentlemen, thank you for your interest and participation. The board will now adjourn for deliberation. We will then forward our recommendations to General Grey and the Federal Judicial Committee for final disposition. This tribunal will reconvene in one week from today to announce the general's decision. This tribunal is now adjourned."

CHAPTER EIGHTEEN

Making Up for Past Mistakes

It was time to return to the task of getting Viper-7 operational. Pop had departed for Sandia Labs several days earlier to arrange to have the engines and the prototype flight computer transported to the Boneyard. Skip's job was to arrange fighter protection for the transport aircraft during the trip to the Boneyard. When dealing with technology of this type, security was imperative. Skip arranged a meeting with Colonel Bass and Major Cooper, now acting Chief of Base One Intelligence, while Lt. Col. Ron Taylor recuperated from his injuries.

"John T., Bud, I just wanted to touch base with you about the upcomin' trip to the Boneyard. I have asked Ahana to be my co-pilot. Since the security level on this project is so high, I wanted to check with you because I don't want anyone makin' an issue about her goin' along."

"We appreciate that, Skip, but I trust your judgment," Col. Bass said. "If you want to take your fiancée along, I don't have any reservations. How about you, Bud?"

"Well, I don't know. Is she stable? The lieutenant has taken on the impossible job of taking care of Skip; she may have lost her mind!"

Bud and Colonel Bass got a good laugh at Skip's expense.

"Very funny, guys, laugh it up. I didn't come in here to get abused, you know."

"I know, but you're so much fun to pick on," Bud said, still laughing.

"Well, I'd like to stay here and poke fun at Skip, but I've got a base to run. Ya'll have a good trip. I hope everything works as advertised. And, I want to see the Viper-7, just as soon as you can get it here."

"Thanks, John T. I'll sit her down right outside your door."

"I sure wish I was going with you, pal," Bud lamented.

"No doubt, we could use your help. But, I guess someone has to keep this intelligence stuff sorted out, and I can't think of anyone that can do it as good as you, 'cept maybe, Colonel Superman."

"I sure hope the boss returns to work soon; I'm ready to go flying."

"I have a feelin' we're gonna be doin' a bunch of that, real soon."

"I'm afraid you're right."

The next morning, Skip and Ahana spooled up a C-130 and headed for New Mexico. While there, Skip coordinated a flight of four F-15's to rendezvous with them, just after departure from New Mexico, en route to the Boneyard.

After take-off, ten minutes out of White Sands, Skip heard their call on the radio...

"Hauler One, Dagger flight, ten miles north, and have you in sight. We'll join up in about one minute."

"Roger, Dagger, this is Hauler One. Tally ho! Welcome aboard."

"Our pleasure, Hauler, thanks for the invite."

For the next hour, it was an uneventful flight. Aboard the C-130 were two of the new engines and a prototype of the new flight computer, various test equipment, and special tools for the engines. Also aboard were three engineers from the Sandia Labs test team and Pop Hackland.

Suddenly, one of the four F-15's went into afterburner and broke formation...

"Hauler, Dagger One, stand by, we're checking out a possible bogie."

Then, without warning, two of the F-15's dispensed chaff and magnesium flares. A split-second later, a missile streaked by, barely missing the C-130. Immediately, another F-15 rolled inverted and dove toward the ground.

"Whoa! Did you see that?" Pop exclaimed. "That was close!"

Just then, the radio erupted:

"Hauler, Dagger Three, hold your course. One and Two are on the bogie. We're still with you and have you covered."

"Thanks. I think our pucker factor just increased about 200 percent!"

"Stand by while we splash this idiot, then you can un-pucker."

A single Mig-31 had come up from below, attempting to shoot down the Herk before being detected by the F-15's. Unfortunately, for the Mig-31 pilot, Dagger Two detected the Mig's weapons radar, getting an indication of the direction of the threat on the Eagle's Electronic Countermeasures Display. The pilot had immediately pointed his aircraft in the direction of the threat. When the Mig's radar locked on, the Mig pilot fired, but the radar locked on Dagger Two. The targeting data from the Mig had already transferred to the missile's on-board radar, so the pilot of Dagger Two led the missile away from its intended target.

Dagger Two then called for backup, and Dagger One immediately responded...

"Two, One, I'm with you at 4 o'clock high."

"One, Two, he's going low! He's going low! Break left."

The Mig pilot was running south, getting on the deck, trying to become lost in the clutter of objects on the ground, and prevent the Eagle's weapons system from getting a lock. Dagger Two was on the Mig; Dagger One was flying in trail, watching Two's back.

"Two, One, I lost him. "

"One, Two, I'm on him. He's twelve o'clock low, five miles. I can't get a tone. He's right on the deck."

"Stay with 'em, Two."

"He's too deep in the clutter. I'm going lower."

Dagger Two dropped to thirty feet above the rolling terrain.

"Two, watch your altitude."

"I've got a tone! I've got a tone!"

"Smoke 'em!"

"Fox One. Fox One."

The AIM-7 Sparrow missile sprinted away from Dagger Two, and seconds later, the Mig disintegrated.

"Splash one Mig-31!"

"Good job, Two, good job. "

Minutes later, Daggers One and Two rejoined the flight. Dagger Two pulled ahead of the flight and completed a victory roll.

"Dagger, Hauler, thanks, guys. Glad we brought you along."

"Our pleasure."

"Glad we could help."

"While you were busy, I set up a pit stop. We link up with a tanker in about thirty minutes."

"We do appreciate that. Might get a bit thirsty later on."

Fortunately, the remainder of the flight was uneventful. Upon arrival at the Boneyard, Skip spoke with the pilot of Dagger One, "When you get back home, go directly to Bud Cooper and tell him that we have a security problem. Our route of flight from White Sands was not briefed prior to departure from Base One. I planned the route while we were at Sandia Labs. The only time that we discussed our route was when I called you on the Net to set up our in-flight rendezvous. Our call was encrypted, so that means that the only place the information could have been intercepted was in the ops room where you received the call."

"You may have something there," the pilot agreed, "we weren't painted by radar before the Mig attacked. It's a good bet he didn't just happen upon us. That smelled like an ambush. I'll relay the message."

"Good. Thanks again for ridin' shotgun. I owe you one. I was hauling some precious cargo."

"I understand your co-pilot is also your fiancée?"

"She's part of that precious cargo I was talking about. Pop was on board too, as well as two of the engineers from the Engine Design Team and one engineer from the flight computer Team, plus the new equipment for Viper-7."

"I think we should ask for a raise," the pilot joked.

"Hell, I'd back you up!"

Later that day, the four Eagles departed for Base One.

Before Skip introduced Ahana to his old friend, Big Sam Thomas, he warned her that Sam had a very serious hatred for terrorists.

"His family was killed in 1996 when a 747 was destroyed by a terrorist bomb. He's one of the best people I have ever known, truly a good guy, but he may be somewhat unfriendly toward you."

"If he is, I will understand. I have always considered bombing innocent civilians an act of cowardice."

"Perhaps you should tell him that if the opportunity presents itself."

"I will. Thank you for giving me the 'heads up' about Big Sam."

"I just don't want you to get hurt, not even your feelings."

"You are such a sweet man. You're spoiling me. You know that, don't you?"

"And I'm lovin' every minute of it!" Skip remarked and kissed her on the cheek.

Skip and Ahana went to the underground offices of the Boneyard, located in the area that was once home for the 41st Electronic

Countermeasures Squadron Headquarters, to arrange for off-loading the Viper engines and equipment. Pop was familiarizing the new arrivals with the facility and getting them set up in temporary quarters, so it was a good opportunity for Skip to find Big Sam. Big Sam was now spending all of his time refurbishing the OV-10E that he had pulled from storage. His duties of acting manager of the Boneyard had been relieved, upon the return of the manager.

Skip and Ahana found him in a small hangar on the far end of the flight line, completely engrossed in his work underneath the center avionics console, behind the pilot's seat. In order to reach it, he had to remove the rear seat, climb into the cockpit, and lie on the floor. Since there was little room for the big man to move, he had positioned a worktable as close as possible to the aircraft and would reach out periodically and feel around until he found the particular tool he needed.

Unable to resist such an opportunity, Skip crept up to the table and patiently waited for Sam to reach for another tool. It was difficult for them to keep from laughing because Sam was talking to the aircraft as he worked on it, and his comments were not necessarily pleasant.

Finally, he reached out, dropped a tool on the table, and began blindly feeling for another one. Skip watched carefully. Just before Sam would touch a tool, Skip would move it slightly.

"What the hell? I know I laid those tools right here," Sam exclaimed, tapping the table with his fingers. "What are they doing, walking around out there?"

At this point, they could barely contain their laughter, so Skip simply handed Sam one of the tools. Sam paused a moment, felt to determine if it was what he needed, then laid it down, and started the process over again. Skip immediately handed him another one, and this time, it must have felt right because he took the tool but then got very quiet. Knowing that Sam felt something just was not right, Skip grabbed two tools and held the tools up along the cockpit ledge, dancing them like puppets in a puppet show.

Then Sam exclaimed, "What in the bloody Hell?" and forgetting his position beneath the cockpit instrument panel, quickly rose up and pranged his head. At that point, Sam came up cursing and banging into everything, with Skip rolling on the hangar floor, laughing.

"I might have guessed it was you!" Sam declared, rubbing his head, "You're worse than my kid brother. Welcome back, you rascal."

"Hi, Sam. How have you been, pal?" Skip asked, still laughing.

"Fine, until a minute ago. Man, I thought I was losing it. I mean, when I start to see tools dancing... And, I think I've got a concussion. Am I bleeding?"

Ahana offered, "Here, let me have a look. No serious damage, just a little scratch."

"Thank you, Lieutenant... who are you?"

"I'm sorry," Skip said. "Sam, this is my fiancée, Lt. Ahana Cohen. Ahana, this is one of my oldest and best friends, Big Sam Thomas. He's also the best Bronco driver in the world."

"Now, I wouldn't go that far." Sam climbed out of the cockpit, smiled, and extended his hand to Ahana. "I'm please to meet you, Ahana. Well... fiancée. Congratulations! You actually *want* to marry this swamp rat?"

"Hey, now! Let's not plant any bad ideas in her pretty head. Ahana said 'yes' and accepted my ring. I'm almost positive that means she's made up her mind."

"Well, my dear, if he gets out of line, just let me know. Back when he was flying Cobras for me, I had to get his attention a few times, and I still remember how."

Glancing at Skip, she replied with a mother-like tone, "Thank you. I'll keep that in mind."

"I'm glad he's finally found a soul mate, but how will he ever support you? If I had you at home, I'd never leave the house!"

She blushed and said, "Thank you."

Skip put his arm around her waist and said, "Isn't she gorgeous, Sam? I am truly a lucky man." Then, he kissed her on the cheek. Ahana was blushing even more, and Skip could see the hint of green in her eyes.

"You love to make me blush, don't you?" she asked, smiling at him.

"Blushin' complements your beauty. That's one of the first things that I noticed about you. Remember?"

"Oh, yes. I will always remember that day."

"So, how did you two meet, anyway?"

"Well, ah, you're not gonna believe this," Skip said, hesitantly, "but, remember the Silver Mustang that I saw flyin' over Owl's Nest on the day that I bounced in Viper-6?"

"Yes, you told me the whole story."

"Ahana was flyin' the Mustang."

"You?" Sam looked at Ahana in surprise.

"Yes, it was me."

"You?"

She and Skip both nodded.

"You were flying the Mustang?" Sam's voice grew higher in pitch with each question.

"I said you wouldn't believe me, didn't I?"

"Just hold it right there. Don't tell me anything else. I'm going to get cleaned up, then we can go to the canteen, and you can tell me the whole sordid story."

"That's a deal," Skip said. "We'll see you there."

"Nice meeting you, Sam," Ahana said sweetly.

"I'm glad to meet you, too, Ahana. Welcome to the family."

As they were walking back to the main hangar, Ahana said, "Sam is nice. I like him. He seems to be very fond of you. Are you related?"

Skip chuckled, "No."

"But, he said, 'welcome to the family.'"

234

"We've been like family for a long time. He was my commander in Viet Nam. He was one of the first black men to command an Airborne Calvary Unit. We rotated back to the States and went to college together. He and his wife, Sarah, helped Holly and me when we were first married. We didn't have much money, so they would invite us over for dinner and take us along on picnics and stuff like that. They treated us just like their own kids. Sarah was really sweet. They had four kids, and I have never known a closer family."

"Where was Sam when the plane was bombed?" Ahana asked.

"They were goin' to meet him in Paris. I helped him through his ordeal, and he was there for me when I lost my family. He's closer to me than my own brother. That's why he referred to us as family."

"You never said anything about having a brother!" Ahana exclaimed, surprised.

"I'm sorry. I'm not tryin' to keep anything from you. Bobby and I haven't spoken in so long... I'm not even sure where he is now."

"You should find him. I miss my brother terribly. You owe it to your family to stay close, and besides, if I am to have a brother-in-law, I want to know him."

"For you, sweetheart, I will."

"Thank you."

"But don't get your hopes up, he could be anywhere, and he probably don't want to see me anyway."

"We'll see...," Ahana replied hopefully, and then asked, "William, do we have time to see the Viper before we meet Big Sam?"

"If we don't, we'll make time. I've been lookin' forward to showing you the Viper."

Ahana and Skip walked to the large hangar where the Viper project was underway. Inside, Pop and the rest of the team had already started to work. Skip told Ahana the history behind the Viper and gave her a close, inside look at the project...

"The Viper in your recon photo was the sixth model in a series of a highly modified McDonnell-Douglas/British Aerospace Engineering

AV-8B Harrier jump-jet. The avionics are the same, with the addition of a hybrid, voice-controlled computer, capable of flyin' the aircraft. The weapons systems are also similar to the Harrier.

"The engines, designated Afterburning Turbofan Experimental, or ABTX-6 and 6A, are similar to the engines used in your Tornado, with the addition of thrust vectoring Hot Nozzles for hover. Since the Harrier engine is larger than the ABTX-6, we were able to squeeze two into the engine nacelle after we widened it a bit. The engines burn JP-8 and operate as a standard after-burnin', turbofan engine in forward thrust mode. Pop added a Thrust Assist modification. The Thrust Assist uses a highly volatile mixture of alcohol and hydrogen, mixed and channeled through a small, super-conductive particle accelerator, which creates a form of plasma. The plasma is directed into the afterburner chamber, where it acts like an oxidizer, augmenting the afterburner output. The result is a 35 percent power increase over a similar after-burning engine, using approximately the same quantities of fuel. Maximum duration of afterburner, with Thrust Assist, is about thirty seconds, due to the heat stress on the engine nozzle."

"This technology is so exotic," Ahana commented. "Are there any problems peculiar to this engine?"

"The main problem with the ATBX-6 is a tendency to flame out if Thrust Assist is not tuned properly. As chief Viper scientist and engine design engineer, Pop tunes the engines. That way, I can blame everything on him!"

Ahana laughed, but Pop heard him too.

"I heard that, you jackass!" Pop shot back, "You won't be able to blame *me* for flameouts on the 'A' series; we've solved that problem."

"I think I should talk a little bit quieter," Skip whispered. "Because we've had such a great success with the Harrier, we wanted to stay with the AV-8, if possible. Fortunately, there were several good ones here in the Boneyard to choose from, so for Seven, we picked the trainer version. The added fuselage length gave us more room for avionics, and it has the extra seat, which might come in handy. There's nothing like an extra pair of eyes in the cockpit when you're in a hostile environment."

"I definitely agree with that."

"The primary avionics modification, as I mentioned, is a highly sophisticated flight computer. The Model I was great, but Model II is gonna be something else all together. Four Hyper-Clock microprocessors, designed by NASA engineers, drive it. The Hyper-Clock chip, which is sealed in liquid helium, runs at a clock speed of 12 gigahertz. The memory consists of 100 gigabytes of RAM, 100 gigabytes of ROM, and 6 900-gigabyte virtual hard drives. Since it has no movin' parts, access time is almost instantaneous. The memory modules, designed by the Jet Propulsion Lab, are in liquid helium too. Most of the software is Pop's. He just loves to talk to computers."

"This is so fascinating. The technology is so advanced; it's almost like working on the space program. I would love to work on this project with you."

"I think I could arrange that."

"Really? Do you think Colonel Bass would approve me to join your project?" Ahana asked, hopefully.

"I don't see why not. He's very excited about the Viper-7, for some reason. I'm not sure why. He has held the purse strings on the last four we've built. This one is gonna be the best, by far."

"I might have known you would be here." Big Sam's voice came from across the hangar.

"We just couldn't stay away," Skip replied.

"I've spent a few hours hanging around here, myself."

"I want to thank you for keeping the project going while we were gone. You and your team did a fantastic job."

"I appreciated the opportunity; it's not often one gets to take a Harrier apart and put it back together with the parts in different places," Sam chuckled.

"Well, how about that drink you mentioned?"

"Let's go, man, I am d-r-y," Sam said.

"Yo, Pop. Let's call it a day. We'll meet you and the crew at the canteen," Skip called.

Pop waved a wrench and replied, "See you there."

That evening, the entire crew visited and got acquainted. After Sam learned Ahana had been a member of Bushmaster, he remained gracious and kind, not showing the least bit of resentment toward her. Sam trusted Skip. If Skip cared enough for Ahana to ask her to be his wife, that was more than enough for Sam.

Time seemed to fly as work on the Viper-7 progressed. Before they realized, it was time to return to Base One and hear the final decision on the requests of Colonel Fronz and his people. Skip and Ahana planned to depart the Boneyard early, arriving at Base One in time to be present for the announcement.

Unable to sleep, Ahana dressed, went to the flight line and began preparing the big Herk for flight. By the time Skip arrived, the preflight was done, and everything was ready to go.

"Good mornin', gorgeous," Skip said as he kissed Ahana. "Couldn't sleep?"

"No…" Ahana sighed, slid her arms around his waist, and laid her head on his shoulder.

"Ahana, it'll be okay, you'll see."

She did not reply, but just held on to Skip a little tighter.

Ahana was preoccupied and did not say much during the flight back to Base One. When they arrived, the general's Gulfstream was already parked on the ramp, so they went directly to the base theater to wait for the meeting to convene.

General Grey had come to announce the decision to the tribunal, in person. Lewis M. Grey was not one to let a memo or an obscure order speak for him.

"This tribunal will come to order. Colonel John T. Bass, presiding."

"Good morning. This has been a very stressful week for all of us, and I will not delay these proceedings any longer. Ladies and gentlemen, our commander, General Grey."

"Greetings, folks. It's good to be back at Base One. I don't get out here nearly as much as I should. I'm glad to see that everyone has taken such an interest in this tribunal. I believe this decision will have far-reaching effects on our organization for years to come.

"Upon reviewing each of the files, I feel that I should clarify some of the details, of which some of you may not be aware. A grave injustice has been done to these people.

"The operation that caused the unnecessary loss of so many of the Red Death personnel was, in fact, an attempt to rid us of the Red Death organization. It was deemed, by a select few, that their services were no longer needed, and the U.S. simply turned their backs on these people. That decision is one of the two most reprehensible acts that I have witnessed in my career. The other happened many years earlier, and it seems that some of us are unable to learn from our mistakes.

"Once before, we turned our backs on friends and allies. Because of that cowardly act, the Vietcong slaughtered the Montagnards, the native hill people of Vietnam.

"It was not in my power to prevent that travesty back then, nor was I able to prevent the injustice previously done to the Red Death organization, but I have that authority today...

"To the former members of Red Death, for your loyal service and sacrifice in support of the security of the U.S., NATO, and our allies, as of this date, by the authority of a federal judicial review board, and by order of the joint chiefs of the Free Forces of North America, I, Lewis M. Grey, chairman of the joint chiefs, hereby grant each applicant full and unconditional asylum. Furthermore, all applications for U.S.-Canadian citizenship have been granted. From the moment you take the oath, you will become members of the Free Forces of North America, assigned to the North American Air Defense Agency at your present rank. Congratulations, and welcome aboard!"

General Grey turned, saluted Colonel Fronz, and then shook his hand. The entire room stood, applauding and yelling in delight and support.

As Ahana and Skip were hugging, he said, "See, gorgeous, I told you everything would be okay, didn't I?"

Aftermath I: The Fight For Survival

Base One had never seen a celebration like the one that occurred that night.

CHAPTER NINETEEN

Into The Snake Pit

It had been two months since the announcement to accept the former Bushmaster members' applications to the FFNA. Base personnel were busy merging the new personnel into various positions throughout the base. Some training and indoctrination was necessary, but for the most part, the new workers were found to be well trained and highly competent.

Christmas was only two weeks away, and everyone was in cheerful holiday spirits. Late one afternoon at the Base One Headquarters building, there was suddenly a great deal of noise, and the wind blew furiously, stirring up a great deal of dust. Everyone in the area came to see what the source of the commotion was.

Colonel Bass came out of his office to find a stealth black, modified Harrier, with 'Viper-7' painted on the nose, sitting in the courtyard directly in front of the building. As Skip and Ahana climbed out of the aircraft, Colonel Bass greeted them, "I know I said I wanted to see it right away, but I don't mind going to the flight line!"

"Like it?" Ahana asked.

"It's beautiful!" Colonel Bass replied as he inspected the sinister looking jet.

"It performs better than it looks," Skip offered. "Wanna go for a spin around the patch?"

"Maybe later. Right now, it's late, and we have some celebrating to do!"

Stepping in between Skip and Ahana, he put his arms around them and escorted them into his office. He poured them a drink and said, "Skip, Ahana, welcome back. I want to thank you for doin' such a great job on the Viper-7 Project. I have been following the project closely, and the reports have all been very favorable. I've been keepin' this under my hat, but just as you suspected, there's a reason that I have taken such a special interest in this project. General Grey wants to equip all of the remote outposts with a Viper. That means I'll need you both on this project to oversee the modification of eight more AV-8's. The general wants six deployed and two available as back-up."

"That is wonderful," Ahana said, taking Skip's hand. "I wanted to work with Skip on the project, but I had no idea it would be this big."

"Fantastic! I'm glad the Viper's finally made an impression on someone with some political power," Skip said.

"Actually, the general had wanted this project to grow for some time, but the resources were not available. Apparently, the same people that were responsible for the loss of the Red Death personnel were also sitting on a big pot of funds. Thanks to information provided to us by Lieutenant Reshond, the general was able to expose a nasty little shell game being played with those funds. I understand the ones involved will be out of circulation for about twenty years or so," the colonel said proudly.

"That is good news, John T.," Skip said. "It's about time the good guys won one for a change."

"Now that I've delivered the good news, it's time to get out of here and go do some real celebrating. The annual Christmas party is tonight. Ya'll go get out of those flight suits, and I'll see you at the O-Club at twenty hundred hours. Just bring yourselves; everything else is on me, General Grey, and Base One."

The Club was filled with cheerful people that night. Candy Simms was finally out of the hospital, and a very attentive Ron Taylor was tending to her like a newborn baby. Candy was in a wheelchair, so

Ahana kept her company, giving Ron and Skip a chance to mix and socialize.

"Ahana, I am so happy that you and Skip found each other. He had been alone for much too long," Candy said.

"I have searched all of my life for William. We desperately needed each other. He has made me so happy. Sometimes, I'm afraid I'm going to wake up and find that all of this was just a really vivid dream."

"Well, I can assure you, it's no dream; this cast and these bandages are all too real!"

Ahana laughed, "I'm sorry, I don't mean to laugh at your misery."

"Forget it. You should have seen Ron laughing at me the first time he saw me trying to scratch an itch inside this cast."

"Have you known each other long?"

"We met about two years ago, here at Base One. I fell head over heels for that guy the instant I saw him, and for the next eight months, he didn't say two words to me. At first, I thought he was a snob, but then I realized he's just really shy. He is very intelligent and focused. It was hard to pry him away from his duties. When I finally got him to notice me and had a chance to tell him how I felt, the change in him was amazing. I really don't think anyone had ever told him that they loved him or that he's wonderful. Since then, he has become the most loving, caring person that I have ever known.

"He is spoiling me too. I keep reminding myself that I am a self-sufficient woman, capable of doing anything I choose. But honestly, I would be content to let Ron take care of me for the rest of my life."

"I know exactly what you mean, dear. I feel the same way about William."

"Speaking of self-sufficient women, Ahana, how did you become a fighter pilot?"

"When I was fifteen, I was living with a family that had graciously taken me in as one of their own children. My guardians were also members of Red Death. Papa Joe, as I call him, is a pilot.

"I have always loved airplanes and flying. I discussed learning to fly with my real papa, and he said, 'Maybe one day.' But, he was very traditional, and I'm sure he hoped that I would grow out of it. But, I didn't. I dreamed of flying and would constantly pretend that I was flying my own airplane.

"Two weeks before I turned sixteen, Papa Joe asked me what I wanted for my birthday. He told me not to answer right away, but to think about it because my sixteenth birthday was very special.

"I didn't even hesitate. I said, 'I want to learn to fly.' Papa Joe didn't hesitate either; that very day, I was flying! He put me in the left seat of Cessna 172. Then, he got the plane off the ground and said, 'It's all yours.' I had never been so excited and exhilarated. I felt like a bird. I flew until the fuel was low; we landed, fueled it up, and took off again. That time, I did the take-off. I flew until the fuel was low again and made a fairly good landing. Papa Joe told me that if he had known that I had such a talent for flying, he would have had me in the air when I was fourteen.

"We flew every day after that, and on my birthday, Papa Joe handed me the keys to the plane and said, 'You're ready to solo. Go have a great sixteenth birthday!' And I have been flying ever since."

"That's a lovely story. Your guardians are really wonderful people."

"Yes, they are. So is everyone I have met here. I'm so glad you came tonight;I'm really enjoying our talk."

"I was a little hesitant to come, but I didn't let on to Ron. He is so happy that I'm out of the hospital that he actually wanted to come tonight. Now, I'm glad I did. I'm really happy to get to know you, Ahana."

"Me, too, Candy. Oh, here they come."

As Ron and Skip were approaching the girls, Skip stopped Ron and said, "Now ain't that two of the most beautiful creatures you have ever seen in your life?"

"Yes, sir, that is precisely correct. We are two of the luckiest men on earth."

"If you're trying to flatter us, it's working!" Candy said, laughing.

"Let's take these two beautiful ladies out of this noisy place and go somewhere a little quieter," Ron suggested. "What do you think, ladies?"

"We're with you, gentlemen," Ahana replied.

For the remainder of the evening and into the early morning hours, the couples shared each other's company and began a friendship that would last a lifetime.

***

Several thousand miles away, in Northern Algeria, a sinister plot was being finalized. If it succeeded, His Majesty Za-Ved Raazmahd, as he now called himself, was certain this would be the last Christmas that the Free Forces of North America would celebrate.

The leader of Bushmaster had amassed a formidable force of planes, pilots, and ground forces. The plan was to launch an overwhelming, mass attack on all six NAADA bases, plus the governmental headquarters of the U.S. and Canada.

His majesty was certain that upon seeing the FFNA take such a fatal blow, the remaining troops and allies would certainly surrender, especially since the object of the attacks would be to detonate a thermonuclear weapon over each of the eight primary targets. FFNA troops around the world would have no leadership and nowhere to run. The date set for the attack was January 1. Ten days and counting...

Day Ten

At Base One, Pop was on the Net, communicating with the Viper project engineers at White Sands. The subject of conversation was the eight new Vipers. Pop had the idea of data linking the flight computers together, so when the Vipers were in flight, the processors could communicate with each other via a radio link. There were a number of advantages with this idea, but primarily, the pilots could communicate via the digital data link without transmitting voice over the radio, and the weapons systems computers could simultaneously share data. The tactical advantages of a system of this type are considerable.

Aftermath I: The Fight For Survival

When the Reaper hit, most communications capabilities were lost. Debris in the atmosphere negated any use of communications satellites and caused severe interference with all forms of transmitted communications. Only buried copper and fiber optics cables were unaffected. Unfortunately, the communication cables only linked voice and data transmission systems into the SatCom Network. It was necessary to abandon the satellites and return to an older technology. More cables installed by the FFNA supplemented the existing microwave links, undersea cables, and existing copper cables. Additional radio links were established using ships as relay stations. The entire system was utilized to form a worldwide communications network called the Net.

Among the people that were utilizing the Net, was a bright young astrophysics engineer and his wife, also an astrophysicist. From their home in Arkansas, Tim and Elizabeth Tenslick were able to provide a number of valuable technical services to a rapidly growing number of clients. Two of these clients were Sandia Labs and the White Sands Test Range in New Mexico.

Bushmaster had tapped into the Net and had been intercepting confidential data for an unknown length of time. With the assistance of Lieutenant Reshond and Pop Hackland, the Tenslicks had developed an encryption method that the Bushmaster hackers were having a lot of trouble breaking.

A data line tap is a very delicate thing. To intercept data, you must tie a sophisticated computer to that line. Thus, your system is also exposed to intruders, and you could become the victim of your own evil.

Tim and Elizabeth had worldwide contacts on the Net. During one of their log-on attempts, their data was inadvertently intercepted and routed into the Bushmaster mainframe. Suddenly, they were in the heart of a system that was just begging to be investigated. They figured, since they had been dragged in the door, it was on open invitation to visit for a while.

Within a span of fifteen minutes, they had intimate knowledge of the Bushmaster organization and the most startling information of all—the plans to launch a thermonuclear attack on North America.

They immediately made a copy of the information and backed out of the system, carefully erasing signs of ever being there.

Pop was online, exchanging comments with one of the engineers at White Sands, when suddenly, Tim and Elizabeth broke into their link....

"Sorry for the invasion, folks, but there is no time for courtesy. Stand by to download an encrypted file. Caution! This file is top secret!"

Seconds later, the file was sent to Pop and White Sands, simultaneously.

"Upload was successful. Good luck, and may God help us all. This link is now terminated."

Once again, Tim and Elizabeth had been in the right place at the right time. Now, it was up to the FFNA and NAADA.

Day Nine

The continuing effort to find the Bushmaster bases was intensified worldwide. It was essential to determine the direction from which the attacks would originate. Due to the loss of Colonel Fronz's unit to the FFNA, Raazmahd was forced, at great expense, to relocate every secret base.

When moving in haste, it is not always possible to remain unseen. Intelligence Agency contacts were providing information from around the world. Bit by bit, the data was assembled, and percentage of probability numbers assigned to various locations over the globe. Each location, depending on its probability percentage, was assigned a reconnaissance priority. Verification would have to be done covertly, by insertion and reconnaissance teams, in hopes that Raazmahd would not move the bases again before they could be destroyed.

Day Eight

It was Christmas day. Unfortunately, it was a typical workday for most NAADA personnel. It had been ordered that every FFNA base keep all pilots on alert and fly no missions, unless necessary. It was essential that the bases maintain the highest possible alert level, in the event that Raazmahd had intentionally planted the information and actually planned to attack at an earlier date.

Four Airborne Warning Alert and Control System (AWACS) birds were flying low altitude orbits, in an attempt to supplement the few operational, but semi-reliable, long-range radar systems. AWACS was slightly more reliable, with severely limited range, due to the low altitude at which they were forced to fly. Normally, it was not advantageous to keep the surveillance birds in the air.

Ron Taylor, Bud Cooper, Lt. Sharee Reshond, and several of the Base One intelligence personnel were hot on the trail of one or more spies, possibly Bushmaster operatives, working on the base. Ron Taylor wanted these people badly. It was suspected that they were responsible for the bombing that killed sixteen base personnel and injured thirty, including Ron and Candy. The only thing Ron had not decided was how he could kill them in cold blood, with his bare hands, without being court-martialed for the crime. Actually, it should be considered serving justice.

The trail led to a technician who had replaced a phone in the Briefing Room of the Operations Building six months earlier. The phone was pulled, checked, and discovered to have an ingenious bug built into the circuitry and virtually undetectable. While the call was in progress, the bug re-transmitted the conversation over the same line on an inaudible sub-carrier. The Secure Voice Telephone Encryption System (SVTES) only scrambled the audio frequencies. The sub-carrier, containing digitized audio, passed right through the SVTES. It would then be intercepted somewhere within the system and converted back to audible voice. A confidential phone call made on the bugged system might as well have taken place on a crowded city bus.

A technician had also been working on a phone in the cafeteria, the morning of the bombing, but no one could recall his description. All of the base civil engineering personnel had checked out clean. There was no record of any telephone repair requests to CE, for the Briefing Room or the cafeteria, despite the fact that repair requests had apparently been sent out.

In an attempt to lure the spy into the open, Intelligence had set up a false, high priority telephone repair request from one of the base Intelligence offices. The hope was that the spy would not be able to resist the opportunity to plant a bug in the heart of Base One Intelligence.

As expected, a technician showed up, complaining about being called out on Christmas Day, and went about his work. The room was being watched via hidden cameras, but the identity of the technician could not be determined. One thing was certain; he did not work for Base One Civil Engineering.

He finished and reported to the secretary that the phone was back in service, "Ma'am, the phone is working, so I'm out of here."

"What was the problem?" she asked.

"The phone was bad and had to be replaced," he replied.

"I hope you don't mind, but before you go, I need to make sure it's fixed... boss' orders," she told him, intentionally stalling.

"Well, I am on overtime, so I guess I can afford it," he nervously joked and went with the secretary, waiting while she checked out the new phone.

"Hmm, that's funny…," she commented.

"What's that, ma'am?"

"The Ops Briefing Room has a phone just like this one."

"Yea, this model is fairly popular."

"But the one in the Briefing Room had some extra circuitry installed," she commented.

The repairman suddenly got very anxious and moved closer to the door, "Really? I can't imagine what that would be for...," he replied nervously.

"My boss said it was used to bug the phone," she informed bluntly.

At that, he quickly turned to run, but only made one step through the doorway where Ron Taylor was already waiting for him. A well-placed right hook sent him flying back into the room. He was out cold before he landed at the secretary's feet.

She looked at the spy, then at Ron, and said, "Wow! Nice shot, boss!"

It was not hard to get him to talk. Apparently, he wanted to live. Actually, he had to write down his statement after he was released from the emergency room. Ron had shattered the man's jaw, and it was wired shut.

At first, he refused to tell them anything. Then, he was told that the fiancée of the officer who had shattered his jaw had been severely injured by the bomb. Further, if he did not confess, they would put him in a room alone with that officer and lock the door. It is truly amazing what the right incentive will do for some people. As it turned out, he was just full of information and willing to tell them everything that he knew.

He was one of three spies on base, and the information that he provided allowed security to apprehend his two accomplices. They had detonated the first bomb and had planted six more bombs, intending to disable the Base Defense System just prior to the attack.

This informative spy unknowingly gave the residents of Base One a gracious Christmas present—their security and, possibly, their lives.

***

Ahana and Skip had spent an uneventful day in the Pilots Ready Room, waiting twelve hours for an alert that never came. The waiting was tense and stressful. The pilots did not necessarily want to be attacked and thrown into an air battle, but given the choice between the inevitable battle and this infernal waiting, they would choose to fight.

The couple's trip home after work included a stop at the gym to work off some of the stress collected during the day. Skip still teased Ahana about the workouts, telling her that she was secretly trying to kill him, but actually, since they had been working out together for the last few months, he could now easily keep up with her. She returned his teasing, telling him that if he really worked hard, she might let him try keeping up with her when she started her full workout program, instead of the light duty version they were presently doing.

Finally, at home, they relaxed on the sofa, listening to Amy Grant's *Home for Christmas* CD. Ahana was lying with her head on Skip's lap, holding his hand against her cheek, but her mind was far away.

"Whatcha thinkin' about, gorgeous?"

"Us... Our lives... I'm just so overwhelmed by it all. I spent last Christmas at the Hidden Base, unsure if I would live to see another Christmas. Now, just a year later, I am an American citizen, an FFNA pilot, engaged to the man of my dreams, and happier than I ever thought I could be... William, pinch me. If this is a dream, I want to know!"

Skip kissed her ever so tenderly and said, "You're not dreamin'; you're in my arms, and we're in our home, spendin' our first Christmas together. This is not a dream; this is a dream come true."

"William, thank you for making this Christmas so wonderful for me."

"Thank you, gorgeous. Up to now, this has been the worst time of year for me. I'd usually crawl into a bottle until it was over. Just hangin' around the Ready Room with you today was a joy for me. Right now, holdin' you, I'm in heaven."

"Merry Christmas, my love."

"Merry Christmas, gorgeous."

Day Seven

This day, Raazmahd began positioning his aircraft and troops for the attack. One by one, over the next three days, Bushmaster fighter and transport aircraft were taken to secret, strategic locations within striking range of their designated targets.

On day six, in an unusual series of unrelated incidents, several aircraft were spotted, either en route or just after take-off. The reports of seeing the aircraft all ended up on the desk of a data specialist working for MI-5, British Intelligence. At first, she did not make the connection, but the reports caught her attention, so she laid them aside, intending to review them later.

That night, as she slept, she suddenly awoke with a start. Realizing the significance of the unrelated sightings, she immediately called the station chief.

"Sir, I'm sorry for waking you at this hour, but I must get a message to the Americans."

"Miss Penninghton, do you have any idea what time it is?"

"No, sir, let me check."

"Wait!"

"It's 03:47 local, sir."

"Thank you, but it was a rhetorical question, dear. I was just trying to suggest that we should be sleeping at this bloody hour!"

"I am really sorry, sir, but I must get a message to the Americans as soon as possible."

"This can't wait just a few hours... it will be morning soon."

"I'm afraid not, sir."

"Very well, meet me at the office in fifteen minutes, and this better be critically important."

"Yes, sir, fifteen minutes."

Miss Penninghton was waiting for the station chief when he arrived. They went directly to her desk, and she showed him the information that she felt was so urgent. The unrelated aircraft sightings that had caught her attention were all SU-27 Flankers. There were six in all, and they had to be six separate aircraft because of the sighting locations.

What troubled Miss Penninghton were the various locations and a report that she had seen several weeks earlier, about six Flankers reported stolen from an air base in Russia. She went to the map and marked each of the sighting locations and the reported direction of flight. Then, she drew a line from the nearest suspected or verified Bushmaster base, to the sighting mark, and continued the line in the reported direction of flight. Four of the six lines intersected Central America.

"Sir, I believe these sightings to be of Bushmaster aircraft, relocating to take part in the attack on the FFNA."

"Excellent work, Miss Penninghton, but very troubling news for the Americans. Those SU-27's have a deadly capability and could have a devastating affect on the air battle. We must notify the FFNA immediately."

"Thank you, sir."

"It's the American pilots that should be thanking *you*, for possibly saving their lives."

Miss Penninghton had been right. In several warehouses located near a secret airstrip, east of Bogota, Columbia, four Flankers were parked, safely out of sight and waiting for the command to strike. Two more Flankers, plus other aircraft, were on the way.

Day Five

Early that morning, the daily briefing included an urgent report...

"Good morning, pilots. It's day five and counting. So far, none of the other bases has seen or heard a thing. However, an MI-5 station chief sent us an urgent message last night that I must pass on to you. There is a preponderance of evidence that Bushmaster has just moved six SU-27 Flankers into Central America."

The room uttered a groan in unison, with a few expletives added.

"I know this is not good news, but we have a solid numerical advantage, plus, we know when they will attack. Just stay sharp, and we will come out on top. This concludes your briefing for day five."

What troubled the pilots was any number of advantages the SU-27 held over every multi-role fighter currently flying. It was as maneuverable as most smaller fighters, despite their higher speed, and considerably more powerful than any fighter. Because of the power-to-weight ratio and advanced flight controls, it was the most maneuverable fighter at slow speeds. Only VTOL type aircraft could outdo the SU-27 at slow speeds.

Then, there were the weapons. The Flanker's advanced avionics, including the most powerful look-down/shoot-down weapons radar, made it virtually impossible to engage the big fighter head-on. Even coming in at twelve o'clock low, the sophisticated radar would pick you out of the ground clutter. That also meant that it was not possible to get low and evade a Flanker if he got on your six.

To make it worse, the SU-27's radar systems shared data while in flight. The radar data from each weapons system was continuously transmitted to the others. During an air battle, the systems not only sorted out the most lethal threat to each aircraft, but potential targets were prioritized in the same manner. It was the equivalent of flying against an armed AWACS bird, except when fired upon, the thing could separate into multiple units and fly off in any number of different directions.

When Pop heard the news, he immediately went to Captain Vanya Petrovich, "Captain, I didn't want to bother you with this, but right now, I need your help."

"How can I help you, Mr. Hackland?"

"Please, call me Pop, and I need your help because I need you to go with me to Russia."

"What?"

"Yes, Russia. I need to see your father, immediately."

"My father? Why?"

"Because he owes me a really big favor. I need to borrow something from him."

"This is a very unusual request. Are you sure you want me to go with you? My father has not spoken to me in five years."

"I realize that you two disagree, but this situation goes beyond personal problems; it may be a matter of our survival. Please, I need your help."

Vanya reluctantly agreed, so the next stop was at Colonel Bass's office and a call to General Grey. Once the approval had been accomplished, Pop arranged to borrow the general's Gulfstream G-4.

The G-4, one of the fastest executive jets ever made, could also make the trip to Russia without refueling. And time was critical…

Day Four

Skip lay beside his love, watching her sleep. It was one of Skip's favorite pastimes. Ahana quietly stirred awake and smiled.

"Why do you love an old, stinky fart like me?"

Ahana chuckled, "*That* was a graphic question!"

"Sorry. But, a legitimate one, nevertheless."

"Quite correct." Ahana sat up and stretched, then faced Skip and crossed her legs. "Hmmm, let's see, why do I love you? I don't know why."

"You don't know?"

"Not really. I believe that our ability to love is a gift from God, but I'm not totally certain why we fall in love with a particular person. I know all of the emotions associated with my love for you."

"Oh? What are they?"

"The first is envy."

"Envy? You envy me?"

"Well, not you, I envy your first wife. You were Holly's before you were mine. I wish that you and I could have been together all of our lives. I would like to have been your first and only love."

Skip was silent.

Ahana leaned forward and kissed him softly. "My love, I'm sorry. It is very painful."

"I still miss her sometimes."

"And you still love her, too." Again, Skip was silent. "Don't be ashamed of that. I understand. In some ways, your love for Holly has made our relationship better. A happy marriage takes hard work. You had a happy marriage, which means you learned how to make it work. And now, I get the benefits of your experience."

"I never thought of it that way, but I guess you're right."

"Next is jealousy. I'm jealous of your career. I don't resent it; after all, flying is my career too. But flying takes us away from each other, and I don't ever want to be away from you."

"I can certainly understand that."

"Next is hate."

"Hate! You hate me?"

"In a very small way. Although you have no control over it, I hate you for not coming into my life when I was younger. I wish I could have met you when I was sixteen."

"I'll bet you were somethin' to see at sixteen. Of course, I was twenty-two and full of myself. I would have gone for you like a kid to candy, been convicted of having sex with a minor, and if your dad hadn't killed me first, I would have lost my wings, been dishonorably discharged from the Army, and sent to Leavenworth."

"Oh. I didn't consider all of that. Well, it is a nice fantasy, anyway."

"Boy, howdy, is it a nice fantasy! But, getting away from the dirty old man in me... what's next?"

Ahaha replied in a provocative tone, "Lust."

"Ooh, I like that one."

"I thought you might. I have a lust for you that goes right to the core of my being. You are so handsome and sexy. I have never been more attracted to anyone in my life."

"Thank you for the compliments. I lust for you for the same reasons." Skip slowly guided his hand up her thigh. "Let's lust together!"

Ahana slapped his hand, "I'm not finished answering your question!"

Skip quickly withdrew his hand, "Oh. Fair enough, please continue."

"Next is want. I have never wanted anyone the way that I want you. I want you inside me."

"I was just about to take care of that when you slapped my hand."

Ahana boinked him on the head, "Not _that_, gutter-brain! I'm talking about you, the spiritual being. Our souls, intertwined."

Skip rubbed his head, "Oh, sorry. I see. Somehow that sounds so erotic."

"Oh, it is! We would share our passions and emotions as one being."

"Hey! That means I could experience your multiple orgasms!"

Boink!

"Ow!"

"Gutter-brain. Be serious. Now, let's see, where was I?"

Skip rubbed his head again and replied, "Well, so far you've covered knots on my head, envy, jealousy, hate, lust, and want."

Ahana rubbed his head lovingly and kissed the hurt, "Quite right. Next is need. I need you more than the air I breathe. I have never known an emotion like this one. I now truly understand addiction. I need you and must have you."

"That almost sounds like a medical condition."

"In a way, I suppose it is. I was the substance abuse counselor for our organization. Occasionally, a patient would ask me how I could help them when I could not possibly understand how it felt to be addicted. I would reply with the standard psychobabble, saying that I was trained to help, and if they would be honest with me about their feelings, together we could beat their addiction. But now, I could say that I understand completely. I like the feeling, and I don't ever want to stop. My addiction doesn't harm me, but now I truly understand their point of view."

Skip smiled deviously, "I'm not a doctor, but I've seen one on TV. I can prescribe an antidote for your addiction."

"Well, for your information, mister, I am a doctor, and I already know that my antidote is right here." As Ahana said that, she lightly touched Skip on the tip of his nose.

"Yep, your prescription is 'on the nose,' all right. But, I don't believe you said, 'psychobabble.'"

"Well, a lot of what I was taught was psychobabble. The first thing that I learned was to throw most of the writings of Dr. Freud and Dr. Spock in the trash. Honestly, I'm not even sure why I chose psychology. It is just that I have always been fascinated by human emotions."

"So, what's next?"

"Like. I like you very, very much."

"Well, of course you do; you love me."

"As obvious as it might seem on the surface, people can actually be in love, but not like each other. I know that sounds like an oxymoron, but it is true. Maybe they feel compelled to care for their mate, to protect them from harm. Often their love is only an extension of their lust. They want this person, so it is assumed that what they feel is love. Sometimes, the emotions run deeper than that. An obligation of the heart, staying together, unsure why, but all the while disliking the one they love. It is the source of so many dysfunctional marriages and most divorces. Love can turn quickly to hate if you don't like your mate very much."

"You know, I can't think of anything that I dislike about you, but I did dislike things about Holly. I just accepted 'em and let it go. How do you know all this stuff? You sure are a smart lady."

"Thank you, you're sweet. It comes from having spent hundreds and hundreds of hours doing research on human emotions. It's a part of the process to become a psychologist."

"Them sheepskins don't come easy, do they?"

"It's 'those' sheepskins. And no, they do not... And now, my last emotion—love." Ahana smiled, "I saved the best for last."

She then grew somewhat serious, "I have never known love like this. I loved my family, but not like I love you. I have been infatuated with others, but infatuation doesn't even come close to what I feel for you. I love you with all of my being. I love you more than life itself."

"I love you, too, gorgeous."

Ahana smiled and kissed him. "Tell me why."

Skip studied her for a moment, "A little while ago, I think I could've given you lots of reasons, but now, I don't know. I know that you are the most beautiful creature I have ever seen. And sexy, well, that goes without saying. You literally radiate sex."

Ahana smiled and blushed. Skip kissed her hand and continued, "And I know, without a doubt, that I love you."

Skip contemplated Ahana for a moment. "More than anything else, I love you, because you are you."

"That is good enough for me." Ahana crawled on top of Skip and kissed him deeply, then ran her hand across his chest and down his belly, "Now," she whispered, "let's stop talking…"

***

A recon team had been dropped into Central America to verify the suspected locations. Orders were given that if a base was discovered, the team was to be extracted as soon as possible. It was essential that Bushmaster have no knowledge of the recon team's presence; otherwise, they were certain to move again.

In Central America, Recon Team Three called in an urgent report and a request to continue surveillance. There was a high probability that Raazmahd, himself, had been spotted at the base, and the team commander believed that this base could be the command center for the attack.

Plans were immediately put into action to take the battle to the enemy. If Raazmahd could be taken out, it might take a lot of the momentum out of the plan to attack North America. In fact, if he continued to be as predictable as in the past, all commands for the attack would originate directly from him.

A mission had to be planned to attack the Central American base. Within the hour, the mission briefing, conducted by Colonel Bass, was in progress. "The mission will be a non-standard four-stage scenario. Recon, then recon with ground attack, second wave ground attack, and finally, damage assessment recon. Due to the time critical nature, this will be a daylight attack. Plus, since Bushmaster's Stealth Net is virtually invisible to sensors, daylight will give us a visual advantage.

"There is one variable. In the event of an unverifiable target from the initial recon, a second recon will be necessary. We cannot afford to waste resources, and we must verify that Raazmahd can be taken out. We might not get another shot at this. We must do it right the first time. This is the mission layout;

"We will stage out of the Boneyard. Command and Control will be provided by an E-2 from the Nimitz. The Hawkeye will rendezvous en route. F-16's, Daggers One and Two, Eagles Two and Three, Mig-29's, Tigers One and Two, will provide cover to and from the target area.

"Point recon will be Phantom 7463, call sign Brighteye One. Tornado GR-1, call sign Brighteye Two, will fly in trail. The RF-4, 7455, call sign Relay, will run an orbit forty miles north of the target. Relay's job is to datalink FLIR and video data from Brighteye One to Hawkeye.

"If photo analysis aboard Hawkeye can spot the target from the real-time data, F-18's, Red One and Red Two, also flying in trail with Brighteye One, will launch Laser Mavericks on the target designated by Brighteye One's Pave Tack laser.

"The next wave of attack, carried out by A-6's from the Nimitz, will hit the target with a combination of ordnance. Brighteye One will also be included in this run for laser target designation. Brighteyes One and Two will then make a final recon sweep over the target for damage assessment.

"I cannot overemphasize the importance of reconnaissance. We must have solid verification of total target destruction. If photo analysis cannot spot the target, Brighteyes One and Two will each make a second recon pass, and all birds will return to the Boneyard. There, we will do another photo analysis, a quick turnaround, and possibly make another run at the target.

"We don't have much data to go on right now. Recon Team Three attempted to send a digital photo of the target, but interference was too high, and the photo is useless. Physical description has Raazmahd's command center located in a stronghold on the west side of a range of mountains ninety miles south of Bogota, Columbia. We will not have any ground-coordinated forward air control support. Recon Team Three was in danger of being discovered and was extracted.

"People, this is day four. We are takin' a big risk and leaving Base One with minimum air defense. Let's get in, take this guy out, and get back home alive. Departure for the Boneyard is in one hour. Good luck, pilots."

By the time all of the aircraft arrived at the Boneyard, were refueled, and armed, it was afternoon. The best time to attack Raazmahd's base would be at night. This would help negate the possibility of an air defense response to the attack. A daytime attack was far more dangerous. However, no air defense aircraft had been seen in the area. Ground anti-aircraft defenses were reported to be light, and the Recon team confirmed that the only access to the area, by aircraft, was a short, rough dirt strip, near the base of the mountain. Thus, it was unlikely weapons had been off-loaded by heavy transports; however, equipment could have been air dropped.

Just before take-off, Ahana and Skip found a private spot to talk. "Ahana, I know that I said I had no right to ask you to stop flyin', but right now, I'm havin' second thoughts. I'm worried that you're gonna get hurt, and I don't know how to deal with it."

"I'm feeling the same way about you, my love. This is our first combat mission together, and it's only natural to be concerned... Hey, fly boy, I'll be fine! We are both experienced combat pilots. We will do the best job we can, take him out, and get out of there. I'll see you back here after the mission, okay?"

Suddenly, the alert sounded for all pilots to mount up. There was only time for one long kiss, and then, it was time to go.

As the aircraft taxied out for take-off, Bud spotted Capt. Jake Spade in Eagle Two.

"How did that jerk manage to get on this mission?"

"Beats me. I'd just as soon that he stayed at home."

Skip lined the Phantom up on the runway. On his right wing, Ahana pulled the Tornado into position for take-off. Skip looked at her

261

and flashed the universal "I love you" sign with his hand. She returned his gesture by blowing him a kiss.

"Okay, boys and girls, let's go make some noise!" Skip said over the radio, rolled on the power of the Phantom's mighty J-79 engines, released the brakes, and lit the afterburners.

The aircraft departed in waves. Recon birds first, attack birds next, and finally, the aircraft assigned as air cover departed last. One hour into the flight, the E-2 Hawkeye and a flight of six A-6E Intruders joined the group. The nineteen aircraft continued on to the target.

One hundred miles north, Hawkeye dropped out of the flight and set up an orbit for command and control. Then, fifty miles out, Relay, the RF-4, 7455, dropped out and set up an orbit, waiting to receive the data link from Brighteye One to be relayed to Hawkeye.

As the flight reached ten miles from target, the Litton Passive Detection System aboard the Hawkeye picked up activity to the east. Instantly, the radar turned on and began tracking the bogies.

"All birds, all birds, Hawkeye. Four bogies out of the nest, 100 miles, inbound at zero nine five degrees, angels one zero. Dagger and Tiger, break left, and intercept."

"Hawkeye, Dagger One. Copy, we're on our way. Dagger Two and Tiger, check."

"Dagger Two, with you."

"Tiger One, on your six."

"Two, check."

"Dagger, Hawkeye. Bogies now at your 12 o'clock, fifty miles, angels one five."

"Hawkeye, Dagger One. I've got 'em painted." (The weapons radar has them on screen, but the pilot does not have a visual.)

"Daggers One, Two. I've got two Mig-25's in sight at 11 o'clock, angels one niner. They're trying to get by us!"

"Dagger, Hawkeye. Confirm. The bogies have split up. One and Two are at 11 o'clock, ten miles, angels two zero. Three and Four are at one o'clock, ten miles, angels one eight."

"Dagger One has them now. Dagger Two, break left on three. One, two, break!"

"Hawkeye, Tiger One. We have two Migs at two o'clock, angels one eight. We're on them. Tiger One has a lock. Fox One! Fox One!"

The Mig-29 launches a radar guided missile. Then, seconds later…

"Splash Bogie! Splash Bogie!"

"Tiger One, Hawkeye. Confirm, Bogie. Three is down. Nice job."

"Brighteye One, Hawkeye. Target is five miles at twelve o'clock."

"Roger, five miles dead ahead, Brighteye One."

"Tiger Two has Bogie Four!"

"Stay with him, Two, Tiger One is with you."

"Dagger Two, I've got Bogie One."

Then, only seconds later.

"Hawkeye, Dagger One. Bogie Two got by me! He's going for Dagger Two! Dagger Two, break left! Break left!"

Just as Dagger Two broke left, Bogie Two fired a heat-seeking missile, but it locked on Bogie One. Seconds later, Bogie One exploded.

"Hawkeye, Dagger One. Bogie Two splashed his own man! He splashed Bogie One!"

"Confirm, Bogie One is down… good job, Bogie Two!"

"Hawkeye, Dagger One. Bogie Two is going for Brighteye One!"

"Brighteye One, Hawkeye. Bogie Two is twenty miles at 8 o'clock, angels one three. Eagle Three, break left, and intercept."

"Hawkeye, Eagle Three. I'm on the way."

"Brighteye Flight, Hawkeye. Break hard right! Break hard right!"

As the combat controller from Hawkeye transmitted the warning, the Electronic Warfare Sensor on the Phantom's front console sent warning tones to the headsets and lit up the display like a Christmas tree. Skip dispensed chaff and called to his flight, "Brighteye Flight, break right on three. One, two, break!"

Just as they turned, a radar-guided missile fired from Bogie Two streaked past, barely missing Brighteye One.

Bud exclaimed, "Damn! I felt the heat from that one!"

"Brighteye Flight, Hawkeye. Your present heading is three five zero. Turn left, and come to one six five. Target will be twelve o'clock, eight miles."

"Hawkeye, Brighteye. Copy, turn to 165."

Just as Skip initiated the turn, Bogie Two got past Eagle Three and made a run for Brighteye Two.

"Eagles Two, Three. Bogie Two got past me! He's going for Brighteye Two. Take 'em out! Take 'em out!

Captain Jake Spade, flying Eagle Two, saw Bogie Two and moved to cut him off. Too close to fire a missile, he opened up with his F-16's 20-mm cannon, but the Mig pilot pressed his attack. Spade continued firing his cannon, turning hard to come head-on with the Mig-25. The Mig pilot fired a heatseeker at Ahana's Tornado. Spade saw it leave the rail and adjusted his turn to put his F-16 directly in the line with the missile.

Eagle Three realized what Eagle Two was doing and screamed over the radio, "Eagle Two! Punch out! Punch out! Punch out!"

A fraction of a second later, the missile hit Eagle Two's fuselage dead center and the F-16 exploded in a bright flash. Less than a second after that, the Mig pilot, amazed at what he had just witnessed, failed to realize that the F-16 had stopped his missile directly in his flight path, and before he could react, flew his Mig-25 directly into the ball of flaming debris and exploded.

"Jesus! Skip, did you see that?"

"No, but I heard it. Spade had time to punch out, didn't he?"

"Yes! It would have been close, but he had time. Why did he do that?"

"I don't know, pal, but he probably just saved Ahana's life."

Amazed, Bud continued to watch as the debris from Spade's F-16 and the Mig-25 scattered and fell, "Why did he do that...?"

"Brighteye, Hawkeye. You're two miles and cleared for the target. Bogie Two is down; Tiger has Bogie Four on the run."

"Copy. Cleared for the target."

As the target approached, Bud began searching the area with the FLIR. Just before they reached the mountain, Ahana turned all of the GR-1's cameras on. As they overflew the Bushmaster base, Bud could see nothing worthwhile on his video monitor, so he contacted Hawkeye. "Hawkeye, Brighteye One. Do you have video?"

"Brighteye One, Hawkeye. We have video, negative target. Repeat, negative target."

Bud spoke to Skip, "I hope this isn't a wild goose chase."

"Considerin' this reception committee we're gettin', I'd be willing to bet he's in there somewhere. That damn Stealth Net is just too good."

Just then, anti-aircraft guns began firing, and several shoulder-fired missiles were launched. The EW Systems in each aircraft again came alive. A series of incendiary flares were launched; the heat-seeking missiles locked onto the flares and exploded harmlessly. The flak bursts made for a bumpy ride, but caused no damage.

"Brighteye, Hawkeye. No joy on the target. Turn to three four five, and set up for another recon over the target area."

The Command and Control Officers aboard Hawkeye vectored the recon birds for a second run over the target. This pass was made at a slightly different angle, to get more recon data for study. Just as the flight of four turned inbound for the target, they again encountered heavy ground fire.

"Hawkeye, Brighteye One. We've got heavy triple-A just west of the target.

"Brighteye, Hawkeye, confirm. Illuminate targets at will."

Bud locked the FLIR onto one of the anti-aircraft positions and fired the Pave Tack Laser Target Designator.

"Red One and Red Two, Brighteye One. Target is painted, fire!"

"Copy, Brighteye, Red One has a lock, Fox Three."

"Red Two has lock, Fox Three."

Two laser maverick missiles dropped from the F-18's and sprinted toward the target, followed seconds later by two bright flashes and several secondary flashes.

Bud saw the hit on the FLIR video and confirmed, "Red Flight, Brighteye. Good hit. Good hit."

Just then, a series of close proximity flak explosions rocked the Phantom.

Suddenly, Ahana frantically called on the radio, "Brighteye One, Brighteye Two. I'm hit! I'm hit!"

One of the triple-A rounds had scored a direct hit on Ahana's Tornado and taken out the right engine.

"Ahana, can you stay with me?"

"Negative. I've lost number two and losing power on number one. I'm going down!"

"Brighteye Two, Hawkeye. The only available landing site is the dirt strip at the base of the mountain at your two o'clock. Can you make it there?"

"I'm looking, Hawkeye. I've got it, Hawkeye, I'll try it."

"Brighteye Two, Hawkeye. Copy you will try for the strip. Heads up for hostiles in the immediate area. Take cover as soon as possible. Intruders will hit the triple-A emplacements in two minutes."

"Brighteye Two copies. Ask the Intruders not to drop one in my lap, please."

"Brighteye Two, Intruder Flight. Ma'am, mark your position with smoke. Repeat, mark your position with smoke. We'll do our best to keep you safe."

"Thanks, Intruder, I'm a little busy right now, Two out."

"Good luck, ma'am."

"Ahana, I'm right with you. Hang in there, gorgeous."

"Hawkeye, Brighteye One. I'm following Two in."

"Brighteye One, Hawkeye. Negative, negative. Return to base, return to base. Red One and Red Two, stay with Brighteye Two as long as you can."

"Hawkeye, Red One. We're already with her."

"Hawkeye copies, Report Two's final ground position."

"Will do."

William, I'm okay, love, just get the recon tapes back home."

"Keep your head down! I'll be back for you, don't worry."

Skip pushed the throttles forward and turned the Phantom to the north.

"Damn it! I should've never let her come on this goddamn mission!"

"She earned the right to be here, partner. She knew the risks. Don't worry, Ahana can take care of herself."

"You might as well be tellin' me I can step out on the wing."

"We'll get her out, pal. Just hang in there."

On the radio, they heard the report from Red One.

"Hawkeye, Red One. Brighteye Two is down. She is out of the aircraft and has taken cover about two hundred yards south of the crash site. We see her smoke marker. We have the hostiles pinned down."

"Red One, Hawkeye copies. Good job. Thank you."

"Intruder, Hawkeye. Report smoke from downed pilot, and attack at will."

"Hawkeye, Intruder. We have the smoke. Let's see if we can thin out a few."

The trip back to the Boneyard required one mid-air refueling. The other pilots let Skip hit the tanker first. When the Phantom had taken on enough fuel to get back, Skip called release, dropped away from the tanker, and went into afterburner.

It was dark by the time they landed at the Boneyard. Hawkeye had relayed a rescue call, and a C-130 was already en route, carrying Insertion Team Three to rescue Ahana. Big Sam had his OV-10 configured with external tanks, plus internal stores, and was standing by as Skip parked the Phantom.

Sam greeted Skip as he stepped onto the ramp, "I heard the rescue call, and when I learned it was for your lady, prepped the Bronco."

"You're a good friend, Sam."

"I knew you would probably steal a bird to get back down there; I was just trying to keep you out of jail."

"Like I said, you're a good friend, Sam."

"Skip, I'll stay with the recon tapes and maybe we can find something that will help us get that bastard. You get Ahana, and get out of there, okay?" Bud said.

"We'll see ya, pal," Skip replied as he headed for the Bronco.

As Big Sam and Skip departed for Columbia, neither one had any idea how they were going to find and rescue Ahana.

As the target area came into sight, plumes of smoke could be seen coming from various locations around the base of the mountain. Sign that the Intruders had left their usual mark.

Suddenly the radio came alive...

"South bound aircraft, Hawkeye. You are entering a hostile area. Identify."

James A. Graves, Jr.

"Hello Hawkeye. This is Bronco One out of the Boneyard. Squawking IFF. We are inbound to assist the downed pilot."

"Roger, Bronco One. We have you. You're cleared to target area. The airstrip is clear, but not secured. We have personnel on the ground. Use caution; hostiles are in the area. Land at your own risk."

"Hawkeye, Bronco. Thanks for the warning."

Sam put the Bronco down on the dirt strip near the wreckage of the GR-1 and taxied into the surrounding jungle.

"Sam, if I'm not back in a couple of hours, you get your ass outta here."

"I'm not leaving without you; just watch your back, son. Find your lady, and we'll all get the hell outta here!" Sam pulled an M-16 out of the back of the OV-10 and headed into the jungle to find a secluded spot to keep watch.

Skip went to pickup Ahana's trail from the point where she exited the crashed Tornado. She had managed to set the GR-1 on the runway, but the right main landing gear collapsed and spun the aircraft off the strip and into the jungle. Picking up her tracks, he followed them to a spot about two hundred yards south of the Tornado, just as the pilot of Red One had reported. The mountain stronghold was across the runway, approximately three hundred yards from where Skip stood.

He was trying to find were she had gone from there when someone grabbed him from behind....

"Identify!"

"Scott, Base One pilot!"

The man released Skip and stepped back.

"Jesus Christ!" Skip spun around, breathless, "You just about gave me a heart attack!"

"Sorry, sir, I saw you land and didn't know whose side you're on. We didn't expect any assistance. I'm Sergeant Allen Brownlind."

"Well, you've got it, Sarge. I'm your assistance. Have you seen Lieutenant Cohen?"

269

"Negative, sir. We believe she has been taken prisoner. We've been looking for a way into the stronghold."

"Tell you what, why don't I show you the way?"

"You know where the entrance is?"

"No, but they'll have to take me in the same way they took Ahana. You just get us the hell out of there, okay?"

"It sounds pretty risky..."

"You have a better idea?"

"No, sir, I don't."

"Well, just hide and watch... and don't call me sir, I'm Skip"

"Yes, sir... ah, okay, Skip."

Skip made his way back toward the Tornado, and then crossed the runway, moving from cover to cover, acting as though he was making his way to a particular destination near the base of the mountain. Suddenly, two Bushmaster guards stepped out of a stand of large shrubs, directly in front of him. Moments later, he was taken down a short path, through a small stone doorway, and along a tortuous, winding trail up the mountain.

Sergeant Brownlind had watched with field glasses as Skip was taken prisoner and marked the location. Within fifteen minutes, the team was assembled and ready to make their move.

Skip had been hustled along a winding trail up the mountainside, to an elevation of about five hundred feet. There, another stone door was moved, and they entered a long winding tunnel. Approximately two hundred feet into the tunnel, after several twists and turns, they began climbing again. Various ladders and crude steps led to a large series of interconnecting rooms and caves. Skip was brought into one of the rooms and thrown at the feet of Raazmahd himself.

"Nice place," Skip commented, sarcastically.

The guard nearest Skip kicked him and said, "You will not speak unless his majesty addresses you."

"His majesty? Congratulations on your promotion."

The guard kicked him again and started to hit him with the butt of his AK-47 when Raazmahd spoke, "Stop. Don't kill him yet. He has an interesting irreverence about him. I like his attitude. It shows he has fire in his character. I admire that. Stand up. Tell me, who are you, and why are you here?"

Skip stood up and brushed himself off. "William Scott. I'm lookin' for a pilot that you shot down."

"Ah! You are the designer and pilot of the Viper aircraft. This is quite an honor. I have been thinking of adding just such an aircraft to my inventory."

"They're not for sale. What about my pilot?"

"I was not planning to buy them. And *your* pilot? I was not aware you were quite so high in your organization."

"It was a figure of speech. The pilot is certainly not *yours*."

"On the contrary, Mr. Scott, she is in fact, *my* pilot. She has simply returned to me."

"Not very, by God, likely!"

The guard nearest Skip stepped toward him and raised the butt of his weapon to strike, but Raazmahd simply held up his hand.

"Now, now, Mr. Scott...temper, temper. Losing your temper is a sign of weakness. You must learn to control your emotions. Let your mind rule your body. You cannot seek happiness; happiness is the way."

"*You* are a fruitcake!"

The sheik's eyes flared. "Simple fool! You will find out who and what I am in just two days. You can wait that long to die. Take him away!"

Below, at the base of the stronghold, Team Three had neutralized the guards at the entrance and were preparing to begin their ascent.

The Bushmaster guards threw Skip into a dark cave and slammed the steel door closed behind him. The room was pitch dark. He was unable to see anything. Realizing that the guards had only taken his side arm and survival knife, but did not search him, he remembered his small 9 mm pistol that he carried in Vietnam and commented aloud, "Well, Einstein, this is a real good time to leave your little nine mil at home!"

Just as he was retrieving a phosphorescent light stick from his survival vest, he heard a faint moan in the darkness nearby.

"Ahana?" Skip whispered and quickly activated the light stick. The room filled with a bright green glow. In the corner of the room, he spotted Ahana.

"Ahana!" He quickly went to her, checked her pulse, and carefully cradled her head with his left arm. Slowly, she regained consciousness.

At first, she tried to resist him, but Skip pressed his cheek against hers and whispered, "Gorgeous! Gorgeous, it's me. It's me. I'm here. I'm here to take you home!"

She smiled weakly and whispered, "Oh, William… I didn't think I would ever see you again…" and started crying.

"Hush, hush," Skip reassured her as he kissed her tenderly. "It's okay now, my love, I'm with you. Hey, gorgeous, I told you I'd be back, didn't I?"

Ahana tried to reach up to touch his face, but she was too weak to lift her arm. Skip gently lifted her hand and pressed her palm against his cheek. Then, he retrieved a small packet of drinking water from his flight suit and gave Ahana as much as she could drink. He checked her carefully for injuries and discovered a poorly bandaged injury on her left thigh. As he removed the bandage, Skip realized that the cut was jagged and deep. It was only then that he noticed that she was lying in a very large pool of blood.

Quickly placing her feet higher than her head, he then placed his survival vest over her upper body. Ahana was in shock from loss of blood, and he almost panicked as the thought flashed in his mind that she could die.

As he applied a new bandage to her wound, he commented, "Thank God I still have my first-aid pack. I wasn't even searched. These guards have got to be some of the dumbest bastards I've ever seen!"

Ahana laughed weakly at his comment and agreed, "Yes, I have that impression too."

Skip was relieved that she was coherent and prayed that was a sign that she would be okay.

"We're gettin' outta here," he said, matter-of-factly, and went to the door to see if he could force it open. "We've got an Insertion Team on the ground. Just hang on… I'll have you back home before you know it."

The door, made from a piece of scrap steel plate, covered an opening not quite waist high. As he tried to force it open, he discovered that a chain secured it to an eyelet imbedded into the stone wall.

Skip listened carefully at the door. In a very short time, he heard the sound of distant gunfire. He had been waiting for that opportunity. He then moved to the far side of the cave and made a run at the door, hitting it full-force with his right shoulder. The impact rattled the chain loudly and jarred him backwards, but the door did not budge.

Skip turned toward Ahana. "Damn! I hope the guards didn't hear that."

Holding his right shoulder lower than his left, his right arm dangling, he continued, "I think I almost knocked it off its hinges… my shoulder that is, that damn door didn't move an inch!"

Ahana tried to laugh, but she was too weak. Skip backed up with renewed urgency and hit the door again. This time it gave way, sending him tumbling out into the corridor. The sound of the door hitting the rock wall reverberated down the tunnel.

A guard heard the noise and came around the corner just as Skip was getting up. The guard kicked him under the chin, sending Skip sprawling backwards; he then bounced off the rock wall and hit the hard rock floor. The guard lunged, trying to hit him in the face with the butt of his AK-47, but Skip quickly rolled and tried to get to his feet when the guard connected with the rifle butt across the top of Skip's left shoulder, sending him down again.

Skip crouched on elbows and knees, his left arm throbbing and going numb. Determined to save Ahana, he concentrated, trying to regain his strength, hoping to anticipate the guard and outmaneuver him. All the while praying that the guard would not lose interest in this cat-and-mouse fight and simply shoot him.

Watching carefully, the guard kicked him lightly in the ribs, checking for a reaction. The guard spoke something in Arabic, and then moved directly in front of Skip, almost straddling his head, and raised the butt of his rifle, planning to inflict a final, fatal blow. Skip summoned all of his strength and swung a powerful right upper cut to the guard's groin. Gasping and groaning, the guard dropped his rifle and collapsed to his knees, holding his crotch.

Skip immediately grabbed the guard's knife. "You shoulda shot me." He then slit the guard's throat, took his side arm, and went back into the cell.

"Thank the Lord," Ahana whispered weakly. "I thought you would be killed."

"Did you catch what that guard said?"

"Yes, he said, 'You are a dead man.'"

"Hmm. I feel pretty damn good for a dead man!"

"You look pretty good too."

"Thanks."

Skip kissed Ahana and gently lifted her into his arms, then headed for the room where he had last seen Raazmahd.

In the corridor, he surprised and shot two more guards. Upon reaching the room where Raazmahd had been, he found it empty. His highness had already fled. Skip spotted a picture of Raazmahd on the wall and placed one round between his eyes. Then, he carefully made his way down the long passageways and ladders, carrying his lady to safety.

Near the entrance to the network of tunnels, the Insertion Team and the Bushmaster Guards were locked in an intense firefight. Skip carefully laid Ahana down in a protected spot, crawled to where one of the guards had fallen, and took the guard's AK-47. He reloaded with a full double-banana clip and opened up on the unsuspecting guards

from behind. Within thirty seconds, the team had secured the entrance, and the young sergeant came through the door.

"What kept you, Sarge?" Skip asked, as he went for Ahana.

"We were just waiting for you to run 'em out to us."

"You know, I'm beginning to like you."

"The feeling's mutual, sir...ah, mister."

"Skip. I'm called Skip."

"Okay, Skip, you can call me Ghost," he said and offered Skip his hand, then turned and yelled an order, "Get a litter up here! On the double!"

"Nice to meet you, Ghost. And thanks."

"My pleasure, Skip."

When they got to the base of the mountain, the remaining Bushmaster guards were trying to pin down the Insertion Team at the entrance. The sergeant tossed a smoke marker grenade, then grabbed his radio and called for help.

"Hawkeye, Little Boy. I've got some unfriendlys just west of the runway, across from the red smoke. We need a sweep, ASAP."

"Little Boy, Hawkeye. Stand by."

Moments later, two A-6E Intruders rolled in, laying down gunfire. As they grew closer to the area where the guards were concentrated, each Intruder dropped two napalm canisters. Instantly, a wall of fire erupted from the jellied gasoline, and the incoming fire ceased. The Insertion Team then spread out and started mopping up.

From the far end of the runway, Big Sam brought the OV-10 toward their location. Moments later, they were in the air, on the way back home.

"Hawkeye, Bronco. Pilot has been rescued. She is injured and has lost a large amount of blood. Blood type is B negative. Please advise Nimitz, we are en route."

"Bronco, Hawkeye. Copy rescued pilot needs B negative. Medics will be standing by."

"Thank you, Hawkeye. Thank you."

"Glad to help. Hawkeye, out."

As Big Sam put the Bronco down on the flight deck of the Nimitz, the medical team was already on deck. They immediately began work on Ahana, where she lay in the cargo hold of the Bronco.

The attending physician spoke to Skip, "As I feared, her blood pressure is too low, and we don't have enough B negative blood. She has gone into deep shock. I have a medivac flight to Base One standing by." The doctor pointed to an S-3 Transport, already spooled up and waiting. "My trauma team will accompany you and keep the lieutenant stable. The Base One trauma team has been notified to stand by. Good luck."

Big Sam said his farewell as Skip boarded the jet, "My prayers are with her, old friend."

Ahana did not come around again during the trip.

At Base One Hospital, hours passed as Skip anxiously waited while the trauma teams from Base One and the Nimitz worked to save her life. Finally, Doctor Jack Rightson came out to find Skip.

"How is she?"

"Well, Skip, she has lapsed into a mild coma due to blood loss. We were unable to find any severe head injuries, but she has suffered some internal injuries, a deep laceration to her left thigh, and she has lost a tremendous amount of blood and body fluids. Right now, we have her stabilized, and we're trying to get whole blood into her system. She has taken six units of blood so far and may need more. Thank God, we had an adequate supply. The next twelve hours will be the most critical. You should know, the first aid that you administered kept her from slipping into a deeper coma and enabled the Nimitz trauma team to keep her stabilized until they arrived here."

"Jack, was she...? Did they...?"

"No, she shows no signs of being molested or sexually abused in any way whatsoever. She has some cuts and severe bruises on her face, upper body, and pelvic area, but those injuries were probably caused by the crash."

"Can I see her?"

"Certainly, she's in ICU, right this way."

Skip stayed by Ahana's side. He held her hand, gently kissed her lips, and stroked her face. He fell asleep sitting by her bed, holding her palm against his cheek.

As Ahana's body slowly absorbed the whole blood and fluids that it needed, her vital signs gradually grew stronger. Finally, the intravenous fluids were taken away.

During the night, the nurses managed to get Skip on the bed with Ahana. As he slept there beside her, holding her palm against his face, Ahana opened her eyes and found her loving William. She smiled, pulled the covers over them, gave him a very gentle kiss, and fell sound asleep.

CHAPTER TWENTY

Target Neutralized

Day Two

Two days had already passed. When the report from the Insertion Team reached Base One, all aircraft had been recalled home.

That morning, the mission debrief was not a happy occasion...

"Well, pilots, we failed to make the mission objective. We managed to do some damage to Bushmaster. The Insertion Team verified the target was a temporary command center. The general, Raazmahd himself, was there but managed, yet again, to escape. The facility has been destroyed. We took out four Migs, a large number of anti-aircraft guns and thirty-eight Bushmaster guards.

"We lost Captain Spade, one F-16, and the GR-1A. Thanks to Skip Scott, Big Sam Thomas, the First Force Insertion Team, and air support from the Nimitz, Lieutenant Cohen is back home. Overnight, her condition improved from critical to guarded.

"All in all, we came out of this licking our wounds and thankful it wasn't worse. We can only hope we get a chance to erase this one from the books. But for now, it is back to twelve-hour shifts, pulling alert stand-by. Hurry up, and wait. It's day two, people. Keep sharp. I want to thank everyone for your brave efforts. Dismissed."

***

The red morning sun peaked through the window of the Intensive Care Unit, and the smell of coffee drifted about, as the staff began their morning duties.

Ahana was awake, watching her hero sleeping beside her. As she gently traced the curve of his face, he slowly opened his eyes.

"Good morning, fly boy," she whispered and smiled. "You have the most beautiful blue eyes I have ever seen."

Skip gently took her hand, kissed the inside of her wrist, and placed her palm against his cheek, "Hello, gorgeous, I was so afraid I had lost you."

Then, he kissed her lips, softly and passionately.

"All right, you two love birds," Dr. Rightson said as he came in the room, "We'll have none of that! Well, young lady, you have made astounding progress during the last twenty-four hours. Thanks to you, I was actually able to get a couple of hours sleep. How are you feeling this morning?"

"Like I was run over by a truck!"

"Actually, that's a good sign. In fact, I think you can be moved out of ICU and into a private room. Maybe we can even find you two a double bed. How does that sound?"

"Wonderful," Ahana said, looking at Skip.

Just then, a nurse brought Skip a cup of coffee.

"Bless your sweet heart," Skip exclaimed.

"That coffee smells so good," Ahana commented.

"You even have an appetite!" the Doctor observed. "I may have to run you out of here earlier than I had planned. I don't see why you can't have anything you like, including coffee."

Skip helped Ahana sit up, arranged the pillows behind her, and placed his coffee cup on the tray for her.

Ahana took a sip of the coffee, "Ummm! William, this is real coffee!"

"I thought it tasted kinda funny," Skip remarked, looked at Doctor Rightson, and asked, "Doc, where did ya'll get real coffee?"

The doctor smiled deviously and replied, "I'm not telling."

"Hey, no fair!" Ahana protested.

"See this bird on my lapel?" The doctor pointed to his collar, "R-H-I-P."

"Okay, Doc. Enough said," Skip admitted.

"Well, young lady, it looks like you're getting the best care possible. So, before I'm forced to reveal the location of my secret stash, I'll be going. Besides, I've got..."

Ahana cut him off, "Don't tell, me... more doctor stuff to do."

"You've got it! I will have you moved to a private room upstairs, and I'll stop by and check on you later." He checked her pulse. Then, he patted her hand and added, "I'm very pleased with your progress and thankful that you're safely home."

"Thank you, Doctor."

"Don't mention it. Patients like you make my job easy."

Skip sat on the edge of the bed, massaging Ahana's feet as she sipped her coffee. She closed her eyes, sighed, and laid her head back on the pillow.

"Are you okay, gorgeous?" Skip asked, concerned.

"I'm fine. Just exhausted. The events of the last few days are so unbelievable. If I didn't know better, I would swear that I had watched all of this in a movie."

"I know how you feel. I never thought for a minute that I wouldn't be able to find you, but lookin' back at what happened, I sure don't see how we pulled it off."

"I was shot down, William! I don't get shot down! I've never even screwed up a landing."

"You did a fine job puttin' the GR-1 on that dirt strip. Did you know there was a hole in your right wing, large enough for me to crawl through? You are a good pilot!"

"Well, I'm not going to become a dead pilot. That's it for me. I've had enough combat. From here on, I am a non-combat pilot."

"Do you really mean that, gorgeous?"

"You can bank on it, partner."

"Will you still be my chief test pilot on the Viper project?"

"Chief test pilot?" Ahana asked in amazement.

"Yes, ma'am. Chief test pilot. You don't think I'm gonna assign a triple fighter ace, with a Purple Heart, Distinguished Flying Cross, and the Air Medal, as just a regular old test pilot, do you?"

"You're not talking about me."

"Yes, ma'am. General Grey stopped by just after you were admitted to the hospital. He has been following our mission very closely. He is very impressed that you volunteered for that recon mission, knowing the high possibility of getting shot down. He is personally putting you in for those medals. He said to tell you that it was an honor to be your commander, and just as soon as you're well enough, he would tell you that in person. I'm a lucky guy; you're quite a catch!"

"I'll have to take your word for it. Right now, I feel like something the cat dragged in."

"You just need a lot of rest and my special tender lovin' care."

Ahana yawned and said, "You'll get no argument from me."

"You just get some sleep now. I feel scruffy. I'm gonna get cleaned up, and I'll be back in just a little bit."

Ahana pulled Skip close to her and said, "Listen, fly boy, you're needed out there. I'm okay now. You saved my life, remember? Don't worry about me. Go get your Viper and help stop that monster. Just be careful and come back to me. I've got plans that include you, mister."

Then, she kissed him and settled comfortably into her pillow.

As she was drifting off to sleep, she said, "Who knows, maybe he's hiding at the Hidden Base... I love you, William."

"I love you too, gorgeous. Sleep well." Skip kissed her cheek, and then reluctantly left her to rest.

Skip got cleaned up, had something to eat, and went to make sure the Viper was ready for flight. All the while, the last thing Ahana had said kept repeating in his mind.

He had the Viper added to the schedule at Base Ops, then reported in to the colonel.

"Sit down, Skip. How is Ahana?"

"Doin' great, thank God. She's resting right now. Man, she is one tough lady."

"Now, that is good news. Can I pour you a drink?"

"No thanks; it probably wouldn't sit so well on top of that so called food I just ate at the O-Club."

"I know what you mean..." Colonel Bass frowned at the thought, and then continued, "Listen, I just want to thank you for rescuing Ahana and getting the both of you back home alive. That was bravery above and beyond the call of duty."

"Honestly, John T., if I hadn't been able to get Ahana out alive, there would've been no reason for me to come back, either."

"I know she means the world to you, pal, but whether you know it or not, we're kinda fond of you too."

"Thanks, John T., that means a lot, coming from you."

"I know I've given you a ration of crap from time to time, but that's just me. I don't discriminate; everybody gets the same treatment from me."

"I guess I'm in good company."

"You got it, pal."

"Somethin's botherin' me, boss. Ahana said somethin' this mornin' that has been rattlin' around my head like a rock, and I just can't leave it alone. She told me to, 'Get back to work, and help stop that Monster', and then she said, 'Who knows, he might be hiding at the Hidden Base.' ...and the more I think about it, the more sense it makes."

"Are you thinking he ran into the fire, instead of away from it?"

"Well, as strange as it may sound, yes. I mean, Intelligence reported that he destroyed the Hidden Base, just after we evacuated. Now, if I was lookin' for a place to hide and ambush my enemy, what better location than a place that's considered uninhabitable. And, better yet, right under my enemy's nose."

"Skip, we need to move on this... but carefully; this is day two. If he is there, and we miss this chance, we may not get another. Hell, we may not be here to get another chance!"

Colonel Bass got on the phone and initiated a mission-planning meeting with Base Intelligence and other senior officers. Within fifteen minutes, the planning session was underway.

"Okay, gentlemen, we need ideas on how we can approach the Hidden Base, determine if Raazmahd is there, and have the fire power to take him out. Suggestions?" Ron Taylor asked.

"What is the reported condition of the base?" Col. Fronz asked.

Bud read from the report, "This Recon Team report shows that ordnance hit the base at approximate runway center. Initial explosions triggered secondary explosions from stored ordnance and fuel. All structures were destroyed and landing strip severely damaged. Also destroyed: one Flanker and one King Air and several vehicles. Several radiation hot spots were detected surrounding the damaged nuclear power cells. They recommend the area be marked uninhabitable and off-limits."

"None of the heavy equipment was listed on that report," Col. Fronz commented. "Apparently, it was overlooked or ignored during the attack on the base. That means that the runway could be repaired, and the damaged power cells could be hauled out and buried," Bud suggested.

"Exactly," Col. Fronz agreed.

"Could we air drop an insertion team and take the base by force?" Col. Bass asked.

"I would not try it, except as a last resort," Col. Fronz answered. "The base is set up with numerous sniper posts and many other defensible positions. It would be easy to lay down enough fire to hold off a large attacking force and allow an aircraft to take off."

"How about a high-speed, low-level air attack? Hit the base in the same way that Bushmaster just did," Skip asked.

"Well, if we could verify that Raazmahd is there, it might be worth the risk. But remember that we programmed our missiles to intentionally miss, in an attempt to confuse Major Blake and his wingman," Col. Fronz answered. "If we had intended to take the aircraft out, we had every advantage. An aircraft must approach from the valley to do any significant damage. It's simply a matter of waiting for an aircraft to approach, and then shoot it down."

"I see what you mean, like shootin' ducks from a blind," Skip replied.

"Precisely. I suspect that Draxon is the one who destroyed the base, knowing that we had already evacuated."

"If we had an Apache gun ship," Ron wished, "we could stay behind cover across the valley and reconnoiter the target with the night vision periscope. If we could remain undetected long enough, we might be able to pop up and launch a missile right down their throat."

Major Vosh interjected, "We must consider that he intends to fulfill his attempt to destroy FFNA bases with nuclear weapons. If the general is at the Hidden Base, he may have those weapons with him and intentionally detonate them if he feels trapped. The radiation cloud could contaminate this base and many areas downwind for thousands of miles."

"The major is right," Bud Cooper agreed. "That bastard is just crazy enough to do something like that. We should put an attack force right on top of the base. And to do that, we need an accurate reconnaissance of the base."

"Why not do it with the Viper?" Col. Bass suggested.

"I would need a FLIR or LANTIRN pod," Skip replied, "mounted on top of the vertical stabilizer. All I have now is an Aft Threat Sensor Array on the tail. The FLIR Ball is a larger unit, built into the Chin Radome."

"Why not install one?" Col. Fronz asked.

"Where do we get one to install?" Bud asked.

"We can use the FLIR pod from Mustang Two," Col. Fronz answered.

"Is it compatible with the FLIR system on the Viper?" Skip asked.

"It should be; we stole it from the U.S. Navy," Major Vosh admitted.

"You're kidding?" Skip exclaimed.

"No. Is that where the Viper's system came from?"

"Yep," Skip answered in amazement.

"Well, then, we've got a FLIR modification to do on the Viper," Col. Bass declared.

"The best crew to do it, unfortunately, is at the Boneyard," Skip lamented.

"Not necessarily," Col. Fronz said. "We have a CIA-trained airframe specialist. He is the one who supervised all of the mods on both Mustangs."

"Get 'em!" Everyone said at once.

Several hours later, a small FLIR pod was mounted on top of the vertical stabilizer of Viper-7.

While Skip sat in the cockpit, the airframe specialist explained the set up. "The ball is not going to be steerable. I was able to tie it into the DC power bus and get the video to your cockpit monitor by using the coaxial cable that was used for your upper UHF antenna. The lower antenna is now your only com antenna, so you may have trouble talking to aircraft directly above you. The FLIR pod has zoom capability, but you will have to position the aircraft precisely in order to point the sensor at the target. It should work okay; just don't try to use the crosshairs as a target designator, because there is not time to boresight it to your weapons system."

"Looks like this will work just fine," Skip observed. "The video is good, and that's all we need. Good job."

"Thank you, sir."

"I'm Skip, not sir."

"Okay, Skip, I'm Greg Hayes," he said and held out his hand in friendship.

Skip shook his hand and asked, "Greg, would you be interested in helpin' me build eight more Vipers, just like this one?"

"Yes, indeed I would," Greg answered excitedly.

"Well, you've got a job. Just as soon as we get Bushmaster out of the way, you tell Col. Bass that I want you assigned as my chief airframe specialist. I'll see you right here in this hangar, deal?"

"Deal. And thanks!"

"Hey, my pleasure, I know a professional when I see one."

As they walked out of the hangar, General Grey's G-4 flew overhead and entered the pattern to land. Suddenly, four Sukhoi SU-37 Super Flankers, in a classic vee formation, roared past, each entering the pattern behind the G-4. The Gulfstream parked in front of Base Ops, and then each of the SU-37's taxied in and parked alongside the G-4 as Pop and ten uniformed Russian Air Force pilots exited the Gulfstream.

It was an awesome sight. Pop stood with his arms behind him, patiently waiting, as the pilots shut the huge engines down and exited their respective aircraft. Skip walked up and stood beside Pop, quietly admiring the unbelievable sight.

"When you do somethin', you don't screw around, do ya?" Skip asked, looking at Pop.

Pop continued looking toward the aircraft and said, "Hello, Junior. I just asked General Petrovich to return a favor."

"What did you do to be repaid like this, kill a dozen or so of his worst enemies?"

"Nope. I just did a little computer work for him."

"Damn! I didn't know you charged so much."

General Vladimir Petrovich, who had been flying one of the SU-37's, approached and greeted Skip, then shook his hand, hugged him, and kissed him on both cheeks.

Then, Captain Vanya Petrovich, who had also been flying one of the SU-37's, walked up to Skip, gave him a hug and a kiss (which he did not mind), and whispered in his ear, "It is a Russian tradition."

"I hoped it was. Looks like you and your dad made up."

"Yes!" she replied excitedly and hugged Skip again.

The other Russian pilots approached but only shook hands and exchanged greetings. By then, Col. Bass was on the scene, along with most of the people in the area. It was like a family reunion, with everyone greeting the Russians, hugging, kissing, and so forth.

While all of that was going on, Skip wandered over to see the four SU-37's. This was his first chance for a close look at the most advanced multi-role fighter in the world. He felt like a kid at an air show.

The Super Flanker's massive vectored-thrust engine nozzles were the most prominent external feature of the menacing birds, but knowing that inside the fuselage was the most advanced avionics and weapons systems known, made the effect even more impressive.

Skip suddenly realized that Bushmaster's SU-27 pilots were about to get their ass kicked in air combat. That old saying, "Now the tables have turned," took on a different meaning. The tables had not only turned… these folks were about to raid the game!

***

The AWACS E-3 had been on station for eight hours, patrolling the Western Defense Zone. High altitude radar coverage was unreliable, due to the dense clouds of ferrous particles in the upper atmosphere, so Big Eye Four was running this orbit at twelve thousand feet.

Since the asteroid's impact, the E-3's had been grounded for the most part. The fleet had been dispersed to all points of the globe, and crews were on hot stand-by. When radar coverage was needed, Big

Eye could be in the air in minutes, sweeping the sky with its powerful Westinghouse APY2 radar for thousands of square miles, from the surface to over eighty thousand feet.

Cruise altitude was determined by atmospheric propagation factors. Sometimes, the ferrous cloud density was low, meaning Big Eye could run the orbit at altitudes above twenty thousand feet. Today was not one of those days, and the crew, for the most part, was very tired of being bounced around.

In the Western deserts, daytime temperatures of one hundred and fifty degrees Fahrenheit were not uncommon. Thermals, generated by the heat, would sometimes be a mile wide. The massive columns of rising air would rush upward at speeds of one hundred mph or more and then mushroom out between ten and thirty thousand feet, spill over the top, and send the chilled air streaming toward the surface at speeds of up to two hundred mph. Previously referred to as clear air turbulence, pilots began referring to them as Super Thermals.

As the Boeing E-3C Sentry plowed through these Super Thermals, it was tossed about the sky like a freewheeling roller coaster. Often, the experience was likened to riding out a cyclonic storm on a battleship. For anyone subject to vertigo, or motion sickness, it was a horrible experience.

For Combat Control Specialist Greg Carras, the past eight hours was now feeling more like eight days. To make it worse, the zone was totally dead. He had not seen one return on his screen all day.

"God, please let this day end soon," he whispered as he watched the screen.

Lt. Ann Brown heard him and reached over from her console, patted him on the shoulder, and said, "Hang in there, sport, we're handing off to a Hawkeye from the George Washington in twenty minutes."

"Since a minute seems like an hour, that is a long time away," Lt. Carras lamented.

Lt. Brown laughed and said, "You'll make it."

As the minutes slowly ticked by, Lt. Carras felt another attack of nausea coming on and started to get his handy bag ready, when four blips appeared on his screen. His nausea suddenly disappeared.

"I've got four bogies out of the northwest, low and hot," Lt. Carras announced into his headset.

"I've got six out of the southwest, looks like they may be turning east," Lt. Brown announced, seconds later.

The alert was immediately relayed to Base One Command Post.

Big Eye One, running an orbit north of the U.S./Canadian border, had also just picked up several bogies making a run toward NAADA Base Two, located in the Southern Saskatchewan Province. Other NAADA bases also received alerts and scrambled interceptors, as well.

At Base One, the alert birds were scrambled, and within moments, two flights of four F-16's and one flight of four F-15's were airborne, heading out to intercept the bogies.

Suddenly, all the radar screens on both Big Eye Four and Big Eye One were filled with targets, moving in all directions and at various flight levels. Then, just as suddenly, they were gone; the screens returned to showing the original ten targets.

"What was *that* all about?" Lt. Carras asked with a confused tone.

"Looked like EW to me; I think Bushmaster is screwing with us," Lt. Brown said. When the Base One interceptor flights established initial contact with Big Eye Four, the combat control specialists had vectored the three flights toward separate targets within the sectors that each specialist controlled.

Then, without warning, the number of bogies doubled. But, regardless of how strange the events had appeared, or whether they were real or not, the radar returns had to be verified. The sudden, apparent increase in bogies required each combat control specialist to redirect the aircraft in his particular sector.

Lt. Carras had Dagger Flight...

"Dagger, Big Eye. Bogies now show eight. Repeat, eight bogies, angels two five, two eight zero degrees, two hundred miles and closing."

"Big Eye, Dagger One. Copy eight. They're multiplying out there?"

"Good question, Dagger. One and Two, turn two seven zero degrees, four bogies, now one hundred miles, angels two five. Three and Four, turn two niner five degrees, four bogies, now one five zero miles, angels two zero."

"Big Eye, Dagger One. Copy 270 at 100."

"Big Eye, Dagger Three. Copy 290 at 150."

"Big Eye, Dagger One. We don't have anything on the screen, confirm heading."

"Dagger One, Big Eye. Confirm four bogies, angels two zero, out of two seven zero, now seven zero miles and closing."

As the intercept flights closed the distance and came within visual range, they began reporting...

"Big Eye, Dagger. Negative contact. Repeat, negative contact. Slate is clean."

"Dagger, Big Eye. Copy, negative contact."

Lt. Brown had Eagle Flight...

"Big Eye, Eagle One. Positive contact, one bogie, turning west, low and hot."

"Eagle One, Big Eye. Copy, one bogie. I show him on the deck at two six five degrees, ballistic. I also have four bogies at your eleven o'clock, angels one three, eighteen miles and closing."

"Big Eye, Eagle One. I have visual on the bogie, ten miles, moving west, ballistic."

"Eagle One has a lock! Fox Two! Fox Two!"

"Eagle Two has a lock! Fox Two! Fox Two!"

The AIM-9 Sidewinders sprinted toward the target, quickly overtaking the Mig. The Mig pilot ejected flares in an attempt to decoy the heatseekers and began evasive maneuvers. Both Sidewinders locked on one of the flares, and the first missile detonated, but the second slipped through the heat bloom, locked on the Mig again, and continued to the target. Seconds later...

"Splash Bogie! Splash Bogie!"

"Eagle, Big Eye. Confirm. Bogie is down.

"Big Eye, Eagle One. We have negative contact on the bogies at eleven o'clock. Repeat, negative contact."

"Eagle, Big Eye. Copy, negative contact. My screen is now clear, looks like it was EW from the bogie. Return to nest. Threat is false. Repeat, threat is false. Return to nest."

"Big Eye, Eagle One. Copy, we'll see ya."

Lt. Brown removed her headsets, leaned back in her seat, and said, "We could have done without that."

The "return to nest" command was given to all intercept aircraft. The threat was logged as an attempt to test air defenses with Electronic Warfare, one confirmed kill. Other bases logged similar reports with no kills. Somewhat later than scheduled, Hawkeye One, from aircraft carrier George Washington, relieved Big Eye Four, and Lt. Greg Carras could finally set his feet on solid ground.

At Base One and the other five NAADA bases, there was great concern over the attempt to test the FFNA Air Defenses and the Electronic Warfare radar jamming that occurred. Only one actual enemy aircraft had been spotted, but radar saw ten, and later, twenty incoming aircraft in the Western Defense Zone alone. Other zones had also reported similar events. Confirmations had to be made visually. Only one of the aircraft that was spotted had been shot down, but Bushmaster proved that FFNA Air Defenses could be fooled and, possibly, led into an ambush.

Expecting a full invasion within the next twenty-four hours, it was not the best time to learn about a major defensive vulnerability. Was Raazmahd also testing Bushmaster's offensive capability or trying to affect the morale of the FFNA pilots? There is an old warrior saying that goes, "If your enemy believes that you can defeat them, your enemy is already defeated."

***

Lt. Reshond had been given a job with Base One Intelligence and, being the type person that liked to stay busy, he was going through paper files and updating the computer database. In the process, he came across some reports concerning the array of unmanned listening stations scattered throughout the Western Defense Zone.

The reports reflected that the listening station equipment had become ineffective, would not be used any longer, and was scheduled to be discontinued. The lieutenant was surprised, to say the least. He had been part of a Bushmaster crew that had searched for, and located, the listening stations in the area around the Hidden Base and along the air routes to and from Base One.

They found the stations to be operational, so, at first, they simply turned them off, to see if anyone would come to repair them. When two weeks had passed, and no one came, they assumed the devices were no longer used. So they modified the units by tapping into the fiber optic signal output and routing it to a small transmitter. At the Hidden Base, the signal was received and used to alert them when aircraft was approaching. The equipment had worked quite well.

Realizing that the listening stations could be utilized to help defeat Bushmaster's electronic warfare false signal radar indications, he immediately reported his idea to his boss, Ron Taylor.

Ron commended him for his innovative thinking and immediately dispatched repair crews, via helicopter, to attempt to restore as many listening stations as possible.

***

Skip's mission to recon the Hidden Base was scheduled for midnight, so he went to get some rest before the flight. Ahana had been moved to a private room upstairs and, just as Dr. Rightson had said, it was complete with a double bed. When Skip entered the room, Ahana was just beginning to stir from a long afternoon nap. Just as he sat on the bed, she smiled, yawned, and stretched. Taking advantage of Ahana's outstretched arms, he slid his arms around her and pulled her close. She felt delightful, almost delicious, if it was possible for a beautiful female to feel delicious. Even if the word did not fit, that was exactly how she felt, and he told her so...

"You feel positively delicious."

Ahana giggled and asked, "How can someone *feel* delicious?"

"Don't ask me," Skip answered as he nibbled on her neck, "I don't explain my five senses; I just enjoy 'em!"

She giggled again and said, "You're certainly in a playful mood this afternoon."

"I wouldn't exactly call it playful. More like, frisky."

"Frisky? As in, sexually frisky?" she asked with playful curiosity.

"I think that nails it... Yep, that's it, all right."

"We can't lock the door, you know."

"Maybe we could put out a 'Do Not Disturb' sign."

"I think that only works at hotels."

"Oh. Well, shucks. I'd sure hate to embarrass one of the staff!"

"And we wouldn't be embarrassed?"

"Not likely... At least, I'm just about positive that you'd be way too preoccupied to notice if the door opens," he boasted.

"I would be too preoccupied. And, what about you?" she asked indignantly.

"When I'm makin' love to you, I wouldn't notice if they moved us, bed and all, into the hallway!"

Ahana looked at the covers on the foot of the bed, and then looked at Skip.

"Well...?" she asked suggestively and winked.

He immediately reached down and pulled the covers up and over their heads. For the next hour or so, no one disturbed them at all. Later, as they lay in each other's arms, Ahana asked, "So, how was your day?"

"I met Greg Hayes today."

"He is very good with airframe modifications."

"As I discovered. So, I hired him to help us build the new Vipers."

"How nice. He will be an asset to the project. How did you meet him?"

"He installed a FLIR pod on top of the vertical stabilizer of the Viper."

"Why would you want FLIR pod up there?"

"Well, it actually started with you…"

"Me? How?"

"Do you remember tellin' me to 'Go to work and help get that monster' this morning?"

"Vaguely."

"How about, when you said, 'Who knows, he may be hiding at the Hidden Base.'"

"I said that?"

"Yep, and then you said, 'I love you, William' and drifted off to sleep."

"All I remember is I was so tired that I could barely keep my eyes open."

"Well, your body may have been sleepy, but your mind was busy. And I got to thinkin' about what you said, so we had a meeting about it, and we decided to go see if Raazmahd really is hidin' at the Hidden Base. The only way we can do it is to spy on the base from a distance at night. That's where the FLIR comes in. It has zoom capability and…"

"Oh, I get it! You're going to use the pod like the night vision periscope on a Cobra or an Apache."

"That's the general idea. The mission is tonight. Bud and I take off at midnight."

Ahana was quiet for a few minutes, and then she said, "I want you to be careful out there, fly boy. I need you. You're going to be my husband!"

"That is a definitely a fact, gorgeous," Skip replied, kissed her, and said, "Please, try not to worry. I just have a score to settle with that monster, as you call him, and he's not gonna get away this time. He'd better have his last will and testament written 'cause tonight, if he's there, he won't see sunrise tomorrow."

Ahana kissed him tenderly and said, "Just come home, William, I've come too far to lose you now."

They fell asleep holding each other, both praying it would not be the last time.

Hours later, Skip was startled awake by the earth shaking sound of several Phalanx systems firing simultaneously. Base One was under attack. Ahana woke up too, but did not say anything; she knew what was about to happen, but did not know how to face it.

She fought back the tears, reached out, and took Skip's hand, pulled him down to her, and said, "You are my hero and my life. I love you more than I can begin to show..."

Skip held her close and said, "I can tell how much you love me. I see it in your beautiful gray-blue eyes. I feel it in your touch and taste it in your kisses. And, like you, I am unable to find the words...'I love you' is correct, but not enough. Maybe there are no words for how I feel about you. Just know that, no matter where I am, I keep you with me. I can see your beautiful face, taste your delicious body, and feel the warmth of your love. I love you with every ounce of my being, and nothing can change it or stop it, and if God allows me, I will be with you forever."

Just one more kiss, and Skip had to go. It was not easy, leaving Ahana again, but he forced himself down the stairs and out the door. Once outside, he appreciated the soundproofing of the hospital walls. The sound of the Vulcan cannons firing was deafening. Sporadically, the cannons were firing around the entire perimeter of the base.

The Base Perimeter Defense System programming had been changed to the highest possible defense level. The system was now set to fire at any movement within the range of the infrared and radar sensors. Someone was out there, in an unauthorized area, trying to approach the base. Apparently, a lot of someones, considering the number of guns that were firing.

Oddly, Skip could not hear, or see, any incoming fire. The Defense System must be detecting the threat at such a distance and keeping the enemy pinned down, so they were unable to get within range to fire. That system was definitely a good idea.

By the time he reached the hangar where the Viper was parked, the flight line crew had pulled the aircraft out of the hangar, and it had been prepped, fueled, and armed.

Skip did not mind doing any of the preflight chores, except charging the hydrogen tanks. The hydrogen fuel was extremely cold, which tended to promote static charge build up. Unfortunately, hydrogen was also highly volatile. A hydrogen fire is invisible. It is not possible to know it is burning, unless you feel the heat, or it begins to burn something that produces smoke.

To work with it, you must wrap up in protective clothing, including heavy gloves and a face shield, because of the extreme cold. Then, if it catches fire, you may not feel that either, until it actually starts burning you. Hydrogen is definitely not a user-friendly element. But it sure was a kick in the ass when that hydrogen/alcohol mix hit the afterburners. The sensation was something like a carrier launch, with the aircraft already traveling at three hundred knots.

Bud had volunteered to run the sensors and joined Skip at the hangar, "Hey, partner. Did the Insertion Team get airborne on time?"

"Yep, they'll be waitin' on station by the time we get there."

They went over the mission scenario one final time before suiting up with G-suits and survival gear. This time, Skip stashed his small 9 mm handgun in his vest. He would not fly another combat mission without that weapon.

In the cockpit, as the two men strapped in, Skip turned on the battery switch to activate the intercom system.

"Here we go... stand by for system power, master switch on."

The flight computer came up instantly...

System initialization is complete, William. Checks in progress; please stand by, sweetie.

"That old fart!" Skip exclaimed.

Bud was laughing so hard that he could not comment. The flight computer's voice was identical to Ahana's voice. Unknown to Skip, Pop had reprogrammed the computer's voice synthesizer, using sound bites from Ahana's voice.

"I swear, he's always up to somethin'," Skip lamented.

"When did he do this?" Bud asked, still chuckling.

"It had to be after the FLIR pod was installed because I brought up the system and reinitialized, so the new pod would be included in systems checks."

"He is a piece of work. Did you know he hacked into the Bushmaster system and installed a software bomb?"

"No. When is it set to go off?"

"Sometime today, I think."

"I would love to see that."

Checks complete, dear. All systems are go.

Skip chuckled, "I told Ahana that she is with me wherever I go, but I didn't expect to actually hear her voice! Thank you, FC. Engine start, please. It sure is gonna be hard to call her 'FC'."

"I feel for you, pal," Bud offered, laughing again.

"Sure you do. I don't know whether to thank Pop or give him a swift kick!"

Immediately the FC advised, "Abuse of the programmer is not allowed. Programmers are perfect and never do anything wrong."

Then, Bud totally lost it.

"I don't believe this," Skip said as he banged his helmet against the canopy.

"Up 'til now... I didn't think... a computer could be... too powerful!" Bud managed to say while laughing.

The engines started in sequence and spooled up.

Ignition sequence complete, dear. I'm ready for full power on your command.

"This is really gonna tickle Ahana," Bud commented.

"Yea, I bet it will," Skip replied as he moved the throttles forward slightly and taxied the sinister aircraft away from the hangar.

"Tower, Viper-7. Ready for take-off."

"Viper-7, Tower. Ah, I thought your lady was in the hospital?"

"That's correct, why?"

"She just called on the radio to advise that you were starting engines!"

"Oh, that's the flight computer's synthesized voice."

"A lady computer. Cool! Viper, wind is calm; altimeter is thirty-two point zero four. You are cleared for immediate take-off. Good hunting."

"Thanks, Tower, we'll see ya. Viper out."

Skip pushed the throttles forward. As the Viper began accelerating down the runway, Skip rotated the Thrust Vector Control for vertical thrust. The Hot Nozzles directed the diverted thrust downward, which began to lift the Viper off the ground. It was then that Skip engaged the afterburners. The response was a solid shove from behind, pushing them into the seats and sending the rate of climb indicator toward the edge of the scale. Airspeed quickly increased to 200 knots indicated, as the Viper passed two thousand feet AGL.

The Base Defense System paused the guns that were shooting in the direction of the Viper's take-off, but below, they could see the tracers streaming out from the other guns as the base quickly faded behind.

Skip rotated the Thrust Vector Control for level flight and issued a command, "FC, ten second boost in three, two, one, go."

The hybrid hydrogen-alcohol thrust boost system worked as advertised, and they were slammed from behind as the indicated airspeed jumped upward from 300 knots.

"Yee ha!" Bud yelled, "That is awesome."

"I love it!"

As the thrust assist timed out, Skip cut the afterburner and pulled the throttles back slightly.

"FC, set Terrain Following Radar to hot stand-by and set cruise at 650 knots, 3000 AGL."

"Compliance, sweetie."

"I think I could get used to this."

"I'll bet this is the first plane that's ever been in love with its pilot," Bud commented.

"I'd say that's a safe bet," Skip replied.

Skip set the Inertial Navigation System coordinates for a valley south of the Hidden Base and gave instructions to the FC...

"FC, confirm INS coordinates. Three hundred miles east of target, descend to 100 feet AGL and go to terrain following."

"Database indicates coordinates are south of Reno, Nevada, located 25 miles due south of Dayton Valley, in the West Walker River Canyon. In the area of TFR mode, terrain elevations range from four thousand feet above mean sea level to eleven thousand eight hundred feet above mean sea level. Expect a rough ride. Suggest you hang on to your shorts, dear."

Bud cracked up again.

"Hang on to my shorts!"

"That is correct," the FC confirmed.

"Well, I guess she told you! I'm sure glad I came along; I haven't had this much entertainment in a long time."

"I'm glad you're enjoyin' yourself."

A direct flight from Base One to the Hidden Base, located in the Reno, Nevada area at six hundred and fifty knots, would normally take about sixty-five minutes, depending on prevailing winds. However, at three thousand feet AGL, the flight path was anything but straight. And at 100 feet above the terrain, the course was a twisting, winding, subsonic roller coaster ride. It was necessary to allow the Terrain Following Radar to control the aircraft while flying in mountainous terrain at high speed and low altitude, especially at night. Although the pilot must let the TFR fly the aircraft, it was not exactly the time to relax and read a book. …unless of course, you routinely read a book while riding a roller coaster.

As they approached the West Walker River Canyon, Skip slowed the Viper and transitioned to vertical flight. After taking a few moments to catch their breath and unwind from the wild ride through the mountains, Skip switched to the Viper's Night Vision System and began navigating through the canyons toward the Hidden Base.

"Stalker, this is Viper," Bud called the Insertion Team aircraft.

"Viper, this is Stalker, standing by."

"Roger, Stalker, we'll have you some data shortly."

"Stalker copies, just say the word."

Upon entering Dayton Valley, Bud immediately started searching the area with the FLIR system, looking for any unusual heat source. Not only did they need to avoid detection, but they also had to watch for an ambush. Raazmahd was noted for being extremely cautious. Thus, it was difficult to know what to expect. The smartest thing to do was expect anything.

Skip searched for a location near the crest of a ridge where they could peek over the rim with the stabilizer mounted FLIR pod without revealing their position.

"I hope none of the listening stations are still tied into the base; I'll bet we're making enough noise to wake the dead," Bud said.

"Well, if they can hear us, we should know pretty quickly."

They found several vantage points, but could not get enough resolution on the FLIR to be of any use. So, they continued searching. Finally, Skip positioned the Viper behind a ridge as close to the Hidden Base as they dared to go.

"Tally ho!" Bud exclaimed, as the infrared video revealed activity within the base, "Hold as steady as you can; the video stabilization is not working very well."

"I'll do my best."

Bud came up on the radio, "Stalker, this is Viper. I've got confirmation."

"Roger, Viper, go ahead…"

"I can see what looks like a Lockheed S-3 Viking. It's on the runway, but the engines are cold. There is also several Yak-36, 'Forger A' variants. One is a 'Forger B', a two-seater, and the engine is running. A number of personnel are moving around inside, and there are six or eight others scattered around the entrance. I'll bet most of the ones outside are armed with Stingers."

"We copy, Viper. We're going in."

"Roger, Stalker, Viper copies."

"Well, if anyone hears us, it would be one of the guards outside," Bud commented.

"So far, so good. You say he's flying an S-3."

"Yea. It looks like the ones the Navy uses to transport VIPs."

"I guess he thinks he's an executive terrorist now. Say, I was thinkin', with only a Yak-36 spooled up, we could make a quick recon run and be gone before they know we're even here. That Yak couldn't catch a crow! What ya' think?"

"I'll go along with that."

"Let's back outta here and get some runnin' distance. We can pop up over this ridge and use the forward FLIR to get a good look at what's in there," Skip said as he began to move the Viper backwards.

"Stalker, Viper. What's your location?"

"We're about ten out from target."

"Stand by for updated target info. We're going in for a closer look."

"Standing by."

They were positioned in a narrow canyon, between high ridges to the north and south. It was necessary to move east, through the canyon, to a saddle in the south ridge. There, Skip could take the Viper through the saddle without being seen. Safely in the wider valley to the south, he could get a running start, allowing a high-speed recon run directly at the hidden base. About a half mile south of the saddle, he turned the Viper around and prepared to make a run for the north ridge...

"Switch to the forward FLIR, and arm the flares; we're gonna get some Stingers thrown at us for sure."

"FLIR video is good; flares are armed," Bud replied.

"Okay, here we go."

Skip pushed the throttles forward and lit the afterburner. The Viper quickly accelerated toward the ridge. As they popped up over the crest of the ridge at 300 knots, they almost collided head-on with a Yak-36.

Reacting instinctively, Skip pulled the Viper into a hard left turn, missing the Forger by a scant few feet, "Damn that was close!"

"I think we occupied the same space in time there for an instant!"

"Hang on! He's going into the canyon!" Reversing the turn to avoid hitting the ridge, Skip dove into the valley on the north side of the ridge and pulled up sharply, attempting to follow the flight path of the Yak.

"There he is! It's the Forger B!" Bud yelled.

"FC, select cannons."

"Cannons are hot."

"Thank you."

To avoid colliding with the south ridge, the Forger pilot had to pull up, which put the aircraft in full view, directly ahead of the Viper.

Skip fired the Viper's 25 mm cannons. Tracers reached out to the target as rounds raked across the top of the Yak's engine nacelle. Suddenly, a large yellow flame shot from the exhaust nozzle as the engine flamed out. The Forger then rolled inverted, spun into the canyon, and exploded.

"Good shooting!" Bud said.

"Thanks. Well, hell, they know we're here now," Skip said as he yanked the Viper around to the north again.

"Stalker, Viper, heads up for bogies; we just stirred up the nest!"

"Copy, Viper, we see the fireworks."

"Stalker, we'll cover you while you clean house."

"Roger, Viper, we jump in one minute."

As they crossed the ridge again, Bud said, "Just a little closer, and I'll be able to get a bird's eye view of the base."

"FC, select Fox Two, and arm," Skip commanded.

Missiles armed and ready, love.

At that moment, the S-3 roared out of the entrance of the Hidden Base.

"Damn it!" Skip said as he saw the S-3 escape and immediately hit the afterburners, initiating pursuit.

Just then, a Yak-36 took off right behind the S-3.

"Watch for another Forger; one just made it out," Bud warned.

Before Skip could ask where he was, a tone in their ears told them the Yak had found them, and the flight computer confirmed it...

Warning! Break right! Incoming missile. Radar guided and locked on.

As Skip pulled the Viper into a hard right turn, the flight computer dispensed a load of chaff, trying to defeat the missile's radar lock.

"FC, thrust boost now."

Just as the Thrust Assist kicked the Viper with another twenty thousand pounds of thrust, the missile streaked by, barely missing its target.

"FC, cut boost."

"Whew! I'm glad it didn't have a proximity fuse," Bud exclaimed.

"Where is he?" Skip asked.

"Aft Sensors show a target at four o'clock low, five miles," Ahana's calm voice reported.

Skip selected an Aim-7X Sparrow and fired...

"Fox One!"

The aft radar data, coupled to the weapons system, sent the Sparrow sprinting in a 180-degree turn to the rear the instant it dropped from the rail. Seconds later, a bright flash indicated the Sparrow had completed its task. Skip and Bud looked back and saw the burning pieces of the Forger as they fell to the desert floor.

"Sensors show target has been hit. Target is no longer a threat," FC dutifully reported.

"Any other bogies come out of the base?"

"Negative contact," FC reported.

Bud swung the FLIR toward the base. "We have people on the ground. It looks like the other aircraft have been disabled."

"Stalker, Viper, what's your status?"

"Situation under control."

"We're outta here!"

"Go get 'em, Viper."

Immediately, Skip turned the Viper in the direction the S-3 had gone, stabbed the throttles forward, and lit the afterburners.

When the airspeed reached 450 knots, Skip ordered, "FC, thrust boost in three, two, one, now."

Another kick in the butt, and the Viper leaped forward.

"FC, cut boost on my command."

Skip let the clock tick past the standard ten-second limit...

"Fifteen seconds. Caution. Exhaust nozzle approaching maximum temperature. Eighteen seconds. Caution. Nozzle at maximum temperature in five seconds... Twenty-three seconds. Warning! Exhaust nozzle in over-temp. Nozzle failure in five seconds..."

"FC, cut boost, TFR on."

Airspeed was now at 940 knots and still accelerating. Skip was determined to catch the S-3 and take Raazmahd down. He held the afterburners on for as long as he dared. They would need fuel to get home, and a tanker might not be available, especially if the main attack came on schedule.

"Hawkeye, Viper-7. Hawkeye, Viper-7."

"Viper-7, Hawkeye."

"Hawkeye, Viper. We're in pursuit of a Viking, west of Reno, runnin' northwest. Can you vector an intercept?"

"Viper, Hawkeye. Negative contact. Repeat, negative contact. Stay on this frequency; we are en route and will assist, if possible."

"Hawkeye, Viper. We're low and ballistic, heading three zero zero."

"Viper, Hawkeye. Copy, three zero zero, low and hot. Good hunting!

"Looks like we'll have to find him ourselves," Bud said.

"There are not a lot of places he can run with the Viking. We'll catch up. "

He cut the afterburner when the airspeed reached 1020 knots. Due to the dense air at this low altitude, the leading edges of the wings began to glow red. Unassisted thrust from the two hybrid engines could not maintain the present airspeed, and the Viper slowed to 930 knots and held. They were running northwest, along the west side of the Sierra Madre, hoping that the S-3 pilot had stayed low and not tried to make a suicide run up one of the winding canyons.

Suddenly, FC reported a target on the sensors...

"Sensors indicate a moving target, three one zero degrees, low, 100 miles."

Skip turned to 310 degrees and went to afterburner. Quickly, the target grew nearer.

"Sensors have target lock, 12 o'clock and 60 miles."

"Target, 12 o'clock and 40 miles. Caution. Excess fuel usage for return to Base One."

"Target, 12 o'clock and 30 miles. Warning! Reduce fuel usage."

Skip cut the afterburner and stayed on the target.

"Target, 12 o'clock and 25 miles."

"Target is descending, 12 o'clock low, and 20 miles."

"Target, 12 o'clock low and 15 miles. Now at minimum altitude."

The S-3 pilot saw the Viper on his aft sensor array and was trying to hide in the ground clutter.

"I have him on FLIR; he is dead meat," Bud reported.

"Target now 12 o'clock low and 10 miles. Select weapons or switch weapon system control to automatic."

"He's so low; I'll bet he's kicking up sand!" Bud commented as he watched the target on his FLIR screen.

"The Pacific is ahead. He's about to run out of places to hide."

"Target is 12 o'clock and 4 miles. Recommend select Fox 2 and fire."

"Your going to chase him down, aren't you?"

"Let's make that bastard sweat," Skip coldly replied.

"Target is 12 o'clock and one mile. Collision warning! Reduce speed or change heading."

Skip pulled the throttles back, hit the speed brakes, and selected the cannons. He waited a few seconds and fired a short burst into the S-3. The rounds hit, producing flashes as the Viking pilot tried to evade his attacker. Suddenly, the S-3 made a hard 180-degree turn and fired on the Viper.

"He's gotta be kiddin'!" Skip exclaimed as he evaded the clumsy S-3.

The Viking pilot returned to his original flight path and accelerated to maximum speed, just over 450 knots.

"He'll blow the wings off that thing if he's not careful," Bud observed.

Suddenly the S-3 pulled up sharply, trying to cause the Viper to fly past, but Skip hit the speed brakes and added vertical thrust. That slowed the Viper instantly, with no loss in altitude.

"Now that was clever," Skip commented sarcastically.

Both aircraft were now flying below two hundred knots as Skip applied forward thrust, accelerating past the S-3. Then, he banked hard, passing directly in front of the Viking.

The Viking pilot fired and turned hard, trying to follow the Viper, but the effort was useless. The 20 mm rounds fell harmlessly into the ocean as the Viking pilot again accelerated to full speed, trying to run.

Knowing the S-3 was unable to maneuver with the Viper, Skip continued toying with the doomed Viking, teasing, but always staying on his tail.

Finally, Skip had played with the monster enough. He positioned the Viper directly along the port side of the Viking. As the Bushmaster pilot looked toward them, they could see Raazmahd himself peering through the window directly behind the pilot's seat. Both men saluted Raazmahd with an upturned middle finger.

Then, setting up an attack position, Skip opened up with the two 25 mm cannons. He held the trigger, letting the guns rip the Viking apart. Pieces began flying away from the S-3 as the pilot tried to maneuver and evade the attack. Suddenly, the right engine exploded, and the wing broke at the pylon, sending the S-3 spiraling into the ocean.

Skip went to full vertical thrust and dropped the Viper to the surface, hovering within a hundred feet of the burning wreckage.

"I told Ahana that if I found that son of a bitch, he wouldn't see another sunrise."

"Target has been neutralized," Ahana's voice calmly announced.

"Thank you, FC."

"My pleasure, love."

"Now, *that* is truly fitting," Bud commented.

"Let's go home," Skip sighed, pressed the throttles forward, and turned the Viper to the east, climbing toward the rising red sun.

CHAPTER TWENTY ONE

The Moment Of Truth

The Army of the Bushmaster had been pressing their assault for hours, trying to get into position to attack Base One. The attack was going sour because the Bushmaster spies had not disabled the Base Defense System as planned. As the combined infrared and radar sensors detected any movement, including incoming missiles or projectiles, the projectiles and any launch point within range was fired on and destroyed.

Eventually, making painfully slow progress, the rocket and mortar crews gained enough positions within range of the base to begin firing for effect. The Base Defense System was then unable to stop the entire barrage of incoming rockets and mortars.

Colonel Bass had ordered that all aircraft on Base One were to be held on alert, to be scrambled in case of an air attack. However, when rockets and mortars began hitting the base, the aircraft designed primarily for ground attack had been shifted to close air-ground support duties.

Most of these pilots were the former Bushmaster aircrews. The aircraft they were flying included two Yak-37 Forgers, the F-3 Tornado, Mustang One, and Mustang Two. While other aircraft, such as the F-15's, F-16's, F-18's and F-5's were multi-role, they would be much more valuable in the air-to-air confrontations.

The attacking aircraft, armed with bombs and air-to-ground rockets, proceeded to attack the Bushmaster invaders. The defenders were met with strong resistance in the form of Stinger missiles and accurate anti-aircraft fire. During the first engagement, one of the Forgers and Mustang Two had suffered anti-aircraft hits and had to land for repairs.

It was during this stage of the battle that Viper-7 returned to the area. Unfortunately, a tanker had not been available, and the FC had been issuing low fuel warnings for the last thirty minutes of their flight.

"Base One, Viper. We're twenty miles west, inbound for full stop."

"Viper, Base One. We have you. Be advised; we remain under attack. Three aircraft are hitting targets to the west and south. The Base Defense Weapons are active. Do not descend below five hundred feet, within five miles of Base One."

"Base One, Viper. We copy. Sounds like you could use some help."

"Viper, Base One. That's a roger. Can you assist?"

"Base One, Viper. We should be able to do a little damage."

"Viper, switch to channel six and talk to Combat Control. Call sign is Ramrod. Good luck."

"Thanks, Base One, we'll be back with you in a few."

"Ramrod, Viper-7. We're five miles out, inbound from the west. Need some help?"

"Viper, Ramrod. Yes, we do! We've got a missile battery, dug in about a mile north of the fence. Use caution; they're deadly."

"Ramrod, Viper copies. Neutralize the bad guy one mile north. Stand by."

As Bud brought up the FLIR and began searching for the anti-aircraft battery, Skip went into hover and positioned the Viper several miles from the missile battery. Suddenly, a bright flash indicated they had just been fired on. The small rocket streaked toward the Viper.

"Incoming!" Bud warned.

"Warning! Incoming heat-seeking missile. Warning! Incoming heat-seeking missile," FC confirmed.

"I have it," Skip replied, quickly ejecting three magnesium flares.

The Stinger's infrared sensor locked onto the intense heat blooms and the rocket turned, following the flares until it detonated a safe distance from the Viper.

Skip selected one of the two remaining Laser Maverick missiles. By firing on the Viper, the enemy had sealed their fate. Bud placed the crosshairs of the FLIR on the target and activated the Pave Tack laser target designator.

"That was nice of 'em to show us their position like that," Skip commented.

"Wasn't it though... Fire!" Bud replied.

"Viper One. Fox Three! Fox Three!" Skip announced on the radio.

Bud held the laser on the target as the Maverick followed the beam to the end. One huge explosion, followed by many secondary flashes, and explosions reported the results.

Then, FC issued another warning. "Warning! Fuel exhaustion in three minutes. Warning! Low fuel."

"Ramrod, Viper. Looks like you've got one less problem."

"Viper, Ramrod. Copy that. Good shooting, and thanks for the help."

"Ramrod, Viper. No problem. We'll be leavin' you now."

"Base One, Viper. We're bingo for fuel. Permission to land."

"Viper, Base. You're cleared for a straight in approach, winds three five zero degrees at two four."

"Base, Viper. We're on the way."

Just seconds before the wheels touched down on the runway, the engines flamed out from fuel starvation and the Viper landed hard.

"Next time, let's set up a tanker," Bud suggested.

"Good idea," Skip replied.

While the Viper was being refueled and re-armed, Skip and Bud went to their ladies to let them know they had returned safely.

Skip ignored the elevator and ran up the steps of the hospital to the fourth floor and Ahana's room. When he opened the door, Ahana was standing by the window, looking out toward the skirmish beyond the base perimeter. She heard someone enter and turned, expecting one of the staff. When she saw Skip, her face lit up with the beautiful smile that he had come to know so well.

"Hi, gorgeous. You sure are beautiful."

She held out her arms, and Skip swept her up, cradling her as they kissed.

"It feels so good to touch you," she said. "I was so worried!"

"I knew you would be, that's why I got here as quickly as I could," Skip replied as he gently placed her on the bed. "I know I could've called, but I needed to hold you and let you see that I'm fine."

"Thank you. You always seem to know exactly what I need."

"Well, like you said, we have bonded. Maybe we were destined to be together. I know I've found a one-of-a-kind girl and a very special love that I've never known."

"I love you, fly boy."

"Will I be able to take my girl home today?" Skip asked as he stroked her hair.

"I think so. The doctor hasn't made his rounds yet, but he seems very pleased with my recovery."

"Good. But, I know one monster who won't recover."

"You got him?"

"Down in flames."

"*Yes!*"

"But, it ain't over yet. Right now, they need our help on the base perimeter. Bud and I are gonna provide close air-ground support. The

Viper has been pulled from intercept duty, so we should be down in a couple of hours. Now, don't worry!"

"I'll try, I promise," she replied, then kissed him and sent him out the door.

As Skip lifted the Viper off for another ground support sweep, the alert sounded to scramble all interceptors.

"Viper, Tower. Contact Ramrod on channel six, ASAP."

"Tower, Viper copies, channel six..."

Skip changed channels on the Viper's radio, "Ramrod, Viper."

"Viper, Ramrod. We need immediate cover for departing aircraft. Set up on the departure end of the runway, and suppress triple-A."

"Ramrod, Viper. We're on it, stand by."

Skip called as he positioned the Viper near the end of the runway, hovering at two hundred feet, "Ramrod, Viper. We're in position."

Bud scanned the area beyond the end of the runway with the FLIR, while the FC scanned the area with the on-board sensors. Skip stood ready to bring all weapons to bear on any target.

Two by two, the intercept aircraft roared into the sky, rushing to stop the Bushmaster air attack. As the first two F-16's passed the ILS Outer Marker, a missile sprinted toward them, barely missing one of the aircraft. Instantly, Bud designated the target, and Skip launched a Laser Maverick. The Marker building and the missile battery disappeared in a large flash.

"Oops!" Skip remarked, "Scratch one baby Sam Site and the Outer Marker!"

"Hell, I never liked flying IFR anyway, did you?" Bud asked facetiously.

"Not really... now that you mention it, screw the Marker!"

Then, two more F-16's roared past, followed by eight more, then four F-18's, followed by five F-5's, four Mig-31's, three Mig-29's, and finally, four F-15's and the four mighty SU-37's. Thirty-six aircraft in all, a combination of fighters that had never fought together before, facing a common, deadly threat.

Suddenly, toward the northwest, a tremendously bright flash lit up the dark horizon. A nuclear weapon had detonated somewhere in western Canada.

"Tower, Viper. Do you have anything on the nuke that just flashed to the northwest?"

"Viper, Tower. Negative, we're checking now, stand by."

Several long moments later, "Attention all aircraft, this is Base One Command Post. The nuke failed to reach the target. Repeat, the nuke failed to reach the target."

Over the radio, a burst of noise and unreadable audio blared as an unknown number of pilots transmitted their relieved comments at the same moment.

...And Command Post replied, "You're welcome!"

Two hundred miles to the west, the attacking Bushmaster fighters had split into pairs. Forty aircraft in all, running low and fast, heading directly for Base One.

Above, the AWACS Combat Controllers had their hands full. Bushmaster had apparently been pleased with the results of their electronic warfare trial runs. They were now using EW in full force.

Big Eye Four and Hawkeye had conflicting numbers of bogies on their scopes and were coordinating with Base One Command Post, using the listening post data, coupled with ground station radar data to verify actual targets. The combination of data was enabling the Combat Controllers to vector the thirty-six FFNA aircraft toward the elusive enemy.

As six unidentified aircraft from the south made their way toward the flight of interceptors, Lieutenant Brown knew exactly what to do...

"Red One, Big Eye."

Vanya Petrovich, flight leader of the four Su-37's responded, "Big Eye, Red One. Go ahead."

"Red One, I have six bogies out of one eight zero, angels one five, three hundred miles. Turn to one niner five for intercept."

"Big Eye, Red One. Copy, one niner five for six, angels one five, three hundred miles. Are these targets our dance partners?"

"Red One, Big Eye. Hawkeye relays high probability."

"Big Eye, Red One. Relay to Hawkeye... If you are right, drinks are on me at Base One tonight!"

"Red One, Big Eye. I will pass it on. Take 'em out, ma'am."

"Will do, Big Eye, will do."

The SU-37's turned to intercept the six oncoming targets. Flying four abreast, they increased the distance between them and initiated the weapons system data link. As the six SU-27's were detected by the Super Flanker's radar, the systems now began operating like a command and control system, analyzing the targets, assigning threat levels, and providing information necessary to neutralize the threats.

The Bushmaster pilots, seeing only four opponents incoming on an intercept course, prepared for an easy victory. Fifty miles out, the 37's weapons systems launched missiles toward the targets. Two of the six 27's went down in flames, and the odds were even.

But as they met, and the remaining Bushmaster pilots saw what they were facing, two of the four immediately abandoned the attack and ran. The Super Flankers, with a thrust-to-weight ratio of 8.7 to 1, were considerably faster and more maneuverable than the Flankers. It was an easy task to chase the cowards down.

The two 27's that chose to stay and fight were not immediately dispatched. It quickly became apparent to the experienced Russian pilots that the Bushmaster pilots were not skilled enough to utilize the full capabilities of the SU-27. At that point, the Russians began playing with the Bushmaster pilots like a cat toying with a bug.

The Super Flanker pilots would bait their opponent, allow him to gain a slight advantage, then immediately turn and pounce. When a Flanker would try to turn into a Super Flanker, the 37 would use the vectored thrust to initiate a considerably tighter turn. Time after time, the 27's were unable to get a missile lock or firing solution.

Aftermath I: The Fight For Survival

The Bushmaster pilots fired blindly, needlessly wasting missiles and ammunition.

Seeing the opportunity to save the valuable aircraft, the Russian pilots gave the remaining four Bushmaster pilots a chance to surrender and be escorted to Base One. Surprisingly, all four of the pilots gave up at the first opportunity.

After learning that Raazmahd had been eliminated, many of the remaining Bushmaster pilots were either shot down as they attempted to turn and run, or surrendered. Then, it was only a matter of determining which of the aircraft were carrying nukes. Those planes were diverted to remote bases where the nuclear weapons could be safely disarmed.

As the FFNA pilots and their Russian allies returned to Base One, more aircraft landed than took off initially. Not only was this day a great victory for the FFNA, it went down in history as one of the most unusual air battles ever recorded. When the numbers were tallied from the six NAADA bases, the enemy had lost thirty-two aircraft, and the FFNA had lost nine but gained twenty-three.

Before the day was over, General Vladimir Petrovich had expanded Vanya's offer and invited the entire crew of Big Eye Four and Hawkeye to the celebration as well.

That night, the general and his daughter were as good as their word. The Officer's Club had never seen a larger group, or a happier one. In fact, thanks to the Russian's fondness for celebrating, the party was just winding down at sunrise on the following day.

***

The decisive moment had come and gone. The good guys had won, but it was not because they had superior weapons or warriors. They had won because of a fundamental desire to win.

In General Grey's analysis of the events, he included the following observations in his report to the joint chiefs of the FFNA, "The American spirit is an interesting study;

"Ask an American to do something that might place them in harm's way, and, if he respects you and your cause, he will do it.

"Order an American to do something, and even if it does not place him in harm's way, he will resist. If you expect any cooperation at all, you'd better have his respect.

"Tell an American that they will be dominated, enslaved, or destroyed, and you will trigger that special trait of the human spirit—the will to be free. That spirit cannot be contained. In the end, you will lose. Oh, it may take a while, but you will lose. It is just that simple."

CHAPTER TWENTY TWO

And So...

In the months that followed the defeat of Bushmaster, the dead were buried, the wounded were healing, damage assessments were made, and repairs begun. Humanity had a long hard battle ahead. Life was still a fight for survival. Organizations such as the Free Forces of North America, the North American Air Defense Agency, and other intelligence agencies would continue to try to stop the vultures who would take advantage of people when they are down. Sadly, there will always be bad guys.

A world tribunal would be held in the coming months to prosecute the captured terrorists for crimes against humanity. But first, the warriors, living and dead were honored in a special ceremony at FFNA Headquarters.

For bravery beyond the call of duty, Medals of Honor were awarded, posthumously, for Major Philip "Phil" Blake, ten other pilots, and twenty-seven members of the Ground Security Forces.

For their unwavering devotion to duty, standing fast against overwhelming odds to uphold the principles upon which our nations were founded, special Medals of Valor were awarded to Colonel Albert Fronz, Captain Vanya Petrovich, Lt. Ahana Cohen, Lt. Sharee Reshond, Sergeant Donald Spiker, and twelve other former members of Bushmaster.

For his selfless sacrifice against the forces of Bushmaster, even the arrogant Captain Jake Spade received a Medal of Honor, posthumously.

Each pilot who served in the campaign against Bushmaster was awarded the Distinguished Flying Cross.

For wounds received in service of the FFNA, Lt. Col. Ron Taylor, Lt. Ahana Cohen, and four hundred others received the Purple Heart.

For their bravery and outstanding airmanship during battles against Bushmaster, Major Brandon "Bud" Cooper, Lt. Ahana Cohen, and eighty-two other pilots were awarded the Air Medal.

For their bravery in actions against Bushmaster, Civilian Medals of Valor were awarded to William "Skip" Scott, Gregory "Pop" Hackland, Samuel "Big Sam" Thomas, Candy Simms-Taylor, Tim and Elizabeth Tenslick, and sixty-two other civilians.

Yes, Candy Simms and Ron Taylor were married, not long after she was released from the hospital. Rumor has it, a little one could be marching into the Taylor household fairly soon. One big clue is that Ron has started shopping for camouflage baby outfits.

A special Medal of Valor was awarded to Russian General Vladimir Petrovich and the other Russian pilots. Vanya was given the honor of presenting the medals. After many years, Vanya and her father are a family again, learning how to be friends. Vanya returned to Russia with her father, vowing to help him reorganize the Russian Air Force and rebuild the Russian economy. She had always been ready and willing to take on the most difficult assignments. No doubt, she would be up to this challenge as well.

Pop was invited to join the Jet Propulsion Research Lab at NASA's Sandia Labs. He accepted and left for New Mexico immediately. His mother would have been very proud. Her son is finally a lab scientist. Pop returned a few months later, just to visit and attend a very special ceremony...

One bright morning, beside the pond at Owl's Nest, on the spot where Skip was standing when Ahana saw him for the first time, they were joined as husband and wife.

A few days before the ceremony, Skip had told Ahana that the Viper project had been put on hold, and for the time being, he was still assigned to the remote outpost. She confided to their friends that she had some reservations about living in such an isolated place, but she loved Skip so much that she would live on the Moon if he were assigned there.

Although he was not being completely honest, Skip asked everyone to keep quiet about it, until the day of the wedding.

After the wedding, the newlyweds were standing alone, admiring the fantastic view…

"It's really beautiful up here, isn't it? I don't think I could ever get tired of this view."

"Yes, I like it too," Ahana replied, trying to be hopeful.

"I guess I'll have to make do with pictures, until we come for a visit…"

"Visit? What did you just say?"

"I'm really sorry, gorgeous, but I've been reassigned to Base One. I know how much you wanted to live here," he replied, with that mischievous smile she had come to know so well.

She hugged him and said, "You rascal! You knew all along that I didn't want to live here, didn't you? You are *so* mischievous! But I love you anyway."

"Besides, how can we raise kids up here?" Skip asked.

"Kids? But you know, I can't…"

"Yes, but I also know that you want to have children. When we get back from our honeymoon, I want you to meet a couple of very special friends of mine. I think they'll be able to help us work this out."

A month later, they waited in their home at Base One. Skip had told Ahana very little about the visitors, only that they were very special friends.

When they arrived, Skip brought them inside and introduced them to Ahana. She was overwhelmed when they walked in the door. Her smile lit up her face.

"Ahana, I would like you to meet Jeremy and Cynthia. Jeremy is four, and Cynthia is two. They lost their parents in the bombing. I've been gettin' to know them for the last few months, and if you agree, I would like for us to be their guardians."

Ahana knelt down, took them into her arms, and said, "Oh, my. Hello, little ones! I had no idea... You are so beautiful! So adorable!"

Then, she looked at Skip with tears of joy streaming down her cheeks and said, "Oh, William, you have made all of my dreams come true."

"Hey, gorgeous, that's why I'm here."

***

In the aftermath of a disaster that almost destroyed our world, new friends had been found in the most unusual of circumstances. And two of those people had found, in each other, the missing parts of their own lives.

Skip and Ahana's love would continue to grow stronger, lasting for the rest of their lives and, perhaps, beyond—in the hearts of a handsome little blonde-haired boy named Jeremy, who loved airplanes and big dogs, and a pretty little girl named Cynthia, with chestnut-brown hair and beautiful gray-blue eyes.

Aftermath I: The Fight For Survival

About the Author

James A Graves, Jr. was born in Pensacola, Florida and grew up fishing, swimming and scuba diving in the crystal clear water of Morrison Spring, Florida and hunting and exploring the swamps of the Choctawhatchee River that runs from Alabama, through the Florida Panhandle, to the Choctawhatchee Bay near Ft. Walton Beach and Destin.

Music was the creative spark that began a lifetime journey as a writer, musician and songwriter. He began writing songs after learning to play guitar at age 10 and continued performing with various rock bands throughout high school and college.

Chasing a fascination with airplanes, James joined the USAF and was selected for an assignment with the Quick Strike Reconnaissance Test Project, Tactical Air Warfare Center, Eglin AFB Florida.

After the USAF, he toured with a professional rock band as second lead guitar. Surrendering to the fact that bills must be paid, James turned to his electronics skills and accepted a job in the defense industry as a field engineer on the US Air Force Air Combat Maneuvering Instrumentation/US Navy Tactical Air Combat Training

System. He also continued pursuing aviation and earned his pilot's wings in 1982. Currently, James is an Airways Transportation Systems Specialist with the Federal Aviation Administration.

His Aftermath Series is an action-adventure blending both science fiction and fact. The characters are realistic, diverse and complex. The stories take the reader on a fascinating journey into the lives of a small group of people who are fighting for survival in a very different world from the one we know, and yet a world to which we can relate... battling terrorism.

Did you like this book?

If you enjoyed this book, you will find more interesting books at

www.CrystalDreamsPublishing.com

Please take the time to let us know how you liked this book. Even short reviews of 2-3 sentences can be helpful and may be used in our marketing materials. If you take the time to post a review for this book on Amazon.com, let us know when the review is posted and you will receive a free audiobook or ebook from our catalog. Email the link to the review, your name, and your mailing address -- send the email to orders@mmpubs.com with the subject line "Book Review Posted on Amazon."

If you have questions about this book, our customer loyalty program, or our review rewards program, please contact us at info@mmpubs.com.

cdp
CRYSTAL DREAMS
publishing

a division of Multi-Media Publications Inc.

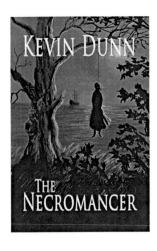

The Necromancer

By Kevin Dunn

Salem, Massachusetts - 1692: The witch hunts begin. Neighbors are turning on one another. A smallpox epidemic has broken out. People are dying. One man is responsible, a warlock of great power - the Necromancer - and he has just seduced one of Salem's purest women into a perdition that will haunt her the rest of her life.

Using actual historical evens as the backdrop for the fictional story of Reverend Ambrose Blayne and Susanna Harrington, it is a novel of passion, horror, love, and the cruelty which man is capable of. It is a deeply disturbing, often graphic depiction of those brutal and uncertain times.

The novel, while primarily set in Salem, sprawls across Europe from witches being burned at the stake in Scotland to spiritual awakenings in the Roman Amphitheater and depraved Witches' Sabbats in the Harz Mountains of Germany. The series of events culminates in the warlock's summoning of a Lovecraftian demon which threatens to unknit the fabric of the world and an ending that will chill the reader's blood.

ISBN-10:   1591460719
ISBN-13:   9781591460718
Price: $14.95

Available from Amazon.com or your nearest book retailer.
Or, order direct at www.CrystalDreamsPublishing.com

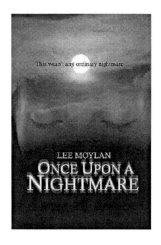

Once Upon a Nightmare

By Lee Moylan

On the night of October thirteenth, the Hunter's Moon descended upon the quiet town of White Chapel. As Sara Bishop drifted off to sleep under its soft illumination, the full moon seemed to have brought with it something far more sinister than a warm glow.

At once, the nightmare started. But this wasn't any ordinary nightmare…

This one seemed real — as if she could smell it, feel it, taste it. It was one of those dreams — one that awakened her witch-like sense — a harbinger of heartbreak and now, horror.

Together with Rebecca Parker, the only other person who understood her gift, someone who had experienced her own strange senses, Sara hoped to come to terms with this ominous nightmare. But her closest friend and next door neighbor was no where to be found — not since the night of October thirteenth.

And so it begins. With little help from her skeptical husband or local police, Sara finds herself virtually alone as her grisly dreams crawl from the darkness to become a sick and twisted reality — a reality where she has become the ultimate desire of a sadistic serial killer.

When the next full moon descends upon White Chapel, he will reveal himself to her. And under its silvery glow, a new nightmare will be born. Will Sara Bishop have to experience death itself to stop this killer? Or will her nightmare never end?

ISBN-10:   1591461960
ISBN-13:   9781591461968
Price: $16.95

Available from Amazon.com or your nearest book retailer.
Or, order direct at www.CrystalDreamsPublishing.com

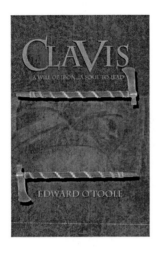

Clavis

By Edward O'Toole

"I have watched you for several summers now, little Clavis; I have watched you more closely than you can imagine. You carry a secret that I had believed was mine alone. Many nights have I spent trying to decide your fate, and am glad I waited. Because I know you can hold your tongue, I have brought you here. As of yesterday, you are a non-person as are the rest in that blasted list you heard cried. You have lost the right to a home and land; you have lost the right to work and to marry. I'm trying to save your life. Here is my deal: I will save your life and you will save my family, my reputation, my Province, and the Kte, I want you to travel to Oksat."

Clavis, a young girl hunted and dispossessed, forced from her home and on a perilous journey to the barbaric lands in the far North. Cursed with a great secret and the Gift of Backsight, she must fend for herself among the druids, witches, barbarians and cannibals, while avoiding those involved with a pretence to the throne.

ISBN-10:   1591460352
ISBN-13:   9781591460350
Price: $12.95

Available from Amazon.com or your nearest book retailer.
Or, order direct at www.CrystalDreamsPublishing.com

Terror in Manhattan

By Ross L. Barber

Jayne Keener is a young, single all-American girl who, like so many newcomers to the world of Cyberspace, finds herself drawn into the shadowy world of cybersex and adult chat rooms. Following the murder of a suave, mysterious Englishman she has met in a Manhattan bar, Jayne finds herself sucked ever deeper into the subculture of Internet chat rooms.

It is in one such room that she encounters Phillip H. Dreedle; professional hacker, convicted rapist and stalker. Suddenly, Jayne's once sane life is turned on its head, and not even her closest friends are what they seem.

ISBN-10:   1591460404
ISBN-13:   9781591460404
Price: $14.95

Available from Amazon.com or your nearest book retailer.
Or, order direct at www.CrystalDreamsPublishing.com

Hunters of the Shadows

By Mark Haeuser

What creature lurks beyond the shadow-rim of imagination, beyond known wickedness? What unspeakable dark force could be so powerful as to unite old foes, one good and one evil, in a quest to subdue it and save a world? Come closer my friend - step in. Traverse the boundaries of time and space to glimpse one possible fantastic future. A future of staggering proportions! Contemplate, as prophesy of old unfolds to wreak havoc on the unsuspecting, the unwary, us! The seconds tick by..... Reader beware! The time has come..... His time!

ISBN-10:   1591460573
ISBN-13:   9781591460572
Price: $13.00

Available from Amazon.com or your nearest book retailer.
Or, order direct at www.CrystalDreamsPublishing.com

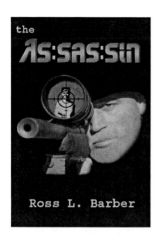

The Assassin

By Ross L. Barber

Cockney schoolboy, Johnny Feltham, has only ever wanted one thing: he longs to be a soldier. He flourishes in the SAS until he is wounded during a mission and is subsequently discharged.

Disenchanted with a military that trained him to be an 'expert killer.' he gets his Green Card and travels to New York City where he sets up his own security franchise. He is soon visited by a man who hires him to do what he knows best.

Feltham's lethal exploits soon earn him the title of "The Assassin." He is ruthlessly pursued by the NYPD and FBI and is always one step ahead of them, until, after a series of twists and turns, fate intervenes.

Hardcover
ISBN-10: 1591460360
ISBN-13: 9781591460367
Price: $19.95

Paperback
ISBN-10: 1591460387
ISBN-13: 9781591460381
Price: $10.00

Monkey Pudding: A Vietnam Hero's Story

By J.B. Pozner

Lieutenant Steve Simmons returned home from the Vietnam war to find his wife Jennifer in bed with another man. In an enraged scuffle, Jennifer falls down the stairs to her death. After psychiatric treatment in a VA hospital, Steve relocates in a new state with a new career and tries to put his life back together.

Then he meets Christina, heir to an international manufacturing corporation. Uncovering a plot on her life, Steve hires a detective and sets out to find the conspirators.

The story begins with gritty combat scenes in the jungles of Vietnam. The battles continue back home as Steve's post-war traumas are intensified by one bizarre twist after another. The fast pace continues to the dramatic conclusion where Steve may at last taste victory.

ISBN-10:   1591460077
ISBN-13:   9781591460077
Price: $12.00

Available from Amazon.com or your nearest book retailer.
Or, order direct at www.CrystalDreamsPublishing.com

A Doctor to Die For

By A.F. Cacchillo

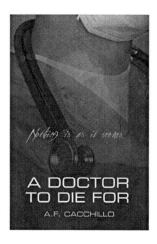

There is a fine line between doctor-assisted suicide and murder, and Dr. Marc Hobson, a physician-psychiatrist, is torn trying to distinguish between the two.

Without laying a malicious finger on a patient, he is able to seal their doom, often using just a telephone and his immense charisma. A pesky priest, himself no saint, is unaware that he is dealing with a sinner far worse than himself when he starts looking into the matter.

"The novel is tight, with no words wasted, in easy-to-read diary form. It truly refelcts a trust misplaced."

ISBN-10:   1591460735
ISBN-13:   9781591460732
Price: $12.00

Available from Amazon.com or your nearest book retailer. Or, order direct at www.CrystalDreamsPublishing.com

LaVergne, TN USA
29 March 2010
177528LV00006B/231/P

9 781591 462484